Eight Inches

Books by Sean Wolfe

Close Contact

Aroused

Taboo

Eight Inches

Published by Kensington Publishing Corporation

Eight Inches

SEAN WOLFE

KENSINGTON BOOKS
www.kensingtonbooks.com

KENSINGTON BOOKS are published by

Kensington Publishing Corp.
119 West 40th Street
New York, NY 10018

All Kensington titles, imprints, and distributed lines are available at
special quantity discounts for bulk purchases for sales promotion, pre-
miums, fund-raising, educational, or institutional use.

Special book excerpts or customized printings can also be created to fit
specific needs. For details, write or phone the office of the Kensington
Special Sales Manager: Kensington Publishing Corp., 119 West 40th
Street, New York, NY 10018. Attn. Special Sales Department. Phone:
1-800-221-2647.

Kensington and the K logo Reg. U.S. Pat. & TM Off.

ISBN-13: 978-0-7582-3432-2
ISBN-10: 0-7582-3432-5

First Kensington Trade Paperback Printing: September 2009
10 9 8 7 6 5 4 3 2 1

Printed in the United States of America

The first true love of my life, and the guy who made me believe in the existence of soul mates, was Gustavo Paredes. He taught me the difference between love and sex, and taught me how to really love another person and allow myself to be loved. He taught me the value of growing up and of commitment and of being true to myself. He was my partner and my life for thirteen years, and everything good and loving in me is because of him. Gustavo Paredes-Wolfe passed away in 2003.

This book is dedicated to you, *Gustavito* ~ *Te extraño y te quiero mucho. Siempre vas estar en mi corazon.*

Thanks and Acknowledgments

Thank you to Austin Foxxe, former editor in chief of *Men* and *Freshmen* magazines, for believing in me and publishing my first erotic stories, and encouraging me to reach for the highest stars.

Thank you to my Angel on earth, Jane Nichols, for believing in me and supporting my dream, even if she can't bring herself to read any of my erotica books.

And special thanks to my editor, John Scognamiglio. You never give up on me, and are always willing to go the extra mile for me. Thank you for giving me the creative liberties that you have. You totally ROCK!!

Introduction

I remember when I was a kid my whole world revolved around my little neighborhood in the small town I grew up in. It was easy, because in Booker, Texas, there was only one school, one small hometown bank, one gas station, and one tiny grocery store. Everyone knew everyone else, and privacy was a myth that we read about in terms of "rights to" and "invasions of." Those terms seemed both ridiculous and strangely elusive to our little town of 500 residents.

"Globalization" for us meant gaining a deep understanding of the intricacies of life for rice patty farmers in China by watching National Geographic specials on TV or by buying imported jalapeños from Mexico with which to top our nachos.

It was hard, if not impossible, for us to understand how our lives could possibly affect that of those rice patty workers on the other side of the world, or even those Mexican neighbors immediately to our south. We were farmers working to fill our own silos; we built our own little churches—nine of them in that small town, to be exact, and we attended those churches every Sunday; and we played the same nine or ten other tiny towns in football every single year. Our little town took care of our own, and the same "village" mentality surely did the same for all the other millions of villages around the world. Our lives meant nothing to anyone outside of our village, nor did anyone else's life affect our own.

Well, I'm not a little kid anymore, and we're not living in that cellular, self-possessed world anymore. In a day and age where we can, and do, travel all across the world simply to go shopping or experience a meal . . . or, even more intimately, adopt children to become a part of our own family, many of us are beginning to realize that we are all part of one family, and that our "village" is much larger and more influential than we once thought.

I do a lot of diversity and inclusiveness trainings and workshops. In one of those workshops I use an activity called the "Circle of Influence." In this exercise, we draw a big circle and write our names in it, and then we draw eight to ten smaller circles around the outside of the bigger circle. Inside the smaller circles we write the names of people or situations in our lives that have affected or influenced us—either positively or negatively—and we reflect on those people or circumstances, and talk about the ways in which they have helped shape who we are now.

It's a powerful exercise, because most of the people in my classes have never given much thought to their circles of influence, and it brings home to them how, although we are all strong and unique individuals, there are a lot of people and circumstances that have helped get us to where we are. At the end of the exercise I ask my participants if their circle of influence is fairly vanilla—if it looks a whole lot like they do—or if it's pretty eclectic. I encourage them to "color up" their circles of influence, to step outside their comfort zone and experience things and people and places and tastes and colors that are new to them. We cannot grow as people by surrounding ourselves with people just like us, or by experiencing the same things over and over again.

My last two books, *Aroused* and *Taboo*, were centered around a central theme. Each story was independent but was connected to the theme. For *Eight Inches* I wanted to do something different. I wanted to demonstrate how each of us is connected to one another in ways that we might never know. But the energy of the universe runs through all of us, and we are all touched by the same energy, and therefore are part of one another.

I had no idea when I began writing this book that we'd be in the beginning of possibly the most exciting time of our history—where we have a leader who commands respect from the rest of the world, and who values and embraces diversity and inclusiveness, and who believes in the power of humanity . . . all of it, and not just those of us who believe the same things that he does. Yes, I really did start writing this book *that* long ago, before anyone really thought this enlightened time in our history was possible!

But this journey that we are on now reinforces my belief that we are all connected energetically with one another, and that our actions, our words, our works, and our love make a difference—to everyone, and not just those to whom we direct them.

Whether we like it or not, we are our brother's keeper. We share the same universal energy, and therefore we have the power to manipulate that force. It's a very powerful idea, for sure. If we want peace, we can—by our actions, our thoughts, and our words—bring it about. By loving unconditionally those around us, we can create a ripple effect of love around the world. And by taking care of one person in need, we can create a chain reaction of compassion and works that can change the world.

Eight Inches is a collection of erotic stories, and so I hope that they will stir you in ways and in body parts that are meant to be stirred by the reading of . . . well . . . fuck stories. I do have a reputation to maintain, after all. But I also hope they help you think about the various people in your life who have helped you become the person you are, and about how you might have influenced—possibly completely changed for the better—the life of others.

Happy reading. And when you see me around, stop and say hi and introduce yourself. We're brothers, after all, and we're sharing energies. Change my life, and I hope I will change yours.

INCH ONE

Street Smart

I.

Carlos was running for his life. It wasn't the first time, not even the first time that week. When he was a full block away and felt it was safe, he stopped and bent over at the waist, taking deep breaths, and looked back at his house. The old Victorian was squeezed between two cookie-cutter low-income apartment buildings, which offered Carlos a clear view of the house without making himself equally visible, especially in the dark of night. The front door flew open and his father stumbled into the front yard, looking frantically to both sides. Carlos took a another deep breath, and turned and continued running.

It was Friday night, almost eleven o'clock, and it was very cold. His breath rose before him in a cloud of fine mist as he ran, and his side hurt immensely. He ran about half a mile before he stopped and wrapped his arms around his chest, trying to warm himself. There hadn't been time to grab his coat before climbing out his bedroom window and fleeing, and now he was feeling the shock of the biting wind.

Carlos had been in the front room watching TV with his younger sister when his parents came home. He heard the squealing tires turn the corner half a block away, and thirty seconds later, the slamming car doors. His parents were fighting in the front yard. His father was drunk, his mother pleading with her husband to listen to reason. The neighbors yelled at his parents to pipe it down, and his father screamed back at them even louder to shut the fuck up and mind their own business.

Carlos and little Rosie looked at each other, a familiar frown dominating their faces. Carlos walked calmly across the room and turned off the TV. He picked Rosie up and hugged her close to his chest as he carried her to their shared room. Pulling the blankets back with one hand as he balanced his baby sister in his other arm, he tucked the young girl into bed and kissed her forehead.

"Good night, princess."

"Why does it always happen like this, Carlos?" Rosie asked sweetly as she looked up innocently into his eyes.

"I don't know, Gorda."

"Is he going to hit you again?"

"No, honey," Carlos said, still feeling the pain from the last fight his parents had had. "Not tonight. Now go to sleep."

"Are you leaving again?"

"I don't know, sissy, I don't know."

"Can I have another kiss, Poncho?"

Carlos knew she was trying to keep him with her as long as possible. "Of course you can, Cisco," he answered, fighting back a tear.

He bent down and kissed his sister on the cheek. The front door was suddenly kicked open, and Carlos jumped.

"Where are you, you little bastard," came his father's drunken voice from the living room. His mother was still pleading with him not to hurt the boy; he was only a child, for God's sake. A loud slapping sound and the thud of his mother falling to the floor got Carlos up and moving.

He ran to the bedroom window and raised it. Halfway out, he turned to his younger sister to blow her a kiss, and saw she was crying. He started to go over and wipe the tear away, but just then the bedroom door was kicked violently open, and Carlos jumped out the window.

Several minutes later he was standing outside a corner liquor store. Looking into the window, he saw in his reflection that his nose and ears were a shade somewhere between pink and red, and his fingers were beginning to turn blue. The old man behind the counter was alone, and he looked very warm. He was eating a pepperoni and double onion pizza recently delivered by Supremo's Pizza, according to the box on the counter, and drinking a Coke. On the shelf behind him, next to the Smirnoff vodka, a small motorized fan blew cool air onto him. He was wearing a short-sleeved t-shirt stained with dark perspiration that covered two-thirds of the sides of the dirty shirt.

Carlos contemplated only a moment before opening the door and walking inside. The old man looked up, frowned, and swallowed the large bite of pizza in his mouth before speaking.

"You can't come in here, kid," he growled. "I know you're not eighteen, so don't even bother pulling out a fake ID."

"I don't want to buy anything," Carlos said, "I just wanted to warm up a little."

"Tough shit. I'm not the goddamned Salvation Army here. Now get lost."

"Please. Just for a minute. It's freezing out there."

"I'm calling the cops now," the old man growled again, even as he took another large bite of the pizza, and picked up the phone.

"Never mind, I'm gone," Carlos said, and walked back into the cold, windy night.

He walked a few blocks north and turned onto Geary Street. The Tenderloin district was well known as the dirtiest, most dangerous, and highest crime-ridden area of San Francisco. Strung-out drug addicts and prostitutes of both sexes lined either side of the large boulevard. The city had long ago given up on "cleaning up" the underbelly of the most romantic city in the country, and the

Tenderloin itself seemed to relish its reputation. Every once in a while a squad car would drive by, but the residents of the boulevard knew all the officers by first name, and more often than not the driver had himself indulged in the merchandise on a semi-regular basis, so the hustlers were not terribly worried about being arrested.

Carlos could sometimes be considered a little naïve, but he was not totally ignorant of the goings-on of Geary Street. He didn't know much in detail, but he knew the people who walked along the street at night were not selling Girl Scout cookies. The people there made him a little nervous, with their pierced bodies, dark makeup, and spiked mohawks. But the street was well lit and most of the kids did not look too cold, and that kept Carlos walking.

In the course of two short blocks Carlos was approached twice to see if he was interested in buying a "dime bag." A few of the more effeminate male hustlers along the street gave him dirty looks. He overheard whispered conversations with the accusatory phrase "fresh meat," and somehow Carlos knew they were talking about him. Just as he was passing in front of the Supremo's Pizza store he was suddenly pulled into the entryway. He was startled, and doubled his fists, prepared to defend himself against an ugly, bearded troll, or even a monster.

"Don't hit me, please." It was a young boy, about Carlos' own age. He was wearing tight blue jeans, a plain white t-shirt, and a single, long, dangling silver earring in his right ear. His eyes were grossly outlined with eyeliner.

"What do you want?" Carlos asked cautiously.

"Well, you look cold and lonely. And there's a cop following you, so I thought I'd pull you in here before he pulled you into his car."

Carlos looked behind him, and noticed the cop car cruising slowly behind him. "Thank you."

"You're welcome. My name's Ricky. What's yours?"

"Carlos."

"Would you like a drink, Carlos?"

"Sure."

He accepted a Coke can from the skinny kid and took a large drink. He swallowed and coughed violently before spitting a mouthful of the liquid to the ground.

Ricky's eyes grew wide in disbelief.

"What the heck is this?" Carlos coughed out.

"Seagram's Seven." Ricky laughed. "It keeps you warm on a cold night."

"Oh," he said, and wiped his mouth with the back of his hand. "What's so funny?"

"Heck is. I haven't used that word since I was three years old. Out here it's called hell and damn and shit, not heck and darn and shoot."

"Oh." Carlos looked around to make sure no one else had heard his childish vocabulary.

"How old are you, Carlos?"

"Eighteen," he lied without hesitating even a second.

Ricky smiled. "Honey, I'm not a cop, so you don't have to lie to me. I'm only sixteen, myself."

"I'm eighteen," Carlos said defiantly as he stared at the street.

"Mmm-hmm. First time on the street?"

"Oh, no. My mom goes to see a doctor a couple of blocks up few times a year. Sometimes I go with her."

"Sweetheart, you've got a lot to learn out here. I meant is this your first time hustling."

"Why do you keep calling me 'honey' and 'sweetheart'? We're both guys."

Ricky looked truly shocked, and raised one eyebrow cautiously as he stared at the newcomer. Because Carlos was walking up Geary Street at midnight, Ricky had assumed he was gay and a hustler. Now he wasn't so sure of either, and thought about the consequences of carrying on and assuming too much. Though Carlos was not built overly big, Ricky was sure he could cause considerable damage to his own scrawny body if provoked.

"Just a term we use. Listen, Carlos, what are you doing out here? You're obviously not a hustler."

Carlos' eyes fell back to the ground and he shifted his feet nervously. He didn't like to talk about his problems with anyone, and especially not strangers. But it was cold outside, and Ricky seemed nice enough. What the heck, he thought, then corrected himself: What the hell?

"Could I have another drink of that?" Carlos asked, and nodded toward the Coke can.

Ricky passed the whiskey to Carlos and waited for him to begin his story. He had nothing better to do, and since it was still early, he doubted he would be picked up for a while yet, if at all. Lately, it seemed all the johns were looking for the masculine type—young and innocent, but masculine. Ricky looked at his new friend and thought how well he would do out there on the street if he really wanted to. He was definitely young, and his jet-black hair, bright blue eyes, and light brown skin gave him an unparalleled beauty. His little peach fuzz of a mustache blessed him with that look of masculine innocence.

Ricky sighed, partly in admiration but mostly in self-pity. He was almost the exact opposite of Carlos. He was three or four inches taller than Carlos, but weighed about the same, possibly even less. Too skinny. He was very pale-skinned, with dirty blond hair and even dirtier brown eyes that rarely, if ever, allowed expression. No mustache, heaven forbid. He wore makeup and girls' jeans, size 1, to enhance his ass, which was much too flat. No sign of masculinity here, Ricky thought, and sighed again.

"I don't know where to start," Carlos said, pulling Ricky out of his trance.

"How about starting by giving me a drink of that and telling me why you're out here," Ricky said as he lit a cigarette.

Carlos stared at Ricky with fascination.

"What are you staring at?" Ricky asked, blowing a mouthful of smoke into the air.

"Your parents let you smoke?"

"Yeah," Ricky said, laughing, "sort of. You never smoked before?"

"No," Carlos answered softly.

"Wanna try?"

"Sure."

Carlos took the cigarette from Ricky and held it for a moment, trying to build the courage to bring it to his lips. Finally he closed his eyes and put the unfiltered tip to his mouth. He drew a small amount of smoke into his mouth and left it there for only a couple of seconds before blowing it out quickly.

"Doesn't do anything for me," Carlos said with a look of distaste.

"Well, I guess it wouldn't unless you inhale it." Ricky laughed.

"What do you mean?"

"Do it again, only this time swallow the smoke."

"Swallow it?" Carlos sounded horrified.

"Sure. Like this," Ricky said, and demonstrated the barbaric act of inhaling smoke into his lungs. He blew the smoke out in rings.

"Wow!"

"Here, now you try it."

Carlos was excited and nervous at the same time, so when he drew in the smoke he pulled in too much, and when he swallowed it, he swallowed too fast. Instead of blowing the smoke out in rings, he bellowed out a cough of smoke and spittle. It sprayed all over Ricky, and his new friend broke into a laugh. Carlos saw absolutely nothing funny in the fact that his lungs were on fire and he was choking to death. When he finally stopped coughing, his eyes were filled with tears. His lungs still burned as he leaned against the wall to breathe in some fresh air.

"Well, what do you think?" Ricky asked, still trying to stop laughing.

"It tried to kill me!"

This brought on another outburst of laughter from Ricky, and he passed the Coke can to Carlos. "Here, maybe this will help."

Carlos took the can and finished off what was left of the whiskey. His throat felt raw from the smoke, and the alcohol burned as it went down. But it was somehow soothing, and he was getting used to it by now.

Ricky had noticed a silver Honda circling the block a few times while he was showing Carlos the fine art of inhaling. It now pulled up to the curb and the passenger window was rolled down.

"I'll be back in about an hour," Ricky told Carlos. "Stick around for a while. When I get back I'll bring a fresh bottle of Seagram's and some food."

Carlos watched, fascinated, as Ricky swished over to the car and leaned into the passenger window. He could see the driver gesturing toward him as he talked with Ricky for a few seconds before Ricky turned around and walked back to him.

"He wants you." Ricky sulked.

"For what?" Carlos asked nervously.

Ricky smiled. "He wants to have sex with you, child."

"Sex?" Carlos whispered. He was astonished. "I've never had sex with a guy before."

"Ever have sex with a girl?"

"Well," Carlos hesitated, " . . . no."

"Then there's no problem, is there? You won't know the difference."

Carlos didn't quite get the reasoning behind that, but the Seagram's had worked its magic on him, and he agreed with Ricky.

"Good. Just lay there and let him suck you off. You don't do anything to him. And whatever you do, don't let him turn you onto your stomach."

"Why not?"

"Because that's my position. Besides, you wouldn't like what happens next if you do." Ricky noticed the guy in the car was getting nervous, so he shook his head yes and continued his lesson to Carlos.

"The going rate is thirty dollars, but you can easily get forty. Hold out for that much. Play it straight; that should be no problem for you. Then make sure he brings you back here when you're through," Ricky said as he nudged Carlos forward.

Carlos' head spun with everything Ricky had told him, and he barely realized what he was doing as he closed the door to the Honda.

II.

The alarm buzzed loudly, scaring Carlos out of his deep sleep. He sat up in the strange bed, causing the sheet that covered him through the night to fall to the floor. He was naked. And hard. Grabbing the sheet from the floor, he covered his lap and looked over next to him. He was relieved to see no one was in the bed with him. He reached over and shut off the alarm just as the bedroom door opened and a middle-aged man came in carrying a breakfast tray.

"Good morning. Sorry about the clock, I know it's kind of obnoxious. I have to meet my sister at noon to go shopping, so I thought it'd be good if we got up early."

"Where am I?" Carlos asked, bringing the sheet up higher to cover his chest.

"We're at my house," the man said, setting the tray in front of Carlos.

"Who are you?"

"My name is Jonathan. I picked you up on Geary Street last night, remember?"

"No."

"Well, I'm not surprised. You were somewhat inebriated. Here, this will help you." He handed Carlos a glass of orange juice. "And there are a couple of aspirin there, too."

"Why am I naked?"

"Because you could not possibly have fulfilled my wildest fantasies as you did last night had you been clothed, that's why. You know, for a small boy, you are very well equipped. Worth the extra ten dollars, let me tell you."

"Extra ten dollars?" Carlos asked, confused.

"Why yes, we agreed on forty." He noticed Carlos' puzzlement, and realized the opportunity. "Or was it thirty?"

"It was forty," Carlos said, the night before slowly unfolding before him.

"Well, like I said, it was worth it."

"Thank you."

"I have to shower now. Eat your breakfast, then you can shower before I take you back to Geary Street. Or was there somewhere else you wanted to go?"

"No. That's fine."

"All right then. Eat up."

Jonathan went into the bathroom, leaving Carlos alone in the bedroom. Carlos popped the aspirin into his mouth and swallowed them with the orange juice. Little by little the events of the night before came back to him. The old man had stripped Carlos naked and just stared at him for a long time before laying him on the bed and rubbing his body. Soon his mouth had enveloped Carlos' dick, sucking and licking it for what seemed an eternity. Then the old man was on his hands and knees and Carlos was behind him, pumping like he had done with girls in his dreams. It felt better than anything he'd ever felt before; it was his first time, after all, and near the end Carlos thought he was surely dying. His heart was pounding extremely fast, and then, without warning, he felt his load erupt from his balls and blast through his rod and deep inside the stranger.

That was the night before, and now, only hours after that vigorous workout, Carlos' dick was harder and fatter than he could ever remember. The sheet created a pleasant friction on his hard cock, and when he reached down to touch it he shuddered. He wrapped his fist around the fat dick and began to slowly pull at it. The sensation was so intense he could not stifle a series of low moans. It took only a few pulls at the readied cock before it shot. Several long streams of warm cum landed on Carlos' face, more landed on his chest and stomach. He instinctively licked a drop that landed on his lips, and kept pumping at his dick until the last drop trickled out of the tip.

It was then that Carlos noticed the old man leaning against the bedroom door. Carlos grabbed the sheet and tried to cover himself.

"That was amazing. The shower's all yours, cutie."

Carlos decided he couldn't hide his naked body forever, and stood up and walked naked toward the bathroom, his cum cooling on his torso and dripping down his hard, flat stomach.

Jonathan reached down and gave Carlos' slowly deflating cock a gentle squeeze as he passed.

Carlos smiled shyly and closed the door behind him as he took his shower.

* * *

Jonathan dropped Carlos off in front of the Supremo's Pizza store where he had picked him up the previous night. Carlos went into the store and ordered a Coke. He finished it slowly, watching the clock on the wall, and waiting until eleven o'clock before getting up to leave. His father left for work at eleven o'clock on Saturday mornings, so it would be safe to go home.

He wondered how bad the fight had been and how badly hurt his mother would be. The fights, which had been going on for as long as Carlos could remember, had become more frequent in the past year and a half, when his father had been fired from his foreman's job at the Burton Jones Welding Company. He had been warned repeatedly, and after showing up drunk on the job for the fourth time, he was fired. Now he worked for his brother-in-law, whom he hated, making ten dollars an hour laying brick. Supporting a family on that salary wasn't easy, Carlos knew. But he also knew it didn't help matters any when every payday his father took his mother out and got stinking drunk.

The fights were always over Carlos, and it took far less than a genius to know why. Mr. Cortez had very dark brown skin, Mrs. Cortez had very dark brown skin, and little Rosie had very dark brown skin. Carlos' skin was a honey-colored light brown. Mr. Cortez had dark brown eyes, as did his wife and daughter. Carlos had bright, electrifying blue eyes, accentuated with long, curly eyelashes. Carlos' father and mother were overweight, and little Rosie was chubby, seeming to follow in their steps. Carlos was, and always had been, lean and muscular.

Less than a full year after her marriage to Juan Cortez, Lydia Cortez began having an affair, quite indiscreetly, with Richard Norman, a local schoolteacher. He was an extremely handsome man, tall and trim, with jet-black hair and crystal clear blue eyes. He also had a very distinguishable birthmark—two small moles on the left side of his chin. It only added to his handsomeness, and many times after making love Lydia would lick his chin and say how cute his "beauty marks" were. The affair lasted three months before Juan found out about it. He had walked in on them in bed together and had beaten the shit out of Richard, causing him to flee town.

Less than a year later Lydia gave birth to her first child. Baby Carlos had skin three tones lighter than his parents. And he had two small moles on the left side of his chin. Later, when his eyes lost that initial gray-black color that all babies are born with, they emerged his present turquoise blue. The fights began two weeks after Lydia brought Carlos home from the hospital, and Juan had never treated Carlos as his son.

That little boy was in front of his own house now, and seeing his father's car gone, he walked inside. His mother and Rosie were in the front room watching an episode of *Superstar Showcase* on TV. Lydia looked up as he walked in, and Carlos noticed a small cut on her lower lip. At least there was no black eye, he thought.

"Hi, honey," she said as she stood up and walked over to him. "Are you all right?" She hugged him tightly.

"I'm fine, Mom. You?"

"Oh, I'm okay. Where did you go last night? I was so worried."

"Hey, Poncho." Rosie ran over to her brother and hugged his legs lovingly.

"Hi, Cisco." Carlos ruffed her hair and returned his attention to his mom. "I went to a friend's."

"You were warm then? It was so cold outside."

"Yeah"—Carlos remembered the night—"I was warm."

"Are you hungry?"

"No, I had breakfast."

"Sure?"

"Mmm-hmm. Who's on *Showcase*?"

"Hannah Montana!" Rosie screamed.

"Gross!" Carlos teased, and Rosie hit him playfully as the three of them sat down to watch his little sister's favorite singer.

III.

"Eat your vegetables, Carlos," Juan Cortez said through a mouthful of instant potatoes. "You can't grow up to be big and strong if you don't eat your green beans."

That meant he'd had five or maybe six beers. Carlos could tell how much Juan had drunk by his moods. Less than five did not affect him at all; five or six made him feel parental, if not loving; six to ten and he was quietly remembering Richard Norman; ten or more made him violent. He was an easy man to read.

"Yes, Dad." Carlos tested his ground. Juan did not flinch at the word. Yes, he was in excellent spirits indeed.

"Could I stay over at a friend's tonight?" Carlos asked as he kept his eyes on his plate until his mother kicked him under the table.

Lydia gave him an aggravated look that seemed to say *how do you expect to resolve this if you're never around?* But Carlos figured if it hadn't been resolved yet, it probably wouldn't be resolved just because he ate his green beans and stayed home and watched *Ugly Betty* with his loving family this particular night.

"Honey, I don't think that's a good . . ."

"Sure, go ahead," Juan finished for his wife. Six beers or not, he still would never turn down a chance to get rid of Carlos so he could spend some quality time with his real family.

"Thank you," Carlos said, and excused himself from the dinner table.

He went to his room and put on a new pair of jeans, a sweatshirt, and his jacket. Tonight he would not need Ricky's Coke can to stay warm. He still had his forty dollars from the night before. He took ten dollars and put it in his pocket, and then put the rest in his sock-and-underwear drawer.

He walked down Geary Street, but it was only eight o'clock and no one was around. Carlos decided to see a movie to pass some time, and walked to the theater a few blocks down on Van Ness Avenue. By the time the movie was over, Ricky would undoubtedly be out on Geary Street.

Carlos enjoyed the movie a great deal, at least what he saw of it. Halfway through it a young man about twenty-five years old sat in the seat next to him, even though the theater was almost empty. Before long Carlos felt a hand rest on his left knee. He stole a glance at the man next to him and saw that he was staring straight ahead at the screen. But his right hand was not so dormant. It was creeping up Carlos' thigh. Soon it was rubbing the bulge in his crotch. Carlos was nervous but did not move the hand away, and in seconds the experienced hand had his dick rock hard. His heart was pounding fiercely, and he barely noticed the man on screen being torn in half by two battling dinosaurs.

Then it was ruined. The guy grabbed Carlos' hand and placed it in his lap. Carlos was shocked to feel the warm, moist skin of a hard cock. He pulled his hand away quickly. The guy removed his hand from Carlos' lap and resituated his own crotch, then got up and left.

Carlos watched the remainder of the movie with only half-interest.

He was still hard and could not concentrate on the story. He began thinking of anything that was ugly in order to make his hardon go away. By the end of the film, he was soft again, and was glad to be out of the dark theater.

He walked down to Supremo's Pizza and was relieved to find Ricky there.

"Love! What happened to you last night?" Ricky screamed, causing several people to look at them, and causing Carlos to blush.

"I fell asleep."

"You what? Child, you do not get paid if you fall asleep."

"After."

"Oh. So, did you bump?"

"Bump?"

"Did you have sex, honey? Do I have to draw a picture?"

"Yes, I had sex."

"Another cherry busted!" Ricky yelled happily. "Tell me all about it, Carlos. I want all the sordid details."

Carlos gave all such details and Ricky listened attentively. When the story was over Ricky gave his congratulations, but began to look around nervously.

"What's wrong, Ricky? You look a little anxious."

"Just waiting for a friend. So tell me, did you like it?"

"I don't really remember how I *felt* last night, just what I did. But I think I liked it. I sure liked it when I played with myself this morning."

"Played with yourself? How cute. It's called jacking off or beating your meat. Whacking off or spanking the monkey. You play with yourself when you are a baby, and from the bulge in your pants, you are definitely no baby."

Carlos looked down quickly, afraid he hadn't concealed himself well enough before leaving the theater. He was still a little naive and was a long ways from realizing that eight inches and almost wrist-thick was well above normal for someone his age.

Just then a black Lexus pulled up and Ricky excused himself.

"My friend," he explained.

Carlos watched as Ricky got into the car and began talking to the driver. Ricky was doing something with his arms and the driver looked around nervously. Then for a brief second, Carlos saw a needle moving toward Ricky's arm. Ricky handed the driver a couple of bills and got out of the car, coming back to Carlos.

"Why did you do that?" Carlos asked Ricky as he lit a cigarette.

"Want to try it again?" Ricky offered the cigarette to Carlos.

"No."

"You mean the blow?"

"No. I mean the drugs you just shot into your arm."

Ricky laughed. "The blow *is* the dope I just shot into my arm."

"Then yes, that's what I mean. The blow."

"I did it because I wanted to. You object?"

"It just makes me nervous, that's all."

"Then don't watch."

"Okay, don't get so upset."

"All right, then. Just don't preach to me. I don't need that shit. What do you say we go get some hot chocolate? There's a donut shop up the block that's open twenty-four hours."

"Sounds good."

They walked to the donut shop and each bought a cinnamon roll and coffee. Carlos didn't like the coffee; he would much rather have had the chocolate, but he didn't want to seem like a child to Ricky again, so he ordered coffee, like Ricky did. When they finished their donuts they walked back to the pizza store. It was eleven o'clock, and the street was alive with its Saturday night traffic.

Ricky was wired from the cocaine and kept dancing out into the street. Carlos was still nervous about being out there, and stayed in the shadow of the doorway. He watched as Ricky danced among the cars parked at the red light and wondered how and why Ricky had grown accustomed to such a life. Probably a drunken father or a sickly mother, he thought.

He saw Ricky leaning into a car and then get inside.

"Be back in an hour," Ricky yelled to Carlos as the car pulled away.

Suddenly it seemed darker outside, and colder. The cars appeared to be vicious beasts with bright eyes, and the people all had fangs. Even the buildings were squeezing together, wanting to swallow him alive. Carlos pulled himself away from the building with teeth and walked to the curb, then leaned against a lamppost and tried to catch his breath.

"I thought you people only did that in books and movies."

The voice had snuck up behind him, scaring the hell out of him. Carlos turned around quickly. The voice belonged to a man who appeared to be in his mid-thirties.

"Did what?" Carlos tried to sound calm.

"Lean against a lamppost. If a cop sees you, he'll bust you for sure."

"For what? I'm catching my breath."

"Prostitution."

"In case you didn't notice, I'm a guy, not a girl," Carlos said haughtily.

"Oh, I noticed all right," the man said, stealing a glance at Carlos' crotch. "Boys can be prostitutes, too, you know."

"That's ridiculous," Carlos said distastefully. He had never thought of a guy as a whore, and the thought that he technically could be considered such did not agree with him at all.

"Then what are you doing out here?" the man asked, smiling.

"Waiting for a friend."

"Me, too. Wanna be my friend?"

"No, thanks." Carlos turned away, indicating the end of the conversation.

"Your loss," the man grunted, and walked away.

Carlos' heart was racing with excitement. His first encounter alone, and he'd actually handled a creep. He mentally patted himself on the back and started thinking about what the man had said. Of course he had been paid for having sex, but that alone did not make him a prostitute, did it? He had seen movies with prostitutes in them, and the terms simply did not apply to him. He wasn't without parents, he didn't take drugs, and of course he didn't have a pimp.

He was about to go back to the donut shop and ponder the question further when he heard a familiar voice behind him.

"Where you going?" It was Ricky.

"Hi! I thought you said you'd be gone an hour."

"He just wanted a quickie in the car. I charged him half price. He was cute."

"Ricky," Carlos blurted out, "am I a prostitute?"

It caught Ricky completely by surprise, and he broke into an uncontrollable laughter.

"Honey, it's called a hustler when you're a guy. A prostitute is a girl, or anything close. You are a hustler, honey. *I* am a prostitute."

"Oh." Carlos still wasn't exactly sure what Ricky was saying, but decided to let it go.

"Why do you ask, Carlos?"

"Because some man called me a prostitute while you were gone."

Ricky laughed. "I haven't been called anything that nice in months."

Carlos smiled.

"Honey, do you plan on spending a lot of time around here?"

"I don't know. It kinda scares me."

"Then, why did you come back here tonight?"

"It's better than staying at home," Carlos answered without hesitation.

"I thought so," Ricky said softly.

"Why do you keep coming back?" Carlos asked.

"It's better than staying at home," Ricky answered without hesitation.

"I thought so," Carlos said softly.

IV.

It didn't matter that he'd been on the streets for almost two months. To say that Carlos felt uneasy in his attire would be a gross understatement. But the promise of $200 had shocked him into agreeing. He would have dressed up like Mary Poppins for $200.

A black leather mask that tied in the back covered his entire face, except for the holes for his eyes, nose, and mouth. Tight leather chaps hugged his smooth, muscular legs. He was wearing nothing else. His thick, hard cock stood out straight in front of him through the crotch in the chaps.

He looked down at the man tied to the four-poster bed. The guy was on his knees on top of the mattress. His arms were tied to the footposts so that he was facing Carlos. His feet were tied to the headposts, but with enough slack to allow minimal movement.

Carlos was a little scared. The man, who was absolutely no younger than forty and probably no older than ninety, had instructed Carlos on how he expected to be treated when he first picked him up on Geary Street. Carlos told the man he didn't think he was big enough to play that part, but the man said that unless Carlos had a pair of socks stuffed in his jeans, then he was plenty big enough where it counted. He told Carlos not to hold back and, no matter how hard he would later plead, not to let up until Carlos had cum twice. About that he was adamant; the first time had to be all over his face, the second time with his cock still buried deep in the man's ass. Carlos was glad his face was covered. He doubted this man wanted to see a scared young boy in front of him.

Carlos cracked the cat-o-nine whip in front of the man's face. The guy flinched.

"This is what you get for looking at me while I'm naked, you slob," Carlos said, a little timidly.

"I'm sorry, Master. Please forgive me."

"Forgive you?" Carlos asked, and slapped the man softly across the face.

"Carlos," the man said, irritated, "you have to hit me harder or it won't work. And don't sound so afraid. You hate me, Carlos. Act like it."

"Shut up!" Carlos yelled as he slapped the man hard across the face. He wanted to get this over with as quickly as possible, and decided to play along. "You speak only when I tell you to. Is that clear?"

"Yes, Master," the man said excitedly as he wiggled his ass in the air.

"Suck my dick," Carlos growled, and moved his cock to within an inch of the man's face. The man reached out with his tongue and licked the head of Carlos' fat dick. Carlos shoved his hips forward and rammed the entire length of his long dick deep into the man's throat. The old guy choked, and Carlos pulled out quickly and apologized.

"Don't apologize. Harder and meaner, Carlos. You hate me."

And suddenly he did. He no longer felt sorry for the old man. He hated this man who wanted him to do strange things and he hated being dressed in these weird costumes. He slapped the guy very hard three times across the face again, causing the man's head to turn and a look of shocked delight to take over his face.

"I said shut up. Open your mouth."

The man had a hungry look in his eyes, and opened his mouth wide to accommodate Carlos' thick uncut cock. Carlos laid the heavy dick on the tip of the man's tongue and slowly began to slide it into his mouth. The guy tried to swallow more of Carlos' dick than Carlos allowed, and was punished with another heavy slap across the face. This time Carlos' cock was halfway inside the man's mouth, and Carlos could feel his dick against the man's cheek as he slapped him. The feeling made his cock throb even more with excitement.

The bound man moaned loudly, and without warning Carlos slammed his big cock all the way down his throat. This time the guy did not choke, and Carlos felt the throat muscles tighten magically around his hot cock. He gasped with the surprise of how good it felt, and grabbed him by the hair, pulling the hot mouth onto his dick harder and faster. He saw the guy's ass moving up and down as he was sucking Carlos, and slapped the heavy end of the whip against the fleshy part of the man's ass. That drew another moan.

"You want me to fuck your ass with this whip?" Carlos asked his servant.

"Yes," the man begged. "Oh, yes, please."

"Did I say you could stop sucking my dick?" Carlos asked roughly, and rammed his dick back down the tight throat. "Well, I'm not going to fuck you with this whip. It's too small."

The man was sucking Carlos for all he was worth now, and despite himself, Carlos was very close to cumming.

"As soon as you get me hard enough, I'm gonna stick my big dick up your ass and fuck you till you cry for mercy. But you'd better do better than this," Carlos said, slapping his face hard again, "because I'm not even gonna stay hard if you don't start suckin' my cock better."

That was a lie. His dick was stretched to its absolute maximum, and the veins were pulsing wildly. Just the sound of his own voice saying those dirty words out loud was enough to push Carlos over the edge. He pulled out of the old man's mouth without warning and sprayed his hot cum all over the old guy's face. The man kept his mouth wide open and most of the cum went inside, splashing forcefully against the back of his throat. But a great deal of it also landed on his eyes and nose and cheeks.

Carlos shoved his cock back into the man's mouth and kept it there until the man had licked him clean and gotten him fully hard again. It didn't take long. He was more than ready.

"Please don't fuck me," the man begged as Carlos worked his way behind him and began to slap his ass. "You're too big. It'll hurt."

Carlos' pulse raced just hearing these words now, and he put the tip of his dick at the hole of the man's ass and slapped his ass cheeks hard. The guy cried out in mock pain as Carlos thrust himself deep inside his ass in one move.

"Shut up, you pig," Carlos said hatefully, and pulled his thick cock all the way out of the man's ass.

"Thank . . ."

He was cut short with a stabbing pain as Carlos roughly shoved the big dick back in to the balls in one single, brutal thrust.

"Carlos, really. Please stop now. You're too big. You're hurting me."

Carlos put his hands on the small of the man's back and forced him to lie flat on his stomach. He fucked him deep and hard.

Half an hour later, Carlos ground his teeth, stiffened his body, and lay perfectly still as his steamy load filled the man's ass.

When he was done he untied the man quickly and apologized for getting carried away. The man said nothing. He paid Carlos ten twenty-dollar bills and offered to drive him home. Neither said a word on the drive back to Geary Street. When they pulled up in front of the Supremo's, the man handed Carlos a business card with his home phone number.

"You did okay for your first time, kid. Any time you want to get those beautiful rocks off, give me a call. Only next time, be a little rougher, okay?"

Carlos left the card sitting on the car seat, saying there would be no next time. The man with the sore ass said that was too bad, and drove off.

Walking briskly up to Ricky, Carlos announced, "I guess I'm a hustler."

Ricky laughed.

V.

The next two weeks flew by for Carlos. He and Ricky had become very close friends, and Carlos had become a bona fide hustler, already commanding more money per trick than any of the others, and getting double the number of requests. He wasn't real sure how he felt about that, exactly, but he was making his own decisions about life, and at least that felt good.

Every evening after his parents went to bed he would kiss Rosie on the forehead and crawl out his bedroom window. He spent every night in front of the pizza store on Geary Street with Ricky. Ricky would spend hours trying to teach Carlos the fine art of hustling, and Carlos would listen politely. But he really only took to heart less than half of what his friend said. They were two very different people and they drew different clientele. Ricky went for $25 and would settle for $15 if he was low enough; Carlos went for no less than $50 for a simple blowjob and as high as $300, depending on how kinky the job was. Ricky was lucky to get one or two tricks per night, and Carlos always stopped after four gigs, but he could easily have doubled that number.

Even though Carlos rejected most of his hustling advice, he valued Ricky's friendship more than anything. He was fascinated with the stories Ricky told and with his sense of humor in what seemed like a humorless life. Carlos tried to get Ricky to talk about his family, but Ricky's favorite put off was, "Honey, we're no Brady Bunch, that's for sure." Carlos told Ricky all about his family, except for the part about Richard Norman, and when his life story began to depress him, Ricky would always put an arm around him and whisper, "It's all right, child. You'll beat it. You've got what it takes." Then he'd offer to treat Carlos to doughnuts and hot chocolate. Carlos always paid, of course, but he didn't mind. He loved being around Ricky.

Carlos saved most of his money, but he did like to buy new clothes every now and then. He would show up with a new sweater or a new pair of shoes and Ricky would praise them all night. Carlos tried to get Ricky to save some of his money, too, but to no avail. Ricky spent all his money on drugs and Seagram's Seven. His mom would find the money and spend it anyway, he said, so why bother?

One night Carlos bought Ricky a new sweater from Saks Fifth Avenue. A john had taken him to New York for the whole weekend, and Carlos had insisted on shopping at the original Saks. He knew Ricky would love the sweater the moment he saw it. It was 100 percent lamb's wool, and cost him $150 on sale. When he gave it to Ricky that night, Ricky cried as he put it on, and that made Carlos very nervous. He'd never seen Ricky cry, no matter how bad things got.

Ricky got high that night, and drunk, too. He passed out on the street and Carlos couldn't wake him up. One of the other queens came swishing over and bent down over Ricky. Carlos' defenses went up immediately, and he was ready to fight. The queens on Geary were very territorial and vicious, and most of them didn't like the others. Ricky had one or two friends out there, but most of the queens teased him and were mean. Carlos was shocked when this queen, whom he'd never seen even speak to Ricky, picked up Ricky's hand and patted it tenderly.

"She looks pretty bad this time. Can you stay here with her for a minute?"

"Of course," Carlos answered, still in shock.

Ten minutes later the queen returned with a friend who had a car.

"I know where she lives, but I can't stay with her all night," the queen said. "If we drop you off at her place, can you stay with her? She's gonna need someone there to hold her when she wakes up."

Carlos said he certainly would stay with Ricky, and drove the few miles to his house with the queen and his friend. He was surprised to discover that Ricky lived outside of San Franicsco, in the suburb of Pacifica.

"His mom will be crashed out already, but the front door is always unlocked. His room is second on the left, next to the bathroom. Take good care of him, okay, kid? He really needs someone to love him."

Carlos noticed the way the queen switched to the masculine form when speaking about Ricky toward the end of the conversation. Underneath all the bullshit about being "girlfriends," they were really two guys who were both hurting and who looked out for one another.

The queen and his friend drove off, leaving Carlos standing in a strange neighborhood at three o'clock in the morning, trying to carry his drunk friend into a strange house. Still unconscious, Ricky was much heavier than he seemed when he was awake.

Carlos propped him up against the porch and opened the front door. Almost immediately he was knocked over by the overpowering smell of dog shit. He held his breath and pulled Ricky into the front room. As he closed the door a small Pomeranian ran up to him and began barking viciously and biting at his pant legs. *They didn't tell me about the damn dog,* Carlos cursed, and hurried to get Ricky into his room. On the way there he stepped in some of the dog shit and tripped over three beer cans.

He finally got Ricky into his room and onto his bed. Fido bit his ankles as he was dropping Ricky onto the bed, and Carlos kicked the dog all the way out into the hallway. The dog yelped and ran back into the front room. Carlos wondered how Ricky's mom could sleep through all the noise as he slammed the bedroom door shut. *Damn dog probably has rabies,* he thought, feeling the pain in his ankle.

Carlos turned on the bedroom light and got Ricky undressed and into bed. When Ricky was covered and Carlos could do no more for him, he sat down on the old lounge chair across from the bed and looked around him. There were dirty clothes thrown everywhere: underwear hanging from the top of the closet door, dirty socks on the old stereo and all over the floor, jeans discarded wherever Ricky had happened to step out of them, and filthy t-shirts peeking out from under the bed. There was a half-eaten bologna and cheese sandwich and a spilled can of beer on the desk next to the CD player. Several cockroaches were doing their best to finish off the sandwich, another lay drowned in a puddle of the spilled beer that had long ago dried up.

Carlos closed his eyes and fought off the tears he felt for his friend. The people who had dropped him off hadn't mentioned Ricky's father, and since Ricky never mentioned him either, Carlos assumed there was no father. His mother was obviously a drunk who didn't care about herself or her son. Carlos suddenly felt guilty about ever feeling sorry for himself. His mother loved him and Rosie very much, and did everything she could to make life better for them. She kept an immaculately clean house, always had a good dinner ready for them, and was always there when he needed her. His own room was spotless and he always had clean, warm clothes, not just old jeans and t-shirts.

Carlos had fallen into a light doze thinking about his home, and was jolted awake when Ricky began screaming hysterically. Carlos ran over to the bed and tried to lay Ricky back down. The screams were very loud and Ricky began to struggle against him. He was sure that Ricky's mom would come running in any minute now, and he'd have to explain who he was and why he was here at three in the morning fighting with her son while he was screaming. But she never came in and Carlos was left to tend to Ricky alone.

"Ricky, wake up. It's me, Carlos."

"Don't do that!" Ricky was yelling over and over.

Carlos slapped Ricky hard across the face three or four times, until he finally woke Ricky up. Ricky opened his eyes slowly and stopped screaming.

"God, what's happening to me?" he asked when he could finally speak. Then he broke down and began to cry.

"Hey, it's okay, Ricky. I'm here," Carlos said, trying to get Ricky to focus on him. Instead, he leaned over the side of the bed and threw up all over the floor.

"There's some hamburger in the fridge," Ricky said as he stopped vomiting. "Go get it."

"What?" Carlos though Ricky perhaps was delirious.

"Hamburger."

"Ricky, I don't know how to cook."

"Not cooked. Raw. It'll make me throw up some more. Gotta get this shit out of my stomach."

Carlos ran into the kitchen and grabbed the hamburger. Halfway back to the bedroom he ran back to the kitchen to get a big pot. On his way back to Ricky's room he was attacked again by Fido the Terrible. Carlos simply hit him over the head with the heavy pot, and walked back to the bedroom, leaving the dog dazed in the front room.

Ricky ate the raw meat and, true to his word, he nearly half filled the large pot. Then he cried and Carlos held him in his arms.

"Don't cry, Ricky. It'll be okay."

"How'd we get here?"

"One of your friends brought us here."

"Oh. Look, Carlos, thanks a lot. I'm okay now. You can go."

"Not a chance. You need me Ricky, and I'm not going anywhere."

"God, Carlos, I'm so fucked up."

"It's okay, child"—Carlos tried to make Ricky laugh by imitating him—"you'll beat it. You've got what it takes. Remember, that's what you always tell me."

"No, Carlos, I don't have what it takes. Look around you, sweetheart. What do you see?"

"A very dirty room, so what. Mine's messy, too," Carlos lied.

"I see a hell with no exit sign, Carlos, and I can't take it anymore. I want out, baby, I just want out." He sniffled.

Carlos cradled his friend and rocked his head gently. He wanted to cry, too, but he couldn't. He had to be strong for Ricky. But he felt so inadequate. He wasn't a psychologist, or even an advice columnist. He was a young boy, with problems of his own. But they didn't seem important anymore. He had to help Ricky. Psychologist or not, he recognized the telltale signs of someone ready to give up, and he was seeing them now in his best friend.

"Ricky, you can get out, babe, you can. Start by having more respect for yourself, man. You're a great guy, you deserve some respect. Then save some of your money and just leave. The only way out of someplace you don't wanna be is to never look back. Look only forward, Ricky. No looking back."

Ricky had stopped crying by now, but Carlos kept rocking him anyway, cradling his head against his shoulder.

"It'll be worth it, Ricky, I swear it will. You just need to know that someone loves you, and I'm telling you here and now that I love you. What do you say, Ricky?"

A soft snore was his answer, and Carlos was glad that Ricky was asleep. He was exhausted himself and desperately needed to rest. He leaned back against the wall and fell asleep with Ricky's head still against his shoulder.

* * *

Carlos woke up about four hours later with a throbbing pain in the back of his neck. He had slept in an upright position with his head against the wall. His arms were still wrapped around Ricky, who was still asleep. He had no idea what time it was; the drapes were drawn and it was dark in the room. He looked around for an alarm clock and couldn't find one. He thought, sadly, that Ricky had nothing of importance for which he would need an alarm clock to wake up.

Carlos felt a heavy pressure in his bladder and knew if he didn't make it to the bathroom quick he would piss his pants and all over Ricky's bed. He tried to move Ricky without waking him, but Ricky was a light sleeper.

"Don't go, Carlos," he said sleepily. "Please don't leave me."

"Just gotta take a whiz," Carlos said as he maneuvered from underneath his friend. "Go back to sleep."

Carlos walked into the bathroom and stepped into a bowl of water that was set next to the toilet. It was obviously for the furball, and he thought seriously about filling the bowl with piss, courtesy of Carlos Cortez. He decided against it at the last minute, and pointed the stream into the toilet bowl instead. He flushed the toilet, which sounded similar to a derailing freight train, and went back into Ricky's bedroom.

Ricky was sitting up in bed, leaning against the wall and smoking a cigarette.

"Gross," Carlos said with a nasty face, "how can you smoke so early in the morning?"

"What time is it?"

"I don't know. I can't find a clock. But the sun is shining through the bathroom window. It must be somewhere around eight or nine."

"Is my mom up?"

"I don't know. The TV is on in the front room, but I didn't see anyone."

"She's up, then. Are you hungry?"

"Starving."

"Come on, I'll introduce you to Mom. I'm sure she'll want to cook for you. Humor her, okay?"

"That's not necessary, Ricky, really. I should be going home. My mom will be worried silly."

"Please, Carlos. Just stay for breakfast."

"All right," Carlos said.

Ricky got up and began changing his clothes. He stripped and walked around the room naked, looking through the mass of clothes strewn around the room. Carlos couldn't help but notice Ricky's body. He was even skinnier than Carlos had thought, and his skin was snowwhite all over. His dick was very small and he had shaven the hair from around it completely. His ass was flat and flabby, and he already showed signs of stretch marks around the hips. Carlos could hardly believe he was looking at the body of a sixteen-year-old boy.

Ricky caught Carlos looking at his body, and Carlos turned his head quickly.

"I haven't always looked this marvelous," Ricky joked. "You should've seen me before I started taking the steroids."

They both laughed, and Ricky finally found some satisfactorily clean clothes and put them on. He put on a fresh coat of makeup and asked Carlos how he looked.

"Fine, but doesn't your mother care that you go around like that?"

"Like what?"

"With makeup on your face."

"Heavens, no, child. She even borrows from me when she's out," Ricky said. The old Ricky was back and he draped his arm over Carlos' shoulder and walked with him into the front room.

Their nostrils were instantly assaulted by the smell of marijuana. The first thing Carlos saw when he entered the front room was Fido. He was lying at the foot of the couch, his head between his paws, and he looked a little cross-eyed. He was either suffering from a headache from the bang on the head last night or stoned from the smoke that filled the room.

The second thing Carlos saw was the mammoth of a woman who could very easily have been mistaken for Mount St. Helens. She was wearing a very old bathrobe that had several stains on it that

Carlos was certain were older than him. Her hair was in rollers and she wore no makeup. In one hand she held a yellow, generic brand beer can and in the other she held a joint. Her eyes were glued to the TV set. A traveling evangelist was warning his early morning audience of the coming doom.

"Good morning, Mom," Ricky said. His arm was still around Carlos' shoulder and Carlos' heart rate sped up when Ricky didn't make a move to remove it before his mother saw.

"Hi, son," the volcano said. "Who's your new boyfriend?"

Carlos tried to swallow, but a giant lump in his throat prevented him from doing so.

"His name is Carlos."

Carlos looked at Ricky in horror.

"He's much cuter than your last boyfriend," she said appreciatively.

"Thank you, ma'am," Carlos said, still trying to swallow.

"And polite, too. You hungry, Carlos?"

"Yes, he is," Ricky answered for him, afraid Carlos would chicken out.

Mount. St. Helens tried to erupt herself from the couch, but was not very successful. Ricky had to go over and anchor his feet against the couch and pull with significant effort to help her stand.

"You boys sit down and have a beer. Breakfast will be ready in about half an hour."

The two friends sat down on the couch and Ricky reached for a beer. Carlos slapped his hand.

"Are you crazy? You're still sick. You can't drink beer before breakfast."

"Why not?" Ricky asked.

"Because it'll kill you. Ever hear of orange juice?"

"Sure. Mom drinks it with breakfast."

"See. It's good for you."

"She says it gives the vodka a little flavor."

"Well, try it straight this once, okay? For me?"

"Oh, all right."

"Ricky, why did you tell your mom I was your boyfriend?"

"I didn't. She told me."

"Well, why didn't you tell her the truth?"

"Because she doesn't understand. She thinks I fuck around with every guy I know. And until you came around, she was right. So I just let it slide."

"Oh, stop exaggerating."

"I'm not. Most guys don't want anything to do with me. Those that do only want one thing. Kinda funny that the one guy I really would like to get involved with just wants to be my friend, huh?"

"What's wrong with being just friends?"

"Nothing," Ricky said. He didn't like arguing with Carlos because he never won. Carlos was too smart and too logical. "Let's watch Preacher Joe."

VI.

Carlos and Rosie were watching *Saturday Night Live*. It wasn't Saturday night at all, only Friday evening. And the show wasn't live, it was syndicated. Rosie's bedtime was eight-thirty, but she'd been looking forward to seeing the show so badly that Carlos said he'd allow her to stay up late to watch it. Fergie was the guest host, and next to Hannah Montana, she thought Fergie was possibly the best thing since cherry Red Vines.

Rosie knew she had Carlos wrapped around her baby fingers, and at five years old, she knew how to fully manipulate her older brother to her full advantage. When she'd first asked Carlos to let her stay up until eleven so she could see Fergie, he'd said no, as she knew he would. She crawled into his lap and cried softly. Within three minutes Carlos had relented, as she also knew he would. When he made popcorn to snack on during the show, she'd asked for extra butter. Carlos did not like butter on his popcorn, but Rosie batted her baby browns, and of course Carlos melted half a stick of butter. He recognized her little games, but was still powerless against them, and if he were honest with himself, he would admit that he liked it that way.

Rosie was halfway through her cute little bump-and-grind

dance to "London Bridge" when her mother came crashing through the front door and fell into the living room. Rosie stopped her dance and stared wide-eyed as Carlos ran to his mother.

"What's wrong, Mom?" Carlos cried as he tried to help her stand. Her face was cut and bleeding, and her eye was beginning to swell shut with what would soon be a very bad black eye.

"Run, baby," she said, and spit blood. "Get outta here and run to your friend's house."

"What happened?"

"Just go, Carlos. He's coming right now."

Lydia was still trying to gain her footing, but kept falling. Carlos helped her to the couch, and turned to little Rosie. She was still staring bug-eyed at her mother, and a tiny tear was falling down her cheek.

"Go to your room, princess," Carlos told her. "Shut the door and don't come out here, okay? Just go to sleep. Everything will be okay in the morning."

Rosie stood frozen in her place, and at first Carlos thought she wasn't breathing. He walked over and carried her to their bedroom. He tucked her into bed and kissed her on the forehead. She was still staring blankly ahead. Carlos thought she might be in shock, but figured she'd probably be all right. He wasn't so sure about his mom, though, and went out to see her.

"Honey, you have to go," Lydia told him. "I'll be all right. Please, just go stay at your friend's house."

"Yes, Carlos," his father yelled from the front door, "why don't you go stay with your little faggot friend."

"Oh my God," Lydia cried. "Please, Juan, don't be like this."

"Shut up, you bitch," Juan yelled.

Carlos had already decided he wasn't going to back down this time. Seeing his mother beaten like that had made up his mind.

"Don't call her a bitch," Carlos said sharply.

"What did you say?" Juan yelled back.

"I said don't call my mother a bitch."

"You little punk," Juan said, and charged Carlos. He landed a punch to Carlos' jaw, and Carlos fell to the ground.

"Stop it!" Lydia screamed.

Carlos stood up and charged back at his father. He slammed his head into Juan's stomach and knocked him on his ass onto the floor. Juan pulled Carlos down with him and threw a fist into Carlos' stomach. Carlos gasped for breath and Juan was on his feet, kicking him in the back. Carlos grabbed Juan's leg and yanked it out from under him. Juan landed on his back and Carlos was up in a moment, kicking his foot into Juan's crotch as hard as he could. Juan's eyes rolled back into his head. Carlos kept kicking his father hard in the groin, and after five or six hard kicks, Juan lost consciousness.

Carlos stopped kicking his father and simply stared at him for a moment as he lay unconscious. Then he collapsed onto the couch and began to cry. His mother pulled him to her chest and cradled him.

"Oh, baby, I'm so sorry. So sorry, baby."

"Mom, what happened?"

"He got drunk again and said he was going to kill you. I tried to talk to him, but he started hitting me. Some guys at the bar pulled him off of me and I ran home. God, Carlos, I'm so scared."

"Don't worry, Mom," Carlos said, drying his own tears and regaining his composure.

"What are we going to do, baby?"

"*We* aren't going to do anything. *I'm* going to leave."

"Carlos . . ."

"No, Mom. He only fights about me. He never hits you or Princess unless he's pissed at me. I have some money saved up and I can stay with a friend."

"Oh, Carlos," Lydia sobbed.

Carlos kissed his mom on the cheek and got up to go to his room. He noticed Juan stirring, beginning to regain consciousness.

"Gotta hurry." He nodded to Juan. "I'll be in touch, Mom. I love you."

Carlos went to his room and took the money from his sock drawer. He counted $1,700 and put it in his front pocket. Then he put some clothes in a paper bag and walked to his window. He stopped at the window and walked back to his little sister.

"I love you, princess," he told the sleeping girl.

With that done, he climbed through the window into the cold night.

* * *

Ricky saw Carlos walking toward him with the paper bag and wondered what was going on. He walked away from the Supremo's entryway and met Carlos halfway. He noticed the blood and the beginning of bruises right away and his heart sped up.

"Child, what in hell happened to you?"

"Family problems," Carlos said, trying to minimize the conversation.

"More like a catastrophe, it looks like."

"Yeah, I guess so. Listen, Ricky, I've got an idea. You said you wanted to get away, right?"

"Yeah."

"Well, I'm leaving home. How would you like to share a motel room together?"

"You mean for good?"

"Well, for a while anyway. We can find a cheap motel and split the rent."

"Are you serious?"

"Yes. I saved up some money. That'll get us started, then from then on out we split the rent fifty-fifty. What do you say?"

"Let's do it!"

They walked a few blocks down Geary Street to the Rainbow Ranch Motel. It was a series of duplex-like rooms consisting of a bathroom, a tiny kitchenette, and a combination living room/bedroom. Ricky had been there a few times with tricks, and a room had cost $50 per night. Because Carlos and Ricky were paying two weeks in advance and told the clerk they'd be staying for a while longer after that, he let them have their suite for $200 a week.

Carlos situated his clothes neatly in the closet and bureau drawers, and the boys decided to wait until the next day to get Ricky's clothes.

"They can wait," Ricky said, "but there's something that can't."

"What's that?"

"Carlos, hon. You're hurting and I can tell you want to talk. What happened?"

"My dad beat the hell out of my mom and then came after me. He got in a few good punches before I knocked him out cold."

"Why did he go off like that?"

"Because he's not my real dad. Right after she married him, my mom had an affair with a white guy. I'm his son. My dad, I mean Juan, can't stand me. Every time he sees me he goes crazy. I've tried to be a real son to him. I've tried really hard. I don't know why he hates me so much. It's not my fault what happened."

"Of course it's not. He's just stupid, that's all."

"Yeah, I know. My mom still loves him though, and I have a little sister. She's his. He's really nice to both of them. The only time he's rowdy is when he's drinking and I'm around to remind him of the affair. He'll take good care of them as long as I'm gone. That's why I left."

"I'm sorry to hear it's such a shitty story, man. But remember what you always tell me? Look only forward . . . no looking back. If anyone can make it out on his own, I know you can."

"What do you mean, out on my own. Now we're in this together."

"Right."

"Ricky, we're gonna have to be careful with our money now. That means you're gonna have to cut down on your drug habit and use the money for rent."

"Yeah, I know. It's gonna be hard, but I'll try really hard, Carlos, really I will."

"Good! Now what do you say we go out and make some money?"

"All right!"

They went back to Supremo's and began their routine. It was already 1:00 A.M., and a very slow night. Carlos got only two dates and Ricky only one. They decided to call it a night at 3:00 A.M. and headed back to the motel. Inside the room Carlos was met with a dilemma he never expected.

"Carlos, love," Ricky cooed.

"Hmm?"

"Do you like me?"

"Of course I do. What kind of question is that?"

"A serious one."

"What's up, Ricky?"

"I want you to make love to me."

"What?" Carlos coughed out.

"I want you to make love to me."

"Oh Jesus, Ricky."

"Carlos, I like you a lot. I feel like you're my only friend. When I go to bed with someone, I don't feel anything. The men fuck me and then get rid of me as soon as they can. I play no part in it whatsoever. They use my ass, pay me, and then throw me away. Just once I want to really make love with someone. I want to feel something for the person who's inside me. Just once, I'd like to cum, too."

"Christ, Ricky," Carlos said, sitting next to Ricky on the bed. "You are my friend. I can't make love to you. I'd feel like I was just another of those men using you."

"But you said you like me. That makes all the difference. None of those other men care for me one way or the other."

"Ricky, if we had sex it would ruin our friendship. I don't have sex for the fun of it, man. I fuck for money, and so do you. Besides," Carlos tried his hand at comic relief, "I wouldn't know how much to charge you."

Ricky didn't laugh.

"You think I'm ugly, don't you? You don't like my body."

"Come on, man, it's not that."

"You have a great body, Carlos, anyone can see that. You have big muscles, a big cock, and a gorgeous face. I know I can't compete with that on the streets, but I thought with you I wouldn't have to look like Prince Charming."

"Ricky . . ."

"Hey, it's all right, Carlos. I understand. Still friends, right?"

"You know we are, Ricky."

"Good. Let's get some sleep."

Ricky stripped and climbed into bed stark-assed naked. Carlos lay on top of the comforter, fully dressed, and stared at the ceiling until sunrise.

VII.

Carlos had been careless, but he didn't realize it until it was too late. The man had driven around the block at least three times, moving slower each time as he passed Carlos and Ricky, then speeding up as he turned the corner to come around again. After the third time, Carlos didn't see him again and thought he'd kept going.

Then Carlos noticed the man walking toward him. Every hustler on the street tried to get his attention. He was obviously rich and obviously interested in purchased sex. The man brushed the others aside thoughtlessly and walked directly to Carlos.

"Would you be interested in spending the evening with me?"

It was the most direct approach Carlos had ever heard. He looked at Ricky, who just shrugged his shoulders.

"Well . . ." Carlos said.

"I'll pay you a thousand dollars."

"He's interested," Ricky screamed, and pushed Carlos toward the man.

"Good. This way, please," the man said, and turned to walk back down the street where he'd parked his car.

Carlos followed him, looking back over his shoulders at Ricky every five steps or so. Several of the other hustlers were throwing him nasty looks and giving him catcalls. He dismissed them and wondered why anyone would pay a thousand dollars when he could easily get it for fifty. But when the door to the Rolls Royce opened and Carlos was eased into a luxurious backseat with full bar, TV, and stereo, he no longer cared. He was in a dreamworld, and he didn't care why.

They drove for almost an hour, and when they left the city limits heading into the Oakland hills, Carlos began to get nervous.

"Hey, where are we going?"

"Don't worry, kid. I live out here."

"Ever hear of hotels?" Carlos asked.

"Don't like them. Besides, they don't carry the equipment I like."

"Equipment?"

"Yes. I like it rough. Slings, whips, leather."

"Oh." Carlos had dealt with this kind before and his experience was good. The older men who liked to be tied up and beaten by young, leather-clad boys were usually pretty strange, but harmless. For a thousand dollars Carlos was willing to play along, even if it meant driving to Sacramento, a couple of hours away.

They pulled into a driveway the size of Interstate 50, and when they stopped in front of the giant brick mansion, Carlos gasped loudly. The next second he felt a sharp pain in the base of his neck, and the world went black.

* * *

When he came to he was in a dark room. His clothes had been removed and he was dressed in a spiked leather vest and chaps. There was a whip behind him. He wore no underwear, and his limp cock was sticking through the hole in front of the chaps. His bare ass felt cold on the concrete floor.

Carlos jumped up and quickly looked around the room. There were chained shackles drilled into the wall. A four-poster bed equipped with handcuffs. From the ceiling there hung a giant leather sling. Tied inside it was a young boy no older than Carlos, possibly even younger. He was blond, thin, and small. He was also naked. A long, thin leather strap resembling a shoestring was his only accessory. It wrapped itself around his cock several times and made a V up to his neck, where it was tied in the back.

"Welcome back," came a voice through an overhead speaker.

"What's going on here?" Carlos yelled. "Where the fuck am I?"

"Why, you're at my house, of course." This was not the voice of the man he'd spoken to earlier. This voice was deeper, and had a thick Latino accent.

"Hey, man, this was not part of the deal," Carlos said, trying to see where the voice was coming from. The room was too dark. He couldn't see anything beyond the kid in the sling.

"The only *deal* was that I would pay you a thousand dollars to spend the evening with me. When you wake up tomorrow morning you will find ten one-hundred-dollar bills in your jeans pocket. You will be sore, but healthy. You will be exactly where I picked you up tonight, and you will not say a word about what happened here to anyone. I will live up to my end of the deal, and you will live up to yours. The measure of a man is in his integrity, my sexy little amigo. In his integrity and nowhere else. I expect much integrity from you."

"I never agreed to this, you sadistic son of a bitch." Carlos was surprised to hear himself talking like this. It was amazing how much he'd picked up from the streets in only a few short months.

"Not yet. But you will. Now, enough talk. I want you to teach this young man a lesson. He's been very bad and I want you to discipline him. The whip at your feet is only somewhat sufficient. He only responds completely to the whip hanging between your legs. Now, discipline him, amigo."

"I won't hit this kid with any whip. And I'm definitely not going to fuck him, either. He's just a kid, for crying out loud."

"You will do it, boy, and you will make him beg you to stop. You will make him cry."

"No, I won't," Carlos said stubbornly.

"You will, or you will switch places with the boy, and believe me, he will not hesitate to cooperate with us. Now pick up the damned whip and get to work."

Carlos picked up the whip and walked over to the young boy. He bent down and whispered into the kid's ear.

"How can we get out of here?" he asked.

"You can't. Just do what they tell you. Be careful with the whip though, it can leave scars if you hit too hard. But feel free to fuck me as hard as you want. I can take it."

"You want me to go along with this?" Carlos was astounded.

"Yes. It's not as bad as it looks, as long as you don't get carried away with the whip. To tell you the truth, it's kinda fun."

Carlos stood up straight, amazed at what he was hearing.

"Enough talking!" came the voice again. The accent seemed a bit thicker to Carlos. "Get to work."

"Are you sure?" Carlos asked the young boy again, quietly.

"Yes. Punish me, and do a lot of talking. He likes that."

Carlos picked up the whip and cracked it in the air a couple of times, a trick he'd learned from earlier S&M encounters. He walked around the sling once or twice, then brought the whip down gently across the boy's exposed ass.

"Why did you do it?" Carlos inquired.

"I didn't do it, sir."

"Don't lie to me," Carlos yelled, and cracked the whip into the air again. The boy's ass was already turning pink after only one slap, and Carlos was worried he might hurt him. The boy, however, showed no concern, so Carlos continued.

"You know what your punishment is for this crime, don't you?" Carlos teased.

"No, please," the boy begged.

Carlos walked up behind the boy. His cock hung limp in front of the kid's face.

"Suck it!"

The boy began to lick the big dick. It didn't take long for Carlos' cock to harden, and when it did, the boy wrapped his lips tightly around the head and sucked. Carlos began to push his cock in and out of the wet mouth. His dick became fat and hard, and grew to its full eight inches in only a couple of minutes.

The boy opened his mouth hungrily and swallowed the entire length. Carlos pumped faster and harder, and the boy sucked just as fast and just as hard. Carlos felt the big vein in his cock begin to pulse wildly and he knew he was getting close. He pulled out quickly.

"You're not good enough," Carlos lied as he bit his lips to keep from cumming. He grabbed his heavy cock and slapped it hard across the blond boy's face. It made a heavy thud and the boy flinched.

"Please don't," the boy pleaded.

Carlos slapped his dick across the smooth, young face and the boy licked it as it hit his mouth.

"You should've sucked me better, little boy, because now I'm gonna have to fuck you. I'm going to ram my dick up your ass deep and hard."

"Please don't fuck me. I've never been fucked before. Don't hurt me, please."

Carlos was already in position. The boy was securely tied, his legs high in the air. His ass was completely exposed. Carlos grabbed a cheek in each hand and spread them apart. The boy's hole was pink and looked very tight. Carlos spit on his huge cock head and slammed it all the way into the boy's smooth ass in one swift jab.

The boy gasped in pain and closed his eyes.

"Please stop. You're too big. God, it hurts."

"Shut up, you scum," Carlos yelled, and slapped the boy's ass. The boy tightened his ass muscles, and Carlos almost exploded then and there. The kid was hot and very tight inside, and the muscles wrapped themselves around Carlos' fat, hard shaft like an electric blanket. Carlos was reluctant to pull out, but anxious to get going at same time. He pulled his cock almost all the way out, until just the head remained inside the hot ass. He slowly pushed the huge pole deep into the ass again, and repeated it faster and with more force.

"When you're almost ready to shoot, pull out," the young boy whispered. "He likes to see you spray all over my face."

"You know this guy?" Carlos asked.

"Yeah, he pays really well. I do this once every six weeks or so."

"It's safe, then?" Carlos asked.

"Enough talking," the unseen voice said. "Fuck him harder."

"Just do it," the boy said, and wiggled his ass around Carlos' hard cock. "Don't make him mad."

Carlos fucked the kid as hard as he'd ever fucked anyone, and the boy was not only *taking* Carlos' big dick, but actually thrusting his ass onto it. He looked up at Carlos and winked, a smile covering his face. He was tightening his ass muscles again, in a steady rhythm, and this time Carlos could not hold back.

He pulled his cock out and pumped it with his hand. A large, hot load of cum poured out of the dick and landed on the boy's face. Three more equally large jets of cum landed on the boy's chest and stomach. The boy's own cock, which was hard, but small, splashed an amazingly large load of its own when he felt the heat from Carlos' load.

"Excellent," the voice all around him said. "Now come over here and stand against the wall."

The boy nodded with his head to the wall closest to them.

Carlos walked over to the wall and stood there silently for a moment. It was pitch dark there, and he couldn't see a thing. A couple of seconds later a hand grabbed him by the back of the head and pulled him closer to the wall, until his head banged against it. It didn't hurt, but surprised him. There was a small hole in the wall, and before Carlos had time to react, a long, hard cock pushed through the hole and pressed against his mouth.

"Suck my cock," the deep voice said.

"I don't do that, man," Carlos said as he tried to turn his head away. "You can suck my dick, but I don't . . ."

"I said, suck my dick!"

The strong hands on either side of the back of Carlos' head pulled him closer to the wall, and against the hard cock. When Carlos tried to say something, the man on the other side of the wall pushed his dick forward and forced it into Carlos' mouth. It was big and thick, and already salty with precum, and Carlos gagged as it pushed deeper into his mouth and past his tonsils.

"Open your mouth and swallow my cock," the voice demanded. "Stop scraping me with your teeth, or I will hurt you."

Carlos believed the man with the deep and accented voice. He was afraid of what might happen if the man was not happy. He'd never sucked a cock before, had never even thought about it much. The men he'd been with had all been older or fat or hairy, or a number of combinations that made them all unattractive to him. The thought of sucking their cocks had never entered his mind, and none of them had ever brought it up either. They'd always seemed content to be used by his instead.

So he was a little surprised when his own cock jumped back to life as the big dick throbbed inside his mouth and slid deeper into his throat. As the big head pressed against his tonsils, Carlos opened his throat wider and felt his heart race as the cock slid all the way inside him. When his nose pressed against the man's bush, Carlos felt a large gob of precum slide out of his own cock head and down the length of his hard and throbbing cock.

"That's it, amigo," the man said, but this time his voice came not from an overhead speaker, but from a couple of inches away. "Suck my cock deep into your mouth."

Without even thinking about it, Carlos wrapped his lips tighter around the big dick and sucked it deeper into his throat. When the man began thrusting in and out of his mouth, Carlos was surprised to see that he was reluctant to let it slip from his mouth, and sucked it back inside him every time it threatened to leave his lips. He loved the way the thick veins felt against his lips and tongue, and the heat from the cock made him hungry for more. He gagged a little the first couple of times the man slid all the way back down his throat, but quickly regained his breath and after only a couple of times, he had his technique down perfectly.

"Oh my God," the man moaned. "I'm cumming."

Carlos moaned loudly, and wrapped his lips tighter around the cock and sucked the man deeper into his throat. He grabbed his own cock and started stroking it as he felt the man's dick grow thicker inside him. After only a couple of strokes, his body became rigid as he sprayed another load all across the wall in front of him.

"Ungh," the man moaned, and shoved his dick deeper still into Carlos, and held Carlos' head tight against his crotch.

Carlos felt the big cock pulse and contract in this throat. He didn't taste anything because the head was deep in his throat and way past his taste buds, but he felt the heat of the man's load as it slid down his throat and into his stomach. After a few shots, the man slid his cock slowly out of Carlos' throat, and he tasted the sweet warm cum as it landed on his tongue and he swallowed it.

It was much better than he'd ever thought it would be, and he was reluctant to let the big dick go. He sucked on it and tried to pull it back into his throat again. A couple of seconds later he felt the familiar sharp pain on the back of his neck, and the world went black again.

INCH TWO

Head of the Class

I.

"You're never gonna make it out there," his father said softly. He took another swig of his beer, and belched loudly.

"I think I will," Justin said. He looked directly into his father's eyes, careful not to look away and to keep his voice even and tremorless. He couldn't afford to show weakness right now. His father had had several beers already and was as vulnerable as he would ever be. The fact that he hadn't already thrown the beer can at Justin's head was proof of that. Now was the time for him to stand strong. "This might just be my ticket," he said as he held up the envelope with the UCLA insignia.

Mr. Bennett pushed his glasses down on his nose and peered over them at his son, in a move that Justin recognized at once. It was the glance that was meant to intimidate him and to silence him and to get him to agree with his father with no questions asked. And for most of his life it had worked. But not anymore. Justin was not the same little boy who had cringed at the slightest raise of his father's voice or who cried when his father slapped him across the face. Those days were long behind him, and he knew that his father knew it as well. He could see it in the old man's eyes as he looked Justin up and down. But even more, he could hear it in his defeated voice as it got more and more quiet with his threats, and as he backed down easier and easier with each passing month.

"Your ticket to what?" the elder Bennett asked with a sneer.

"The real world."

His father laughed, and spit out a mouthful of beer as he choked. When he regained his composure, he glared at his son with contempt. For just a few seconds, Justin saw his old father, the one who slapped and beat him regularly and who kept him living in fear. His heart beat a little faster, but he struggled to match his father's stare and stretched his shoulders backward to stand taller and stronger.

"If you think *that's* the real world"—his father sneered as he looked away from Justin—"then you're a bigger idiot than I thought. *This* is the real world, Justin." He waved his arm drunkenly around the living room.

Justin followed his father's arm and looked at the room around him. Two of the bulbs in the three-way lamp were burned out, but it still provided enough light to take in the filth around him. A dirty bathrobe and an even dirtier pair of jeans lay tossed across the tattered sofa. There were two empty TV dinner trays strewn across the glass coffee tabletop with the crack that ran across the entire length, and a third still had the vegetables in their compartment, dried and browning even as he looked at them. Two cereal bowls serving as ashtrays overflowed and spilled onto the stained carpet. The 19-inch television was powered by a set of rabbit ear antennae wrapped in aluminum foil, and rested on a compressed wood shelf atop several cinder blocks that had been spray painted red and black to match the Spanish design on the cheap sofa and matching recliner in which his father now sat.

"Not mine," Justin said quietly.

"What the hell did you say?" his father asked, and leaned forward in his chair as he tried to look as if he weren't intentionally flexing his biceps.

It was another of the moves that had been designed to manipulate and frighten him into submitting to every will and whim of his father, and that had worked quite well up until that very moment.

"I said"—Justin raised his voice and took a step forward—"it's not *my* reality." He noticed his father flinch and hunch backward slightly. As much as he wanted to revel in the delight of seeing his father back down and frightened of him, he couldn't. A part of him still expected the old man to stand up and deck him, as he'd done so many times in the past. A part of him was still afraid. But he couldn't show that part. "This is my ticket out of this hell, and there's not a damned thing you can do about it."

He slapped his father across the face with the envelope before he could stop himself. His heart beat fast and his knees threatened to give out on him. When they didn't, he backed away from his father and never took his eyes off of the old man. When he reached the stairs, he turned around and walked up them quickly and directly to his room.

* * *

"Dude, what the fuck happened?"

Justin looked at his best friend and prayed he wouldn't break out in tears. "Just drive," he said. He looked behind him and saw the shadow of his father behind the curtains, walking toward the door. "Now. Just go!"

Dusty gunned the accelerator and grinned as the tires squealed just before jetting the Camaro forward.

Justin kept looking out the back window until his best friend made a quick left turn and then a right and another left a couple blocks away. When he was certain his father was not following them, he turned around and stared straight out the passenger window.

"You okay, man?" Dusty asked as he slowed the car down and took a deep breath. "What's goin' on?"

"I don't know what came over me, dude," Justin said. He continued to stare out the window, and turned the envelope over and over in his hands. "I told him that this was my ticket out of this hellhole of a town and that I wasn't gonna waste my chance."

"What's so wrong with that?"

"I slapped the old man across the face with the envelope."

"It's not like the bastard didn't deserve it. It couldn't have hurt more than his ego."

Justin turned and looked at his friend. "I haven't opened it yet."

"What?"

"I couldn't do it, man. I have no idea what it says."

"Are you fucking kidding me?"

"No."

"What if you didn't get in, Justin? It was a really slim shot to begin with, you know that."

"Yeah, I know."

"Dude, you played your trump card with the slap. If you didn't get in, you're fucked. You can't go back to that asshole and continue living with him."

"I know that, Dusty. Fuck! You're not helping anything here, you know."

"I'm sorry. Sorry, man." Dusty pulled into the parking lot of their favorite bar. "You gotta read it, Justin. You have to know what to expect."

"I can't. You should feel my heart, dude. It's about to fuckin' explode in my chest."

"Then I'll read it. But we both need a beer to deal with this shit. Let's go."

The two friends ordered their beers, and sat at the bar. It wasn't until their fourth Michelob that Justin finally pushed the envelope toward his friend.

"You sure, man?" Dusty asked as he opened the envelope.

"No. But I have to know sooner or later. Just read it."

Dusty pulled the letter from the envelope and read it to himself. Justin watched him carefully, trying to read his expression, but couldn't get a clue. Finally, Dusty folded the letter slowly, and slid it back into the envelope.

"Fuck, dude," he said as he took another big swig of his beer. "I don't know what you're going to do . . ."

Justin took a deep breath and lowered his head.

". . . without me. Because I'm gonna be slaving away in Philly while you're living the high life in Los Angeles."

"What?"

"You're in, man. They're offering you a half scholarship for the first two years. After that, if you prove yourself on the field and keep your grades decent, they'll pick up the other half of your first two years, and then sail you through on a full scholarship for the rest of your time at UCLA. Fuck, dude!!"

Justin looked up just in time to catch his friend as Dusty flung himself into his arms.

"You made it, Justin. You're outta here!"

Justin held his breath and hugged his friend as he struggled to remain on the barstool. After a couple of minutes, he helped Dusty back into his own seat, and accepted a round on the house from the female bartender that Dusty had been trying to lay for the past year. When he finished his fifth bottle, Justin excused himself and stumbled to the restroom.

The door barely closed behind him before he felt the tears building up behind his sinuses. He'd taken such a risk with standing up to his father like he had earlier. What if the letter had begun with, "The Board of Regents regrets to inform you," instead of, "is happy to inform you"? What if his father had been drunk enough to stand up to him? Would he have had the guts to hold his ground, and if so, would that have resulted in one of them being seriously hurt? What if his dream of a better life was flushed down the toilet with the opening of that one little letter?

Justin walked to the urinal, pulled his cock out, and leaned against the wall in front of him as he pissed. Before he knew it was coming, he began to cry. It started as a silent sob, but within a few second, he was crying openly, and struggled to keep his piss stream inside the urinal.

"Dude, are you okay?"

Justin turned around and looked at his best friend. He tried to wipe his tears, but ended up crying even harder.

Dusty walked over and hugged Justin, pulling him close to his body. "It's all right, man. You're gonna be getting away. You're gonna be free."

Justin felt himself collapse into his friend's embrace, and hugged him back. After just a few seconds, he felt his cock harden in between them. He panicked, and tried to pull himself away, but Dusty pulled him even tighter against him. He struggled weakly for a few seconds, and then froze in place when he felt Dusty reach down and squeeze his cock.

"What the fuck are you . . ."

Dusty pushed him back a couple of steps, and dropped to his knees.

Justin looked down at his friend and wondered if he was dreaming, or perhaps hallucinating. He didn't have a big dick by any stretch of the imagination—a little less than six inches at full mast, and no more than average thickness. He'd seen several more that were much bigger in the locker room at school, but had never given it much thought. He never had any complaints from the chicks he fucked.

But Dusty's face was only a couple of inches from his throbbing cock, and he was staring at it as if he were afraid it would bite him at any moment. He looked to Justin like he was frightened and about to piss his pants.

Justin was about to ask him again what the fuck he thought he was doing, when his best friend licked his lips and then leaned forward and sucked the head of his cock into his mouth. His head spun as the wet heat of Dusty's mouth enveloped his cock head and sucked the first couple of inches inside. He was confused, and with five beers in his bloodstream, he should not have been able to get hard at all. But it was hard, and throbbing and his friend's clumsy sucking was making it harder with every passing second.

"Fuck, man," he moaned as he thrust his cock another inch deeper into Dusty's mouth.

His friend gagged and spit as he pulled his mouth off Justin's cock. But then he took a deep breath and grabbed the cock roughly and shoved it back into his mouth. He groaned loudly and choked a couple more times as he stubbornly attacked the dick.

Dusty would never win a cocksucker award, Justin thought. He was rough and noisy and awkward. His teeth scraped the skin of Justin's rod a couple of times, but not enough to hurt, and so he let him continue. At this point, the whole scene was turning him on more than he'd ever imagined, and he didn't dare say or do anything that might jolt his friend back to reality and cause him to remove his warm, wet mouth from his hard cock. He'd never thought about another dude sucking his dick, and certainly not his best friend, but the sight of his cock sliding into Dusty's mouth was turning him on.

"Suck my dick, dude," he moaned, and thrust his cock all the way inside the wet tunnel.

Dusty wrapped his index finger and thumb around the base of Justin's cock and squeezed as he sucked his friend's rod. He bobbed his head up and down the length of it, ignoring the gag reflex that caused him to cough and spit around it and trudging along courageously.

"You like suckin' my dick, don't you?" Justin said, as he grabbed the back of Dusty's head and pulled it deeper onto his cock. When his friend moaned his response, Justin smiled and thrust his cock in and out of the mouth slowly at first, and then a little more rigorously.

In just a couple of minutes, Justin felt his knees begin to shake and knew that he was getting close. He started to warn Dusty, and then changed his mind. Instead he tightened his grip on the back of his friend's head and after a couple more bobs on his cock, pulled the mouth tight against his pubes. He moaned loudly as his legs quivered and threatened to collapse on him. He felt his cock thicken inside Dusty's mouth, and a second later bright pins of light exploded behind his eyes as he emptied himself in his buddy's mouth.

Dusty gagged and coughed, and struggled against Justin's grip. But Justin held on tight for a few sprays of his load, and only let go of Dusty's head when he felt the panicked mouth and teeth bite down on his still-throbbing cock.

"Fuck, dude," Dusty yelled as he fell backward onto his ass, and scooted a couple of steps away from Justin. "Why the fuck did you do that?" He spit out a mouthful of cum, and wiped his mouth frantically.

"What do you mean?" Justin said. "You can't tell me you didn't know that was gonna be the end result."

"Not in my mouth, man. Fuck! That's gross, dude."

"Shut up, faggot. You wanted it."

"No, I didn't," Dusty said defensively, and spit into the sink. "You could have cum all over the floor, asshole."

"Hell, no. I can do that at home by myself," Justin said as he pulled up his jeans. "It's not every day your best bud sucks your cock."

"That's just not right," Dusty said weakly. He pulled his cock out of his jeans and waved it in front of Justin. "Your turn."

"Fuck, no!"

"Come on, man. It's only fair."

"Fuck that, dude," Justin said, and stepped backward. "I didn't ask you to do that. You wanted it."

"Please," Dusty pleaded. "Just suck it. I'm already close. It won't take long."

"No way. But I'll beat you off if you want."

Dusty looked down at his cock. Justin could see the wheels spin-ning in his friend's head. He could tell the way Dusty's cock was bouncing up and down that he was close. And he could see the frustration in his red face. He knew what the answer would be.

"Okay," Dusty said, and scooted closer to Justin, and wrapped his arm around his friend's waist.

Justin wrapped his fist around his buddy's cock and squeezed it softly. He'd seen Dusty's naked cock in the shower and locker room at school, but it had always been soft, and so he was surprised at how long and thick it was now. Even more surprised was he at the tingle of electricity that ran through his body as he felt the heat of the hard cock as he slid his hand up and down the length of it. His own cock began to strum to life again, and he was glad for the safety of his jeans.

"Oh, God, man," Dusty moaned. "That feels fuckin' incredible."

Justin tightened his grip on the cock and began to stroke it faster. He was afraid someone would walk in, and now that he'd al-ready cum, he wasn't as invested in the whole process as he'd been earlier.

"Here I cum, dude," Dusty said hoarsely. "Get on your knees."

"No way . . ."

Dusty grabbed Justin by the shoulders and pushed him roughly to the ground. A second later, he pointed his cock at his buddy's face and sprayed his load all over him.

"Fuck, du . . ." Justin started to protest, but stopped midsen-tence when a large load of Dusty's spunk landed on his tongue. He pushed himself away from Dusty's exploding cock, and stumbled to his feet. He wanted to go off on his friend, tell him that what he'd done was fucked up and that he was going to kick his ass. But he couldn't take his eyes off the thick cock that was still spraying out thick streams of jizz all over the floor and sink.

"Man, that was hot," Dusty whispered as he shook the last of his load to the floor and stuffed his shrinking cock back into his jeans.

"That was sick, man," Justin said softly and without looking into his friend's eyes. "You didn't have to cum on my face."

"Shut up, faggot," Dusty taunted. "You know you wanted it."

II.

Justin sat on the cool grass in the middle of Spaulding Field, clutching his knees to his chest and trying to catch his breath. The rest of the team had been excused twenty minutes earlier, and were now showering up across the plaza at the sprawling Acosta Athletic Training Complex, which housed the Knapp Football Center. But he'd had a really shitty practice, and was pissed at himself and way too wound up to shower it all off and move on with the rest of the evening's activities.

For Justin, those activities consisted exclusively of studying his ass off, and he definitely wasn't looking forward to that, and so he'd stayed behind and ran several laps around the field as fast and as hard as he could. He'd thought that if he ran fast and long and hard enough, that he'd feel better about himself and his lackluster performance. It didn't work out that way, though, and instead he realized that he'd let himself go over the summer and was out of shape. His throat felt like sandpaper, and excruciating pain shot up through his ribs, which felt like they were on fire. He didn't dare try to stand up yet, because he was sure his legs would not support him.

He felt so removed from reality. The first six weeks at UCLA had been an eye-opener, and not one he particularly welcomed. Back home at Haverford High School, in the quaint Philadelphia suburb where he'd grown up, he was the superstar quarterback who could do no wrong. He was the guy that every girl wanted to claim as her own, and with which every guy wanted to be seen. The trophy case in the main hallway had numerous trophies bearing his name, and even the teachers treated him with a sense of respect and awe.

Los Angeles was a whole other world for him, and he felt like E.T. trying desperately to get back home. Despite his six foot two frame and 210 pounds of solid muscle, he was treated as a little kid at UCLA. Upperclassmen teased and harassed him, and most of the girls pinched his cheeks and looked at him as if he were a lost and mangy puppy. They were all after the same guys who taunted Justin. And to top it all off, he wasn't even being considered for a quarterback position at UCLA. He was alternating between center and wide receiver, and he didn't like either of those positions.

School itself was much more difficult than he'd expected, too. He took the minimum number of courses, and those that were considered easy and "blowoff" classes. Everyone else seemed to be sailing through them with no problem, but Justin was barely squeaking by, and that was with him studying hard for three or four hours a night after football practice.

He lay down on his back on the grass and stared up at the darkening sky. It was just past dusk, and the stars were beginning to peek out from the advancing darkness. No matter what was happening in his life, how bad things got or how much he wished he were someone else, watching the skies and the stars always calmed him down and helped him put things in perspective. He grabbed a couple of handfuls of grass from the field and threw them high into the air. When the blades were within a couple of inches from his face, he blew them up and away from him.

"Bennett, is that you?"

Justin startled, and sat up as gracefully as he could. "Coach Wynette?"

"What's going on here?" the offensive coach asked as he walked over and sat next to Justin. "Why aren't you off fucking your girl-friend or something? Practice ended almost an hour ago."

"I just thought I'd get in a couple of extra laps, you know, with-out all the other slowpokes getting in my way."

Coach Wynette laughed. "Right. You have penis envy or some-thing? Can't see the other guys in the shower without getting a boner?"

"No!" Justin said quickly. "I just felt like I was a little sluggish today, and wanted to put in a little extra time."

"You were more than a little sluggish today, Bennett," the coach said, and put a piece of gum in his mouth. "You sucked a big old donkey dick this afternoon. It looked like I was watching a high school junior varsity game or something."

"Come on, it wasn't that bad."

"Like fuck it wasn't, kid," Coach Wynette said, and kicked at Justin's feet. "What the hell is up with you? I saw you play three different games back in Philly, and you were brilliant. You weren't that same kid out on the field today. Why not?"

"I just can't get into playing wide receiver, coach. I haven't played anything other than quarterback for the past three years. It's in my blood."

Coach Wynette laughed. "That's ridiculous, son. It's not in your blood. We can tell when it's 'in your blood,' that's what we're trained to look for. And it's easy to spot when it is there. It's like an aura around your body, if you believe in that shit. But it's there even if you don't believe in it. Well, for guys who do have it in their blood, it is. It's not there for you, Bennett."

Justin flinched.

"Don't get your panties in a wad," the coach said. "It doesn't mean you can't be a damned good football player. Obviously it doesn't mean that, or we wouldn't have brought you here on a scholarship. It just means that you aren't quarterback material, not on a college level, or at least not on *our* college level. But you might make a decent center or a better-than-decent wide receiver. If you can get your shit together, that is."

"I'm trying, coach, really I am," Justin said as he stretched his legs. "It's just that it's harder than I thought it would be."

"What is?"

"School. I wasn't expecting it to be this hard. I barely had to study at all back in high school, and I sailed through. Here, I study my ass off and I'm barely scraping by."

Coach Wynette snickered again. "Boy, they grow 'em naïve back in Philly, don't they?"

"What do you mean?"

"You sailed through high school because you were the star athlete, and they needed you more on the field than they did in study hall. And your good grades would make you more marketable to good universities, which in turn looks good for the high school. Or at least it would if you were to become a star college player as well."

Justin looked stunned.

"Don't worry, the same thing can happen here, Bennett. We can sail you on through the classes here, too. But not until you become more valuable to us. Not until you become a star player for us like you were for your high school back home. We have to be getting something in return for the favor. Do you know what I mean?"

"Yes, sir," Justin said, even though he really didn't have a clue.

"Good. So you just do whatever it takes to keep scraping by if you have to. But you better dig deep down and find whatever it takes to make you a superstar on this field. Do you hear me? Whatever it takes. When you do, and when you make a name for yourself here, and when pro scouts start mentioning your name, then you'll see that school just starts magically getting easier. Capiche?"

"Yes, sir."

"Good," Coach Wynette said, and stood up. "Now get your ass back to your room and start studying. And I goddammed better see a better practice out of you tomorrow."

III.

Justin had intended, with every ounce of his being, to apply himself and to do better in school since his talk with Coach Wynette almost a month ago. He wanted more than anything to be that superstar athlete his coach had spoken to him about. And he knew deep down that he could be that person.

But knowing he could be that person and actually becoming that person were two very different things, and the latter was proving to be much more difficult than the former. He tried to study, to understand the words he read in his books, to make sense of the psychological and philosophical crap that his professors insist he read. But it all just gave him a headache, and he couldn't get out of his head all of the laughter and fun that everyone else on his floor seemed to be having without him.

"Are you even listening to me right now, Bennett," Professor Reid said, "or are you daydreaming like you do in class?"

"What?" Justin said sleepily. Goddam, Reid sounded a lot like the invisible teacher in the old Charlie Brown cartoons. "Huh?"

Professor Reid laughed, and shook his head. "Get out of my classroom, punk. You just failed this class."

"No," Justin said, suddenly snapped back to the present. "No, please, Professor Reid. I can't fail this class. I can't flunk *any* class. I'm barely getting by, and if I fail any classes, then I can't play ball."

"Not my problem, Bennett. I've tried everything I can think of with you, but nothing is getting through. You're just not trying. You don't give a damn about this class, or any other I would venture to guess."

"That's not true," Justin said, and scooted to the edge of his seat. His heart was beating fast and hard, and he felt the tears threaten to burst through at any moment. "I do care, Coach . . . I mean, Professor Reid."

The professor laughed and shook his head again as he leaned back in his chair. He could sense that his student was on the verge of tears, and knew exactly how to play his hand. "You're pathetic."

"Please, Professor Reid," Justin begged just as the first tears began to fall. "My entire future rests on this. I can't fail. Please, just give me another chance."

"I've given you a million chances already, Justin. And you haven't taken advantage of a single one of them. If you aren't willing to do any of the work, then I'm not willing to continue giving you any more chances."

"I will try," Justin cried, and wiped the tears from his eyes. "I'll do anything, Professor Reid. Just give me one more chance."

"Anything?" the teacher asked.

"Yes," Justin said hopefully, and brushed the tears away quickly. "Anything. Just tell me what I need to do. I promise, I'll show you I care. Just give me one more opportunity."

"Come over here."

Justin stood up quickly and walked over to his professor's desk. He wasn't sure exactly what he expected—maybe a thousand-page book that Reid would demand a book report on in a week, or maybe a billion-word thesis on the esoteric value of the meaning of life. Or something equally ridiculous. But at this point, Justin didn't care. He'd do anything for another chance at passing this stupid class.

"Get on your knees, Bennett."

"What?" Justin asked, and blinked rapidly to clear the tears.

"You heard me. I've got a big cock, but it's not quite that big. You won't reach it from up there."

Justin just stared at his teacher, and struggled to catch his breath.

"You said anything, Bennett."

"I know, but . . ."

"Never mind, then. Get outta here."

"No!" Justin said quickly, and dropped to his knees in front of Professor Reid. "No, I'm sorry."

"That's better," the teacher said, and spread his legs apart. "Get over here and suck my cock."

Justin took a deep breath and scooted closer to Reid's chair. He unzipped his professor's trousers and dug around clumsily inside for his dick. Almost a minute later it was out and lying semi-hard against the inside leg of the trousers.

"Suck it!" Reid ordered.

Justin leaned forward and took another deep breath as he licked the thickening cock. He only got a couple of licks in around the head before he began sobbing.

"Shut the fuck up, bitch," Reid said. "You can't cry. How the fuck am I supposed to get hard if you're crying like a fucking little baby?"

"I'm sorry," Justin said, and wiped the tears from his eyes again. "I'm sorry." He leaned down again and licked at the cock more vigorously. After a few seconds, he lifted the dick with his fingers, opened his mouth, and took half of the shaft inside. He sucked on it tentatively at first, concentrating on not gagging or vomiting.

"Watch your teeth, Bennett."

Justin opened his mouth a little wider, hoping to pull his teeth away from the cock. He closed his eyes and bobbed his head up and down the length of the shaft. Reid had an exaggerated vision of his own cock—it wasn't big at all, maybe six inches at its hardest.

Not that Justin was complaining. He was thankful, in fact. He'd never sucked a dick, and was afraid that if it were any bigger that he'd gag on it, and he was sure that Professor Reid would not be happy about that.

"That's it, baby," Reid moaned loudly as he stretched his long legs out farther in front of him. "Take that giant cock all the way down your bitch throat."

Justin wrapped his lips tighter around the cock and sucked on it as carefully as he could. He had no idea if he was doing a good job or not, but Reid was moaning and tightening his legs, so he figured it wasn't completely horrible. After a couple of minutes, he wrapped one hand around the rod and squeezed it as he sucked around the head. When the teacher moaned louder and thrust his dick inside Justin's mouth faster and harder, Justin took that as his cue. He reached down with his other hand and squeezed the hairy balls.

"Oh yeah, man," Reid grunted loudly. "Suck my fat cock, man." A couple more thrusts, and then, "I'm gonna shoot!"

Justin loosened his lips from around the cock, but kept squeezing with his hand, and tried to lift his head from it. But Reid grabbed him by the back of the head and held him tight to the base of his cock as his body stiffened. Justin panicked when he couldn't breathe, and struggled for a couple of seconds, and then his eyes bulged as he felt the first few squirts of warm liquid splash against his throat and land on his tongue. His professor bucked and grunted and made a theatrical production of emptying his load into Justin's mouth. Justin gagged as the first couple of shots slid down his throat, and then swallowed it as quickly as he could before he had time to think about it.

"Fuck, that was hot, man," Professor Reid said hoarsely. He pushed Justin away from him, and stood up to tuck his cock back into his trousers. "Now get the fuck out of my classroom."

"Are you going to pass me?" Justin asked softly as he stood up and walked toward the door.

"I said I would, didn't I? But don't forget, this is only mid-term.

There are still several exams between now and your final grade. You're not so stupid that you don't get what I'm saying, are you?"

"No, sir," Justin said as he stared at the floor.

"Good. Now get out of my face."

Justin walked out the door of the classroom and then ran to the nearest restroom. He locked himself in one of the stalls and beat himself off quickly, and then vomited in the toilet and cried. When he had no more vomit and no more tears, he left the restroom and walked back to his room at Evergreen Hall in De Neve Plaza.

IV.

"Dude, what the fuck happened out there tonight?" Jeremy asked as he grabbed a beer from the mini-fridge and plopped onto the futon. "You were on fire!"

Justin laughed, and grabbed a beer of his own and stretched out on his bed. "I'm always on fire, bitch. You're just too stupid to notice."

"Fuck you," Jeremy said, and belched loudly as he finished his first beer and took another. "Seriously, what's gotten into you? It's like you're a whole different player than you were just six weeks ago."

"I've just been more focused, that's all. I know that this is my only chance, and I have to make the best of it."

"And you didn't know that six weeks ago?"

"Yeah, I did," Justin said, and concentrated much harder on peeling the paper label from his beer bottle than was necessary.

"Well, then, spill it, dude. What's your secret? Steroids?"

"Fuck, no," Justin said, and threw the empty bottle at his friend as he stood up to get another. The past few weeks had been very stressful on him.

On one hand, he didn't have to worry about his grades any-more, and he was able to focus and put all of his energies into football. And he was getting better with every passing week. Several of his teammates had commented about it to him, and a few others glared at him with a mix of suspicion and envy. But more important, his coaches had taken notice and had given him more and more field time.

On the other hand, he was keeping a secret that seemed to be taking on a life of its own and was getting out of hand. Professor Reid had obviously not been discreet about their encounter. In the week following their first session, two of Justin's other professors approached him and offered to sail him through their classes as well if he blew them. With the three of them in his back pocket, the only other problem class he faced was Economics, and there was no way he was going to fuck Professor Birch. She was ninety years old if she was a day, and even Justin had his limits, and he could afford to fail one class, if it came to that.

He hated his male professors that blackmailed and forced him to suck their cocks, but he hated himself even more for getting hard and needing to rub one out after each session. He struggled with himself and his secrets, and had often wished he had someone to talk to about it.

"Can you keep a secret?" he asked Jeremy as he stretched out on his bed and leaned against the wall.

"Of course," Jeremy said as he leaned forward to pay closer attention.

Justin took a big swig of his beer, and then inhaled deeply. "I don't really have to worry about passing my classes anymore. So I can concentrate on football a lot more now."

"What do you mean you don't have to worry about classes anymore? Did you discover some kind of smart pill or something?"

"Not exactly," Justin said, and took another swallow of beer. "I'm blowing a couple of my professors."

Jeremy was bringing his beer bottle to his mouth to finish it off, but stopped midway there. "What?"

"You know Reid, Gonzales, and Matthison?"

"Yeah."

"Well, I was failing my Sociology and Spanish classes, and right on the fringe of flunking History. Reid cornered me one day and promised to pass me in all of his classes if I sucked his dick."

Jeremy stared at his friend, stunned. "And you did it?"

"Of course I did. It was mid-term, and failing that one test would have failed me for the entire course. I couldn't afford that. It would have put me off the team."

"Fuck," Jeremy said, and got up to get both of them another beer.

"He must have told his cronies, because the following week, both of them pulled the same shit on me. They threatened to fail me if I didn't blow them, and promised to sail me through if I did. So of course I sucked their dicks."

"What are you gonna do? Go to the dean?"

"What? Fuck, no! And you can't, either. You have to promise me you won't say a thing to anybody."

"Why not? What they're doing is wrong . . ."

"Promise me!"

"Okay, okay. I won't say anything to anyone."

"This is my only chance to play ball, man," Justin said as he took the beer from Jeremy, and swallowed half of it. "I'm not smart at all. I barely made it through high school, and college is totally overwhelming me. Or at least it was when I had to spend every spare minute of my time studying and writing papers I didn't understand. Football is my only ticket, and without it I will be right back home with my abusive father and his poor white-trash trailer. I will not let that happen."

"Wow, man," Jeremy said, moving over to Justin's bed and sitting next to his friend. "I had no idea. But there's gotta be another way to play ball. Surely this isn't . . ."

"There's not another way," Justin said sharply. "Not for me. So you better not fuck it up for me."

"I'd never do that, Justin. I gave you my word."

"Thank you."

"But I still can't believe it. I had no idea those professors were gay."

"They're not," Justin said. "Reid and Gonzalez are married, and Matthison has two women pregnant at the same time."

"Then why . . ."

"Because they're pigs, and they know a desperate guy who will do anything to pass their classes when they see one. And they especially know one who will not go squealing to the authorities. Girls are much more likely to tell someone and go to the police, so they stick with dudes. I'm sure this isn't the first time they've done this. But they aren't gay," Justin said wearily. "And neither am I."

"That's too bad."

"What?"

"I was hoping you were," Jeremy said, staring at his empty beer bottle. "Because I am, and I have really wanted to get together with you since our first team practice."

Justin stared at his friend for a moment. "Are you fucking serious?"

"Yes," Jeremy said. He scooted closer to Justin and leaned in to kiss him.

Justin pushed him away and jumped off the bed. "What the hell are you doing?"

"I just want you to know that you don't have to be alone in this, and that it doesn't have to be creepy or disgusting, like it is with those other guys."

"Jeremy, I'm not gay," Justin said, and ran his fingers through his hair. "It's cool with me that you are, I don't care at all. But I'm not. And I don't suck my professors' cocks because I like it, or even because I want to like it. It's all business for me. I need their help to get through school and stay on the team. That's it."

"Come on, Justin," Jeremy said, standing up and walking over to his friend. He pulled Justin close to him and began unbuttoning his shirt. "That doesn't have to be all it is. It could be a lot of fun. With me."

Justin pushed Jeremy away from him again, and quickly moved around to the other side of the bed. "Oh shit, I made a mistake by telling you this. Fuck."

Jeremy took a deep breath, and looked around uncomfortably for his jacket. "No, you didn't make a mistake," he said. "I did. I'm sorry."

"Please don't tell anyone," Justin begged, and tossed Jeremy's jacket to him.

"I said I wouldn't, and I won't. But if you ever change your mind, and want someone there to help you through all of this, I hope you will let me be that person."

"Jeremy, you're my best friend here at school. I can't possibly imagine trying to get through this without you."

"Yeah, whatever," Jeremy said, and walked out the door.

V.

Justin sat alone at the small round table in the coffee shop in the Student Activities Center, drinking his steaming Zebra Mocha latte, pushing his notebook around the table aimlessly, and trying to slow his heart rate to something resembling normal. In the past four weeks since he'd shared his secret with Jeremy, things had changed dramatically for him. Jeremy barely spoke with him anymore, and when he did it was always in group situations, and as little as possible. Justin was getting more and more time on the field, and was even allowed to practice in the quarterback position a couple of times, a move that suggested he might be considered for the position in a year or two.

The most dramatic change, however, was Justin's recent but intense obsession with his Psych professor. It hit him suddenly and unexpectedly, and he reeled from its effects on him. In class he couldn't stop staring at Professor Norman's stylish salt-and-pepper hair and his piercing blue eyes. The professor was tall and lean, but powerfully built—it was obvious he spent a significant amount of time in the gym. His strong jawline made Justin's breathing become erratic, and when Norman smiled, Justin's knees buckled beneath him and his cock hardened instantly.

He was confused about his reactions to Professor Norman. He'd never been attracted to another man before. He'd let Dusty suck his cock, and he was sucking three of his professors' cocks while attending school this year. But he'd never been sexually attracted to a dude before, and he certainly didn't consider himself gay. And so his hard cock at the sight of Professor Norman and the depth of his desire for the man baffled him.

Justin had never taken a psychology class in high school, and never really had in interest in it. He took the class only because it was required, and he never expected to do well in it. After only a couple of classes, he began thinking that he wouldn't mind sucking Professor Norman's cock to keep his grades up, and after a couple of weeks, he found himself wondering why the psych teacher hadn't approached him yet and wishing that he would. But he discovered that he actually really enjoyed psychology, and he did well in the class all on his own. He carried an easy B with almost no study time at all. He thought briefly about dummying up his performance in the class, just so he could have the chance to add Norman to his cocksucking list, but wasn't so stupid as to really believe that was a good idea.

Instead he decided to just take the most direct route and ask Professor Norman if maybe he could fuck his brains out. So, after class the day before, he'd asked his teacher if they could meet at the coffee shop, and here he was waiting and hoping his heart wouldn't explode from his chest.

"Hi, Justin," Professor Norman said as he walked from behind Justin and squeezed his shoulder before sitting down.

Justin felt a tingle that started at his shoulder where Professor Norman touched him and extended down his left side, down his rib cage, and ended at his cock, which grew fully hard in just a couple of seconds.

"Hi," Justin squeaked out, and then cleared his throat even as he felt his face grow red with embarrassment. "Hi, Professor Norman."

"Please don't tell me you're studying on such a beautiful Saturday morning," Norman said as he nodded toward the stack of papers in the manila folder Justin brought with him.

"Yeah, a little bit," Justin said with a shrug. "Gotta keep the grades up in order to play football."

"I can't imagine that'd be a problem for you. You're doing great in my class. You seem to be a very bright kid."

"Thank you," Justin said, and felt his cock twitch in his jeans. "I like your sweatshirt. It's really cool. What does KLP stand for?"

"Kappa Lambda Phi. It was my fraternity when I was your age and at Yale. We're a very close fraternity, and stay pretty active even as alumni. I can't seem to let go of the 'good old days' and I buy a new sweatshirt every year. I have a whole closet full of nothing but these damned sweatshirts."

"It's great. And it looks incredible on you."

Professor Norman laughed. "Thanks. I'm sure it looked much better when I was actually in school and in a lot better shape. But I try."

"You look incredible."

Professor Norman blushed and shifted in his seat. "So, what can I do for you, Justin? Why did you ask to see me this morning?"

He'd dreaded that question almost as soon as he'd asked Norman to meet him. He'd gone over in his head a thousand times how to answer it, and right then, with the question face to face, he blanked out and couldn't remember what he'd decided upon. "I was wondering if . . ."

. . . I could suck your cock until you spray your load all over my face
. . . you could suck my cock until I spray my load all over your face
. . . you'd let me slide my dick inside your ass and fuck you
. . . we could run off together and get married

All of the other possible scenarios he'd contemplated the night before came flooding back into his mind a millisecond before he finished his question.

". . . we could maybe go out for dinner sometime soon?"

Professor Norman cleared his throat and shuffled his feet as he rearranged his position in his chair. "I don't think that's a great idea, Justin," he said as he looked around the almost-empty coffee shop. "I'm your professor."

"So? I know it's not exactly encouraged, but you can't tell me it doesn't go on all the time anyway. And worse, even."

"That's true, it probably does. But not with me."

"Please, Professor Norman," Justin said as he kicked off his flip-flops and stretched his leg out to squeeze between his teacher's legs and caress his crotch with his bare feet. "I can't believe I'm doing this. It's actually very hard for me to ask you. But I really like you a lot and I want to spend some time with you."

Norman tightened his body and looked around nervously, making sure no one was watching this young student massage his cock with his bare feet. But he didn't move away from the advance. "Really, Justin, it's not a great . . ."

"I'm not asking for any favors, Professor Norman," Justin said, and increased the pressure on his teacher's crotch. "You said yourself I'm doing great in your class already, so I don't need you to fix my grades. I don't want your money or anything else that some people get involved with their teachers for. I just want to know what it feels like to hold you in my arms and to kiss you and to make love to you."

"It's not . . ."

"Yeah, I know it's not a great idea," Justin said, and leaned in to kiss Norman on the lips briefly. "But I won't take no for an answer." He could feel his professor's cock hardening against his bare feet. And he could see him staring deep into his eyes and then sizing up his body as if he'd never seen it before.

"Let's go," Professor Norman said, and walked to the door without looking back or waiting for Justin to follow.

*   *   *

They'd barely walked inside the door before Justin pinned Professor Norman against the wall and kissed him softly on the lips. When the professor returned the kiss, and slid his tongue inside Justin's mouth, Justin whimpered quietly, and felt his knees threaten to betray him. He wrapped his arms around his teacher, and held him tightly as he opened his mouth a little wider to take more of Norman's invading tongue. He'd never kissed another man, and was worried that he wasn't doing it right or that it didn't feel good for his professor. He sucked on the tongue softly, and when the teacher moaned and pressed his hips against Justin's, he knew that he was doing it right and had nothing to worry about.

Justin ended the kiss and pulled the sweatshirt off Professor Norman's torso carefully, and then took his time kissing the teacher's neck and chest and nipples. The professor gasped and his entire body quivered at the touch of Justin's tongue against his hot, smooth skin, and Justin smiled at the power he seemed to have over his professor. He could feel the older man's cock throbbing against his legs, and an uncontrollable urge to take it into his mouth and deep into his throat overcame him.

He dropped to his knees and pulled Professor Norman's sweatpants down to his ankles. The thick cock was unconstrained by underwear, and bounced in front of Justin's face, begging for attention. Justin looked at the cock for a moment, and felt his own dick throb to life inside his jeans at just the sight of the teacher's fat cock. It was long and thick, with a mushroom head that turned from a deep shade of red to a darker purple in just a couple of seconds. A thick vein ran the length of the shaft from the pubic hairs to the ridge of the fat head. Several smaller veins branched off from the main one, and reminded Justin of maps of the Amazon River he'd seen in school. Large, hairy, low-hanging balls hung heavily beneath the big dick.

Justin took a deep breath and sucked just the head into his mouth. He flicked the head with his tongue a couple of times, and smiled internally as he felt Professor Norman's legs shake and saw him brace himself against the wall with his hands. Then he rolled the big balls between his palms a couple of moments, and swallowed two-thirds of the big dick deep into his throat. He might be uncertain about his kissing skills with another man, but he had no doubts about his cocksucking talents. He'd been a quick learner after starting with Reid several months ago, and his practice with Gonzalez and Matthison had honed and perfected his skill. They'd all let it slip a few times and told him how amazing he was, but he didn't need that reassurance. The way their bodies shook and the increasing quickness with which they exploded into his mouth let him know that he was an expert cocksucker.

"Come here," Professor Norman said, and lifted Justin to his feet.

He kissed his student passionately on the lips for a moment, and then took his hand and led him into the bedroom. Once there he slipped off Justin's flip-flops and slid his jeans off his long legs, and then pulled off his shirt and tossed it to the floor. He laid Justin down on the bed and kissed him again as he lay on top of him.

Justin moaned and wriggled beneath Norman, thrusting his hard cock against his professor's. "Suck my dick, Professor Norman," he moaned deeply. "Please."

The professor slid down Justin's body and between his legs. The young student's cock was hard and throbbing against his belly. It was fairly average, about six and a half or seven inches long, not very thick, and cut. The skin was smooth and pink, and looked to Norman as if it were begging to be sucked. He obliged. He licked around the head for a few moments, lapping up the thin precum that covered it, and sliding his tongue into the slit at the top of the head. When Justin moaned loudly and thrust his hips off the bed, Professor Norman squeezed the hairy balls and pulled them farther between Justin's legs, and slid his cock deep into his throat in one swift swallow.

"Oh, fuck!" Justin moaned as he clutched the blankets on either side of him and slid his cock in and out of his professor's mouth. "Suck it, dude."

Norman continued squeezing the small balls and lapping at the juicy cock for several minutes. He loved the taste of the spurts of precum that slid out of Justin's cock head every couple of minutes, and swallowed it hungrily. It was obvious his young student didn't have a lot of experience sexually, and he had to pull off the hot cock several times when he saw that Justin was about to shoot his load.

During one of these breaks, he spread Justin's long, hairy legs apart, and then lifted them high into the air, forcing his ass up and wide open. He felt Justin's entire body tighten, and try to wriggle out of the position.

"Relax," he said softly as he looked up between the spread legs to look into Justin's face. "I won't hurt you, I promise."

Justin took a deep breath, and relaxed his body. A second later he felt Professor Norman's hot breath against the hole between his ass cheeks. He tightened up again, and then took another couple of deep breaths. As he exhaled his second breath, he felt Norman's warm, wet tongue lick around his hole, and flick against it quickly several times.

"Oh my God!" Justin moaned loudly.

He lifted his ass higher off the bed, hoping to get more of the hot tongue inside him. He wasn't disappointed, and when the teacher spread his cheeks with his hands and slid his tongue deep inside his ass, Justin thought his heart would stop. The room spun around him and there was a loud ringing in his ears. He was shocked to feel his ass twitch and squeeze around Professor Norman's expert tongue, as if it had proclaimed mutiny of itself from the rest of his body, and demanded to be filled.

"Fuck me," Justin blurted out, and then wondered when his mouth had joined his ass in the treason.

Professor Norman stopped in mid-lick, and looked back up at Justin's face from between his legs. "What?"

"I want you inside me."

"Are you sure?" Norman asked, but was already lowering Justin's ass and positioning it in front of his hard and throbbing cock.

"Yes. Fuck me," Justin panted, and grabbed at the blankets on either side of him again. "Please."

Norman reached above and behind Justin to grab a condom from the nightstand next to the bed. He slipped it on quickly, spit on the head of his cock, and then pressed it against the convulsing hole between Justin's ass cheeks. "Relax," he instructed again.

Justin took a few quick, deep breaths, and then nodded his head. A second later, he felt his ass rip open, and thousands of bright, colorful lights exploded behind his eyes and spread out to fill the room. "Oh God, it hurts," he whimpered. "Take it out."

"Just take a deep breath and relax," Professor Norman said, and pressed another inch inside Justin's tight, hot hole. "It'll only hurt for a moment, I promise. Breathe."

Justin closed his eyes and breathed like those women he always saw taking Lamaze classes. It made sense to him—this had to be what it felt like to give birth to a thirty-pound child. He felt every inch of Norman's cock as it slid deeper into him, and was sweating profusely by the time he felt his teacher's pubic hair tickle his ass.

When he was buried to the balls inside his student, Professor Norman leaned forward and kissed Justin on the lips. Justin's face was red and covered with sweat, and his mouth and lips were hot to the touch.

But he sucked Norman's tongue into his mouth hungrily, and kissed him passionately. He wrapped his arms around his teacher's neck and held him close and tight to his own body. He couldn't get enough of the feel of Professor Norman's warm and hairy skin against his own sweaty and smooth, and he ran his hands up and down Norman's muscular back and ass, pulling him deeper into him.

"Fuck me, Professor Norman," Justin moaned as he lifted his ass to get even more inside him. "I want you to fill me up."

The teacher slowly slid his cock out of Justin's clutching ass until only the head remained inside. When he saw Justin's eyes bulge and shake his head "no," he slid even slower back inside, and then slammed the last couple of inches into his student's hot tunnel.

"Yeah, man," Justin grunted, and squeezed his ass tighter around Norman's thick cock inside him. "That's it. Fuck me."

Norman kissed Justin again, and began sliding in and out of his student's tight, hot ass slowly. He loved kissing almost as much as he loved fucking, and Justin's mouth and lips and tongue mesmerized him. The young man's kisses were sweet and strong and loving and desperate, all at once. He could feel the vulnerability and the strength and the fear and the hope of Justin's emotions behind his kisses, and they made him want to get lost in them.

For Justin, this moment was an epiphany. He felt free and alive and on fire for the first time in his life. Every time Professor Norman slid all the way inside him and stabbed that one place deep in his guts that made him feel like he'd experienced heaven, he wanted to stop time and stay in that split second forever. When Norman began to slide out of him, he felt like his world was being pulled away from him cruelly, and felt his heartbeat increase dramatically at the thought of losing a part of himself. And then with sweet mercy, he was rewarded with another several inches and seconds of pure bliss.

The two men quickly found a magical rhythm, and moved together like a machine. Professor Norman slid in and out of Justin's ass as the younger man clutched onto his teacher's long, thick cock with his ass, releasing it reluctantly to fate, and then accepting it warmly back inside him as his teacher kissed him and brought him closer and closer to ecstasy.

"I'm close, baby," Professor Norman whispered into Justin's ear as he slowed his thrusts and moved from side to side when fully inside Justin's ass. He nibbled on the soft ear in front of him as he said this, and felt his heart stir into a place he'd not been before.

"Oh God," Justin moaned loudly as he thrust harder onto the cock inside him. "Me, too." He bucked awkwardly up and down on the bed, desperate to take as much of his professor inside him as possible.

"Ungh," Norman moaned quietly as he shoved his cock to the hilt into Justin's ass. He remained perfectly still as he kissed his young student and emptied his load deep inside him. Every contraction of his cock seemed to drain his soul, and he prayed the condom would hold the massive load that erupted from his cock.

"Oh FUCK!" Justin yelled, and held his teacher close to his body. He hadn't touched his own cock at all since Norman entered him, for fear that he'd shoot too soon and end the fuck before he was ready. But now, with Norman's body pressed against his and rubbing against his cock, he was ready. His entire body convulsed, and his cock exploded its load between his stomach and Norman's. "Oh . . . My . . . GOD..." he panted, as he felt his ass grope around the thick cock inside him like a vise grip with every spurt of cum from his cock.

When both men had spent themselves, they remained embraced, with Norman's cock still inside Justin's ass for several minutes. When his cock finally began to soften, Professor Norman slipped it out of Justin's ass slowly. He slipped the condom off carefully, tied it in a knot, and tossed it into the wastebasket a few feet away.

"Wow, that was . . ." He looked down at Justin, and saw he was crying. "Hey, are you all right? What's wrong?"

Justin wiped the tears away quickly, and started to sit up. "Nothing," he said. "I'm good."

Professor Norman pulled Justin back to the bed and wrapped him in his arms. "Bullshit. Something's wrong. Tell me. Did I hurt you?"

"God, no," Justin said, and hugged his teacher tightly. "You were great."

"Then what's wrong?"

"This is. This whole thing is wrong. Two guys together is wrong."

"What?" Professor Norman said, and untangled his arms from

around Justin and moved to look him in the face. "You seriously believe that what we just experienced is wrong?"

"Yes."

"Then why did you approach me and ask me to fuck you if you believe it's wrong? I don't get it."

"I don't know. I don't get it, either. I just know that I had an overwhelming attraction to you, and I couldn't think about anything else but getting to know you and having sex with you. It was paralyzing."

"And at your very core, you think that's wrong?"

"I don't know," Justin said, and buried his head in his hands. "Everything I've ever been told and taught is that being gay is wrong. It's a sin. It's a mental illness. How can that be right?"

"It's not," Professor Norman said, and kissed Justin on the back of the head as he massaged the back of his neck gently. "What you've been told is not right. There comes a time in every person's life where he has to choose for himself what he believes and what he does not believe about what others have told him. A lot of people will tell you that it's your gut feeling that dictates those beliefs. But I disagree. I think it's what your heart and your mind tell you. You listened to your heart earlier this afternoon. Do you honestly feel that what we did . . . what we just shared . . . is wrong?"

"No," Justin said softly, and leaned up to kiss his teacher. "No, I don't."

"I didn't think so," Norman said as he held Justin's face in his hands and returned his kiss.

"But my dad . . ."

"Your dad is wrong."

"And the team . . ."

"Fuck the team. Well, not literally. I'd rather have you all to myself. But they can't discriminate against you for being gay. It might be a little harder for you, if word even gets out. But it'll only make you stronger."

"You want me for yourself?" Justin asked, and sat Indian-style in front of Professor Norman on the bed.

"Yeah." Norman laughed. "At least I'd like to give it a try and see if we both continue to feel the same way as we do now."

"Me, too," Justin said, and kissed him again. "But what about the whole teacher/student thing."

"Well, I can't be your teacher anymore. You'll have to test out of my class, with another professor administering it, or just drop out and take other psych courses with other professors. But as long as I'm not your teacher, no one can tell me who to date, or who to love."

"They can't?"

"No."

"Good."

"So, do you still think it's wrong?"

"No," Justin said, and hugged Norman. "I guess maybe I never did."

"See, you're thinking for yourself already. Doesn't it feel good?"

"Yeah," Justin answered, "but I have a feeling I'm gonna need a lot of help with my Sociology, Spanish, and History classes really soon. Think you could spend a little time tutoring me?"

"Yeah, of course," Professor Norman said. "But why do you think you're gonna need that?"

"I dunno, something just tells me that thinking for myself might not translate into great grades for me in those classes."

Professor Norman gave him a quizzical look.

"No more questions," Justin said, and reached for the teacher's cock. "Lemme have another go at this for a few minutes, and then it's my turn to fuck you. See if I can give you a passing grade in both positions."

INCH THREE

Politico

I.

Governor Benavides popped the cork on the champagne bottle and poured two glasses, and carried them over to the sofa. He handed one to Rafael Suarez, and clinked glasses with him, and then offered the newly elected candidate a cigar.

"Omar, my friend, you know I don't indulge in that poison."

Benavides rolled his eyes and sat in the chair next to the sofa where Suarez sat alone. "Yes, I do know that. It's my job to change that nasty habit and to bring your attitude down a notch or two. Or don't you remember that that is what PAN hired me for?"

"Of course I remember." Rafael laughed. "You never let me forget it, and neither does anyone else in the party."

"That means I'm doing my job well. It would look as if I'm doing even better and be a personal favor to me if you actually listened to what I say and heeded some of my advice."

"A true leader does not need someone else to advise him on his beliefs or his virtue, my friend. The measure of a man is in his integrity. In his integrity and nowhere else."

"I'm so sick of that little nugget of wisdom, *my friend*. You really must come up with something else. Something new."

"You see, right there is another piece of advice that I will not take to heart."

Governor Benavides took a deep sigh and shook his head. "It would behoove you to be a little more appreciative of the National Action Party, Rafael. They have gone out of their way to accommodate your eccentricities and to be supportive of your ambitions."

Rafael Suarez took his time finishing his glass of champagne, and set it down carefully on the coffee table. "Let's be candid, Omar. You and I both know that PAN only has the best interest of PAN in mind. Every political party has the same mindset. It doesn't matter if it is in Mexico, America, or Nigeria. PAN had no choice but to get behind me, because the movement of the people of Mexico overwhelmed them. I am a force of nature, Omar. The people want me. And when PAN recognized that the will of the people could not be stopped, they begged for my alliance. So, let's not play games and pretend that the party is doing me some kind of favor. It is the other way around, my friend."

The governor looked at his friend with a mixture of fascination and trepidation. They'd been compadres since elementary school, and Omar was sure he knew the certain future president of Mexico better than anyone in the world. He remembered a time when Rafael Suarez had been easygoing and fun and even a little mischievous. As young boys they'd skinny-dipped in Lake Chapala, stolen candy from the local dulceria, and set off firecrackers under their teacher's desk and then laughed when she peed in her dress. When Omar's father passed away, Rafael returned from university in the U.S. to comfort him and to make sure his family had everything they needed.

But his father passed away twenty years ago, and the other things had happened even much longer ago. The Rafael Suarez sitting next to him this evening was not that same person. This Rafael Suarez was arrogant and calculated and self-obsessed. When Omar looked into those dark eyes, he had to strain to get a glimpse of his old friend. He was in there, Omar knew, and every once in a while he would catch that old familiar smile that he had known and loved for so many years. But then Rafael would realize his indiscretion, and would pull it back in with an intense resentment.

"We all know that you are popular, Rafael. More popular than probably any politician in Mexican history. You're a celebrity. Unless there is some enormous conspiracy and fraud, you will be our next president. I'm just saying that it might not hurt to play by some of the rules of the game. It doesn't hurt to have very powerful people and political parties actually like you."

"They don't have to like me, Omar," Suarez said. "They only need to stand behind me."

"And what about the Mexican people, my friend? Do they not need to like you, too?"

"What do you mean? The Mexican people adore me."

"But they won't if you continue to spit into their faces, to mock them."

"I have no idea what you're talking about, Omar."

"Mexican men smoke and drink and raise hell. We are macho. It's our history. It's who we are. You won't smoke a cigar to celebrate your victory, you drink very little, and you refuse to swear or say a bad word about anyone."

"And this is a bad thing? Is that what you're telling me?"

"Yes," Omar said as he ran his fingers through his hair frustratingly. "Yes, it is a bad thing when it looks like you think you are better than everyone else. Sooner or later the Mexican people will tire of your arrogance and self-importance. We want to feel hope, not to be made to feel like we don't deserve our president."

"There is nothing wrong with our history, Governor, as long as it remains our history. Our future can only be better if we take a stand. The measure of a man is in his integrity. In his integrity and nowhere else."

"Cut the crap, Rafael. I don't need to hear your campaign slogan. It makes me want to vomit." Omar knew he was treading dangerous ground, but the use of his title by his old friend, and the tone with which it was used, just pissed him off.

Rafael Suarez raised an eyebrow at the governor of Jalisco, and allowed himself a smile.

"God, you know how to get me riled up," Omar said with a laugh. "You know I'm your biggest fan . . . I mean, supporter," Omar said with a smile of his own. "That's why it's so important that you embrace your heritage."

"I embrace my heritage, my friend," Rafael said, softening his tone. "I just don't have to be imprisoned by it."

"You might be forgiven for not smoking or whistling at women as they walk by you," Omar said quietly as he looked at his shoes, "but you won't be forgiven not having a family."

He felt the air in the room chill and be sucked out of it by some invisible vacuum. When he looked up at his friend, he was met with piercing eyes that looked as if they wanted to stab the governor.

"We will not discuss this topic again, Omar."

"Yes, we will," his old friend said. "If you want me on your team, and especially as your top advisor, then we will discuss it. Because it is the very issue that will make the difference between you being our next president and being run out of the country."

"I already know what you're going to say, so we don't need to go over it again."

"You know that I don't personally have a problem with your lifestyle, Rafael."

"How very kind of you not to have a 'problem' with my life, Omar. It's not a lifestyle, it's a life."

"You know what I mean. Don't twist my words around to make me look like the bad guy, because I'm not. But ninety percent of all those people who adore you *will* have a problem with your sexuality, and one hundred percent of the PAN party will have a problem with it. You cannot afford to let this get out."

"I'm very careful, and you know that. No one is more discreet than me."

"Yes, I do know that. But that's not enough. People are starting to talk. Not too loudly, and only among friends. But still, talk is talk and it will eventually get out of control if we don't curb it right now. You need a wife. Mexico needs a first lady."

Rafael sighed deeply. He knew his friend was right. As much as he hated to buckle under the pressure of his country's outdated cultural and ethical ideologies, he knew that this was one that would not give an inch. The Mexican people would never elect, or tolerate, a gay president. He'd known for several years that he was destined to lead his country, and likely the entire Latin America, and so he'd been extremely careful with his sexual rendezvous. He was quite certain that no one would have access to any of the skeletons from his closet. But there was still the matter of not being married, and as ridiculous as it was, he knew that his being unmarried would fuel the gossip fires, and the last thing he wanted was to have to defend himself in that particular arena.

Omar Benavides saw the wheels spinning in his friend's head, and moved in to close the deal. "I can take care of it for you."

"How?"

"Leave it to me."

II.

The modest stage atop the floor of the famous arches at the end of El Malecon, and the giant red, white, and green fold of fabric draped across the arches themselves, looked no more prestigious or important than the design sets of some of the ballets and other performances that graced the space every weekend. It was essential to Rafael Suarez's message and image that this speech in Puerto Vallarta address and reflect the simplicity of the resort town—the laid-back coziness that made it one of Mexico's main tourist attractions. The citizens here were modest and humble, hardworking people who were cosmopolitan enough to welcome and host international visitors from every country on earth—and yet intensely proud of their own Mexican heritage and culture, and refusing to let their little corner of the world become overly commercialized.

The tranquil appearance of the venue was all smoke and mirrors. There were no fewer than two hundred Mexican Secret Service agents, local and state police officers, and private security personnel scattered strategically throughout the massive crowd of a couple thousand spectators. Dozens of snipers dotted the rooftops of every other building along the stretch of the famous boardwalk. They were the one group of security that were not discreet or out of eyesight of the crowd below, but instead stood grandly with their legs spread wide, their rifles drawn and ready, and the binoculars securely attached to their heads and blinking with red lights as they scanned the throng.

The large audience stretched halfway down the mile-long board-walk, and spilled over into the narrow streets on one side and onto the beach on the other side. Many of the people more than a block away had their binoculars raised to get a better view of the candidate, and when the Mexican national anthem began to blare over the loudspeaker, the crowd surged forward as one entity, pushing closer to and into the person in front of and next to them.

"Ladies and gentlemen," the announcer said as the music faded to allow him to speak, "please welcome to the stage, the next president of the United States of Mexico . . . Rafael Suarez!"

The crowd exploded into thunderous applause, stomping their feet, pounding on metal trash containers dotted along the malecon, and blowing into various noisemakers. Car horns blared from a couple of blocks away from the barricaded area, and several bugles and trumpets heralded a welcome from somewhere near the stage.

Rafael Suarez took a deep breath and counted to ten, waiting for the roar to hit the perfect decibel level, and then stepped out from behind the curtains with his hands clasped and raised above his head. He smiled graciously and waved at the crowd, clapping along with them for several minutes, and then holding his hands together with his fingers spread out in front of him, and bowing to the appreciative audience humbly. It was his signature gesture to show that he was ready to begin, and the throng knew to bring the applause to a halt and to listen up, because El Suarez had something of significance to say.

"Thank you, compadres," he said into the microphone, immediately establishing a rapport with his audience. He'd taken Omar's words to heart, and was making a conscious effort not to appear an elitist or think himself above his fellow Mexicans. "Are you ready to make history?"

The audience roared its answer, and became rabid in their response. Some of the older buildings rattled with the reverberating noise, and the snipers above tensed just a little as they carefully scoured the crowd for anything suspicious in the middle of the overwhelming noise.

"Me too, mis amigos," he said warmly. "Me too. I am ready to tell the world that we are no longer receptive to being seen as a 'third world' or developing country. We are intelligent, we are brave, we are capable, and we are ready to not only be in the same room as the international superpowers, but we are ready to take a leadership role with them!"

This brought on another rousing round of applause, and as the speech went on, and people in the crowd began to nod more at his words and to hold the hand of the person next to him or hug his neighbor, Rafael knew that he had them in his back pocket. Bringing Mexico onto the international political stage as a leader and elevating his country's status among those superpowers was his main platform. It played into Mexico's macho and patriotic vigor, and at the same time it recognized where they were at now, and how much hard work it would take to get to where he wanted to take them.

And it reiterated that he, and only he, was capable of the big task. His Yale education and flawless command of the English language, the two years he'd lived and interned in Japan, and his close friendship with the newly elected Chancellor of Germany supplied him with the perfect picture of international competence. If the Mexican people really did want to be in the middle of international prominence, then Rafael Suarez was the only person to get them there. He knew it. But more important, he was convincing people all across Mexico of it, too.

As he drew his speech to a close, he sensed that the people were with him. They loved him. They supported him. And they wanted him to be their leader.

"And in conclusion," he said grandly, "let us remember how important each and every one of our roles is to this process. The measure . . ."

". . . of a man is in his integrity," the crowd roared to finish his sentence. "In his integrity and nowhere else."

* * *

The Presidente Intercontinental Hotel was not unaccustomed to tending to the needs of visiting presidents, royalty, and other dignitaries. But in their many years of operation, they'd never been faced with the security and privacy challenges that came along with Rafael Suarez's visit. Hordes of paparazzi from Mexico, the U.S., and across the globe, and screaming fans and curious onlookers crowded around the hotel entrance, trying every way imaginable to get inside, and stretching the hotel's security personnel to their limits.

And so, when Rafael walked into his suite and saw the silhouette of an unknown person sitting on his sofa behind the flicker of several candles, he panicked for just a moment. There were two Secret Service agents just outside the door, but that was easily twenty feet from where he now stood. A trained assassin would have no trouble killing him. Where the fuck was Omar? He was supposed to have been waiting for Rafael here in his room. That alone could not be a good sign.

"Good evening, Presidente Suarez," the soft female voice said.

He'd seen both *Kill Bill* movies, as well as *Mr. & Mrs. Smith*, which was one of his favorite films, and so the quiet, feminine voice was not all that comforting.

"I'm not the president yet," he said evenly, and mentally counted the number of steps to the front door.

"Semantics," the woman said, and stood. She walked slowly and deliberately toward Rafael, and when she was close enough, handed him a glass of chilled champagne.

At this close range, Rafael could see that she was in her midthirties. She wore an elegant black dress that dipped just below her knees and hugged her body enough to accentuate her curvy figure, but not enough to cheapen her classic beauty. She was tall and slender, with just the right amount of curves to satisfy her Latina heritage. Her skin was a beautiful copper color, and flawlessly smooth. Her slightly wavy black hair fell gracefully and rested against her neck and shoulders. When she smiled, dimples dotted her cheeks, and a bright white smile demanded attention and respect. Her large, almond-shaped brown eyes were soft and kind, and told Rafael at once that she was not carrying a machete under her dress, nor had she laced his champagne with rat poison.

"What are you doing here?" he asked. He made a mental note that any other man would stroke her smooth skin, draw her into him, and kiss her passionately. Instead, he finished off the glass of bubbly in two large swallows, and set the glass down on the table. "How did you get in here?"

She sipped at her own drink slowly, and smiled. "Governor Benavides arranged it," she said. She took a step closer, and caressed Rafael's cheek. "I'm here to take care of you."

"I don't need taken care of," Rafael said gruffly, and walked away from her. He stepped out onto the balcony and stared out at the sea and the city lights in front of him. When she followed him out into the warm night and wrapped her arms around his waist, he tensed up and pulled away from her. "What's your name?" he asked as he turned around to face her.

"Lorena."

"You're a very beautiful woman, Lorena," Rafael said matter-of-factly.

She smiled, and stepped closer as she leaned in and kissed him softly on the lips.

Rafael returned the smile, and forced himself not to snicker. "I'm afraid there's been a mistake, Lorena."

"No, there hasn't," she said softly, and intertwined her fingers with his. "I understand perfectly your . . . dilemma," she said as she squeezed his hand. "You are safe with me, President Suarez. There is no one more discreet than me."

Rafael's heart sped up and he felt his face flush. What the fuck had Omar told her? Who did he think he was? How could he not understand how this could destroy him? "I told you, I am not the president yet. Are you so dense that you don't comprehend this? Are you all beauty and no brains?"

Lorena didn't flinch at the attack. Instead she smiled, and wrapped her arms around his waist, and pulled him closer to her. She leaned in and whispered into his ear as she kissed it lightly, "You will be. With me by your side, you will be the next president of Mexico."

Rafael took a deep breath, and looked into her eyes. They were kind and soft and beautiful, and again he noted that there wasn't a hint of malice in them. Though he didn't know her at all, something told him that she would never betray him. He didn't trust her by any stretch of the imagination; that came with time and experience and history. But he was certain she would never be disloyal to him, and that her priority was to protect him and to help him. He needed people like that around him. And in order to become president, he needed a woman on his arms and by his side, and it wouldn't hurt at all if she was beautiful and expressive with her affection for the future president.

He took a deep breath, and then pulled her closer to his body, and held her to him as he slid his tongue into her mouth and kissed her roughly.

"Slow down," Lorena said as she pulled away and caressed his face. "Come with me," she said as she pulled him with her and walked toward the bedroom door. When she saw his nervousness and felt him hesitate, she smiled. "Relax," she said. "I won't bite. I promise."

* * *

He'd never felt more out of control or nervous in his life. He'd been in many situations that had required immense courage and strength, and was known both in Mexico and internationally for his fortitude and determination. The pounding in his heart and the sweaty palms were very uncharacteristic of him.

Lorena smiled at him from the bed all the way across the room. She'd already slipped out of her high heels, and had shed the flattering dress, and was now lounging on the king-sized bed. The white lace panties and enhancing bra stood out in stark contrast to her glimmering copper-colored skin. She had long legs and a flat stomach and the perfect ass that every Latina dreamed of possessing.

Rafael knew that any straight man in the world would consider Lorena a very beautiful woman, and the ultimate prize. They would have raging erections at the mere sight of her fully dressed; seeing her in nothing but the provocative lingerie would surely have them empty their loads into their pants. But his reaction was different. Though he recognized her intense beauty, it had no effect on him whatsoever. His cock didn't harden as she spread her legs ever so slightly and beckoned him to come to her, and in fact, he felt a little repulsed.

But if there was anything that Rafael Suarez was not, it was foolish. He knew what was at stake here, and stubbornly gave in to it. He unbuckled his trousers, and slid them down his ankles. "Come here," he ordered as he leaned against the bureau and spread his legs.

Lorena scooted off the foot of the bed and sauntered over to him. When she reached him, she leaned in and kissed him softly on the chin as she cupped his bulge in her hands. She tried to kiss him on the mouth, but he moved his face away, and she didn't push. Instead, she dropped to her knees, and pulled his boxers down to his ankles as she knelt in front of him.

Rafael looked down and watched disinterested as she cupped his balls and squeezed his cock. His dick was long and thick and uncut, and had been the source of much pleasure and awe from the few men and young boys he'd fucked over the years. It didn't take much to get it fully hard; or at least it usually didn't. He watched

Lorena pull the foreskin back and stick out her tongue to lick the head.

She continued to squeeze his balls and stroke his cock as she took more and more of his cock into her mouth. When her lips brushed his pubic hair, she choked a little, and pulled a couple of inches off of his cock.

Rafael knew she faked the choke. He wasn't even half hard, and was only about six inches long at this point. Fully hard he'd be a little over nine, but he knew that he wasn't going to get anywhere near that length that night. And Lorena was no amateur. She was classy and obviously educated, and very refined. But she was a whore, nonetheless, and any choking going on with a cock in her mouth was done for the benefit and ego of the client she was servicing.

He closed his eyes and tried to imagine the warm mouth around his cock attached to the hard body of the beautiful young man he'd glimpsed from the corner of his eye at the rally earlier that afternoon. The boy had worked his way from the back of the crowd to near the front, where Rafael had noticed his thick eyebrows, striking eyes, and sexy stubble on his chin. As he spoke from the podium, Rafael discreetly glanced at the young man a few times, and was rewarded with a sexy smile.

His cock began to thicken and grow inside the hot mouth as he remembered the young man.

"That's it, baby," Lorena said as she came up for breath and kissed the head of his cock dramatically. "Let me make you feel good."

And then his semi-hardon was gone. Just the sound of her voice jolted him out of his fantasy, and back into the reality of his present.

"I'm sorry," Rafael said as he gently pushed her away from him, and pulled up his shorts and pants. "I can't do this."

Lorena quickly got to her feet, and wrapped her arms around Rafael's waist. "Don't worry, Presidente Suarez," she cooed as she leaned up to kiss his ear. "We can take it slower. There's no rush."

He laughed, and pushed her away again, holding her firmly at arm's length. "It's not going to happen, Lorena. No matter how slowly we take it, it's not going to happen. Surely you understand that."

He kicked off his trousers and dress shirt, and changed into a pair of jeans and a pullover short-sleeved shirt.

"Yes," she said softly. "I understand." She reached for her dress.

"Excellent," Rafael said, as he tucked his shirt into his jeans and slipped on a baseball cap. "I assume that Omar has . . . made arrangements for you?" he said as he walked toward the door.

"Yes," she said demurely, and avoided eye contact with Rafael.

"Very good. It was nice to meet you, Lorena," he said as he walked out the door.

* * *

It wasn't easy convincing the Secret Service agents to leave him alone. But when Rafael Suarez was determined, very few people could dissuade him. He told the two agents that he wanted to go out to meet an old friend and that he needed a decoy to lure the paparazzi away from him. He convinced them to dress the bellboy up as himself and that the two Secret Service agents needed to flank him every step of the way in order to fool the waiting crowd outside. The Intercontinental Hotel was located several miles south of downtown Puerto Vallarta. Rafael told the agents to drive to the northern end of the town and to spring the decoy on the unsuspecting reporters only when they reached the Marriott Casa Magna in the northern marina district of the city.

Though skeptical and resistant at first, the agents finally hesitantly agreed. They ushered the bellboy into the black Lincoln Town Car quickly and under the guise of night. Rafael watched a couple dozen giddy reporters clamor around and jump in their own cars and speed after the decoy. He laughed to himself, and then ordered a simple and unassuming car for himself.

He drove the few miles into town with the top down on the Jeep, and enjoyed the wind on his face and the sound and smell of the ocean to his left. When was the last time he'd driven himself anywhere? Hell, when was the last time he'd been alone for any amount of time, outside of his bed? He wanted to be president more than anything, and he knew that that meant he would have very few moments like this. His heart raced, his palms were sweaty, and he found it hard to breath regularly. But it felt great to feel alive again, and he found himself smiling.

Rafael drove to the Zona Romantica, and parked the Jeep in front of one of the many sidewalk cafés on one of the side streets of the larger Olas Altas Street. He hadn't thought out where he might go once he got to the old town area, and just started walking. He was surprised how much had changed since he'd last been there, and even more surprised at how he found himself walking toward his old haunts without thinking about it.

It had been several years since he'd been to Paco Paco's, the famous gay club. In his younger days, long before he began to be famous, he'd frequented the bar often. The three-level club had two large dance floors, a pool table and video game room, no fewer than six bars serving liquor at any given time, and world-renowned female impersonator and hot male stripper shows. On weekends the club was packed to the rafters with patrons. It drew a very eclectic crowd—young and not-so-young; Mexicans, Americans, and Europeans; drag queens, gay-for-pay strippers; and hustlers of every age, shape, and gender identity.

He couldn't go there, of course. He'd be recognized immediately. Puerto Vallarta was one of the "happening" cities in Mexico, where pop culture ruled. And as much as Rafael was a politician, he was even more a celebrity. All it would take was one gay boy to spot him, and the news would be all over the bar . . . and all over Puerto Vallarta in a matter of seconds. He calculated how long it would take the gaggle of paparazzi to get from up north to the cozy Romantic Zone, and didn't like the answer.

He stopped at the park only a block away from Paco's, and sat on one of the iron and wooden benches. He hadn't driven all that way just to sit alone in a dark park. But he couldn't go to his favorite haunt, either. His free moments, away from the press and advisors and staff and the public, were rare, and he wanted to make the most of it. But how?

"Hi, handsome," he heard from a few feet away. "You looking for a friend?"

Rafael looked over at the young boy sitting on the brick ledge built around a tree trunk a few feet away. He couldn't have been more than seventeen or eighteen. He was a little under six feet tall. He wore a pair of faded skinny jeans with holes in both knees, tennies, and a plain white t-shirt that should have hugged a pair of gym-sculpted pecs, but instead hung loosely on his thin torso.

Rafael was about to say no, but was silenced when the kid took a drag on his cigarette, lighting the night air enough for Rafael to get a decent look at him. His facial features were soft and beautiful, almost feminine, but with enough masculinity to cause Rafael's cock to plump in his jeans. His hazel eyes glowed bright orange with the spark from the cigarette, and were large and almond shaped, with long, curly lashes hanging on the lids. The smooth tanned skin shimmered with a thin layer of perspiration, and seemed to light up from somewhere deep inside him. After exhaling a mouthful of smoke, the kid smiled, and Rafael's cock throbbed against the inside of his thigh as he watched snowy white teeth appear between the most beautiful, full lips he'd ever seen.

"What are you doing out here?" Rafael asked, and immediately regretted it. God, he sounded so much like his father and grandfather. Though the three generations were all currently playing well with each other for the sake of the upcoming election, it was no secret that there was not a lot of love lost between the Suarez men. Rafael hated even the slightest reminder that they shared the same blood and often were much more alike than any of them preferred to acknowledge.

The young boy snickered. "I'm the park security guard," he said, and took another deep drag on his cigarette. "Can't you tell?"

Rafael shook his head slowly, and lowered his head into his hands so the kid wouldn't see him smile. Young people were such smartasses, and their asses were getting smarter and smarter with each passing decade. They all thought they were invulnerable and immortal and that they knew everything. He remembered being that young once, and thinking the same things. The difference was that for him, those things were true, and for everyone else it was just a silly idealistic perception of themselves. Still, it was hot to hear a confident young guy speak like that. But he couldn't let the kid know that.

"Put that thing out," he said slowly as he nodded toward the cigarette in the kid's hand. "It's disgusting and it will kill you."

The boy sneered at Rafael, and took another defiant drag. But when he looked into Rafael's eyes, he wasn't able to hold the glare, and tossed the cigarette across the sidewalk as he exhaled.

"What's your name?" Rafael asked.

"José," the boy said quickly.

Rafael smiled. "What's your name?"

The kid stood up and shoved his hands into his jeans pockets, and shuffled his feet a couple of times. "Israel," he said softly after a long moment. "My name is Israel."

Rafael smiled, and stood up and walked over to Israel. He leaned in and kissed him on the lips, and pulled him tight against his body. He felt the boy's body trembling against his own, and smiled inwardly as he pressed himself even tighter against him. "Do you feel my cock, Israel?" he asked as he broke the kiss.

"Yes," Israel answered with a quivering voice.

"I need to have it inside your ass. Do you know of someplace where we can go? Someplace discreet."

"I work at a hotel not far from here," Israel said. "There are a couple of vacant rooms. We can go there."

"Will there be people around?" Rafael asked. "I need not to be seen."

"Yes, there will be people there. We have a pool party every night that lasts until eleven o'clock. And I need not to sneak you into my room. I don't know you. You could be a serial killer, for all I know."

Rafael laughed. "I am not a serial killer, Israel." He pulled the young boy closer, and kissed him again, more passionately this time. "You have no idea who I am, do you?"

Israel looked embarrassed, and blushed. "You look a little familiar. Are you an actor?"

"No," Rafael said. "I'm not an actor. But I do need to be very discreet. I will not hurt you, I promise."

"I'm gonna need payment up front," Israel said boldly, and thrust out his hand.

Rafael looked at him as if he were speaking Martian. Of course he'd known Israel was a hustler, but the conversation of money and how that might look had never crossed Rafael's mind. This was not the type of person Rafael Suarez had reason to socialize with, and he was completely ignorant of how they navigated the particulars of their business deals.

"Five hundred pesos," Israel said stubbornly, and thrust his hand out again.

"Five hundred pesos?" Rafael said disbelievingly.

"Three hundred?" Israel answered uncertainly.

"Three hundred pesos will not even buy you a decent pair of shoes," Rafael said. "Are you honestly telling me that you will allow a complete stranger to fuck you for less than a pair of shoes?"

"I don't need much," Israel said uncomfortably, and looked around nervously.

"But you deserve more, Israel," Rafael said. "You deserve better. You can't possibly survive on that."

"I also work at the hotel."

"Of course, and how much do you make there?"

"Two hundred pesos a day."

Rafael scratched his head and paced back and forth for a moment. Having gone to school in the States, he couldn't help but convert the currency into dollars. Two hundred pesos translated to approximately twenty dollars. How could anyone survive on twenty dollars a day? Dinner alone cost that much. No wonder so many of the kids in Puerto Vallarta had to hustle to make ends meet. As much as he didn't want to play politician right then, he couldn't help but wonder how he could make it better for Israel and the millions of others just like him in Mexico.

"Look, maybe this was a bad idea," Israel said nervously. "I don't like to talk about money out in the open like this, and I am not going to go any lower than three hundred, so maybe we should just . . ."

Rafael pulled Israel to him again, and kissed him passionately on the lips. "It's not a bad idea," he said as he pulled away. He reached into his wallet and pulled out ten 500 peso bills. "This is for you."

Israel looked at him suspiciously, and didn't take the money. "Five *thousand* pesos? Why would you pay me five thousand pesos when I only asked for five hundred?"

"Because you are worth more than five hundred pesos, Israel. Don't you understand that?"

"How do you know what I'm worth? I haven't even sucked your dick yet."

Rafael was torn. Part of him wanted to hold this young man and to help him make a better life for himself and to show him that anyone could be anything they wanted to be if he only believed in himself and applied himself. The other part of him wanted to take the boy and fuck his brains out, and hearing Israel talk like that only made it harder to ignore that particular part.

"Well then, why don't you show me how much you're worth," Rafael said as he took Israel's hand and allowed him to lead the way to the hotel.

* * *

The Vallarta Cora was more than just a hotel. And it was more than just a clothing-optional gay resort. It was a movement, an icon of gay life in Mexico. The hotel itself was rather small. It consisted of twelve one-bedroom apartments in two three-story buildings that were intersected by the small pool between them. A poolside bar with porn videos playing all around it served cheap drinks during the famous Happy Hour and pool party from four o'clock in the afternoon until midnight. Behind the pool and bar were a hot tub, a dry sauna, and a "black room" that didn't even try to disguise its purpose of luring naked men into raw, animalistic public sex.

When they approached the front gate, Rafael heard a few men splashing in the pool several feet behind the office in front of them.

"I can't go in there, Israel," he said as he stopped at the gate.

"Why not?"

"Because those people in there will recognize me, and that cannot happen."

"You don't even know who's in there," Israel said as he opened the gate. "They might not know you."

"They will know me, Israel, believe me," Rafael said, and leaned in to kiss Israel on the ear. "Get rid of them." He handed the boy another handful of bills.

Ten minutes later Israel returned, and took Rafael's hand and led him past the empty pool and the loud music behind it and upstairs to Room 202.

"This is my apartment," Israel said as he opened the door. "I'm going to shower," he said as he walked to the bathroom without closing the door or turning on the lights. "Get comfortable. I'll be out in a couple of minutes."

Rafael looked around the apartment, taking note of every detail, as was his way. It looked as he imagined every other apartment in the complex looked, with cheap art pieces on the walls and indigenous sculptures on the tables and counters. There were a couple of posters of Britney Spears and Thalía on the walls, and several photos of Israel and some friends taped to the borders of the mirror on his bureau, but other than that there was nothing that would let him know that someone actually lived there, rather than renting it out for a few days while on vacation.

He walked over to the larger-than-king-sized bed, and quickly undressed and then lay down on top of the comforter. He stretched out his long legs and pulled on the balls lying between his legs and stroking his cock.

"Shouldn't you leave that for me?" Israel asked.

Rafael looked over at the boy framed in the bathroom doorway, silhouetted with the light behind him. He was long and lean, as he looked in his clothes. But he had more muscles than Rafael had expected, and was tight and toned. His body was completely smooth except for the thick bush right above his crotch, and the small patch of short black hair right between his pecs. Though he'd brushed his hair back with hands, several mutinous strands fell across his forehead and neck, dripping with water. Standing there naked and wet, he looked more masculine than Rafael expected, and it caused his cock to stir.

"Come here," he ordered.

Israel walked over and crawled into the giant bed with Rafael. He immediately slipped between the older man's long legs, and tried to push them farther apart.

But Rafael had something else in mind, and reached down and hooked his arms under Israel's armpits and pulled him up so that he was lying directly on top of him. He pulled the boy's face down to his own, and licked Israel's lips slowly with his tongue, and then slipped it slowly into his warm mouth. He slid it in deep, and then pulled it out slowly, and then back inside again. When Israel sucked on it, Rafael felt his cock thicken and grow longer against his leg. But when he switched positions, and pulled the young boy's long tongue into his mouth, and tasted its sweetness, his cock throbbed to full life and he found it hard to breathe.

He rolled Israel onto his back, and maneuvered himself so that he was lying on top of him. He slid his cock between the youngster's legs and made a couple of short thrusts against them, shuddering when the lean legs squeezed against his cock. The smooth body beneath him felt incredible, and he rubbed his hands up and down every inch that he could touch.

"God, you feel so good, papi," Israel moaned as Rafael slid his cock between his legs and caressed his body. He kissed Rafael's chin and neck, and ground his hard cock against the older man's tight and lightly hairy abs.

Rafael kissed Israel on the lips again, and then slid down the length of his body until he was between the tall boy's legs. He lifted both of the boy's legs into the air, so that his knees rested against his chest, and his ass was pointing straight into the air. Staring down at the puckered hole below him, Rafael felt his heart beat erratically in his chest, and struggled to take in enough air as he breathed. The ass, and indeed, both legs supporting it, were completely hairless, and as smooth and soft as baby powder. The hole looked small and tight, and Rafael wondered how his big cock would fit inside. And yet, a couple of seconds later, it began to twitch and wink at him—opening up and then closing tightly again—seeming to beg for him to fuck it with everything he had.

He held both of Israel's feet together at the ankles, and bent down so that his face was only a couple of inches from the boy's quivering ass hole. He blew softly at it, and grinned when Israel moaned loudly and squirmed beneath him as his breath wisped across his fuck cavity. Then he lowered his head even farther, and stuck out his tongue. When only the very tip of it touched the puckered skin around the hole, he felt a tingle begin at the tip of his tongue and travel into his mouth, down his throat, and into his stomach. The silky soft skin and faint smell of baby oil was more than he could take, and he grabbed both ass cheeks and spread them farther, and then kissed the center of Israel's universe.

"Oh, God, that feels good," the young hustler moaned. "Fuck me, papi," he groaned.

"Don't call me that," Rafael said, coming up for a quick breath. "I hate that word."

"Okay," Israel agreed. "Just keep doing that."

Rafael licked and kissed around the hole for another few moments, flicking his tongue around it playfully until Israel moaned louder and bucked beneath him, and then slid his entire tongue deep inside the tight hole.

"Oh, fuck, pa . . ." Israel gasped, and stopped when he realized what he was about to call his john. ". . . baby," he corrected himself. "Give me more, baby."

Rafael tongue fucked him furiously, spreading his ass farther apart, and replacing his tongue with a couple of fingers when his jaw got sore. His cock bounced up and down in front of him frantically as his heart beat faster and faster, and when it grazed the smooth skin of Israel's ass and lower back, he thought he'd blow his load all over the bed before he ever got inside the tight ass.

It had been more than three months since he'd last fucked a hot boy. He had been on a trip to Thailand, and had arranged for the get-together through a trusted colleague. The boy was only fourteen, but had already been a high-priced call boy for almost two years. He was fairly tall for his age, and thin, with smooth copper skin that begged to be caressed. His ass was tight and insatiable, and he was very skilled at taking a big cock. He also was not well educated, and it was obvious that he had no idea who Rafael was, and so Rafael felt safe and comfortable fucking him rough and hard, and going a little further than he usually dared. He never really hurt the boy, though, and compensated him extremely well, and so he didn't feel overly guilty about fucking the boy so intensely.

Israel reminded Rafael of that Thai boy, and the memory of that other boy, and the smell and feel of Israel currently in front of him, drove him over the edge. He stood up so that he was standing over Israel's upturned ass, and spit down onto the center of the hole. When he saw the hole open up and swallow the spit hungrily and then close tightly again, he pressed his cock head against the hole and slid it across the opening a couple of times.

"Fuck me, baby," Israel groaned, and lifted his ass higher to slide across Rafael's cock head.

Rafael slipped the head of his cock just inside the clutching sphincter with every intention of sliding in slowly and carefully, allowing Israel a chance to get used to the length and girth of his big, uncut cock. But after only the first half of his head slipped easily inside, Israel's ass muscles gripped Rafael's cock and pulled it deep inside him in one forceful tug. Rafael held on tightly to the boy's legs as his cock was drawn deeper and deeper into the fiery hot tunnel, and his body collapsed onto Israel's legs and ass.

"Do you like my ass?" Israel asked, between gasps for air.

Rafael regained his balance, and slid his cock in and out of Israel's ass slowly, careful not to spend himself too quickly. The kid's ass was phenomenal; it grabbed his cock like a vise grip and squeezed it with what seemed like thousands of tentacles and sucked him in deeper and deeper to his seemingly endless ass. The muscles were hot and moist and relentless in their appreciation of his cock. Though he would never be in the record books for the size of his cock, it was still by any definition very large. He'd measured it a few times, and it always fell about a couple of inches short of a full ruler, and was almost as thick as his wrist. When he pulled the foreskin back, the head was purple and hard and looked like a proud crown. His thick rod was riddled with fat veins that throbbed like the heart of a separate entity. More than a few guys had been unable to take Rafael's cock at all, and a handful had been reduced to tears as he fucked them relentlessly.

The Thai boy a few months back had been an exception to that statistic, and had taken his cock valiantly, although he seemed stunned and a little unaware of his surroundings after Rafael had spent himself inside the boy, and was unable to speak for almost an hour. Rafael had been a little concerned, and wondered if he'd caused permanent emotional damage to him. But after a while he began to come around again, and so Rafael had felt comfortable enough to drop him off on the street corner and drive away knowing he'd never see the boy again.

Israel reminded Rafael of that other boy, at least physically, with a couple of exceptions. One was that he had an impressive cock himself, easily eight inches or a little more, and almost as thick as Rafael's own. The Thai boy had a small, cut penis that wasn't any thicker than Rafael's fingers. Another difference was in their eyes. The Thai boy had sad brown eyes that never looked Rafael in his own, and seemed constantly to be looking at the floor or scoping out a possible escape route. Israel's eyes were light hazel, and sparkled with life and energy, and insisted to looking deeply into Rafael's as he drove deeper and deeper inside him.

Both boys also had incredible, smooth asses. But that was also their biggest difference. The Thai boy was able to take Rafael's cock in its entirety, and to his credit he didn't cry or beg for it to be taken out, as did many others. He lay perfectly still, and rolled over into all of the positions in which Rafael had instructed him, but once in position he lay perfectly still, seemingly in a coma as Rafael fucked him relentlessly. He allowed himself to be kissed, but did not return it, and he never touched himself or seemed intent on his own release.

Israel, on the other hand, couldn't get enough of Rafael's cock. From the second Rafael placed his cock head at his ass hole, Israel grabbed onto it and sucked it deep inside him, and it felt to Rafael as if the young boy never planned on letting go. He slid his ass up and down the length of the big cock, squeezing it and milking it with his hot muscles. And when Rafael finally caught his breath and started ramming into him harder and faster, Israel matched his pace, thrusting his ass up to meet each plunge with equal force and vigor.

Rafael had never fucked anyone who could take everything he gave . . . and still ask for more. It felt surreal for him, and for a moment he lost his rhythm as he wondered what to do next.

"Come on, pa . . . baby," he said as he groaned and thrust himself deeper and harder up onto Rafael's big cock. "Give me more. I want it all."

Rafael grabbed Israel's ass from underneath and pulled him harder up onto his cock. When the boy whimpered, he slammed his cock all the way in up to his balls, and ground his hips. He leaned down and licked the head of Israel's cock, pulling some of the slick precum into his mouth. He sucked on it for a moment, and then swallowed it, and was surprised to find that he liked it. Israel's cock was long and thick, and stretched a couple of inches past his navel, which made it easy for Rafael to lean down and take several inches of it into his mouth. He sucked furiously on it as he slammed in and out of the tight ass. His balls bounced off Israel's ass cheeks as he fucked him deep and hard.

"Oh, God," Israel moaned. His body went limp and he shook his head from one side to the next as he grabbed Rafael's ass and pulled it deeper into him. "Stop . . . I'm so close . . . don't . . ."

Israel's ass spasmed around his cock, and he felt the dick in his mouth thicken and the veins throbbed against his tongue and the roof of his mouth. A second later the first squirt flew from Israel's cock and splashed against the back of Rafael's throat. He swallowed it before he could think about it, and pulled his mouth off the big cock. The next several shots of cum sprayed across his face, covering every inch of it.

"Oh FUCK!" he yelled, and bit down on Israel's neck to stifle the scream. He was buried deep inside the boy, and Israel had his cock in a vise grip from both inside and with his hands cupping his ass cheeks and keeping him pressed tight against his own ass. There was no way he could pull out in time, and before he knew it he was releasing his load deep inside the kid's ass. "Take it, baby."

After several shots, he collapsed onto the bed, still buried inside Israel. He hugged the boy close to him for several minutes.

"Are you okay?" Israel asked.

"More than okay," Rafael said, and kissed him tenderly on the lips.

"Can I pull off now?"

"Oh, God, sorry," Rafael said, and slid his half-hard cock out of Israel's ass. When he did, a thin stream of cum slid out of the hole with the cock. "Wow, that's hot," Rafael said as he watched the cum slide down Israel's ass and the inside of his legs.

Israel flexed and then relaxed his ass, and smiled when he felt another large gob of cum slip from his ass, and saw Rafael's reaction. "So, do you still think I'm worth five thousand pesos?"

"No," Rafael said, and stood up to get dressed. "But we can stop at an ATM and I can get the rest for you."

III.

Ramon Mendoza sat in the oversized wing chair in front of the fireplace, alternating between puffing on his Cuban cigar and swirling the crystal cognac snifter dramatically in front of him so that he could see the fire glow through it. Every five minutes or so he would pull at or run his fingers through his thick black mustache, and check himself out in one of the huge mirrors on either side of the fireplace. Rafael was certain the leader of the PAN party had a hardon from looking at and feeling himself.

"I hope dinner was satisfactory," Mendoza said in his deep baritone voice, and curled his lips into the most ridiculously fake smile Rafael had ever seen.

"Superb," Rafael said, and smiled back. With anyone else, he would have expounded upon the statement, extolling the virtues of the fine meal. But he knew that would only stroke the already-oversized ego of his host, and he couldn't bring himself to do it. And he knew that the statesman would not let it go without comment, even if he himself had to make the comments.

And he was right. "You could search the whole world over and not find a finer meal than good old Chihuahua grown beef,"

Mendoza said with a smile, and then took another large toke from his Cuban.

Rafael waited for the ex-senator to pound his chest and grab the nearest woman by the hair and drag her off into an adjoining room. When he didn't, Rafael smiled back, and raised his own glass up for a toast. "Well, it's certainly up there among the best," he said. "But we shouldn't undervalue Maine lobster, or French escargot, or Japanese eel." He watched the commissioner's eyes twitch and his lips quiver. "They are all pretty damned good, too."

Mr. Mendoza sighed deeply, and stood up to refresh his drink. He glanced at Rafael's empty glass, but didn't offer to refill it. "I don't think it's any secret that I am not one of your legions of fans, Mr. Suarez," he said with his back to the candidate.

"No, Mr. Mendoza, it is no secret at all. Thankfully, over ninety percent of your party is on my bandwagon, and are rabidly supportive of me and my candidacy."

"Yes," Mendoza said, and turned to face Rafael. "There is that. Lucky for you."

Rafael was well-known for his patience and his diplomacy, but even he had his limits, and he just wasn't in the mood to deal with Mendoza right then. "I assume that there was a reason that we enjoyed this delicious meal together, Mr. Mendoza."

"Undoubtedly. I can certainly understand your wish for privacy in your personal life, Mr. Suarez. None of us is eager to air our dirty laundry in public."

Rafael's heart raced, and he felt a giant lump block the airway in his throat. Visions of hidden camera videotapes of him and any number of one-night stands, including the one with Israel just the night before, looped through his head. He'd paid them all well for their discretion, but he knew that there was always the possibility that that might not be enough. Mendoza wouldn't blink about paying twice—or ten times the amount he himself had paid the hustlers—for some proof of his indiscretions. He made a concerted effort to breathe normally, and to swallow while he figured out what to say to get things back in his favor.

"I mean, I have five mistresses on the side myself," Mendoza said with a laugh. "They're draining me goddammed dry. Their houses, their clothes, their cars, and their kids. Jesus Christ, I can only spend so much money without my wife getting suspicious. She's sneaky that way."

Rafael looked at him with one raised eyebrow. "Excuse me?"

"Oh, don't get all worked up," the older gentleman said as he downed his fifth drink and poured another. "I know your little lady isn't a mistress. You're still young and naïve enough to believe you'll fall in love and live happily ever after with just one woman. And you want to protect her from all of us mean, nasty people who will corrupt and demoralize her. I understand that, and I say good for you. That's exactly what your adoring public will love about you. They'll eat that shit up."

"What the hell are you talking about?" Rafael asked, and stood to fill his own glass without waiting for his host to offer.

"I'm talking about the fact that it's time you stopped being so secretive, and you bring your little who . . . your girlfriend . . . out into the open. I understand you've only been dating her for about six months now, and you are still 'watching over her.' That's very cute. But that's got to stop, and stop now. It's time the public meets her, and you must ask her to marry you. The election is only eight months away. You can introduce her to the world, and announce your engagement at the same time. In six months you will get married, and Mexico will have our first lady when you take office a month later in December."

"You're absolutely mad," Rafael said.

Mendoza chuckled. "That would be convenient for you, but no. And the rest of the party and I might disagree on many things, and most things regarding your candidacy. But on this we are in one hundred percent agreement. They have asked me to convey their mandate. We have a press conference scheduled on Wednesday. It is at that press conference that you will introduce your . . . future fiancée to the Mexican voting public."

"And just where did you get your information, Mr. Mendoza?"

"It took some convincing, but your campaign manager, Governor Benavides, finally spilled the beans. The party is quite united on this issue, Mr. Suarez, and the good governor is embarrassingly dedicated to seeing you in office. He told us about your relationship, and about your desire to keep it all under the radar. He all but begged us to drop it and let it go, not to insist on bringing her out in the open. But as I said, our minds are as one on this, Mr. Suarez. You will not be elected to office, and you will not have the support of the Partido Accion Nacional behind you if you do not share this 'amazing woman' with your adoring public and if she is not Mrs. Rafael Suarez at least six weeks before you move into Los Pinos."

"You have lost your mind, Mr. Mendoza," Rafael said as he finished his cognac and set the empty glass on the bar. "You cannot dictate who and how and when I marry."

"I'm sorry you feel that way, Mr. Suarez," the ex-senator said, and smiled smugly as he lit another cigar. "You have been wrong on many occasions, but never more so than with that statement. I can . . . we can . . . dictate exactly that. At least we can if you truly wish to become the most powerful man in all of Latin America. It's cutting it close, but it's not too late for us to find, endorse, and groom another candidate. All it would take is one little scandal with your name attached to it. I'm sure that wouldn't be too terribly hard to manage."

"You're fucking with the wrong man, Senator."

"I really don't care about that, Mr. Suarez. As long as you're fucking with the right woman. The image of our first lady is very important. She must be first class. I hope to God your girlfriend isn't a total whore."

"This conversation is over, Mr. Mendoza," Rafael said, and walked toward the door.

"Wednesday afternoon, Mr. Suarez. Governor Benavides has all the details."

Rafael glared at the senator, and slammed the door on his way out.

* * *

"Who the *fuck* do you think you are?" Rafael said between gritted teeth as he barged into the living room.

Governor Benavides sighed deeply and turned around to look at his old friend. He'd seen Rafael angry before, and at various levels of upset, and even really, really pissed off. But the crimson color in the face before him, and the veins popping out on the candidate's face, and the spittle flying from his mouth were all new to Omar, and he wondered if this might be the final straw for the candidate.

"Good afternoon, Rafael," he said calmly.

"Don't fucking patronize me, Omar," Rafael yelled as he leaned in closer to his campaign manager's face. "What were you thinking? Did you honestly think that telling the party that I was dating someone would satisfy them? Did you not know that they would demand her presence?"

"Yes, Rafael, I did know that they would insist on seeing her."

"Then what the hell were you thinking? There is no 'her,' Omar. I have not been dating anyone, let alone a woman, for the past six months, and you know this."

"Yes, I do."

"Well then, please tell me what is going on in that feeble little head of yours. I understand that you've scheduled me for a press conference in two days, and that I am to present my fiancée to the world at this grand event. Are you planning on entering the perfect qualifications of the First Lady of Mexico into a computer like they did in that old movie *Weird Science* and hoping that she materializes?"

"Don't be ridiculous, Rafael," Governor Benavides said with exasperation. "That's a fictitious movie, and this is real life. It's already taken care of."

"And how is that?" Rafael asked as he settled heavily into a chair next to the sofa.

"Good afternoon, President Suarez."

Rafael looked in the direction of the female voice. Lorena was standing in the doorway that separated the living room from the hall that led to the bedrooms of the hotel suite. She was dressed in a simple black dress that came down just below the knees and elegant black high heels. Her jewelry was expensive but not overstated, and complemented the rest of her attire perfectly. Her hair fell to her shoulders gracefully. She looked like the perfect first lady.

It had been almost a month since their first and only meeting, but the memory of it was burned into his head. It now made his stomach tighten into a knot. "Lorena," he said uncomfortably. "It's nice to see you again."

"It's my pleasure, Mr. President."

Rafael laughed softly. "Omar, you have got to be fucking kidding me, right? You don't honestly expect me to present Lorena to the world at the press conference and pretend that she is my fiancée."

"I expect exactly that," Omar said flatly.

"Well, it's not going to happen."

Governor Benavides stood up and walked over to Lorena, and took her arm and led her to the sofa, where he helped her sit. "Yes, it is. At least it is if you want me to stay on as your manager. And it is if you want to become the next president of the United States of Mexico."

"Are you serious? You will resign if I don't go along with your idiotic scheming lie?"

"Yes, Rafael, I will," Omar said heavily, and sat next to Lorena. "It is the absolute only way that you will win the presidency. With Lorena by your side, you cannot lose. You are guaranteed the highest office in the country. Without her you don't stand a chance, Rafael. Despite your rabid popularity, you will not be elected president without a beautiful and graceful wife at your side. You will lose and you will lose badly. And as much as I love you, I will not be dragged down politically by a loser, and especially not one with a scandal."

"Omar . . ."

"I'm serious, Rafael. You have a decision to make, and you have to make it right now. My bags are packed and I am ready to leave. But I can unpack them very easily and quickly, if you make the right decision."

"Omar, please," Rafael said, and leaned forward with his elbows on his knees. "I appreciate your honesty, and your dedication. But this plan will never work. Lorena is beautiful and graceful, and she'd make the perfect portrait of a first lady. But she knows next to nothing about me. We have only two days before the press conference. That's not nearly enough time for her to get to know me well enough to convince the PAN elite, and the entire nation, that we have been intimate for the past six months and that we are engaged to be married."

"I know that you grew up in Guadalajara. Your father was a metalsmith, and your mother sewed sports uniforms for local school athletic programs. You were brilliant in junior high and high school, and caught the eye of a very wealthy businessman named Reynaldo Perez, who took you under his wings and groomed you for politics and public service."

Lorena leaned closer, and held Rafael's hands in her own. "He also paid your way to Yale University, which is where you and I met for the first time," she said in perfect and only slightly accented English. "I was studying Economics and you were in the Political Science program. We met through mutual friends and saw each other socially a few times with other friends, but never dated then, and lost touch soon after I returned home to Mexico to help take care of my ailing father. After Yale, you traveled extensively to Europe and Japan, where you lived for two years."

"That is all public information, Lorena," Rafael said, and removed his hands from hers. "Anyone with access to the Internet can gain that information."

She reached out and took his hands again, stubbornly holding them tightly in her own. She switched back to Spanish. "I know all of that public information, Mr. President. I even know all of the names and personal information on all of the significant people in your life. I'm intimate with the details of the rift you have with your family members, and would respectfully decline any comment on such matters, saying only that family is extremely important to you and that you and your family are committed to reconciling, and that they support you one hundred percent in your candidacy.

"I also know that you have a birthmark in almost the exact shape of the state of Jalisco on the inside of your upper right thigh. Your penis is just under twenty-three centimeters and is uncircumcised, and you release a large amount of precum very soon after becoming fully hard. You are a very tender and passionate lover, and love to kiss. Of course, I would never share this with anyone, especially the press. But the details are permanently burned into my brain, as are the details of much, much more. Ask me anything."

Rafael watched Lorena with amazement. "What was the name of my statistics professor at Yale?"

"Thomas Benson. You hated him intensely."

"When did I have my appendix removed?"

"July 12, 1992. In Japan."

"Who was my first intimate relationship?"

Lorena hesitated for only a couple of seconds. "Steven Collins, in your second year at Yale. You dated for a little over a year and he asked you to move in with him. But you didn't because you were focused on public life and feared the consequences of being found out. He couldn't handle the closeted relationship, and broke up with you."

Rafael blinked rapidly and struggled to catch his breath.

"But that's not what the public will hear, of course," Lorena said, and patted his hands. "They will know that your first and only real girlfriend before me was Sofia Villareal, a school teacher from Guanajuato who was tragically killed in a car accident on the very afternoon that you planned to propose to her. After her death in 1988 you were so distraught that you never dated anyone seriously until you ran into me again almost a year ago. We reconnected slowly, and began dating a little over six months ago. I have all of the details committed to memory, including the intimate ones, if you care to hear them."

Memories of their last meeting flooded back into his mind. "No, that's perfectly all right. I trust implicitly that you have them correct."

Omar leaned forward and took a deep breath. He looked back and forth from Rafael to Lorena. He didn't speak, but raised an enquiring eyebrow at his old friend.

"All right," Rafael said, and leaned back defeated in his chair. "Let's do it."

IV.

With seating capacity of more than 100,000, the Estadio Azteca is the largest soccer stadium in Mexico. On this late afternoon, it was filled to capacity and beyond, and the roar of the crowd was deafening as they yelled with excitement and stomped their feet in anticipation. The Mexican people were electing their new president, and for the first time possibly since the Mexican Revolution in 1910, they felt a hope for real change, for moving forward out of poverty and hopelessness into prosperity and optimism, from a government infamous for fraud and distrust into one of integrity and true global leadership.

The crowd was rabid, and the loud stomping from close to 120,000 people shook the structure visibly. Police and stadium officials tried unsuccessfully to quiet the raucous mob, frightened that they would get out of control and wondering if the giant stadium might collapse under the pressure of the anxious energy. A couple dozen Secret Service agents paced nervously around the president-elect, and begged him to cancel the speech. It was a logistical nightmare, and the opportunities for disaster were too great.

"Unthinkable," Rafael said, and peeked out from behind the

curtain to take in the crowd. "This isn't my moment," he said. "It's theirs. And I'm not going to deny them it." He pulled Lorena closer to him and whispered into her ear, "Are you sure you're ready for this?"

"It's too late to change my mind now," she said with a nervous smile, and leaned up to kiss him on the cheek, making sure that she and her future husband were being watched by stadium personnel and the throng of reporters with them backstage.

"Ladies and gentlemen," the announcer blasted over the loudspeaker, and waited for the crowd to quiet. When they did, he continued. "Please welcome the next president of the United States of Mexico, Rafael Suarez!"

The roar was immediate and vociferous, and caused several people backstage to cover their ears as the floor and walls around them shook. Rafael took a deep breath and stepped from behind the curtain and onto the stage to thunderous applause, high-pitched whistles, and blinding flashes of camera lights. He made sure never to let go of Lorena's hand, and when they reached the podium they both waved and smiled to the crowd. Rafael laughed nervously and pulled his fiancée to his torso and kissed her lovingly, just as they'd practiced a hundred times over the past month. Though seemingly impossible, the bellow of approval grew even louder.

He clasped his hands in front of him with his fingers spread and bowed to the massive audience before him. He bowed humbly and grinned faintly to himself when they quieted almost immediately. He had them in the palm of his hands, and the feeling caused his cock to harden inside his pants.

"Thank you, compadres," Rafael said warmly, making sure to acknowledge people in every corner and in front and behind him. "This is a very special day for Mexico and for the Mexican people. I could not be more proud to accept your election and to begin working hard for you as president of the United States of Mexico!"

The applause lasted a full five minutes before he was able to continue. Throughout his forty-five minute acceptance speech, Lorena stood two steps behind him, and stepped up next to him and hugged him at precisely the right times. Over the past six months they'd appeared on the cover of every magazine in the country, and several in the U.S. and overseas. The country was infected with Rafael and Lorena fever, and they couldn't get enough of the beautiful couple. They were more popular than the biggest pop and movie stars. When they were married six weeks earlier, millions of people packed the streets of Mexico City and every other major city in the country, and massive celebrations erupted simultaneously and lasted the entire weekend.

"We've got a lot of work ahead of us, my friends," Rafael said as the applause and noise finally started to quiet a little. "And I say we intentionally because this is a combined effort. I can lead you, and I can sit at the international table and represent you, and I can pass the laws that will protect you and help make your lives better and more productive. But none of that will make a difference if you don't become an active participant in this process of improving your own lives and take an active role in moving Mexico forward in the world stage. I am only your representative, compadres. You are the real agent for change. And you are the real hope for our great republic."

The audience rose to its feet and shook the foundation of the stadium again, even more frantic this time because they sensed the end to Rafael's speech.

"We are in for a wild ride, my fellow citizens. We will be successful because we are an honorable country and we are filled with courage and integrity."

The crowd stomped their feet wildly and shouted in unison:

"The measure of a man is in his integrity. In his integrity and nowhere else."

* * *

Rafael rode with Lorena back to their home, and kissed her tenderly on the cheek as she got out of the car, but he didn't get out with her and he didn't go inside. Instead, he instructed his driver to take him to an address on the other side of the city. The nondescript two-story stucco building had no signs or identifying sources. It was nestled a couple of blocks behind an eight-foot wrought iron fence and several tall and leafy trees. Rafael's chauffeur rolled his window down and entered in their private code, and drove through as the gate opened and then closed quickly behind them as he entered the underground parking structure, safely out of the eyes of any paparazzi or other curious onlookers.

"Good evening, Mr. Smith," the woman said as she smiled warmly and held her hand out to Rafael. She was dressed in an expensive tan pantsuit and black high heels. Her shoulder-length black hair was stylish and framed her face perfectly. Though Rafael knew she was in her early sixties, she could easily have passed for twenty years younger.

"Maria," Rafael acknowledged, but pushed her outstretched hand aside and hugged her affectionately. "It's so good to see you again. It's been too long. I've been a little busy the past few months."

"Yes, sir," Maria said, and allowed herself only a trace of a smile. Though she made no moves of affection or other signs of familiarity with Rafael, she seemed comfortable when he wrapped his arm around her waist and walked with her into the building from the underground parking structure. "Congratulations," she whispered as the sliding glass doors closed behind them.

* * *

The two boys on the large bed were perfect, and exactly what he'd ordered. They were thin and smooth and though he'd specified to Maria that he wanted them to be between eighteen and twenty years old, he doubted very much that they were even that. One of them had longer black hair, not quite to his shoulders. His eyes were large and exotic with long black lashes. He had a constant smirk on his thin lips that caused Rafael's cock to twitch. The other boy looked frightened and nervous. He had shorter dark blond hair and hazel eyes that darted around the room as if searching for an escape route. He had thick, full lips capped with deep dimples, and Rafael wanted desperately to kiss him.

Rafael wore a leather hood that hid his face and head, and nothing else. His cock was fully hard within a couple of minutes of setting eyes on the two boys, and it swung heavily in front of him as he walked toward the bed.

"What are your names?" he asked the boys as he reached the big bed.

"I'm Uriel," the blond boy said. He looked frightened, and squirmed on the bed.

"And you?" he asked the boy with longer hair.

"What do you want my name to be?" the kid said coyly, and got onto his knees and crawled toward Rafael's cock.

The new president-elect pushed the young boy away. "Don't be a smartass, kid. What is your name?"

"Nestor," the boy said, and rubbed his shoulder where Rafael had pushed him.

"Well, Nestor," Rafael said, "you're a very beautiful boy, but you're very cocky. You need to learn a lesson."

Nestor rolled his eyes, and Rafael wondered if he even realized he'd done it. But the boy's cock also sprang to life with the thought of his punishment, and he wriggled his ass in anticipation.

Rafael crawled into the bed between the two boys. "Suck my cock, Nestor."

He spread his legs enough for Nestor to crawl between them. The young boy attacked his cock like it was an ice cream cone. Rafael moaned as Nestor licked the head and shaft slowly and teasingly, and then wrapped his lips around the fat head. The kid had a talented mouth, and sucked the cock head lovingly for several minutes before slowly taking inch after inch of the thick shaft deeper into his throat, until he'd swallowed the whole thing.

"Fuck," Rafael moaned as Nestor tightened his throat muscles around the big dick and slid his mouth up and down the length of it. His mouth was hot and wet and relentless in its mission of milking him dry.

As Nestor worked over his cock, Rafael pulled Uriel closer to him and kissed him on the mouth. The boy's lips were full and soft, and Rafael had never been kissed more tenderly and hungrily at the same time. When he slipped his tongue inside Uriel's mouth, he tasted a mix of milk and honey and peaches that made him never want to stop kissing the boy. Rafael wanted to protect him and love him and keep him close to his side forever. He was intoxicated with the feel, the taste, and the smell of the young boy. Everything about Uriel was tender and innocent and soft.

Except his cock. He rubbed his crotch against Rafael's leg, and it startled the newly elected president. He looked down and gasped. Easily ten inches long and thicker than Rafael's own cock, it seemed half as big as Uriel himself. It throbbed against his leg and a thick string of precum oozed out of the head and slid down the big shaft.

Nestor was still working over Rafael's cock, and bringing him closer to orgasm. His tongue flickered around the bulbous head a few times and then he swallowed the entire cock deeper into his throat. Rafael slid his cock in and out of the hot mouth several times, and knew he couldn't take much more of the expert service without blowing his load.

"Come here," he told Uriel. "I want to suck your dick."

Uriel straddled him and slid his huge cock just barely into Rafael's mouth. He let it rest there for a few minutes, allowing Rafael to get used to its size. When the president began sucking it deeper into his mouth and more expertly, the young boy slid it in and out slowly. "Let me know when you want me to cum," he told the president.

Rafael loved the feel and taste of Uriel's huge cock in his mouth. And the feel of Nestor's tight hot mouth on his own cock was drawing him closer and closer to ecstasy. "Oh, God," he moaned as he let Uriel's cock slip from his mouth. "I'm gonna cum."

Nestor started to pull off Rafael's cock, but the president-elect grabbed him by the back of the head and pulled it back onto his cock until it was buried in the boy's throat. His body shuddered violently as he emptied his load deep into Nestor's throat.

"Can you cum now?" he asked Uriel.

"Anytime you want," the boy said as he stroked his huge cock.

"Now!"

A second later the first spray of cum splashed across his face. Nestor gagged on the flood of jizz that poured down his throat, and squirmed to release himself from Rafael's grip. But the president was harder and more excited than he could ever remember being, and with each new gush of warm cum from Uriel's cock, his grip on Nestor tightened, and caused him to gush even more of his own cum down the boy's gullet. His face was coated with the warm sticky fluid when the young blond boy pulled away, and only when Nestor began choking and flailing in earnest did Rafael release his grip and allow him to sit up.

"That really hurt, man," Nestor said as he sat up on his haunches. "I can't believe you made me swal . . ."

Rafael grabbed him by the waist and flipped him onto his knees. Nestor yelped, and as Rafael leaned in and began licking his hole, the yelps turned to moans. The president licked around the sphincter tenderly for a few moments, and then slid his tongue inside and fucked the tight hole. He slapped both sides of Nestor's waist and then pushed and pulled the boy onto his tongue.

When Nestor's hole was dripping with Rafael's saliva, the president got onto his own knees and slammed his hard cock deep into the boy's ass roughly and in one long stroke.

"Fuuuuuuck!" Nestor yelled.

Rafael pushed Nestor's face into the mattress and thrust his cock in and out of the tight ass violently. The boy moaned and groaned beneath him, and tried to squirm his way out from beneath the president. But Rafael had a firm grip on him, and was relentless with his cock sliding in and out of him.

"You," he said to Uriel. "Get over here and slide that big dick of yours up my ass."

Uriel fumbled quickly to his knees, and slid into place behind Rafael. He placed his cock against the crack of the president's hairy ass, and slid it slowly and carefully across it. He looked frightened again as he glanced back and forth from his friend and the president.

"Fuck me, Uriel," Rafael said. "Slam that big cock up my ass and fuck my brains out."

Uriel spit on the head of his cock, and thrust it deep inside Rafael's ass as roughly as Rafael had done with Nestor a moment earlier.

Rafael ground his molars together and tightened his grip on both sides of Nestor's ass, but didn't groan or yell out in pain, even though sharp needles of excruciating agony shot up through his ass and spread to the very end of every extremity on his body. He stayed perfectly still, not daring to slide an inch inside or out of Nestor's body as he took a few deep breaths and got used to the feel of the giant cock deep inside him.

Uriel also remained motionless, not even daring to breathe. His eyes were wide and blinkless, and it looked as if he might cry at any moment.

The moment hit Rafael like the Acme safe falling from the sky in the old Road Runner cartoons. His body convulsed as the pain turned to pure bliss. He moaned loudly and began thrusting his cock in and out of Nestor's ass, which also caused his ass to slide back and forth onto Uriel's thick cock.

"Fuck me, kid," the president ordered as he slammed his dick deeper into Nestor's ass.

Nestor groaned and struggled against Rafael as he fucked him. But the president was much bigger and stronger, and he easily overpowered the boy. He took a deep breath, and then slowly lay down on the bed, limp and surrendered.

Rafael tightened his ass around Uriel's cock and pulled him

down with him as he fucked Nestor fast and hard. Uriel didn't even have to move. As Rafael moved in and out of Nestor's ass, he also slid on and off of the young boy's giant cock. The feel of Nestor's warm tight ass wrapped around his cock, and of the heat and hardness of Uriel's cock deep inside him was more than he could take for too long.

"I'm gonna cum," Rafael moaned loudly.

"Do you want me to cum, too?" Uriel asked.

"On my . . . back," Rafael said between gritted teeth as he thrust himself deeper into Nestor's ass and lay on top of his ass and back. He closed his eyes as his cock thickened and jet after jet of his load sprayed deep into Nestor's ass.

Uriel pulled his big dick out of the president's ass, and he rested it between the cheeks, pointed straight into the air. The first gush flew way over Rafael and Nestor's heads, and the next six or seven landed across Rafael's sweaty back and his ass.

Rafael waited until the last of Uriel's load was sliding down his sides and between his ass cheeks before he pulled out of Nestor's ass, and rolled onto his back on the bed.

"Holy fuck!" he whispered as he pulled Uriel in closer to him and kissed him tenderly on the lips.

"Did you like me, mister?" the shy boy asked.

"That is an understatement."

"What about me?" Nestor asked as he leaned up carefully onto a sitting position.

Rafael laughed. "You're cute."

Nestor raised an eyebrow, and then sneered at the president.

"Can you take off that mask?" Uriel said. "I want to see your face."

"That's not going to happen," Rafael said, and took a deep breath as he stood up to get dressed.

The two young boys crawled next to one another, and cuddled on the bed as they watched the president slip into his pants and button his shirt.

"Your payment is at the front desk with Maria," he said to Nestor. Then he leaned down and kissed Uriel on the lips again. "This is for you," he said, and handed the boy a handful of bills.

"Normally I'd say that the measure of a man is in his integrity," he said to the kid as his cock began to grow with excitement over holding so much money. "But in your case, the only measurement that matters is this beautiful work of art between your legs."

He squeezed the huge cock one last time, and then walked out the door.

INCH FOUR
Frat Frenzy

I.

Corey Scott-Baker sat cross-legged in the middle of the room. All of the lights were out, making the room completely black save for the faint glow of candlelight from the circumference of the perfect circle around him. He wasn't one prone to crying, but in the past two weeks he'd found himself doing just that at least half a dozen times. He'd tried everything he could think of to stop it—running as fast as he could around the track, hitting the punching bag in the gym in the basement of the house, and even swimming several laps as fast and as hard as he could until he couldn't take another breath. None of it helped.

But sitting completely naked in the middle of a circle of candles in this otherwise totally dark room—that helped. Breathing deeply and inhaling the aroma of the candles and watching the flames flicker around him helped. Shutting out all the noise and the sights of the world around him helped.

He never really considered himself all that spiritual, and he certainly wasn't one to believe in or play around with the metaphysical. He'd stumbled upon the new ritual by accident one evening when he had one of his crying fits and found himself escalating in anxiety, and when nothing else seemed to work. All of his frat brothers were downstairs, partying as usual. He had no escape, and since nothing else had worked in the past, he crumpled to the floor and curled up in a fetal position. After a couple of minutes, he felt trapped, and tore his clothes off rapidly. He felt himself calming a little, but also becoming anxious because of his fear of the dark. The couple of candles in his room helped, and fifteen minutes later he wasn't crying anymore and he felt his normal self again. He bought several new candles after that first time, and created the circle of light around him shortly after, and it worked miraculously. His friends would laugh uncontrollably and accuse him of being stoned if they ever saw his little ceremony. But he didn't care; it helped him stop crying, and that was all that mattered to him.

His eyes were adjusting to the dark around him now, and he could make out some of the items in his room. Several sports trophies lined shelves on the walls. Pictures of family and friends adorned the bureaus and hung from the walls. His letter jacket was slung carelessly across the chair in front of his desk, and slips of paper with phone numbers from more than a dozen girls were strewn even more carelessly across the desk and dresser.

Corey couldn't remember a time when he wasn't the most popular guy in any situation in which he found himself. Even when he was born, the doctors and nurses at the hospital stood around his crib and ooh-ed and ahh-ed about how beautiful and "special" he was. In preschool all of the teachers fussed over him, and even at that age all of the other kids seemed to instinctively know that Corey was the kid to be seen with. In elementary school he received more Valentine's Day cards than all of the other kids combined. In high school he was voted most likely to everything, and there wasn't a single girl in five surrounding school districts that didn't try desperately to lose her virginity to him.

Most people outside of Corey's tax bracket might believe that his extreme popularity was a by-product of his huge inherited wealth, but that thought never crossed Corey's own mind. It didn't take a genius to realize that he was beautiful. Anyone who looked at the trendy teen magazines at the supermarket or who watched the popular television shows could see instantly that Corey Scott-Baker had the "it" factor. At 6' 2", 185 pounds, with perfectly styled blond hair and Caribbean Sea blue eyes, charming smile with dazzling white teeth, and a hard, chiseled body, he was ninety percent of the general population's picture of the ideal young man.

It didn't hurt that his parents were close personal friends with Bill and Melinda Gates, or that they hosted parties in which the Rockefellers, the Waltons, and the Gettys were frequent guests and often not the wealthiest in the room. Certainly it helped him get into the best schools and bought him anything he needed or wanted. But even without that advantage, Corey would have been a huge success. He knew instinctively that greatness was his destiny, and believed that membership into his biological family was only a part of that formula.

He was Midas in everything that he did. Everyone wanted to be around him, and he had to fight to find very few moments alone in his days. He wasn't at Yale a full two weeks before even the quarterback of the football team and the editor of the *Yale Law Journal* were scrambling to spend time with him and fighting for their own Kodak moments with him. He was the first sophomore ever to be voted president of *any* Yale fraternity, let alone Kappa Lambda Phi, the most prestigious and popular on campus.

And so, one might deem it more than a bit odd to find Corey Scott-Baker sitting naked in the middle of a circle of flickering candles, his body wracked with sobs. How could anyone with all of Corey's advantages have anything to be sad about? With everything that he had, what more could he possibly want? With the entire campus population adoring his every move and breath, what could warrant the tears and the convulsing sobs?

But they didn't really know Corey, and that was the problem. No one at Yale knew who he really was. The only person who truly knew Corey, and who loved him for who he was at his very core, was Roger. His parents moved a few doors down from Corey's parents in the Pacific Heights district, San Francisco's wealthiest neighborhood, and the two couples became close friends. The boys were born half an hour apart, and had grown up closer than brothers. They got their first visit from the tooth fairy together, scraped their elbows together on their first attempt at riding a bike, and had their first experiences of masturbation, blowjobs, and fucking together.

Corey and Roger both dated girls all through high school, but neither of them were into girls at all. They didn't have sex with their girlfriends, much to the girls' dismay. Instead, they allowed the rumors about their sexual prowess, spread by the girls themselves, to go unchallenged. It worked to their girlfriends' advantage, since getting it on with the two most popular and hottest guys in school elevated them to goddess status. And Cory and Roger were glad not to have to answer any embarrassing questions or address any ugly rumors. Instead, after dropping the girls off after their dates, they went home and fucked each other until they were covered in sweat and struggling to catch their breath.

In their junior year, Roger revealed that he was in love with Corey, and fell just short of begging him to become lovers. Corey laughed him off at first, but when he saw that his friend was serious, and that he was hurting, he stopped joking around and spoke seriously. He had a plan for his life, a big plan, and it did not involve having a gay lover by his side. It was fine that they continue being discreet and having fun, but nothing more serious could ever come to fruition between them. His life in politics would never allow him to be in a committed relationship with another man, and he'd never command the respect from the general public that he needed for that successful career, with Roger, or any other man, by his side.

They remained best friends for the rest of their high school years, but something changed between them after that. They still fucked a couple of times a week, but Roger wasn't the same. It seemed to Cory that his friend was only going through the motions, and that the passion was gone. A couple of times he caught Roger crying as he fucked him, even though Roger tried to hide it. When it came time to decide colleges, Roger became very quiet and didn't want to talk about it at all with Corey. It didn't come as a surprise at all that he chose to attend Berkeley, even though he could easily have joined Corey at Yale.

The past four years had been difficult. Though still best friends, Corey felt as if he and Roger had drifted further and further apart. When he first arrived at Yale, they talked on the phone three or four times a week. Now they spoke only once a month or so. Even so, he still considered Roger his best friend, and he still felt no one knew him or understood him better. He really mis . . .

The loud banging on the door caused him to jump. "Come on, man," one of his frat brothers yelled from the other side of the door. "Everyone's here. We're all waiting for you."

"I'll be right there," Corey said, and sighed as he began blowing out the candles around him.

II.

Corey walked down the stairs slowly and deliberately. He was completely naked, and loved the feel of the air on his skin. His hard cock throbbed and led the way almost ten inches in front of the rest of his body. He took a couple of steps down the stairway, and his cock was the first part of his body to be illuminated by the dimmed lights of the living room below. A couple of audible gasps echoed their way up the stairs, and Corey smiled as he watched his thick cock swing heavily up and down in front of him, and imagined the faces of the pledges below as he descended down the stairs and into the living room.

When he reached the landing, he scoped the room around him. Eryk, Bryson, and Gavin were his fellow officers on the executive team of the fraternity, and were lined up military fashion in front of the fireplace wall. They were fully dressed in jeans and t-shirts, but even from his vantage point on the stairwell landing all the way across the living room, he could see that Eryk and Gavin were sporting full hardons. The vice president and secretary stared straight ahead, but they were both bouncing up and down on their feet and Corey could see they were anxious to get started. Bryson, by far the shyest of the group, stood perfectly still, with his hands behind his back, as ordered, and his eyes darted nervously around the room, even though he was instructed to stare straight ahead.

Directly in front of the trio, on their knees in the middle of the room, were the two new pledges, also fully dressed. In the past three years as president of Kappa Lambda Phi he'd seen several guys who had looked frightened, and a few who looked excited. And he remembered his own initiation into the elite fraternity four years ago. He knew these two new pledges were struggling to catch their breath, and that their hearts were pounding uncontrollably in their chests. They looked much more frightened and surprised than excited, and that made Corey's cock throb even harder, and bounce up and down in front of him frantically.

"Who said you could look at me?" Corey barked at the pledges, and smiled to himself as they quickly turned their heads to look at the other three frat members, and then lowered their heads to stare at the floor. Corey nodded to his frat brothers.

Eryk, Gavin, and Bryson broke out of their military stance and moved toward the pledges. They pushed the two boys on their stomachs. Eryk pulled two bandanas out of his back pocket, and quickly blindfolded the two newcomers, who were shaking visibly. Gavin brandished several long strands of black leather straps, and made short task of tying their hands together. Bryson looked around nervously again, and took a pair of scissors from his back pocket. Corey could see them shaking in his friend's hands as the treasurer began cutting off the t-shirts and jeans from the pledge's bodies. He looked up at Corey questioningly, but when his president nodded his head, he went back to his assignment. A couple of minutes later, the two boys were lying naked in the middle of the room, their cut and torn clothes tossed into the wastebasket in the kitchen.

"Get the fuck up on your hands and knees," Corey ordered the pledges. He watched as they struggled into position. It wasn't easy, he remembered from four years ago. With one's hands tied in front of him, it was awkward, and even more so with the nervousness of being naked in front of a group of strangers.

The two boys in front of him were both beautiful, but couldn't have been less alike. One of them was about five foot eight, with smooth light brown skin and the hard muscled body of a champion gymnast. His head was shaved and looked as smooth as the rest of his body. He was the first to get into position, and his ass wiggled just slightly in what Corey figured was closeted anticipation. It was smooth as glass and perfectly muscled, and the sight of it caused a long, thick stream of precum to drip from Corey's cock head. Big, heavy balls swung between the caramel ass cheeks, and the boy's cock was long and thick and uncut, and jutted out almost a foot in front of him. With the blindfold on, his features couldn't be seen, but Corey remembered his almond-shaped eyes, and straight, ta-pered nose from their previous meetings. He reminded Corey of the artists' depiction of what King Tut probably looked like, and from their very first encounter, Corey knew he would be fucking the boy on this night.

The other guy was about six feet four inches tall. He was thin and lanky, with strawberry blond hair and hazel eyes. He had a farmer's tan, but the areas that weren't blushed by the sun were milky white. His ass was one of those areas untouched by the sun, and was bony and a little hairy. His smile was a little dopey, but charming. He reminded Corey of a grown-up Opie, from the re-runs of *Mayberry R.F.D.* that he used to watch back in high school. It didn't take the class valedictorian to know that his daddy was a very successful farmer who wanted only the best education for his son, and that he had been sent to Yale very much against his will. He had enormous hands and feet, but was clumsy and awkward. He was still struggling to get on his hands and knees when Corey motioned for his three frat brothers to strip.

Gavin and Eryk instantly made a beeline toward the tall blond boy. No surprise there. The girls they dated were all tall and thin and could easily be Miss America contestants. The boys they fucked around with were all white jocks with freckles and a little to be desired in the brains department. Opie was perfect for them.

Bryson walked confidently up to join Corey and Tut. He started to get in front of the bound boy's face, but Corey stopped him.

"Get over here and suck my cock."

Bryson stopped in his tracks and stared at his friend dumfoundedly. The pledge crawled around toward the sound of Corey's voice. "Not you," Corey said to the kid who was now dripping a string of his own precum. "I want my frat brother to suck my cock."

"But . . ." Bryson stuttered.

"Shut up and get on your knees and suck my cock!"

The KLP treasurer dropped to his knees and looked up at Corey, his eyes brimming with tears. This was not part of the script, and Bryson was as anal as they came. It had been difficult enough for him to be totally on board with the thinly disguised hazing ritual when he was actually one of the initiators. He was not at all okay with having to so the same things that the new recruits had to do. He'd barely gotten through his own pledge initiation a couple of years ago. It just wasn't right that he had to do this.

Corey knew his frat brother was nervous and frightened and would give his left nut to be able to get up and leave. But that was not an option, and they both knew it.

"Don't make me tell you again," Corey said, as he took a step toward his friend and slapped his heavy cock against Bryson's cheek. "Suck it."

Bryson stuck out his tongue and licked the head of Corey's cock uncertainly. He licked the sticky precum from the head, and opened his mouth wide enough to take the entire head inside. He sucked on it for a minute, and then gagged as Corey pushed forward and slid two or three inches of his thick cock inside.

"Come on, guys," Tut whimpered as he crawled a couple of steps closer to the sound of Bryson slurping on Corey's cock. "I'm the one pledging here. Let me have some of that."

"Turn around," Corey said.

"Who are you talking to?" Tut asked as he faced the sound of Corey's voice.

"You. Turn around and stay on your hands and knees."

Corey dropped to his knees, too, and helped maneuver the boy into position. He looked at Bryson, and pointed to his cock again, and then slid Tut's ass cheeks apart and leaned in to lick at the hole as Bryson lay on his back on the floor and sucked Corey's cock deep into his mouth. He flicked his tongue across the smooth mocha ass a few times, and when the new pledge moaned and wiggled his ass, he slid his tongue deep inside.

"Oh, God," Tut moaned loudly as he frantically slid his ass deeper onto Corey's tongue.

Corey attacked the ass as if it were his last meal. He'd never seen an ass so hungry and anxious to be rimmed. It twitched and contracted, begging to be entered, and when Corey licked around it, the hole grabbed hold of his tongue and sucked it deep inside. Once inside the ass, it was massaged and tugged deeper inside. The ass wall was warm and moist and as strange as it sounded, it tasted undeniably like orange and mint. Corey's head spun with delirium as he ate the ass, and his cock thickened and hardened inside Bryson's hot mouth, causing the treasurer to gag as it slid deeper into his throat.

Afraid he'd blow his load way too early, he pulled his mouth off of the ass. He grabbed Tut by the waist and roughly turned him around so that they were face to face.

The kid was still moaning, and his copper brown skin had a pink flush to it. His whole body quivered, and his cock bounced heavily between his legs, still dripping with precum. He licked and bit at his lower lip, giving it a glossy sheen.

Corey thought he'd never seen a more perfect mouth. It was full and pink and begged for attention. He leaned in and licked at the lips, and Tut's mouth opened up slightly and sucked his tongue deep inside, just as his ass had done a couple of minutes earlier. The boy's mouth tasted exactly the same as his ass did, and in this context Corey identified the taste immediately. It was the citrus flavor of the same mouthwash he himself used. Apparently Tut douched with it as well as cleaned his mouth, and for some odd reason that turned Corey on immensely. He wrapped his hand around the back of Tut's head and pulled him closer so that he could kiss him deeper and more intimately.

Just beyond the blindfolded boy on his knees in front of him, Corey saw Eryk and Gavin skewering Opie. Gavin was fucking the pledge's mouth, his hands locked behind Opie's head and pulling him harder onto his cock. Eryk's hands were locked behind his own head, and he slid his cock deep and hard into the boy's ass, his head leaned back and his eyes shut tightly. He was biting his bottom lip, and it looked as if he was trying hard not to blow his load deep into the boy's ass.

Watching his frat brothers fuck the boy senseless and hearing him moan almost on the verge of crying got Corey's cock even harder and his heart beating faster. Most of the time, he could fuck for a couple of hours without fear of shooting his load too early. But he knew that that night was not going to be among those times.

"You ready to get your ass fucked?" he asked as he looked down between his legs.

"Oh, God, yes," Tut moaned huskily.

"Not you," Corey said, as he tried not to laugh at the desperate tone in the boy's voice. "You," he said, and scooted Bryson out from under him.

"What?" Bryson screeched in a high-pitched voice. His eyes were wide and his bottom lip trembled.

"No," Tut groaned, and sat down on his ass with his arms limp at his side. "That's not fair. I'm the pledge. I should be the one . . ."

"Don't worry," Corey said. "You're gonna get your ass fucked, too. But first I want to watch you fuck my friend, here."

"Corey, you can't be serious," Bryson said. He was shaking his head as he stared at Tut's huge cock, which was bouncing up and down excitedly in front of him. "I can't take . . ."

"Shut up!"

Bryson did as he was told, and dropped his head.

"Get on your back."

The treasurer lay down on his back on the floor, and turned his head to one side, breathing rapidly. His hands played nervously with the tassels of the rug beneath him.

Corey lifted Tut up from the floor by the armpits, and maneuvered him into position between Bryson's legs, and helped lower him to the ground. "Fuck him," he ordered.

The pledge spit on his cock and slid it around the head with one hand, and with the other felt his way to Bryson's hole. He moved tentatively until the head of his cock was resting against the hairy fissure, and once there he leaned forward and slid his big cock deep inside, until his balls rested against Bryson's ass cheeks.

"Oh SHIT!" Bryson yelled. "Take it out. It hurts. Take it out."

"I don't think so," Tut said between gritted teeth, and continued fucking him.

Corey laughed softly. He knew that he should scold the big-dicked pledge and remind him who was in charge here. But the kid was so fucking hot, and watching him blindfolded and pounding Bryson's ass relentlessly got his cock throbbing and his blood roaring through his veins. He liked the cocky kid, and loved watching him in action. He'd let it slip this one time.

He walked over to Eryk, and slipped his hard cock into his friend's mouth. He slid in and out slowly, allowing Eryk to get used to his large size. Watching his two friends fuck Opie into oblivion was turning him on and making it difficult to hold back much longer. Luckily, Eryk was not a great cocksucker; he was clumsy and scraped with his teeth a few times, making it easier for Corey to pull out and move on.

"You ready to get your ass fucked, Tut?" he asked as he pulled

his cock out of Eryk's mouth. The young pledge still had his blindfold on, and continued fucking Bryson. Cory laughed, and walked
up behind him, caressing his chin and neck and leaning in to kiss
him on the neck. "I'm talking to you, punk."

"Yes," Tut moaned loudly. "Please, fuck me now."

Corey shoved Tut deeper inside Bryson's ass. "Keep your cock
deep inside him, bitch," he whispered into the boy's ear. He got on
his knees behind the pledge, and leaned his body against Tut's, sliding his long, thick cock between the kid's smooth, sweaty cheeks.
Then he slapped the mocha globes several times, and when Tut
moaned louder and he felt the ass cheeks relax, he slammed his
cock in to the hilt inside the hot, tight ass.

"FUCK!" Tut yelled, and stopped mid-thrust inside Bryson's
ass. His own sphincter tightened, and he tried to wriggle from beneath Cory.

"Shut up and take it," Corey said, grinding his teeth. He shoved
his cock in again, pinning Tut between him and Bryson's naked back-
side. The ass was tight as a blood pressure cuff, and he worked up
a sweat trying to slide in and out of it for a few minutes, until the
kid finally relaxed. Then he thrust in and out furiously, slapping
Tut's ass and loving the way the kid's ass raped his cock.

As he fucked Tut's ass, the kid slammed just as feverishly into
Bryson. Corey loved watching his friend get fucked. The frat treasurer alternated between moaning and licking his lips to crying,
and Corey found this amusing. For as much as Bryson begged and
pleaded not to be fucked, Corey knew he actually loved it. They'd
messed around several times over the last year, and a couple of
times he'd woken up in the middle of the night to find his friend
sucking on his cock and then impaling himself on it. So seeing him
cry now, with real tears, as Tut fucked him frantically, entertained
him immensely.

Eryk and Gavin were yelling profanities and fucking Opie, who
was completely silent and almost motionless as he took both cocks,
at an increasingly frenzied pace. Both of his friends were red and

sweating, and Corey could tell by their possessed fucking that they were very close. Eryk's moans and grunts became higher pitched, and a few seconds later he screamed as he pulled his cock out of the redhead's ass and sprayed his load all over the boy's ass and back. Gavin wasn't far behind, and he pulled Opie's head tight against his crotch as his body stiffened and he convulsed all over. A few seconds later, he pulled out, and sat on his ass in front of the pledge. Opie crumpled to the floor silently, and curled up into a fetal position. Corey thought to himself that he should not be turned on by watching what looked like a quart of cum dripping from the seemingly comatose pledge's mouth, but he couldn't help it.

"You ready, baby?" he asked as he leaned in and kissed Tut's ear and neck. "I'm about to explode all over you."

"Fuck yeah, man," Tut moaned loudly, and slid his ass harder onto Corey's cock.

Corey slammed in and out of the tight ass a couple more times, and then pulled out quickly. His cock head barely cleared the sphincter before it sprayed its first couple of shots all across the puckered hole. The next three or four spurts flew over Tut's back and head, landing on Bryson's face, and the last couple of jets fell on the pledge's back and then rolled down his sides.

Corey fell forward and rested on Tut's back and ass.

"Oh, shit!" Tut yelled. His entire body began to convulse, starting at his legs and then moving up his ass, across his back, and up to his head. He pulled out of Bryson's ass with an audible "plop," and leaned up so that his cock was pointing directly over the crying frat brother. "Ungh," he grunted as he sprayed his huge load all over Bryson's face and chest, and several stray jets landed on the rug on either side of his face and over his head.

Corey wrapped his arms around Tut's neck and chest, and kissed him again on the neck. "Your room is the last one on the left on the third floor, next to the bathroom. Welcome to Kappa Lambda Phi. Now get out of here."

"Yes, sir," the pledge said, and took off the blindfold and ascended the stairs.

"You okay?" Corey asked Bryson.

"Yeah," his friend said. "But you fucking owe me one, dude. That would have been really fucked up if I didn't want his fat cock so badly."

Corey laughed. "Help them get him dressed and back to his dorm." He nodded toward Opie. "He's obviously not ready for Kappa Lambda Phi."

"Sure thing. You cool with the new guy?"

"Yeah. You guys did make sure his room is ready, right?"

"Yep."

"Good. Make sure this one's not hurt," he said, and kicked at Opie. "I'll see you tomorrow."

Corey watched his three frat brothers help get the rejected pledge dressed, and then walked up the stairs. He went directly to his room, and lit all of his candles and placed them in a perfect circle in the middle of the room. He stepped into the center of the circle, and then curled up into the fetal position. Five minutes later he was snoring.

III.

Corey boarded the plane ten minutes before the general seating was called, and found his seat in the first-class section. He looked out the window and watched the workers below pack the luggage into the underbelly carriage and drive around in the carts, trying to look important. He felt a little uneasy about this trip—not nervous, really, and not second-guessing his decision. Just a little uneasy. He wasn't used to feeling uncertain or out of control in any situation. When it was his own life that seemed to be spiraling into maelstrom, he was even more uncomfortable. It was not his style to run from conflict or stress, and he told himself over and over that he was not doing that now by returning home for a couple of weeks. In fact, it was by going back home that he was dealing with it. He needed to get centered, and he needed Roger and home to get there.

His KLP frat brothers didn't understand at all, and acted as if the world were now rotating backward when he told them his plans for a two-week hiatus.

"What the hell do you mean you're leaving?" Eryk said with a squeak.

"What part of the statement is confusing for you?"

"Don't be a smartass," his friend said. "You know what I mean. Next week is our first mixed social. You can't miss that. You're the KLP president, for chrissake."

"Which is exactly why I can miss it. I'm the president. I can do whatever I want. You're the vice president, and next year you'll be president. Take over. It's good practice, and you're gonna need it."

"I'm not ready for that kind of responsibility, Corey. Come on, man. Just wait and go home after the social. Hell, if you can wait for another couple of months, we'll be on spring break, for crying out loud. What can be so important that you can't wait until then?"

"I am," Corey said, and continued packing.

"I don't understand."

"Well, you don't really have to," Corey said stubbornly. "I'm going, and that's all there is to it."

He knew that if he told Eryk and his other brothers that he was falling apart and thought he might be going crazy, that everything around them would implode. As much as he knew he had to take care of himself, he didn't want their world to crumble around them, too. He'd done a great job over the last four years of establishing himself as the ultimate leader and success story. But he hadn't done a very good job at all of empowering his friends and frat brothers to become their own leaders and successes. He felt responsible and irresponsible at the same time.

"You can do this, Eryk," he told his friend, and hugged him tightly. "Probably even better than I can do it myself."

"Yeah, right. You're freaking me out, you know that, don't you?"

"Yeah, and I'm sorry. But I have every confidence that you can do this. You need to do this, and I need to go home and take care of some stuff. So don't make me feel guilty about it, okay?"

It wasn't okay, and Corey knew it. But there was no other way around his going home. He'd mulled it over for over a week, and he'd debated several options. He always came up with the same result. Go home.

He put in his earplugs, closed the window beside him, and

stretched his legs out as he leaned his chair back as far as possible. Five minutes later, when the coach passengers began boarding, he was already asleep.

* * *

"Honey!" his mother yelled as she dropped her tennis racket and bounded down the stairs of the Victorian mansion three at a time.

Corey couldn't help but smile as he watched her spring down the stairs and across the expansive front yard. Her short blond hair hid the headband until she was only a couple of feet from him. She was wearing white tennis shorts, a pink tank top, and a diamond bracelet that Corey knew cost more than a decent midsized sedan.

"Hello, Jo," he said warmly, and hugged his mother. "Are you just heading out for a match, or just getting back?"

"I'm just heading out, honey. You should have told me you were coming home. I could have met you at the airport. And I certainly wouldn't have scheduled a match with Danielle and the Gettys."

"And how is Ms. Steel?"

The famous romance novelist was their next-door neighbor, and one of Jo Scott-Baker's closest friends. She was Corey's godmother, and Jo was the godmother of Danielle's daughter, Vanessa. Together they were an unstoppable force of nature, and were in the middle of every fundraiser and social activity in the city. If their photo and a highly complimentary article were not included in San Francisco's big newspapers any given week, they strategized over several bottles of wine on how to change that for the following week.

"She's as incorrigible as ever," Jo said with a heavy sigh. "It's no wonder she went through five husbands. I honestly don't know how anyone could endure her for more than a couple of hours."

"You seem to have done a pretty good job with her for many years."

"Yes, well, she *is* my best friend. It's my duty."

"And what about Mrs. Emerson?"

"Oh," his mother said exhaustedly, and shook her head. "The

same as always. That will never change. Danielle thinks Bonnie is a stuck-up bitch, and Bonnie thinks Danielle is superficial and shallow, and even worse, a horrible writer. They just can't be in the same room together, or it turns into a rabid dog fight. Honestly, I don't know why I tolerate either of them."

"Give me a fucking break, Jo." Corey laughed. "You thrive on the drama. You wouldn't know what to do with yourself if you weren't constantly in the middle of their tug-of-war."

His mother covered her mouth with one hand and giggled into it. "You're right. Life would be dreadfully boring without them, wouldn't it?"

"Thank God Roger and I don't take after the two of you."

"We're not *that* bad," Jo said, as she slapped him playfully on the arm. "I can cancel my match if you want me to."

"Oh God, I'd never hear the end of it from Ms. Steel. Go on, have fun. I'm tired anyway, and am gonna take a nap. Later tonight I'm heading across the Bay."

"That's nice, dear. Roger will be so glad to see you. Bonnie tells me all the time that he asks about you. Did you two have a fight?"

"We're not in elementary school, Mother," Corey said, and kissed her on the cheek. "I've just been really busy at school, and we're three thousand miles apart now. Now get out of here, you're gonna be late. And beat the shit out of those pretentious Gettys, will you?"

"Watch your mouth, son," Jo said sweetly as she kissed him back on the cheek and swatted his ass. "What will the fucking neighbors think?"

Corey watched as his mother jogged next door, and then hurried inside before his godmother answered and saw him. She'd never let him get away without a two-hour conversation and at least a dozen pinches on the cheek. Jo was right, she was incorrigible.

"Martina!" he yelled as he walked into the kitchen.

"Mi amor!" the Scott-Baker housekeeper screeched. She dropped the mop and ran up to him and hugged him tightly. "Why didn't you tell me you were coming home? I could have made you a cheese-cake."

"That's the last thing I need," Corey said as he patted his stomach.

"Whatever. You're as lean and strong and beautiful as always. And you know it."

"Yeah, I suppose I am, huh? But I'll be here for two weeks, so there will be plenty of time for your famous turtle cheesecake."

"Two weeks? What happened? Is something wrong?"

"No, nothing's wrong," he said, and pointed to the barstool. When Martina sat, he went to the counter and pulled out a frying pan. "I just need a little R and R. I've been a little stressed lately."

Corey continued talking with his beloved housekeeper as he methodically made them both a grilled cheese sandwich. He carefully fried four thin slices of tomato and added them to the melted cheese on Martina's sandwich before closing the two pieces of bread together, and then made his own with only cheese and a little mustard. He put them on plates with a handful of potato chips. Then he poured himself a Diet Coke and poured Martina a glass of Merlot with a splash of orange juice.

"Oh, baby, I can't drink *wine* right now," Martina whispered. "It's the middle of the day," she said, even as she took a giant swallow. "Your mother wouldn't . . ."

"We both know that mother will be gone for at least four hours. After their tennis match, she and Danielle will head over to the Laurel Court bar for several glasses of champagne if they win or Bloody Mary's if they lose to the Gettys. By the time Arthur drives them back here, mother will be much too . . . happy . . . to care, or even notice that you had one glass of wine."

"Well, maybe two," Martina said as she finished her first glass and tipped it in Corey's direction to refill, and giggled.

The two friends ate their sandwiches and drank their respective beverages, and then Corey helped her finish mopping the kitchen floor and dusting the great room and library. She'd been with his family for almost thirty years, long before Corey came into the world. She had practically raised him, and felt much more like his best friend than his housekeeper.

"How's your love life, baby?" Martina asked as she dusted the library shelves. "Do I have a potential new son-in-law in my very new future?"

"No," Corey said. "I've dated a couple of guys, but nothing serious. I think they're more interested in the idea of being my boyfriend than they are in the real me. Either that or they are more interested in my family's money than they are in me."

"Well, you guys *are* richer than God," Martina said with a little slur, followed by a hiccup.

"I know," Corey sighed deeply, and plopped down onto the leather sofa. "But I'm an old-fashioned kinda guy, you know that. I want a guy to love me for me, and not for my money or any fame that might come along with it."

"Yes, I do know that, cariño," Martina said as she sat next to Corey and wrapped her arm around his shoulders and hugged him. "That's what I love about you the most. Don't worry, your Prince Charming will come along. They always do, to good guys with good hearts."

"I know," he said, and rested his head on her bosom. "You sure you won't have that sex change and be my boyfriend? The offer still stands."

"Oh, baby, you could not handle me. But you could handle Roger, if you wanted to."

"Martina!"

"I'm sorry," she said quickly. "I know I should keep my mouth shut, but I just can't help myself, especially with two glasses of wine in my belly. You shouldn't have let me drink like that."

They both laughed.

"I'm tired, Martina," Corey finally said. "I'm gonna go up and take a nap."

"What time do you want me to wake you up?"

"About four, I guess. I'm gonna go visit Roger a little later."

"Oh, thank the baby Jesus, I'm gonna have that little grandbaby, after all."

Corey looked at her sharply.

"I'm sorry," she said, and shrugged as she giggled uncontrollably. "But it's your fault. You should not have given me that second glass."

* * *

"I can't believe you're here," Roger said excitedly. "And I can't believe you didn't tell me you were coming."

"I didn't really know myself until I was practically on the plane this morning."

"What's going on, Corey? It's not like you to just jump on a plane and show up out of nowhere." He dumped the cup of cheese sauce over the basketful of chips and waved the waitress over to order another round of margaritas. "You never even take a breath without weighing the consequences and planning out your next fifty moves."

Corey shrugged. "I just needed a change. I needed to catch my breath a little."

"And you came *here* to catch your breath?" Roger asked as he popped a cheesy chip into his mouth.

Corey looked at his best friend, and felt his heart begin to beat faster as his cock stirred inside his jeans. Roger had always been a good-looking guy. Even without his association with Corey he would've been among the most popular and sought-after guys in any school. That had never been good enough for Corey, though. He'd never been willing to settle for second best. As much as Roger had tried to get him to get serious together, he was never willing, never able to do so. He always thought there had to be something better, something more, out there for him. But the last four years had proven just the opposite. As much as he wanted to let Roger go and to put him in the back of his mind and find the perfect guy, the true love of his life, he hadn't been able to. And now, looking at

Roger shoving cheesy chips drizzled with salsa into his mouth, he realized that he'd never find that perfect guy in anyone else *but* his best friend.

"Yeah, I know, it's a little crazy, right?"

"Mmm-hmm," Roger said as he chased the chips down with half a blackberry margarita.

Corey couldn't stop staring at Roger. He'd bulked up a little, and had a sexy stubble on his cleft chin and strong jaw. He looked much more like a young man and less like the little boy that shared his treehouse club with him and was the first person to suck his cock. His blond hair fell carelessly across his forehead, and his light blue eyes sparkled as he talked and laughed. Corey's cock throbbed against the inside of his leg as he stared at the thick blond hair sticking up through the top of Roger's button-down shirt, and the dimples crease his cheeks when he smiled. His friend seemed a lot stronger and more confident than Corey had ever known him, and that was driving Corey crazy with lust.

"So what's been going on with you?" Corey asked, eager to change the subject about his sudden and unexpected trip home, and to get his mind off Roger's studly chest and the memory of his hot mouth on his cock.

"Not much, man. Just struggling to get through school and not take myself too seriously."

"You seeing anyone?"

Roger diverted his eyes from Corey, and stared at the table as he made a production of swallowing his chips and finishing off his drink, and then waved at the waitress for yet another round. "No, not really," he said as he cleared his throat. "I've dated a few guys, but nothing serious."

"Why not, man? You're looking really good, dude. Better than I've ever seen you. I'm sure you're beating the girls off with a stick."

"Seriously, Corey?" Roger said, and lifted his eyes to look into Corey's. "Are we really so uncomfortable with one another that we're gonna resort to that closeted internalized homophobia?"

"I'm sorry," Corey said, and this time it was him who dropped his eyes. What the fuck was wrong with him? He knew without a doubt that he was in love with Roger, and he knew just as certainly that the one thing that pissed his friend off more than anything else was his macho bullshit closeted behavior. "I'm sorry. I didn't mean that."

"You fucking infuriate me, man. I am not seeing anyone seriously because . . ."

"I know," Corey said hurriedly, and looked away as he shuffled his feet. "I gotta pee," he said before Roger could say anything else, and walked quickly to the restroom.

IV.

Corey felt like an idiot after the dinner with Roger. How could he have fucked everything up as badly as he had? He'd gone to the dinner with every intention of confessing his love for his best friend, and to see if there was any way they could make something a little more serious work out between them. But Roger hadn't said five words to him on the drive back to campus after the dinner, and he slammed the car door as he left.

Corey didn't really have a lot of time to work through it all or to come up with a plan to fix it. The next evening, Jo was hosting a large fundraising event for one of her pet charities, and she insisted that Corey attend with her. As much as he loved his mother, and as fun as she could be most of the time, once she made up her mind about something, no one could talk her out of it.

"Jo, you know I hate these fancy charity events."

"But Lisa Boujet will be there. I've been trying to get you two together since high school. You shouldn't keep putting her off. It's really quite rude, you know."

"And playing matchmaker for two people who don't like one another isn't?"

"What in the world are you talking about? Lisa likes you," Jo said as she applied lipstick to her lips. "She told me so just the other day."

"Lisa Boujet likes any guy who drives anything better than a second-hand Mercedes."

"The subject is closed." Jo put her foot down. She kissed him on the cheek and then wiped the lipstick off of it.

Corey went to the party, but didn't stop complaining the entire time, even though he knew it wouldn't do any good. Corey noted the twinkle in his mother's eyes as he danced with Lisa, and saw her point him out to several of her high-society friends, and realized he would do almost anything to see that twinkle.

During a slow dance after dinner Lisa maneuvered Corey into a back corner, away from everyone else. She pressed herself closer against him than was socially acceptable, and when she was certain no one was watching, she reached down and cupped her hand over Corey's crotch. She massaged his dick slowly and increased the pressure as she whispered into his ear.

"I can make you feel really good, Corey."

"Really?" Her massage was not getting the response she expected, and Corey smiled at the control he had over his body. He could get rock hard at the drop of a dime, but he could also hold off an orgasm for hours if he wanted to. He could also obviously keep from getting hard. Lisa saw him smile and misinterpreted it as pleasure.

"Rhonda Peterson says you're really big," she whispered huskily. "I like big."

"She did?" He wondered how Rhonda Peterson knew he was "really big." He'd only dated her twice, on double dates with Roger and Carol Purcell back in high school, and he certainly hadn't fucked her. She'd never even seen him naked.

"Oh, yes. Wanna go to your car?"

"There's no room. I drive a Ferrari," he said, and then smiled as he watched her squirm and moan.

"Really?" Lisa feigned surprise. "I have a pass key to the game room."

"That sounds good." The song was over. "Why don't you go ahead and go to the game room. Leave the door unlocked and wait for me. I'm gonna tell my folks I have to make a phone call. I want you ready for me when I get there. Is that clear?"

"Oh, yeah." She was hoarse with lust.

"I want you naked and spread out on the pool table. I want to fuck you on top of every game in that room. Are you up for that, Lisa?"

"God, Rhonda was right. You are an animal!" She turned and began walking toward the door. Halfway there she lifted her dress a few inches and broke into a slow trot. Corey watched with amazement and laughed softly as he walked over to his parents' table.

"Hi, son," Jo said cheerfully. "Where's Lisa? You two seem to be hitting it off well."

"She went to the bathroom. Listen, I'm gonna go now. I promised Roger we'd see a movie tonight."

"But the dinner . . ."

"I stayed through dinner and half the dance. Let's compromise, okay?"

Jo started to protest, but Mr. Baker patted her hand and nodded.

"Well, all right," Jo sulked.

"Thanks, Carl. Thanks, Jo," he said and kissed his mom on the cheek.

He walked out to his car and started the engine. He wondered if Lisa was naked in the game room yet. How long would she actually lie there on the pool table, waiting for him with her legs spread? He laughed out loud, threw the car into gear, and peeled out of the parking lot.

He drove aimlessly around town for about half an hour, thinking about Roger and how he could make things right with him. He didn't really have an idea of where he was going, or what he would do for the rest of the evening. But when he found himself in the middle of the Tenderloin, he wasn't surprised. It wasn't his first time there.

Geary Boulevard was not a place people of his social status frequented. But Corey was never one to allow his social standing rule his actions. His first time on the broad street had been back in high school, and it was quite by accident that he wound up there. It was late at night and he'd been fascinated with the street life he saw there. The female prostitutes on one side of the street and the male hustlers on the other side were unsettling, but mesmerizing. He kept coming back. At least a couple of times a month since the first time he'd wound up there by accident he drove up and down the street, watching the people who called it home.

He wondered, with a dull ache in his heart, what drove these kids, most of them younger than him, to live such a life. Where were their real homes and their families? Didn't their parents worry about them? Weren't they afraid they'd be killed?

Though unsettling, the life on Geary Boulevard also enthralled him. These kids didn't own *any* car, let alone a Ferrari. They didn't sleep on satin sheets and pillows, and they didn't have an upstairs maid to make their beds every day. Instead they met a new man every night and had sex with total strangers to get them through the cold nights.

The thing that bothered Corey the most was the way the boys looked. Even on his very first drive down Geary he was able to place every single boy into one of two distinct categories. One was muscular, kept a cigarette dangling from his lips even if it wasn't lit, and wore a t-shirt to show off his bulging muscles and tattoos. He wore tight faded jeans accentuating a bulge that he doubted was even real.

Then there was category number two. He too wore tight faded jeans, but they were usually girls' cuts and sizes, and were much more honest in their advertising; they accentuated nothing. These boys also wore t-shirts, or muscle shirts, but there were no muscles to show off. The shirts were usually a size or two too large for the skinny, malnourished bodies. The only tattoos on their arms were needle marks. They wore makeup and earrings and they walked with a swish that put Paris Hilton to shame.

Corey had driven the street maybe thirty times over the last few years, watching with bewildered fascination the nightlife of these young street kids. Not once had he seen a boy who did not fit comfortably into one of these two categories.

Until now.

He couldn't tell how old the boy was, but he was young. About five foot seven inches tall and 140 pounds. He was wearing what looked like a new pair of jeans and a nice sweater. Though there was a very large bulge in the jeans, it didn't look disgusting or grotesque, and something told Corey this one was real. The boy was Latino, with light brown skin and a soft, budding mustache. There were no earrings or makeup, no cigarette or tattoos. The kid laughed unselfconsciously and exuded a rare innocence.

He stood out in the crowd, as if a spotlight were shining directly on him. Corey watched the boy for a long time. The traffic light turned green, but Corey didn't see it. He was staring intently at the young Latino. Several cars honked their horns, causing some of the hustlers to turn and glare angrily at him.

Three or four of the more feminine hustlers began to swish hungrily toward the Ferrari, but one of them pushed past the others and ran to his open window. The kid scared Corey. He had dirty blond hair, and was so thin his bones seemed to be poking through his skin. His teeth were stained and crooked, and when he smiled it gave Corey the creeps.

"Hey, handsome," the hustler said as he leaned into the window of the Ferrari. "You looking for company?"

"Yes," Corey said. "Do you know that guy over there?" He pointed to the kid in the sweater, who was watching him and the scarecrow.

"Yeah, he's my best friend," the skinny kid said excitedly "You can have both of us, if you want. Two for one."

"No, thanks. I'm just interested in him."

The hustler snorted, and then shrugged and turned to walk toward his friend. After a short verbal exchange, the Latino boy with the nice sweater walked over and made himself at home in the passenger seat of the Ferrari without saying a word.

* * *

On the drive back to his house, Corey discovered the boy's name was Carlos, and that the pleasure of his company would cost Corey two hundred dollars an hour. And that was pretty much all he found out from the beautiful kid. He wasn't much of a talker, and after several one-word answers to his questions, Corey stopped asking.

When they got to the Pacific Heights mansion, Corey checked to make sure his parents' car wasn't in the garage. Then he came back and held Carlos' hand as he guided him through the dark and through the living room. Halfway up the stairs to his room, he heard a noise, and turned to see Martina standing at the bottom of the stairs.

"Baby, what are you doing?" she whispered to Corey.

Corey put his fingers to his lips, signaling Martina to keep quiet. Then he continued up the stairs and to his room.

"Take off your clothes and lay on the bed," Carlos said quietly as he closed the door behind them.

Corey stripped slowly and timidly, his heart racing inside his chest the entire time. He was used to being the one giving the orders, and being the dominant person, and being on the other side made him uncomfortable. But it also excited him. He crawled into bed and covered his crotch with a throw pillow as he leaned against the headboard, and stared at the beautiful boy in front of him.

Carlos slowly removed his clothes. He didn't make a big production of it, and certainly didn't look like a stripper in doing so, but with just enough tease to make Corey feel as if he would explode if he didn't see Carlos' naked body in the very next second. The last item of clothing discarded was his jeans, and when Carlos kicked them off and toward the dresser, Corey took a deep breath as he stared at the Latin god before him.

The boy was even more muscular than he looked in his clothes. He was no bodybuilder, but his muscles were developed and toned, and perfect. When he breathed, his smooth copper chest expanded and caused his tiny nipples to harden. His stomach was flat, with the slightest hint of washboard muscles, and a thick trail of black hair descended from his belly button down to his pubic hair. His cock, though limp, hung low and thick, its head peeking through the short skin covering it.

"What do you want?" Carlos asked quietly, even as his cock began to thicken and grow.

"You," Corey whispered hoarsely.

Carlos walked over and crawled into bed. He curled up between Corey's arm and chest, and cuddled with him. He traced a line across Corey's chest and down his stomach, and when he reached the hard cock at the belly button, he squeezed it tenderly, and then continued with his fingers down the shaved balls and between Corey's ass cheeks.

Corey moaned and shuddered as Carlos' fingers barely touched his skin as they traced every inch of his body. When they made their way to his face, Corey pulled Carlos up to him, and kissed him softly and gently on the lips. He slipped his tongue tentatively into Carlos' mouth, and felt a large stream of precum slip out of his cock head when Carlos wrapped his lips around his tongue and sucked it deeper into his warm mouth.

Carlos broke the kiss after a couple of minutes, and lay on his back, stretching his long legs in front of him, and clasping his hands behind his head.

Corey gasped as he stared at the hard cock lying across Carlos' belly. Though he'd seen plenty of big dicks in his time, he'd until now not seen one that he would call perfect. The silky skin peeled back from the head, allowing a thin trail of precum to slide down the long and thick pole. It was easily as long as Corey's own, which

also was a rarity, and a long, thick vein ran the length of the underside, pulsing it to life. He could barely wrap his fist around it.

Corey moved his head down between Carlos' legs and began
licking his thighs. His tongue licked along the inner leg and lightly
touched one of the large smooth balls. When Carlos squirmed and
moaned softly, he sucked the entire ball into his mouth, tickling it
with his tongue, and Carlos moaned even louder.

Corey let the ball slip from his mouth, and slid his tongue slowly
up the length of Carlos' thick shaft. He licked the underside, playing with the large vein that pulsed against his wet tongue. When he
reached the tip he opened his mouth wide and swallowed the big
brown head, swirling his tongue around it. He slid his tongue underneath the foreskin and licked around the inside of the skin, tickling Carlos' cock head with the tip of his tongue.

Carlos gasped for breath and grabbed the sheets with both hands.

Corey slid his tight lips slowly down the big rod. He loved the
taste and feel of Carlos' thick, uncut dick. Halfway down the long
shaft he opened his throat, and felt the entire cock slide deep into
his clutching throat.

"Oh, God!" Carlos gasped again, and grabbed Corey's blond
hair and held his head down on his cock.

Corey tightened his throat against the thickness and began to
move his lips up and down the big dick. He loved the feel of
Carlos' monster dick filling his mouth and throat, and took his time
to make his new friend feel good and moan loudly.

Carlos pumped his dick in and out of Corey's mouth slowly at
first and then with increasing speed.

Corey could tell he was getting close. He wasn't ready for this to
end, though, and pulled himself off the hot, thick dick quickly.

Carlos was still on his back as Corey sat up and straddled his
chest. His long cock pointed straight out at Carlos' mouth, but before Carlos could reach out and lick it, Corey leaned back and took
Carlos' hot cock into his hands.

Corey positioned his ass at the head of his cock and began lowering himself on the long, thick cock. It took him a minute or so to relax. He wasn't used to getting fucked by a big dick like that, and he bit his lower lip to keep from yelling out in pain. The head popped in, and he moaned softly as he felt his ass burn against the thick cock head. He took a deep breath, and at the same time, slid all the way down Carlos' huge cock. He looked down at Carlos' eyes, which were wide with surprise. He imagined that not many guys had been able to take his cock in one move like that without crying out in pain. But Corey was determined not to whimper at all.

He squeezed and moved his ass around the big cock, causing it to rub against the inside muscles of his ass. It felt better than anything he'd ever experienced, and his own cock dripped with thick, silky precum. He wasn't even touching his dick, and yet he felt as if he could shoot at any second.

He lifted himself slowly up Carlos' cock and slid back down onto it. With each ride down the huge cock, Corey felt the inside of his ass tingle and grip the cock harder. When he pulled himself back up to where only the fat head was still inside him, he felt as if he was being abandoned, and as he lowered himself back onto the big dick, he felt as if the love of his life was returning home to him after a long absence. He leaned down and kissed Carlos on the lips, squeezing his ass around the thick cock as he did, and held the boy close to him.

Carlos picked up the rhythm and lifted his hips so that his dick pumped into Corey's ass. It was obvious to Corey that the kid had fucked a lot of ass, and knew what it took to make his partner feel incredible. Shouldn't he feel repulsed knowing that this street hustler had fucked hundreds of guys? Shouldn't he be concerned about catching something from the boy? Shouldn't he feel above the poor young whore who associated with drug addicts and common thieves and crossdressers?

"Fuck me harder, Carlos," he whispered into Carlos' mouth as he kissed him. "Shove that big cock deep inside me and fuck my brains out."

Well, there was that. He never was one to follow societal norms and rules.

Carlos slid in and out of Corey's ass slow and deep, teasing him and making him beg for more. Then he slammed in faster and harder, until both of them were sweating and panting for breath.

It didn't take long before both boys were ready to shoot.

They came at the exact same time. Corey moaned loudly and leaned back on his hands as spray after spray of his cum splashed onto Carlos' chest and face. Carlos shoved his dick deep inside Corey's ass one last time, and left it there as he lay perfectly still and emptied his cum into Corey's spasming ass. Both boys were breathing very heavily, and neither moved. They lay perfectly still, Carlos' dick still inside Corey's ass, and both still hard as a rock.

Finally, Corey started laughing, and rolled off Carlos.

"What's wrong?" Carlos asked sleepily.

"Nothing's wrong. Everything's right, Carlos. It's just that I've never had sex like that. I mean, I've had plenty of sex in my life, and most of it has been really good. But that was amazing!"

"Yeah. You wanna go again? It's been less than an hour, you still have some time."

"I'd love to. But let's wait for tomorrow."

"Tomorrow? You want me to spend the night at two hundred dollars an hour?"

"Yeah. Money isn't an issue."

"I can see that," Carlos said, and cuddled up between Corey's arms and chest again. "I guess I can give you a little discount. Since you just wanna sleep," he said as he yawned, and hugged Corey tighter.

"I'm exhausted," Corey said sleepily. "But you can wake me up in the morning the same way you put me to sleep tonight, if you want."

"Good night, Corey."

"Good night, Carlos."

* * *

The next morning they were awakened by a knock on the bedroom door.

"What?" Corey said sleepily. Carlos squirmed in his arms and cuddled next to him even closer.

"Baby, breakfast is ready," Martina said from the other side of the door. "I told your parents you had company and Mrs. Scott-Baker asked me to set an extra place at the table."

"Oh, Jeeezus," Corey moaned. He could hear the excitement in her voice, and could only imagine what she was thinking. "I'm not ready for this."

V.

The plane ride back to Yale was almost intolerable. Not because it was particularly turbulent, in fact it was as smooth a ride as one could hope for. And not because it was overly crowded. There was only one other passenger in first class, and so there was plenty of room to breathe and stretch out. It wasn't because the person next to him wouldn't stop talking to him and leave him alone. The truth was, Corey would give his left nut for someone to chat with at the moment. He felt more alone than he could ever remember. And that was what was most intolerable.

Carlos had stayed with him the entire two weeks. They'd made up a story about Carlos' parents being out of town for a few days at a conference, and how he didn't like staying at home alone. Corey's parents loved him instantly. Though they'd never heard Corey mention him before, they didn't question when the boys said they'd been good friends in high school, even though Corey was sure his parents knew that the boy was still in high school himself. They never asked why he slept in Corey's room instead of the guest room. They had Martina cook his favorite dinner, which she gladly did while she and Carlos conversed in Spanish. They even made him promise to stop by and visit at least once a week, even while Corey was at school.

Corey couldn't remember ever having a better time in his life. He and Carlos spent every minute of every day for those two weeks together. Long before the halfway mark, Corey knew he was in love with Carlos, and when Carlos was awake, Corey was the happiest guy on earth. But when Carlos fell asleep, Corey lay next to him in bed, watching him slumber like an angel, and became sad and cried. He knew the time was fast approaching when he'd have to leave Carlos and return to school, and that was most inconvenient when falling in love.

"Please don't," Carlos said quietly as he fidgeted with his hands.

"Come on, babe," Corey said, and hugged him closer. "I have to go back. I have exams next week, and I've already missed way too much. I'll never catch up as it is."

"But I need you here."

"Please don't do this to me, Carlos. You knew I was going to go back to school. This isn't a surprise. Don't make me feel guilty."

Carlos curled into a ball and laid his head in Corey's lap, and said nothing.

"But don't worry, babe," Corey said, and leaned down to kiss Carlos. "I'm gonna take care of everything. I don't want you going back to the streets."

"What?" Carlos asked, and sat up to look at Corey in the eyes.

Corey smiled excitedly, and pulled an envelope from his back pocket and handed it to Carlos. "Open it!"

Carlos opened the envelope slowly, and looked inside. "What's this?" he asked as he held up a key.

"It's the key to your new apartment. I knew it'd be

hard for you to get a place on your own. So I rented a cute little one-bedroom place in Noe Valley. The first six months are paid for. And there's two thousand dollars in the envelope, too. Just to get you started."

"What are you talking about?"

"I'll be coming home once a month or so, and we can spend the whole weekend together when I come back. I can get you more money as you need it."

"Fuck you," Carlos said, and stood up.

"What?" Corey said, stunned. "Babe, what's wrong?"

"Who the fuck do you think you are?"

"I don't understand."

"Do you think you're my knight in shining armor? You're my hero?" Carlos said, and walked around the room collecting his clothes and putting on his shoes. *"Well, guess what, Corey. I don't need to be rescued. I'm not your little heroine in distress."*

"Don't get upset," Corey pleaded, and tried unsuccess-fully to get Carlos to stop getting dressed. *"I didn't mean to . . ."*

"I don't need your money, Corey. And I don't need your apartment, either. I've got over eight thousand dol-lars saved up from the disgusting work I do on the streets, and I can pay for my own fucking apartment anytime I want, thank you very much."

"But babe . . ."

"Fuck you, Corey. I'm not your own little Julia Roberts. I want you here because I love you, not because I need your money or your fancy car or your fucking cute little apartment in Noe Valley."

Carlos stormed out the door, and headed down the stairs. He stopped and kissed Martina on the cheeks, and then left the house. Corey had tried to stop Carlos from leaving, but was not successful. He was just glad that his parents weren't home to see the argument. He'd never be able to explain it. He'd called Carlos several times before leaving, but Carlos never answered his calls, and he didn't show up to accompany Corey to the airport.

*   *   *

The lead flight attendant announced their decent into JFK International, and Corey collected his carry-on baggage and laptop. He couldn't get off the plane soon enough. He was anxious to get on the ground so he could call Carlos again. Hopefully his call wouldn't go unanswered this time.

The second the door opened, he was on the jetway bridge and walking steadily to the gate and the open air of the terminal, where he hoped he would be able to breathe easier. The terminal was busy with hundreds of people frantic to get to their gates on time. But the ceilings were high and the halls were wide and spacious. So he didn't feel alone or trapped, and that was a vast improvement over the plane.

"Babe," he said loudly into his cell phone to be heard over the noise all around him, "I'm so sorry. I know I fucked up. I didn't mean to, though. I wasn't trying to buy you or imply that I am any better than you. I only hoped to show you how much I love you and want to spend more time with you. I know you can take care of yourself. You've obviously been doing a great job way before I met you, and that's why I fell in love with you. I know you don't need me to rescue you, but I need you to rescue me. I need you, Carlos, and that's why I got the apartment. I just wanted a place with you in it to call home. I screwed up big time, I know. Please forgive me, and please call me. I love you."

He hung up, walked to the limo service counter, and twenty minutes later was on his way back to campus.

VI.

"Dude!" Eryk yelled as Corey walked in the door. "Fuckin' welcome back!"

Corey laughed. "Thanks, man. It's good to be back."

"You missed it, man. We had the best fuckin' social *ever*!"

"See, I told you you could do it. All you needed was a little push and a little self-confidence. You're every bit as ready to take over here as any incoming president I've ever known."

"Thanks, Corey. The other guys helped, but I pretty much did it all myself. I mean, I made all the important decisions." He stuck his hands in his pocket and looked around nervously.

"Like I said, it's good practice. How would you like to get started a little earlier than planned?"

"What do you mean?"

"I'm stepping down."

"Shut up!" Eryk laughed, and punched him on the arm. "I did an okay job, but not that good."

"I'm serious," Corey said. "I'm moving out. I'll stay through the rest of the month, and I'll be available to help out with anything you have questions about. But I'm out, man."

"What the fuck happened while you were in California, dude?"

Corey could see the panic on Eryk's face. The color drained from his skin, and his lips trembled. "It didn't happen while I was in California. It's been happening for a while now. But my trip home helped clarify things for me, and made me realize I need to get out of this environment. And I'm in love, and I can't be a part of the goings-on here anymore. I need to take myself a little more seriously, and I need to respect the guy I love."

"The *guy* you love?" Eryk said incredulously. "We don't love guys, dude. We love girls. We just fuck around with guys every now and then when we're drunk or to humiliate them, man."

"No, that's what you do. Not me. I'm gay, Eryk."

"Shut up," he said less forcefully this time. "You've been the leader of our group for the past three years. You've tortured and humiliated more guys than any of us. Hell, more than all of us combined."

"I know, and it sickens me to think about that. I've been completely untrue to myself, Eryk, and I've become someone who is not me at all. That person repulses me. I'm gay and I'm in love with another guy. And I have to get out of this house and live alone so I can get my shit together and be respectful to him."

"I can't believe this shit, man," Eryk said as he scratched his head. "It's like you've been brainwashed or something."

Corey laughed. "I haven't been brainwashed, buddy. And I'm not crazy, either. I'm still the guy you've known and loved the past three years." He noticed the shocked look on Eryk's face, and the way he shuffled his feet awkwardly. "Don't worry, dude. I don't mean that you loved me *that way*. Although, I do remember that one time . . ."

"Fuck you! That is not funny."

"Come on, baby," Corey teased, and leaned in for a kiss. "I want you. I need you."

"You're an asshole, you know that?" Eryk said, with a laugh. "You deserve whatever the fuck you're getting into."

"Yeah," Corey said with a smile, and walked into his room to prepare to pack.

INCH FIVE

Tick Tock

I.

"I am not happy, and I want to know what you are going to do about it."

The woman might have stood five feet three inches if Payless made a four-inch pump strong enough to hold her three hundred and fifty pounds. Instead, she wore a pair of tattered flip-flops with gray duct tape wrapped around the toe separator and a cheap cotton muumuu that had a large coffee stain around the neck and an even larger dried egg yolk nestled between her mountainous bosoms. She was missing one tooth from her bottom row, and another from the top, and those that were still connected to her skull were various shades of gray and brown. Adam counted nine thick black hairs dangling from her chin, and her mustache rivaled Tom Selleck's. She reminded Adam of Ursula from *The Little Mermaid*.

"I'm sorry, ma'am," he said with a sigh. "There's not really anything I can do about it."

His lower right molar throbbed in his jaw and reverberated up his sinuses and across the crown of his skull. *Not again*, he thought, and rubbed the outside of his jaw until the spiders he saw crawling across the woman's face disappeared and the vibrating buzz he felt and heard in every bone in his body dissipated.

"What do you mean, there's nothing you can do about it?" the woman said. She didn't seem to notice the stream of spittle that slithered down the crease between her lips and chins. "Look at these pictures. The top part of their heads is cut off in almost every single one. And there's a finger going across three of them. These are pictures of my baby's birthday party, and they're ruined. I want you to fix it. Now." She crossed her arms, which gave Adam a quick glimpse of the patch of black hair under each of her armpits.

"I'm sure you do, Urs . . . ma'am," Adam said, and closed his eyes. The spiders were now lizards, and they were crawling all over her face, biting deep into her fatty skin, and drinking her green blood. He couldn't watch them anymore. "But this is Walgreens, not Billy Bob's House of Magic. And I get paid minimum wage, which is not nearly enough to deal with your shit right now."

The woman took a step back and gasped, pulling a mouthful of saliva into her throat, and causing her to choke.

Adam rolled his eyes and rubbed his jaw again. "Please go away, please go away," he whispered.

"I will *not* go away," the woman yelled as she braced herself against the shelves holding potato chips on one side of her and baby food on the other. "I demand that you develop those pictures again, and I want them right this time. And I expect them to be free. I'm not paying for your sloppy work."

"My work is not sloppy, lady. Your fingers are too fat to fit outside of the lens range, which means you're covering up half of the picture with your porky little sausages. And you obviously need glasses so you can see where your chubby little son's head ends and can get it all in the frame. How old is he, anyway? Nine?"

"He's four!" the woman screeched, and lunged at Adam.

He took a step back, and watched as she slid into the counter between them. Her eyes popped out of their sockets, and thousands of cockroaches swarmed out of the black space where they once were. She ricocheted off the counter, and landed on her ass on the floor.

"You sick son of a bitch," she screamed as she struggled to get to her feet. "I demand to speak with the manager. I'll have your job, goddam it."

"You wouldn't want it," Adam said, and laid her pictures on the counter. "I'm fifty years old and working at Walgreens for minimum wage and a nickel." He looked her up and down for a moment. "On second thought, I suppose that would be a step up for you."

"What's going on here, Pollard?" the manager asked as he rounded the corner and stared at the woman still on her knees and turning purple with the strain of getting to a standing position.

"She's upset because her fingers are in the way of the pictures, and she cut off the top of her son's head."

"He fucked up my baby's birthday pictures," the fat lady yelled. "And he assaulted me. I demand that he be fired!"

"*I* attacked *you*?" Adam said. "I was calm and respectful behind the counter. You are the one who charged me, lady. And the security camera will prove it," he said, and pointed at the camera above him. "Take a look at it, Perry."

The woman jerked her head to look at the camera, and crossed her arms as her face turned red.

"Take a break, Pollard," Perry said, and nodded toward the employee door that led to the back room behind the photo area.

"But, boss . . ."

"Go!" the manager said sternly.

Adam shoved the door open and stormed through it, leaving Perry to handle things with Jabba the Hutt. Charlotte, one of the cashiers at the store, was on her break, and had half of a peanut butter and jelly sandwich in her mouth when the door slammed against the wall. She jumped to her feet, and squeezed past him to exit the same door he just burst through, and Adam noticed her eyes were bugged. She looked frightened and as if she was about to cry.

When the door swooshed back inside the room, carrying the putrid mixture of Skippy peanut butter and a cheap Chanel No 5 knockoff past his nostrils, Adam yelped, and jumped on top of the nearest chair. Hundreds of thousands of cockroaches swarmed into the break room. When the floor was completely covered, the bugs began to climb on top of one another and layer themselves so that they were quickly closing the space between the floor and the ceiling. These were ordinary roaches. They were snot-green with giant purple teeth and glowing red eyes. Their long, sinewy antennae were capped with tiny pinchers that opened and shut rapidly. By the time the sea of bugs reached halfway up to the seat of the chair, Adam could see their razor sharp incisors opening wide and then clamping shut hard enough for him to hear the "snap" of their jaws meeting, and to see the tiny droplets of blood ooze from the place where their teeth dug into their own gums.

"Oh my God," Adam cried as he stepped up from the chair and onto the table. He opened his mouth to scream, but just then the door swung open again. Perry walked into the room, and the million cockroaches immediately began retreating from the room, running backward at astounding speed.

"Pollard!" the store manager said sternly as he stared at Adam and scratched his head. "What the hell are you doing up there?"

Adam looked around frantically. There wasn't a single mutant roach in sight. Charlotte stood safely behind the beefy manager, still bug-eyed and still devouring her sandwich. "Nothing, sir," he said, and climbed down from the table. "One of the lightbulbs was loose and blinking. Just thought I'd change it."

"No, it wasn't," Charlotte said, and took another nibble from her PB and J.

Adam glared at her, and smiled to himself as she turned around and retreated into the belly of the store.

"Go home," Perry said flatly.

"What?" Adam said. "No, Perry, come on. That bitch was trouble from the time she walked in the door."

"I don't care. You never argue with a customer like that, and you certainly never call her names or insult her kids."

"But . . ."

"I'm worried about you, Pollard," the manager said. "You don't look well."

"I'm fine, Perry," Adam said, and brushed his fingers through his hair. "Thanks for the concern, but I'm good."

"You're not good. You're a long ways from good, Pollard. So you're going to go home now and relax. And I want you to take tomorrow off, too. Just get some rest and get your shit together."

"You've got to be kidding me. Are you firing me?"

Perry took a deep breath and let it out noisily. "No, I'm not firing you. But this definitely warrants a disciplinary warning. See a doctor or a shrink or someone. You'll be on probation for six weeks. It's company policy."

"Perry . . ."

The store manager crossed his beefy arms across his chest and nodded toward the door. Adam stormed through the door and slammed his fist on the front counter as he walked out the door.

* * *

Standing in the hall outside his apartment, Adam could hear the bugs on the other side of the door. From the sound of it, there were thousands of spiders running restlessly around his living room, and possibly a million roaches in the kitchen. That didn't count the buzzing he heard coming from the direction of his bedroom. Wasps.

He wanted more than anything to turn and run as far from the building as he could. But he couldn't do that. He had nowhere else to go, and he needed what was on the other side of that door. He needed what the wasps were hell-bent on keeping him from getting.

Adam took a deep breath, and shoved the key into the lock. He needed another breath to steady his shaking hands, and then turned the key. Once the lock turned, he rushed into the foyer and turned on the light, even though it was only three in the afternoon and the daylight sunshine still illuminated the apartment. He propped the front door open, then ran through the entire apartment, switching on every light and lamp. It wouldn't do any good, he knew. The bugs weren't afraid of the light, and it wouldn't keep them away. But it made him feel better to have the lights on, and so he didn't stop until the last one was on.

He allowed himself to catch his breath, and then walked into the bathroom. He stared at his reflection in the mirror for a moment. It only took a few seconds before he saw the first long, thin, hairy leg poke tentatively out of his ear. A couple of seconds later, the cockroach head peered around the corner of the ear, and then the six-inch-long bug slipped out of his ear and scurried down his neck and into the collar of his shirt.

Adam quickly opened the medicine cabinet and grabbed two bottles. He poured out six pills, and swallowed them without the benefit of water. When he looked back into the mirror, he saw a shorter, thicker and hairier insect leg snake its way out of his left nostril. A moment later, the rest of the gigantic tarantula crawled out of his nose, and slithered between his lips.

He shut his mouth quickly, and ran into the bedroom. He pulled the covers down and crawled underneath them. "Please go away," he begged as he pulled the blankets tight around his neck and chest. Five minutes later he was asleep, and bug free.

II.

Adam Pollard opened the door of his brand new 1979 Cadillac Seville, and stepped out onto Elm Street. He looked at Farnam Hall and Battell Chapel, and smiled. He'd had some pretty damned amazing rendezvous in Farnam in his first couple of years at Yale. And though he wasn't a religious person by any stretch of the imagination, he couldn't help but be in total awe of the century-old chapel with its old stone façade that felt oddly welcoming and comforting. After a summer away, it felt good to be back on campus and among the familiar and comfortable.

"Oh shit!"

Adam was thrown to the ground hard enough to knock the breath out of him, and was acutely aware of the kid on top of him.

"I am so sorry," the boy said as he struggled to get to his feet. It wasn't easy with the heavy skates.

"What the fuck?" Adam said, and jumped to his feet quickly, brushing off his clothes before anyone saw him.

"Please forgive me," the boy said with a strong Spanish accent. "I am so sorry. I am not very good with the skates yet."

"Well, you should really be . . ." He stopped as he looked up at the kid who'd run him over.

Adam had seen many gorgeous dudes during his first two years at Yale. The school seemed to be a magnet for beautiful people, and he supposed the exorbitant wealth that ninety percent of the student population enjoyed probably helped make them so attractive. But even among the uber beautiful, this guy was in a class all his own. He stood almost six feet tall, with a slim build that still promised plenty of tone and definition. His black hair fell almost to his shoulders, and had a slight curl at the bottom. His eyes were hazel and had long, curly eyelashes, and when he smiled, his teeth sparkled and sent tiny shockwaves throughout Adam's body. His caramel-colored skin was smooth and smelled lightly of musk and baby oil.

"It's no big deal," Adam said. He knew he was staring, and wished desperately that he could stop. But he couldn't. "I mean, I didn't get hurt or anything. It's cool."

"Are you sure you are okay?" the boy asked, and touched Adam on the shoulder.

Adam's cock hardened instantly, and he found it difficult to swallow. "Yeah, I'm fine."

"I should be more careful. I can hurt someone the next time. I am just learning the skating, and still am a little . . . how you say . . ."

"Clumsy?"

The boy laughed, and Adam felt a thin stream of precum ooze from his cock head, and the hair on his arms stood up. "I'm Adam," he said, and held his hand out.

"My name is Manuel," the boy said, and shook Adam's hand.

"It's really nice to meet you, Manuel," Adam said, and prayed to God that his voice didn't really squeak as much as he thought it did or that his cock didn't leak enough precum to stain through his jeans and betray him right there in the middle of the busiest intersection on campus.

"The same with you." Manuel looked at him for several long seconds, and stuffed his hands into his pockets as he smiled awkwardly and tried to keep his roller skates from sweeping his feet out from under him.

"Okay, so I'm totally making an idiot of myself, and so I'm gonna shut up now," Adam said, and laughed to himself as he scratched his head. "But, I am pretty damned good on wheels, dude. I could totally teach you a trick or two. Before you know it, you'll be zippin' around Xanadu with Kira, and trust me, that's way hotter than greasin' it up with Sandra Dee."

"Huh?" Manuel said. "Who is Kira? I am afraid I don't know Sandra Dee."

Adam smiled and shook his head. "That's okay, man," he said, and put his arm around Manuel's shoulders, holding him steady as he led him down the street. "Stick with me, kid, and you'll be a roller derby champ in no time."

* * *

"I'm still not sure this is a good idea, dude," Wylie said as he tossed socks and underwear from the top drawer of his dresser. "Where the fuck did I put that weed?"

"Chill out, Carmichael," Adam said, and reached into the drawer and pulled the baggie of pot out from under a pair of plaid boxers. "It's a great idea. He'd be a great addition to Kappa Lambda Phi. He's mondo, man."

"I don't know, Pollard. We've never had a spic in KLP before."

"You're a disgusting motherfucker, you know that? Spic is a hateful word, and it doesn't apply to Manuel at all. He's from Colombia, not Mexico. Surely you know the difference. I mean, you *are* attending Yale."

"Whatever. He can still barely speak English."

"*You* can barely speak English, Wylie," Adam said. He lit a joint, took a toke from it, and passed it on to the frat president. "Manuel speaks very good English. Yeah, he has an accent, but he has better grammar and vocabulary than you do."

"Don't get so heavy, man," Wylie said as he exhaled a lungful of smoke. "I already said he could pledge. He'll be here in an hour with the rest of the slugs. So, have another toke, man. Take a quaalude or something."

Adam took another lungful of smoke and held it for almost a minute before he blew it out in smoke rings above his head.

"Why does this beaner mean so much to you, anyway?" Wylie asked as he tossed his t-shirt onto his bed and stepped out of his jeans.

Adam watched his friend as he stood in front of the full-length mirror and admired himself. Wylie flexed his biceps and stared at them for a long moment, and then kissed each one slowly. Adam's cock began to stir, and he tried to look away, but couldn't. He was mesmerized as the frat president tweaked his nipples and slid his hands slowly down his chest and across the deep ridges in his abs. He'd seen his friend lounging around the house in nothing but boxers on several occasions over the past two years, but he'd never seen Wylie's cock. He'd often fantasized about it, and beat off to that image more times than he could count. His eyes darted between the long, muscular legs, eager to catch a glimpse of it now.

It was much more impressive in Adam's fantasies. There it was long and thick and pink, with fat veins roping around the big shaft. In reality, Wylie had to pull on the head and stretch it out for several seconds before it could even be seen in front of the blond bushy pubes.

Adam sighed in disappointment. But the rest of his friend's body was perfection, and he contented himself to admire it while Wylie did the same.

"He doesn't mean that much to me," Adam said, and stretched out on the bed as he continued watching Wylie touch himself for a few more moments, and then get dressed. "I barely met him three weeks ago, but he seems pretty righteous. And since you're outta here at the end of this year and I will be president next year, I want to start off with a strong crew."

That wasn't completely the truth, but it was as close as Wylie was going to get to it. Adam and Manuel had spent almost every day of the past three weeks together, becoming good friends and growing more and more intimate. Adam had been very slow and careful in his seduction of the sexy Latino. He knew he was in love with Manuel after their first afternoon together, but getting Manuel to the point of recognizing that and on the same page was requiring a careful and detailed game plan. He was almost there. Though they'd started out as just buddies, over the past week Adam had let his knee graze Manuel's, and then applied more and more pressure when it wasn't met with resistance. A couple of times, while watching television together, Adam inched his hand closer and closer to Manuel's, and eventually intertwined his fingers with the boy's. And the night before, as they finished their studies together and were walking from the library back to Manuel's dorm, Adam leaned in and kissed him. He wasn't sure what reaction to expect, but was relieved when Manuel pulled him closer and returned the kiss.

"Whoa, dude," Wylie said, picking at what seemed to be an imaginary spider crawling down his left thigh. "What do you mean, 'strong crew'?"

"His father is the second wealthiest man in Colombia, and will probably be the country's president."

"I thought Reagan was our president," Wylie said slowly as he held out his hand and steadied himself as he took the five steps to his bed, and scooted Adam off.

"Oh my God, dude," Adam laughed. "You're totally wasted."

"No, I'm not," Wylie said, and swatted at unseen bugs or alien invaders that seemed to be diving at his face. "Wake me up when they get here."

* * *

The four pledges were blindfolded with their hands tied behind their backs and lined up in a row in the middle of the living room. Tommy, the frat secretary, and George, the treasurer, stood in front of them with their hands behind their backs in front of the fireplace. Adam was there with them as well, and couldn't take his eyes off Manuel. His heart raced erratically and his knees trembled slightly. The frat execs had been cruel and rough with some of their pledges in the past, and he didn't want them to hurt or humiliate Manuel too much.

Wylie began descending the stairs slowly, and Adam could tell he was buggin' out big time. His eyes seemed to be focused about three inches in front of his face. He held on tightly to the railings on the stairwell, and took each step tentatively. A couple of times he even went to take a step and then quickly pulled his foot back up and waited a few second before continuing.

"Dude, you okay?" Adam asked as he walked up and helped Wylie down the last few steps.

"Yeah, man," Wylie said, and then broke into uncontrolled laughter. "I'm prime time, chico!"

"I'm not sure this is such a great idea, bro. Maybe we should wait and do this another time."

"Fuck, no!" Wylie yelled, and waved Adam away. "I'm here, they're here, let's get this party started."

Adam shrugged and took his place back in the line in front of the fireplace with the rest of the frat execs.

"Get down on your knees," Wylie barked, and pushed the four pledges down to the floor roughly. "You," he said to the first guy in line on his knees, and slapped him across the face, "lean back."

The pledge leaned back as far as he could bend without falling backward. Wylie ripped the boy's shirt off and threw it to the ground. The boy panted rapidly and trembled visibly.

Adam felt sorry for the kid, but he noticed that the two frat brothers next to him were getting excited about the whole scene. They bounced on their feet rapidly and giggled nervously as they watched their president light a long taper candle and walk back to the pledge.

Wylie held the candle over the boy's torso, and when it accumulated enough melted wax to satisfy him, he tilted it and waved it in a circular motion, causing the hot wax to fall and land on the pledge's naked chest. When the boy whimpered out loud and wriggled around to escape the hot wax, Wylie broke into hysterical laughter and dropped the still-lighted candle onto the pledge's bare stomach.

"Careful, Wylie!" Adam yelled, and lunged forward to swipe the candle to the floor.

Wylie rolled around on the floor for a moment, laughing and trying to catch his breath. Then he stood up in front of the group of recruits again. "Darren"—he waved the secretary over—"take this one into the bathroom and make sure he doesn't leave until it sparkles. You know the routine . . . make sure he is naked and uses the toothbrush below the sink."

Darren grabbed the boy in the middle and dragged him off into the bathroom at the end of the hall behind the kitchen.

Wylie picked up the candle again, and lit it, then walked in front of the pledge on his knees next to Manuel. "Open your mouth, punk," he said as he grabbed the guy's hair. "Get ready for something hot."

The boy opened his mouth and stuck out his tongue as he leaned forward at Wylie's crotch level.

"Holy shit, man," Wylie yelled, "this faggot wants my cock." He looked back at his frat brothers and pointed frantically at the pledge on the floor beside him. "Did you see that, guys? He wants my cock."

"But you told me to . . ."

"Shut the fuck up, punk," he said, and grabbed him by the hair again. "Let's try this again. Open your mouth and stick that fucking tongue out."

When the pledge did as he was told, more tentatively this time, Wylie tilted the candle and watched as several drops of the hot wax landed on the boy's tongue.

"Fuck!" the boy yelled, and struggled to get to his feet with his hands still tied behind his back.

"Who said you could get up?" Wylie asked, as he dropped the candle and pulled the boy into place on his knees directly in front of him. "You want my dick, you're gonna get it."

He held the boy's head in one hand and unbuttoned his jeans with the other. He pulled his cock out and slapped it across the pledge's lips a few times. "Open up and take it, bitch," he ordered the pledge.

"Wylie, what the fuck are you doing?" Adam asked. This was way further than they'd ever gone before. They'd often made recruits dress up as girls or clean the bathroom in the nude or streak up and down the middle of Elm Street in the middle of the busy early evening. Certainly humiliation was not a stranger to Kappa Lambda Phi pledging ceremonies. But they'd never made a recruit perform sexual acts with another dude. "This is not cool. You need to . . ."

"No!" Wylie yelled as he shoved his half-hard cock into the pledge's mouth. "You need to shut up. Both of you grab one of these boys and get to it," he said and waved Adam and Ryan toward the two remaining pledges.

The frat treasurer took a couple of steps toward Manuel, but Adam grabbed him by the arm and pointed him toward the other boy. "That one's mine," he told Ryan.

As much as he knew it was wrong, and knew he should put a stop to it, he wanted to see Manuel naked and feel his cock buried deep inside his ass even more. He knelt on the floor with Manuel, and when he was sure Wylie and Ryan weren't watching him, he leaned in and whispered in his buddy's ear. "It's me, Manuel. Just try and relax. I'll be very gentle with you."

"What?" Manuel asked. "You must not be serious."

"He's really high right now, and he's out of control," Adam whispered as he began undressing Manuel. "He's dangerous, and could cause a lot of trouble for both of us. So just go along with it."

"No, I can't," Manuel said, and struggled to scoot away from Adam. But with his hands tied behind his back, it was impossible.

"Stop fighting, Manuel," he whispered, and kissed him softly on the lips. "I won't hurt you, and I won't let anyone else hurt you, either. But we gotta do this or things can go downhill very quickly."

Adam laid him on his back, and pulled his jeans and underwear off, and tossed them to the side. He struggled to get the shirt off because of the rope tied around Manuel's wrists, and after a couple of minutes, he ripped it off impatiently and tossed it over with the jeans and briefs a few feet away.

He was enthralled with the sight of Manuel's naked body in front of him. His caramel-colored skin was soft and smooth and begged to be caressed. His chest was tight and toned and tapered down to the perfect "v" highlighting his ridged abdomen. There wasn't a sign of hair anywhere on his torso except for the thick patches of black hair under his arms and the sexy trail that snaked from his belly button down to the thick pubic hair. His fat uncut cock lay limp between his legs, and big hairy balls rested between the heavy cock and his ass cheeks. In contrast to his torso, his muscular legs were covered with coarse, short black hair. His feet were large, perfectly manicured, and hairless.

Adam's cock throbbed to life inside his pants, and he quickly kicked his way free of them. He looked over and saw that Wylie was still face fucking the first pledge, with his back to him, and Ryan was moving his assigned recruit into position on his back. He leaned forward and kissed Manuel on the lips. When Manuel didn't return the kiss, and in fact lay perfectly motionless beneath him, his heart sank.

"Come on, babe, don't act like this," he whispered as he continued kissing him.

"Don't call me that," Manuel said between gritted teeth, and turned his head to avoid another kiss.

"Manuel, please," Adam said. "I'm trying to protect you. It would be much worse if Ryan got you."

He kissed Manuel's neck and continued down his smooth chest and washboard abs. He reached between the thick, hairy legs and cupped Manuel's fuzzy balls as he sucked the limp uncut cock into his mouth. It began to grow as Adam sucked on it, despite the uncooperative attitude that Manuel refused to let go of. When it was fully hard, he couldn't keep it in his mouth without gagging on it. He pulled off it and stared at it, and his heart raced painfully in his chest. It was the longest, thickest cock he'd ever seen, and it made him drunk with desire. He dove back down on it, and sucked as much of it into his mouth as he could take.

"Dude, what the fuck are you doing?" Wylie asked from a few feet away.

"What?" Adam said, confused and inebriated with his desire for Manuel.

"That shit is for fags," the frat president said. "You don't suck his cock, man. That's gross. He sucks your cock, and you fuck his ass."

"And that doesn't make me a fag?"

"No, Sherlock," Wylie said as he slammed his cock harder into the mouth in front of him. "Get with the program, dude."

"I'm sorry, Manuel," Adam said as he rolled him over onto his stomach.

He spread Manuel's smooth, hard ass cheeks apart and spit a mouthful of saliva in between them. When he pressed his cock head slightly against the puckered hole, Manuel tensed up. "Take a deep breath, baby. I won't hurt you, I promise."

"Fuck you," Manuel groaned, as he took a deep breath.

When he did, Adam pushed forward until just the head of his cock slipped inside Manuel's ass. He almost shot his load that very second. His cock was instantly enveloped in tight, wet heat, and squeezed magically. He moaned and leaned forward to kiss the back of Manuel's neck.

"Oh God, I love you," he whispered into Manuel's ear as he slid the rest of his cock deep into his ass.

"I hate you," Manuel cried softly.

"Please don't say that," Adam said as he pulled his dick all the way out of the tight ass and then slammed it back in to the balls. "I love you."

He slid in and out slowly at first and then picked up his pace. Every nerve on his body seemed to explode with millions of tiny fireworks. He felt himself losing control and fucking Manuel deeper and harder than he intended. He didn't want to hurt him, and so he concentrated on slowing down and being less forceful.

"Tell me you love me, Manuel."

Manuel clinched his back molars and tightened his lips, refusing to say anything.

"Say it, dammit," Adam said, and slapped Manuel's ass lightly as he picked up his pace and fucked him faster.

"No."

"God!" Adam yelled. "Why are you being so fucking obstinate, dude?" He pulled his cock all the way out and then thrust it back in hard, and ground it around inside the warm ass. "Say it."

"I hate you," Manuel spat out.

"Say you love me, bitch!" he grunted as he fucked Manuel ferociously. He slapped the smooth ass hard enough to leave a red handprint this time. When Manuel still refused to do as he was told, Adam grabbed him by the hair and pulled his head up. "Say it, Manuel, or I'm going to hurt you."

"Hurt me, then," Manuel said between gritted teeth. "I will not say it."

Adam grabbed him by the tied wrists and pulled him roughly into a doggie position. He shoved his face into the floor and pulled his ass higher into the air so that he could slam deeper and harder into the tight ass. He looked over and saw Wylie picking up his pace as he slid in and out of the first pledge's mouth, and felt the first stirring of his load stirring in his balls and gut.

"Oh Jesus," he moaned. "I'm gonna cum, baby. I'm really close. Please just tell me . . ."

"You are disgusting and I hate you," Manuel spat out as he collapsed to the floor.

Adam thrust his cock deep into Manuel's ass and dropped to the floor with him. He kept his cock buried in the twitching ass as he felt stream after stream of his load shoot from his rod and into the warm ass. After a couple of minutes he caught his breath and felt his dick shrink even as it was still inside Manuel.

"Get that thing out of me," Manuel said.

"Oh my God, Manuel," Adam whined as he slid out of Manuel and sat up. He still couldn't take his eyes off of the beautiful ass, though, and when he saw a thick stream of white cum seep out of the twitching hole and slide down Manuel's hairy balls, he felt himself start to get hard again. "I'm so sorry, babe," he said as he forced himself to look away. "I didn't mean to, I swear I didn't. I'm so sorry."

"Dude, that was hot as fuck, man!" Wylie said as he shoved his own pledge to the floor.

"Shut the fuck up, asshole," Adam said, and stood up and ran to the bathroom.

Inside the bathroom he fell to the floor in front of the toilet, and vomited for several minutes. What had he done? That was not the way he envisioned and dreamed about his first time, or any time, with Manuel. He did love him, he was sure of that. But who the fuck blurts it out like that during the first time they have sex with the person they love? No one, that's who. What was he thinking? What had gotten into him? He'd dreamed about making love with Manuel a dozen times, and in every one of them he was passionate and loving and tender with his lover. He didn't slap him and pull his hair and call him names. And he certainly didn't insist on making Manuel say that he loved him when that was obviously not the way he felt. Yet.

He had to make this right. He stood up and splashed water across his face and rinsed his mouth. After a couple of deep breaths he walked back into the living room.

"Where's Manuel?" he said as he looked around the room and saw everyone there except for his lover.

"He left, man," Wylie said slowly. "He couldn't hang. *These* are our new frat brothers." He pointed and waved at the other three recruits. "Wipe my spunk off your mouth, dude," he said to the one he'd just mouthraped. "It's disgusting."

"What?" Adam said, dazed. "No, that can't be. Where'd he go?"

"Fuck if I know, man. I untied his hands and he was out the door faster than Flash Gordon, dude. A real bummer."

"You can't be serious," Adam said, and pushed the screen door open and ran out into the yard. He looked in every direction, but didn't see a trace of Manuel. He ran back into the house. "Did he say anything?"

"Who?" Wylie asked as he collapsed onto the couch.

"Manuel, asshole. Manuel, the guy who was just here and then just left. Did he say anything?"

"He said, 'fuck you all' and then he grabbed his clothes and ran out into the yard completely naked. Fucked-up downer, man. I don't think he's right in the head."

Adam looked over to the corner where Manuel's clothes had been. They were all gone.

"I can't believe you, man," he said to Wylie. "You're a bogue asshole."

"What did I do, man?" Wyle said as he scratched his head. "I thought I did good. You got your rocks off, right?"

"Fuck you, man."

"Now you sound just like the spic."

Adam lunged at him, but the other brothers grabbed him and held him back.

"Chill, dude," Darren said. "Let it go."

Adam wrested free from them and flipped Wylie off as he kicked the screen door open and walked out into the yard and down the sidewalk toward Manuel's dorm.

Halfway there he saw the t-shirt he'd ripped from Manuel's torso lying in the middle of the street. He picked it up and brought it to his nose. He could still smell his lover's sweet, musky scent on it. God, how he loved him!

"Manuel!" he yelled into the dark night. "Babe, where are you?"

When no one answered after several more inquiries, Adam curled up into the fetal position in the middle of the sidewalk and cried himself to sleep.

III.

Adam moaned loudly and struggled to push his way up to consciousness. Every muscle in his body ached, and he couldn't move his arms or legs for several minutes. He blinked his eyes open slowly, allowing them to adjust to the little bit of lingering afternoon sunlight that peeked through the bent horizontal blinds on his window, even though they were drawn tight. When he felt the first needle sting in his legs, he slid them off the side of the bed and banged them a couple of times on the wooden floor. He needed to get the blood flowing. If the spiders and roaches and bees attacked again, he'd need to run, and run quickly. Having his legs and arms asleep would not get him off the bed and out the door fast enough.

After a couple of minutes, he felt confident enough in his walking ability to get up and move around. He went into the kitchen and pulled a diet soda from the fridge, and downed it all in several swallows before setting the empty can on the table.

He looked at the clock on the kitchen wall. Four-thirty. What day was it? How long had he slept? The last thing he remembered was arguing with that fat woman about her photo prints at work. Was that earlier today? Yesterday? The pressure in his bladder was overwhelming, so he went to the bathroom and relieved himself. On his way into the living room, he noticed the red light on his answering machine blinking, and pushed the button to listen to his messages.

"Pollard, this is Perry at work."

Adam sensed some tension in his boss's voice. God, he hoped the fat lady hadn't caused him too much grief. Perry could be a real bitch when he was in a bad mood.

"What the fuck is going on with you? I know you've been having a rough time of it lately, but this is ridiculous. It's company policy to give someone a written warning if they don't show up for work and don't call in for one day. Any more than one day, and we consider it job abandonment. This is day three, Pollard, and there is absolutely no reason why I shouldn't just be calling you and telling you that you're fired. But I think I know you well enough to know you wouldn't abandon your job. You can't afford it. And as much as I wouldn't call you a friend by any stretch of the imagination, I certainly don't like to entertain the idea of interviewing a dozen people and then having to train someone else. So, I need to know what is going on with you, and I need you to call me. Immediately."

"Three days," Adam said aloud as he scratched anxiously at his neck. "That's impossible. I just laid down for a few minutes."

He walked over and sat on the sofa, and clicked on the television. He turned it to the TV Guide channel, which also showed the date and time. Thursday, 4:55 P.M. How is that possible? he wondered. The confrontation with the fat woman at Walgreens had happened on Monday. He remembered that because he'd just finished unloading the delivery truck right before Jabba the Hutt came into the store, and deliveries were always on Monday. That was the last thing he remembered. How could it be Thursday already? He needed to call Perry, and to beg him not to fire him. He needed his job. He was barely making his rent the way it was, and being unemployed would send him into the streets. But before he called Perry, he needed an excuse for missing three days of work without calling in.

Adam flipped through several channels as he tried to formulate a believable story. He stopped on one of the local news channels, and dropped the remote control as he felt a hot dagger stab him in the chest. He couldn't breathe, and when he tried to swallow he found himself choking.

"The new president-elect of Mexico will be speaking to an estimated audience of over 10,000 people at Justin Herman Plaza tomorrow at 11 A.M.," the afternoon anchorwoman said. "Rafael Suarez will take office as Mexico's leader in just two weeks. But before doing so, he will speak with the citizens of San Francisco, both Americans and native Mexicans alike, about the reforms he plans to make for our closest neighbor to the south."

"Manuel," Adam whispered, and scratched frantically at his head. "Baby, you came back for me."

"Suarez Fever is rabid in Mexico, and all across Latin America. The president-elect is a celebrity of the highest status, and commands larger crowds and Internet hits than the biggest movie star or pop singer in the country. His leading man looks make women of all nationalities swoon, and his sharp wit and intelligence draw dignitaries and leaders of the largest nations in the world to him like magnets," the anchorwoman said.

Adam looked at the picture of Rafael Suarez on the television screen, and began crying. His body racked with pain, and he trembled almost violently on the couch. He scratched all over his body, and lay on the sofa so that he could rub his back against the seat, to get to the itches he couldn't reach with his hands.

"I'm here, baby," he cried. "You found me, and I won't let you go again."

"Mr. Suarez is stopping in San Francisco as part of a three-day tour through the U.S. and Canada, meeting with our presidents and political leaders. The president-elect says that rebuilding strong relationships with the other North American leaders and nations is his most important priority. His speech begins promptly at 11:00 tomorrow morning, and by 12:30 he'll be on his plane bound for Corpus Christi before finishing his day in New York City."

"What?" Adam said, and sat up quickly on the sofa. "But you just got here. You just found me. You can't leave already. You can't go."

He continued watching the anchor as she transitioned to the next story. He saw her lips moving as the picture of Mexico's president-elect was replaced with that of a two-legged dog, but no sound came out of her mouth. She opened her silent mouth to laugh at something in the story, and when she did a long, thin salamander slithered out of it and crawled down her neck and disappeared into her bosom. Adam gasped at the sight of the prehistoric-looking amphibian, and how in the world the pretty newswoman could sit there perfectly still and not panic and beat at the lizard frenetically as it left a trail of greenish-yellow slime behind it on her creamy white skin.

Adam tried to sit there calmly and continue watching the news-cast, because he was afraid he'd miss more information about Manuel's visit. But when a tiny red spider crawled out of the anchor-woman's eye socket, and then grew longer and fatter as it kicked its back legs out from the eyeball and stretched across her face, he'd seen enough. He jumped from the couch, grabbed his jacket from the coatrack next to the door, and slammed the door behind him as he left the building and rushed outside into the cool and fresh air.

He ran as quickly as he could the four blocks from his apartment to the BART station without looking behind him. He was afraid of what might be following him if he did. The cockroaches and spi-ders and bees were getting more numerous and they were getting bigger. And now there were mice and bats and lizards added to the mix, and their teeth were getting larger and their eyes stared di-rectly into his when he looked at them. There wasn't a doubt in his mind that they were behind him and in pursuit. He couldn't chance that a backward glance would embolden them and give them the extra burst of energy that would allow them to pounce on and devour him right in the middle of the crowded street.

Adam bounded down the stairs of the transit station four at a time, and squeezed through the closing doors of the train just before they slid tightly shut behind him. He took a couple of deep breaths as he leaned against the wall and watched millions of bugs and rodents and lizards of every species flood down the staircase and envelop the train. In just a few seconds the inside of the train turned completely dark as the animals clawed and scratched and bit at the windows and doors. Adam started to scream, but noticed that no one else on the busy train noticed the darkness or the attack. He held his hand over his mouth, and concentrated hard on not screaming out loud. Only when the train accelerated out of the station, and the millions of fanged vermin suddenly retreated backward in one swift and singular wave off the train and back up the stairs did he move his hand away from his mouth and get his breathing under control.

He exited the train at 16th and Mission, and looked around carefully as he walked up the stairs from the underground station and into the cool air of the busy street. It was now a quarter til six, and most of the shops along hectic Mission Street closed at six. He had ten minutes to get to the store, which was five blocks away, and he wasn't one hundred percent sure he remembered exactly where it was at. He'd only passed by it once before, a couple of weeks ago, and hadn't written the address down. It was right around the corner from one of his favorite South American restaurants, and so he was fairly confident he could find it. But he had no time to waste.

Adam walked quickly up Mission Street for a couple of blocks, and when the crowd thinned out a little he broke into a jog. He hooked a right on 18th Street and stopped right before reaching Guerrero Street. He stood outside Morales' Gun & Pawn Shop for a moment, trying to catch his breath and slow down his heart rate. It wouldn't do for him to go in there breathless and out of control. There was too much at stake, and he had to be sure not to blow it.

He wasn't completely under control when he opened the door and walked into the gun shop, but his watch now read three minutes before six, and he could see the old man behind the counter making the final preparations to close up.

"We're just about to close," the man behind the counter said, as he stepped into the middle of the store. He looked to be in his mid-sixties, and walked with a heavy limp and with the assistance of a cane.

"I know," Adam said, and smiled. He hoped it looked genuine as he smoothed out his shirt and glanced at his watch. "I'm sorry. I tried to get here as quickly as I could before six. I won't be long, I promise."

The clerk looked at Adam intently for a moment, and then sighed deeply. "All right, I suppose," he said in a tone that said unmistakably that he was annoyed at the last minute shopper.

"Thank you so much," Adam said. "I need . . . I mean, I'm looking for a handgun. A small one, but with decent power."

The man stared at Adam for almost a full minute. He looked right into Adam's eyes and didn't blink even once.

Adam prayed that the barbed-legged scorpion he felt just behind his left eye would not deem it necessary to crawl out of his eye socket at that very moment. He made a feeble attempt at smiling, and was relieved when the guy waved him over to a glass case near the front of the store.

"Depends on what you're looking to use it for," the guy said as he waved one arm over the long display case. "What *are* you gonna use it for?"

"My sister," Adam spat out. "She was mugged a couple of weeks ago, and is scared to death to leave her apartment anymore. I just wanna give her a little something to build her confidence again.

Nothing too drastic, but something that could definitely take care of things if she ever found herself in that situation again."

"I see," the clerk said. He pulled three handguns out from behind the case and set them on top of the glass counter. "Any of these should serve your purposes."

Adam looked at the guns and felt his legs begin to quiver. He took a deep breath and carefully monitored his speech to make sure he didn't sound frightened or hysterical. He picked each one up tentatively and held it in his hand. When he slipped his finger across the triggers, he felt a sharp stabbing feeling in the back of his head. But he also felt his cock harden in his pants.

"Which one will do the most damage?" he asked.

The clerk raised one eyebrow as he stared at Adam uncertainly.

"If it comes down to my sister having to fire it, I want to make sure she only has to shoot once. I don't want an attacker to get the best of her again this time. He needs to be stopped unquestionably with the first shot."

"I don't know that that is necessary," the man said. He blinked rapidly as he looked uncomfortably around him. "Usually just the sight of a handgun will scare an attacker away."

"She's handicapped," Adam said quickly. "In a wheelchair, and she can't move her legs. She's completely helpless."

The clerk with the cane gasped, and looked at Adam intently. His lips tightened and his left eye began to twitch slightly.

"This one," he said matter-of-factly, and pointed to the largest of the three guns in front of him. "It's light, easy to handle, and has very little kick. But it will get the job done. The son of a bitch won't ever be a menace to society again. Taking advantage of a helpless handicapped woman," he said sadly as he shook his head. "Asshole deserves exactly this gun."

"Thank you," Adam said, and smiled. "I'll take that one, then. And a couple of boxes of bullets."

The clerk put the other two guns back in the glass case and

locked it, and then pulled a couple of boxes of bullets from a shelf behind the counter.

"I just need to see your permit, please," he said.

"Permit?" Adam said.

"Yeah, thanks to the damned commie Democrats, you have to fill out these here forms for a background check through the FBI, and you have to have a permit to buy a handgun. You do have one, don't you?"

"Of course," Adam said, and put his hands in his pocket, pretending to retrieve the permit. "But I'll be able to take the gun with me today, right?"

"Oh, heavens, no. It'll take a day or two for the FBI to get back to me." The old man leaned forward to get the background check forms.

Adam looked around to make sure no one was watching from outside. Satisfied that they were not, he grabbed the old man by the back of the head and slammed his face into the top of the glass counter case. The guy moaned, and held his head as he stumbled backward, but didn't fall or lose consciousness.

"Shit," Adam said quietly.

He ran quickly behind the counter, and grabbed the old guy's arms before he could reach the baseball bat leaned up against the filing cabinet a few feet away. He punched the old man in the stomach, and as the guy slumped to the floor, he kicked him hard in the face, forcing his head backward. The clerk landed on the floor with a thud, and remained perfectly still in a growing pool of blood.

Adam grabbed the pistol and bullets, threw them quickly into a paper bag, and ran out the door. He didn't stop running until he reached the BART station several blocks away.

IV.

"Dude, what the fuck are you doing?" Wylie stood in the middle of the doorway, scratching his balls as he watched Adam throwing clothes hastily into his suitcase.

"I told you," Adam said, shutting the suitcase and zipping it shut. "I'm outta here. I can't do this anymore. I didn't sign up for this bullshit, Wylie. I didn't join this fraternity to rape anybody."

"Rape?" Wylie squealed, and shifted from one foot to the other several times. His eyes were wide with fear, and darted around the room nervously. "What are you talking about? You didn't rape anybody. Nobody raped anybody."

"Yeah, well, you can say that all you want," Adam said, and pulled several jackets and sweaters from his closet. "But it was rape, and it was wrong, and I can't stay here another day and pretend it didn't happen. I'm moving to an apartment off campus. And I'm going to the dean and tell him what happened here last week."

"No, you're not," Wylie said calmly, and moved inside the room and closed the door behind him.

"Yes, I am, Wylie," Adam said. "What are you doing?"

Wylie took a couple of steps closer. "Our three new recruits will vouch that nothing inappropriate happened during their initiation. And certainly the rest of the brothers won't say anything to the contrary. And your precious little Manny has just disappeared and is nowhere to be found."

"What did you do with him?" Adam asked between clinched teeth.

Wylie laughed. "I didn't do anything with him. God, you sound like some stoner who can't hold his drugs, man. But the truth of the matter is, your little boyfriend is gone, and no one else here will corroborate your story. It's your word against . . ." he waved his arm at the door ". . . all of ours."

"Fuck you!" Adam said, and tried to walk past the frat president.

"No, fuck you," Wylie said, and pushed Adam to the floor. He stood over his friend, straddling his legs. "You're a faggot, and I'll be damned if I'm going to let you bring this fraternity down."

"What are you doing?" Adam said, and started to get up.

Wylie kicked him back to the floor, and pushed his jeans down to his ankles. "I've seen how you stare at my cock, dude," he said as he stroked his soft dick. "You've been jonesing for me since you were initiated into the house. I thought it might just be a phase and that you'd get over it with enough college pussy behind you. But it wasn't just a phase, and you didn't get over it, did you? You're a faggot, and you fell for that little spic, didn't you?"

Adam blinked rapidly, and tried hard not to stare at Wylie's thickening cock, but couldn't do it. It was fully hard now, and turning dark pink. Even though it wasn't very big, and he hated his former friend at the moment, Adam found his own cock beginning to harden.

"I didn't . . . it's none of your . . ."

"Suck my dick, faggot," Wylie said, and took another step closer to Adam. He grabbed his friend by the hair, and pulled his face to his crotch. When Adam didn't immediately start sucking his cock, Wylie slapped it against his cheeks and mouth. "I said suck it!"

Adam licked the head of Wylie's cock, and then opened his mouth to suck on the head. But Wylie wasn't really looking for anything slow and careful. He shoved his hips forward and forced his cock all the way into Adam's mouth. As much as he didn't want to, Adam found himself tightening his lips around it and sucking on it.

"That's it, bitch," Wylie moaned, "suck that big dick." He thrust it in and out of Adam's mouth faster and harder. "You want it bad, don't you?"

Adam sucked the dick, and reached below it and tugged on Wylie's hairy balls. This elicited a low moan from the frat president, and Adam swallowed a large dribble of precum. He wanted not to enjoy sucking the dick, but he was getting turned on more than he cared to admit. He sucked it harder and squeezed the shaft teasingly. After a couple of minutes, he felt Wylie's cock thickening and getting even harder, and tasted several thicker streams of precum on his tongue. He could tell Wylie was getting close.

Suddenly Wylie pulled his cock out of Adam's mouth, and took a step backward. He grabbed Adam by the arm and roughly pulled him to his feet, and then threw him onto the bed on his stomach.

"What are you doing?" Adam asked even as Wylie grabbed him by the back of the neck and held his face into the bed.

"Shut up, bitch," Wylie said roughly. He kept a knee planted in the middle of Adam's back, and quickly pulled his pants off and threw them to the floor. He spit a mouthful of saliva into the crack of Adam's ass, and spread the cheeks roughly.

"Stop it, Wylie," Adam protested. "Get the fuck off of me."

"Not gonna happen, dude," Wylie said, and moved between Adam's legs, and spread them forcefully with his own. "You know you want it. You're a fucking faggot, and you want my cock up your ass."

"Get off of me," Adam screamed.

Wylie grabbed him by the hair and thrust his face deep into the blanket, and then shoved his cock into Adam's ass in one quick move. When Adam tensed up and screamed into the bed, Wylie slapped his ass hard and pulled his cock all the way out and then shoved it all the way back in. "Take it, punk. Take my cock and shut the fuck up."

Adam struggled against him, but Wylie was much too strong. The more he fought, the more Wylie was turned on by the resistance, and the harder he fucked Adam. The cock inside him was small, but it hurt incredibly. He'd never been fucked before, and the hard cock stabbing around his hole felt like a splintered soda bottle sliding in and out of him, leaving sharp pieces of it deep inside him.

"You're pathetic, man," Wylie panted heavily as he slammed his cock in and out of Adam's ass. "What do you think your precious basketball team will think when they find out their captain is a queer? And how long do you think the student council will stand behind you when they hear that you take it up the ass?"

"Please," Adam cried into the blanket on his bed. "Get off me, Wylie, please. I'm sorry. I won't say anything."

"Goddam right you won't say anything, punk," Wylie said as he continued pounding Adam's ass. "Cuz you like getting fucked like a bitch, and you're nothing but a skanky cocksucker. How dare you threaten me."

"I'm sorry," Adam repeated. His body went limp, and he lay on the bed completely motionless, his eyes staring into the blanket beneath him. "I'm sorry."

Wylie pulled Adam's head up by the hair, and held it pulled back tight as he increased his rhythm as he slid in and out of Adam's ass. "Oh, God," he moaned as he slid into the ass one last time before keeping himself buried deep inside his former friend. "Fuck yeah!"

Adam felt the cock grow thicker inside him and felt the inside of his ass grow warm and wet. He lay completely still as Wylie emptied himself inside of him, and when Wylie pulled out and stood up, Adam fell limp to the floor next to the bed. He stared at the ceiling, emotionless.

"You're right," Wylie said as he shook the last couple of drops of cum from his cock and onto Adam's face. "You don't belong here anymore. It is time for you to go. But you were wrong about telling anyone about what happened here. You are not going to tell anyone anything about the goings on here. Because if you do, I will destroy you. Do you understand me?"

Adam remained completely still and said nothing.

"I take that as a yes. That's good. Now get the fuck up and finish packing. I want you out of the house in an hour."

Wylie left the room, and left Adam alone in the room. He curled up into the fetal position and cried for several minutes. When he finally stood up, a large stream of Wylie's cum slid out of his ass and down his legs. He walked into the restroom and took a long, hot shower, and then got dressed.

An hour later he threw two suitcases into the backseat of his Seville, and pulled away from the frat house. He never looked back at it, and didn't stop driving until he ran out of gas a couple hundred miles from Yale and everything he knew. Going back to his family was out of the question, and school was definitely not an option anymore.

Adam pulled into the parking lot of a Denny's along the highway, and laughed hysterically until he fell asleep inside the car.

V.

Justin Herman Plaza had been transformed into a world-class staging area. The stone fountain made a dramatic backdrop to the stage, which was draped in Mexican and American flags. There were dozens of uniformed police spread out throughout the entire plaza, some of them carrying rifles. Police helicopters shared the airspace with television news choppers, who transmitted images of the spectacle back to audiences at home, and stressed the visible and nonvisible security forces that were in place.

Even at 10,000, the local authorities had severely underestimated the size of the crowd that would gather to see and hear the popular president-elect of Mexico. They started showing up before sunrise, and by 8:00 A.M. the police had to stop letting people in, and turned them away in disappointment. They filled the plaza to standing room only, and almost every window in the buildings surrounding it was filled with onlookers staring down at the crowd and the stage below them.

At 10:45 the crowd began chanting, "Pre-si-den-te." It started out as a murmur, but grew louder with every passing minute. By the time the mayor of San Francisco walked onto the stage to introduce her close friend Rafael Suarez to the crowd, the chant was deafening.

"What an amazing, beautiful, and positive world we are living in, right?" the mayor said, and smiled brilliantly as the crowd roared in agreement. "In just two weeks, our beloved and cherished neighbor to the south will inaugurate its new president, and will take a giant step toward a more hopeful and more prosperous future. When a country . . . and people . . . have faith and believe in themselves, they become unstoppable. And when a leader emerges who can help identify and instill that faith and hope and belief in oneself, we realize how lucky we are and how powerful we are."

Adam Pollard stood in the crowd about halfway to the stage. The energy and the noise around him were deafening and intoxicating at the same time. To think that all of this hoopla was for his long lost lover was overwhelming. He was so proud of Manuel, and couldn't wait to wrap his arms around him and to kiss him and to tell him how much he loved him.

"Ladies and gentlemen . . . damas y caballeros . . . please help me welcome to the stage the next president of the United States of Mexico . . . Rafael Suarez!!" the mayor said loudly and proudly. She stood aside and clapped enthusiastically as the president-elect strode across the stage confidently. He kissed her on the cheek and waved to the crowd humbly.

"My friends," Rafael said in his deep baritone voice as he walked up to the podium, "welcome to the first day of a world filled with hope and with positive change and with promise."

The crowd roared its approval and stomped their feet frenetically. It had been a long time since most of the people in the audience had heard those words in more than just a wishful tone or ridicule. For many it was the first time they'd felt they had permission to express or experience those promises. And they were rabid with the hope for their fulfillment.

"We can bring about that world," he said in perfect English with almost no trace of an accent. "Together, you and I can create that Utopia by demanding the best, and nothing but the best, from ourselves and from our brothers and sisters sharing our corner of the world with us."

Adam began to cry. He'd lived in a world where high expectations were discouraged, and in some cases even forbidden, for so long that he forgot how exhilarating it could feel to have those expectations of yourself and those around you. The fear of litigation and liability and accusations of slander and discrimination had made things like hope and high standards and accountability for our actions things of the past.

But here was his lover, whom he hadn't seen or heard from in thirty years, inspiring this huge crowd to depths of emotion around these promises of change, and engaging them to be the impetus of change in their world. God, how he loved Manuel. Never in his wildest dreams had he ever thought that the man he'd loved for three decades would turn out to be the most powerful man in Latin America, and standing in front of him now, bringing thousands of Mexicans and Americans alike to the brink of an emotional orgasm.

Adam had to get to the front of the crowd. He'd wanted to give Manuel a little room, because he knew that he was an important man now, a leader of millions who had many demands on him. He didn't want to appear clingy, not to Manuel or to the adoring public who watched and dissected his every move. But now he needed to step up. He needed Manuel to see him and to know that he was with him now, and that indeed he'd never left him. And he needed the public to see him stand next to his man. They'd be watching the new president and his life partner very closely from here on out, and it'd behoove them to get to know him now and to get used to him being at the forefront of everything that Manuel would be doing, in public and in private, from here on out.

He pushed his way through the dense crowd, elbowing past

them or pushing them to the side when they didn't move away and allow him to pass on their own accord. A couple of people yelled at him and pushed back, and after a couple of minutes a rumble of annoyance rippled around him and swelled toward the stage. Adam saw several uniformed police and obvious undercover agents looking his way, and beginning to move toward him.

Now was the time to make his move.

"Manuel!" he yelled loudly. He was only a few feet from the stage, and everyone on it swung their heads and looked at him. "Baby, it's me. It's Adam."

"Well, hello *honey*," Rafael said with a laugh, but looked around himself consciously. "It's good to see you, Adam. But my name isn't Manuel. It's Rafael."

The police were moving toward him faster, and with more determination. Adam pulled the handgun from the waist of his jeans and waved it frantically in front of him. Several people around him screamed, and a few threw themselves to the ground.

"Don't lie to me again, Manuel," Adam screamed loudly, and aimed the gun right at Rafael.

The mayor and one of her aides on the stage rushed toward the president-elect and tackled him to the floor. They lay on top of him, protecting every inch of his body.

A loud shot rang out, and people began screaming and running in every direction. The plaza was so tightly packed that it took a few moments for the swell to move at all, but once it did it was quick and disastrous. Several people fell to the ground, and were trampled by others as they scrambled to get away from the lunatic with the gun.

Adam was thrown to the ground by the force of three officers jumping on him.

"Manuel!" he screamed. "Don't let them do this to me, baby. It's me, Adam. Don't leave me again. I love you. I need you."

The stage emptied quickly, as Rafael Suarez was whisked away by a throng of police and secret service agents.

"Manuuueeeeellllllllll!" Adam yelled as his arms were twisted behind his back and handcuffed roughly. "Don't leave me again, baby."

INCH SIX

DudeSearch

I.

Harmon Bernacke was a study in irony. His short, wavy blond hair, sapphire blue eyes, tiny upturned nose and full, pink lips would have looked perfectly in place on the cover of the most trendy entertainment magazine. He normally sported a three- or four-day stubble on his face, and his dimples were deep enough to fall into and get lost in. He was not unaccustomed to people, both women and men alike, doing a double take as they passed him on the street. His eyes were soft and gentle and had broken more than a few hearts, and his plump lips were almost always curled into a smile that melted a person to his core and begged to be kissed.

As beautiful, soft, and tender as his face was, his body was just the opposite. At six foot five, he towered over almost everyone around him in any situation. His legs were bulky and hard as tree trunks, his muscled chest puffed out powerfully in front of him and strained the buttons on his shirts, and his thick biceps and forearms were riddled with muscles that seemed to be grown on top of other muscles with little rivers of veins snaking between them.

At twenty-five years old, most of Harmon's friends were busy partying and still mooching off their parents, and figuring out what they wanted to do with their lives. But Harmon had always had a very strong idea of what he wanted to do, and had never let anything stand in his way of getting there. He was passionate about justice and in rehabilitation and in providing people chances, and sometimes second or even third chances, in improving their lives. He powered his way through college in three years, getting a degree in Criminal Justice, with the idea of becoming a parole officer in the near future. But before going that route, he wanted some practical experience, and had for the past year and a half been working as a guard at San Quentin prison.

He only had six months left for this part of his career training. Upon completion of two years at the Q, he had a cushy job waiting for him with the San Francisco District Attorney's office. He was looking forward to the new career, for sure. But unlike many of the other guards there, he also enjoyed his position at the prison. He had a unique way of commanding respect from the inmates while developing a good rapport with them. Despite their misfortune, most of the prisoners found it easy to laugh and joke and make the best of their situation.

"Hey, Bernacke," one of the inmates yelled from down the hall, "why don't you get off that fat ass of yours and bring me some cigarettes."

Harmon recognized the voice at once, and laughed.

At six foot two and well over three hundred and fifty pounds, Gerald Pruitt was one of the biggest guys on the floor. His face was hardened and tough and covered with scars and tattoos. Most of the other inmates stayed away from him and avoided eye contact.

But Harmon was still bigger, and once Gerald learned that he wasn't intimidated, the two developed a friendly bond.

"You know the rules, Pruitt," he yelled back from his desk.

"Only in the yard, and only when you've earned merit points. The rate you're going, you'll die old and fat and wrinkled before you taste another cigarette. Besides, I'm not your bitch."

"That's not what you were moaning last night, baby."

Familiar laughter and catcalls broke out all across the hall, and Harmon let it go on for a few moments before cutting it off.

"All right, guys," he said forcefully, even through his smile. "That's enough. Lights out in five."

He waited almost an hour. "Tiny" Murphy, who would surpass five hundred pounds before the weekend, had a bad case of insomnia, and was always the last one to fall asleep. His cell was the second one from Harmon's desk, and when he started snoring, Harmon knew everyone else was asleep.

Everyone, that was, except Adam Pollard, whom he suspected never slept. Harmon checked his keys and gun, and then walked slowly and quietly halfway down the hall to Pollard's cell.

"You awake?" he whispered.

"Of course."

"You still wanna do it?"

"Sure," Adam said softly. "It's not like I have anything better to do. Bubba here is out like a light, and . . . well, even if he weren't he's not the most exciting conversationalist."

Harmon laughed softly and unlocked the cell door, then stepped aside so Adam could walk out and into the hall. The two men walked quietly and wordlessly and worked their way through a maze of hallways. When they reached the last door at the end of one of the halls, Adam stood to one side and watched as Harmon unlocked the door. Both men stepped inside the room, and closed the door tightly behind them before they turned on the light.

"I don't know why I always get so nervous doing this," Harmon said softly as he took a deep breath. "My heart is beating like crazy."

"Because you could lose your job," Adam said coolly as he took a seat at one of the desks and turned on the computer. "Me? I'm already in one of the most infamous prisons in the country, and I'm here for life. What more could they do to me?"

Harmon laughed uneasily, and sat at the second desk and booted up the computer there.

"So why do you do it?" Adam asked as he quickly typed in the URL address. "I mean, why do you let me out and bring me here to play. With so much at stake, what gives?"

"I like you, Adam," Harmon said as he typed in his username and password. "You're a nice guy. I mean, I know that you attempted to murder . . ."

"Tsk tsk," Adam said quietly.

"I'm sorry. I mean, that you had no intention of killing the president of Mexico, and that you were only carrying the gun to protect him against any possible lunatics in the crowd. But you're a nice guy. And once they diagnosed your . . . mental disorder . . . and got you medicated, you chilled right out and have been really mellow and a model inmate. You're harmless, and it's just not right that they keep you locked up like they do. You deserve a little break."

"Well, thanks. You know I appreciate it."

"Besides, you introduced me to DudeSearch, and I'm frickin' addicted to it now. And it's more fun to be on here when I have someone to talk to while I play around."

Adam laughed as he entered the site. "You're a disturbed motherfucker, you know that?"

"Nah, just a lonely geek with nothing better to do."

The two friends spent the next fifteen minutes checking their email and browsing the profiles of some of the inhabitants in the DudeSearch Bay Area room.

"Oh my God, Adam," Harmon whispered loudly. "He's here."

"Of course he's here," Adam said with a sigh, and rolled his eyes. "You told him you'd be on tonight at this time."

"I know, but I sometimes think maybe he's not interested and won't show up. I'm always a little surprised to see him on."

"You're like a little teenage girl waiting to be asked to the prom."

"Shut up, he's typing something," Harmon said excitedly.

<Hey babe. Good to see you. How are you?>
<<I'm good>> Harmon typed back.
<I missed you>

Harmon's heart raced and he felt his face flush and that stupid smile that made him look like Gomer Pyle on steroids spread across his face.

<<I've missed you, too. Seems like forever since we chatted.>>
<LOL. It was two days ago. But you're right, that's too long.>
<<How was school today?>>
<Good, but a little rough.>
<<Why?>>
<I started thinking about you in Poli Sci class and popped a boner that hasn't gone away all day.>
<<Poli Sci class? That's at 10 AM>>
<Yep>
<<It's midnight now>>
<Yep>
<<You've had a 14-hour hardon?>>
<Almost. I beat off a couple of times and it went down. But it keeps coming back about an hour later. I'm hard again right now, and dripping precum.>
<<Oh fuck, you know what that vision does to me.>>
<Yep>
<<You're cruel>>
<I'm strokin' now. Why don't you pull it out and beat one off with me?>
<<OK>>

Harmon reached down and stroked his cock through his pants. It was already hard, and formed a line a quarter of the way down his left thigh.

"Adam," he moaned.

"Right here," Adam said, and dropped to his knees between Harmon's legs. He unzipped the uniform pants, and reached in with his hands. A few seconds later he pulled the thick cock out.

"Take it, man," Harmon moaned as he thrust his hips up.

Adam stuck his tongue out and licked the fat head. It was red and throbbing, and he loved the taste and feel of it on his tongue. He wrapped his lips around the head and sucked it into his mouth, and slid his tongue down the underside of the shaft as he took more and more of the big dick into his mouth.

<Are you stroking your big dick, baby?>
<<Yeah, man.>>
<Slide that hand up and down that thick shaft. Pretend it was my lips.>
<<I am>> Harmon typed, and slid his cock deeper into Adam's mouth.
<You like how I suck your cock, Harmon?>
<<You know I do.>>

Harmon grabbed Adam by the back of the head and pulled him all the way down on his cock. He didn't have an exceptionally long dick, just under seven inches. But it was almost as thick around as it was long, and covered in fat veins. Not too many guys could take him without gagging, as Adam was doing now.

"Come on, Roger, suck my cock," Harmon said as he thrust deeper into the wet mouth.

"I'm not Roger," Adam said, coming up off the cock for a breath. "I'm Adam. That's Roger," he said, and pointed at the computer monitor.

"I'm sorry," Harmon said. "I didn't mean . . ."

"It's okay. Just lean back and lemme drain this fat snake for you."

Harmon did lean back, and let his favorite prisoner work over his cock. The guy knew what he was doing, and it wouldn't take long for him to shoot his load. He usually came pretty easily anyway, but with the expert mouth and lips tasking his dick, it'd be even quicker. And especially because he was chatting with Roger and dreaming that it was his mouth and his tongue and his lips sucking the juice from his thick cock.

Adam licked around the head for a moment, and then sucked most of the shaft into his mouth, and tightened his lips around it. He carefully lifted Harmon's heavy balls out of the zipper of the pants, and massaged them gently in his hands as he took the last inch of the thick cock into his throat.

"Oh shit, man," Harmon moaned loudly. "I'm gonna shoot. Careful."

In the nine months Adam had been at San Quentin, he'd sucked Harmon's cock five or six times, and in each time he pulled his mouth from the cock and let the jizz splash all across his face. But this time he decided not to pull off. Instead he wrapped his lips tighter around the shaft, sucked harder on the dick, and tugged harder on Harmon's shriveling balls.

"FUCK!!" Harmon groaned as he tightened every muscle in his body and grabbed the arms on the chair until his knuckles turned white.

He felt his cock shoot seven or eight spurts of cum into Adam's mouth. He always shot huge loads, and could tell that this one was even larger than usual. Adam gagged a couple of times, and Harmon could feel the inmate's legs shaking. But he clamped down harder on the cock and kept sucking on it until every last drop of cum was milked from it.

"Damn, dude," Harmon gasped as he caught his breath. "That was hot. You've never done that before."

"I just thought I'd take it up a notch. You know, to show you how much I appreciate your kindness and bringing me in here for a couple of hours a week. It helps me from going completely insane."

"Well, you deserve a little diversion. I didn't make you feel like you had to swallow, did I?"

Adam laughed. "No. I don't know what came over me. I just really wanted to eat your cum tonight. I hope you didn't mind."

"Fuck, no! It was hot, dude."

There was a "ding" from the computer monitor, and both men look toward it.

<Did you cum, baby?>

<<Yeah, man. Big time.>> Harmon looked down at Adam and winked.

<Good. So I was thinking . . . Do you wanna finally meet in person? I mean, it's been six weeks since we started chatting. It's about time, don't you think?>

"Oh fuck," Harmon said. "He wants to meet. Like, in person."

Adam laughed. "Well, then, like, say yes. For fuck's sake, you've been flirting with him for over a month now. Don't be a cock tease."

Harmon looked hurt. "I'm not a tease."

"Prove it. Say yes. Meet him."

<<OK. Yeah, sure>> Harmon typed. <<I might have some time in the next week or two.>>

<Two days ago you said you had tomorrow off. Did that change?>

"Fuck!" Harmon scratched his head and stuffed his cock back into his pants. <<No, it hasn't changed.>>

<Good. Tomorrow at 7:00 then. Meet me at my apartment. It's right off campus. You still have the address?>

<<Yeah, I have it.>>

< Good. Meet me at 7. Just walk on in, don't bother knocking. We'll work up an appetite and then go grab a bite to eat.>

Harmon's heart was beating so fast it hurt, and he felt his face warm up. He knew it was turning red like it always did when he got nervous. His palms were sweating, and he felt as if would faint any minute.

<<Cool>>
<See you tomorrow, baby. Sweet Dreams.>
<<G'nite>>

"Holy shit, Adam, what am I going to do? What if he doesn't like me?"

Adam snorted. "You're an idiot, man. He's gonna like you. Everyone likes you. It's physically impossible not to like you. The fact that you're oblivious to that only makes you that much more adorable. I hate you for that."

"You can't hate me. You just said it was physically impossible to hate me."

"Yeah, but I'm certifiably insane. I don't follow the rules."

Harmon switched off both computers, and turned off the lights as they left the room.

"Seriously, though, Adam, what am I going to do tomorrow? I'm not used to going out on dates."

"I know. That's because you build up this wall around you and people tend to find you intimidating. You're too big and you're too beautiful. That's hard for a lot of people to deal with."

"Well then, why am I even trying?"

"Because Roger isn't intimidated. I think he sees you for the real you, and he likes what he sees. And he seems really nice, and he's really cute. You'd be an idiot not to see what happens. You deserve someone like Roger."

They reached Adam's cell, and Harmon opened it quietly. When Adam was inside, he shut the door and locked it.

"Thank you," he whispered as he leaned into the bars on the door.

Adam leaned forward and kissed him on the lips. "You're welcome. And I wanna hear all about it on Monday."

II.

Harmon pulled up to the address and turned off the car. He had to double check his notes. Roger had said he lived in one half of a duplex, and so he was expecting something smaller and unassuming. Though technically the two identical buildings could be considered a duplex, it definitely wasn't small and even more definitely wasn't unassuming. The two brick buildings looked like mini mansions, with sprawling second-story terraces, lighted water fountains, and a large perfectly manicured garden between them.

But it was the address that Roger had given him, and so Harmon walked up to the door. He'd been given very specific instructions: walk in without knocking, don't turn on any lights, and be as quiet as possible while working his way to the bedroom. When he turned the front door knob, and it opened with no resistance of a lock, he knew he was in the right place.

All of the overhead lights in the main level were turned off, but there were a few soft accent lights under a couple of tables, behind some plants, and in the fireplace. They illuminated the room enough for Harmon to navigate the furniture without tripping over something, or probably even more purposefully for him not to break anything. The décor and furnishings looked really expensive, and though Harmon wasn't an art expert, he knew instinctively that the stuff in this room cost more than he made in a year. Maybe more than he made in five years.

He took his shoes off and set them next to the front door, and then walked carefully around the first floor. The living room could easily fit fifty people comfortably. A large crude stone fireplace covered two-thirds of the main wall, plush sofas and chairs were spread out throughout it, and a large, fully stocked bar dominated one corner. The kitchen was massive, with stainless steel appliances, hanging pots and pans and a large island in the middle. The "half bath" on the main level was the size of Harmon's living room.

"What the fuck am I doing here?" he whispered to himself. "This is way out of my league."

He walked past the tree in the stairwell that towered over him, and walked slowly and quietly up the stairs. When Harmon reached the top of the landing, he looked around him, and allowed his eyes to adjust to the darker lighting up there. There was a closed door on either side of the hallway, and then beyond one of them, an open door that revealed a large, full-sized bathroom. The door at the end of the hall on the left was opened, and he saw candlelight flickering from the room behind it.

Harmon took a deep breath and tried to ignore the rapid pounding in his chest. He took several steps toward the door, but stopped just outside of it.

"Are you just gonna stand out there all night, or are you gonna come in here and fuck me?"

Harmon gasped. Roger's voice was deep and commanding, and much sexier than he expected. His cock instantly began to harden as he listened to the voice and thought about meeting Roger in person for the first time. The dark and mysteriousness of the situation only added to the excitement, and it didn't take long at all for his cock to reach full hardness.

He took a deep breath and turned the corner and walked into the room. He stopped dead in his tracks and prayed that his heart wouldn't stop and his legs would continue to hold him upright.

Roger was lying spread-eagle across the king-sized bed. He was completely naked, and his arms and legs were tied to the bedposts of the four poster with black leather straps. He was blindfolded, and his cock was fully hard and throbbing against his stomach. Several strands of his light blond hair fell across the blindfold. His lips were full and pink and he licked them sensuously.

Harmon ripped his clothes off quickly and kicked them over to one corner of the room. His cock throbbed in front of him as he walked over to the large bed.

"God, you're beautiful," he whispered.

"Kiss me," Roger said.

Harmon leaned down and kissed him gently on the lips. He was surprised at how soft and tender Roger kissed him. With the bondage scene and his commanding voice, he had expected a frantic and demanding kiss. Instead, Roger moaned softly as he sucked lightly on Harmon's tongue and flicked his own around Harmon's lips.

The big guard broke the kiss, and moved down Roger's neck and chest. He could tell that Roger spent a lot of time in the gym, but also that he didn't live there. The chest was strong and powerfully muscled, and so smooth that Harmon could tell it had never been shaved. It was just naturally soft and silky and perfect. The tiny nipples were hard and begged to be licked, and Harmon obliged. He nibbled them softly for a moment, and flicked at them with his tongue, and then sucked them into his mouth.

"Yeah, baby, that's it," Roger moaned.

Harmon paid equal attention to both nipples, and then snaked his way down Roger's torso. His tongue dipped into the ridges across his abdomen, and before he reached the belly button, he came mouth-to-head with Roger's cock. It was fat and hard and a deep shade of red, and when he wrapped his lips around it and sucked it into his mouth, Roger moaned loudly.

"Oh, God, baby," he said breathlessly. "Suck my cock."

Harmon slid his lips down the entire length of the cock, and was shocked at how easily the long cock slid past his tonsils and down his throat. His own cock bounced up and down frantically as he moved his mouth up and down the length of the uncut dick. He loved the way the extra skin slipped along the shaft with his mouth, and the feel of the thick veins that ran along it. He slipped between Roger's spread legs to get a better position, and deepthroated the big dick as he pulled lightly on the smooth balls and tickled the sensitive area between them and Roger's smooth ass.

"You gotta stop, man," Roger said huskily. "I'm getting really close."

"Are you sure?" Harmon asked. "I can finish you off."

"Hell, no. We've just started. Come up here and let me suck your dick, dude."

Harmon moved cautiously up Roger's legs and torso, careful not to bruise him along the way. He straddled the smooth chest, which wasn't an easy task with his thick, muscular legs.

"Holy shit, dude," Roger gasped. "Just how big are you?"

Harmon laughed. "I told you I'm a big guy. Is it too much?"

"Hell, no. It feels really hot. Lemme have your cock, man."

Harmon leaned forward and barely touched the tip of his cock against Roger's lips. He slid it across them, teasing Roger with just the smallest taste of precum.

"Give it to me," Roger begged.

Harmon slid his cock all the way in to Roger's mouth, and moaned as he felt Roger's lips wrap around it and his tongue slide up and down the underside of it. He got really turned on by seeing Roger tied up and blindfolded and all spread out on the bed, and began fucking his mouth slowly at first, and then more quickly.

Even under normal circumstances, Harmon was not one to take a while to shoot his load. He usually struggled to keep it off for at least ten minutes, and was successful about half of the time. But tonight was anything but normal, and he could tell he wasn't going to last anywhere close to ten minutes.

"I'm cumming, man," he almost yelled.

He pulled his cock out of Roger's mouth just in time. Just as the head slipped from Roger's lips, the first shot of cum splashed across his lips and nose. The next few shots landed on the headboard and across the black blindfold covering Roger's eyes, and another couple slipped from the cockhead and down his lips and chin.

"Oh my God," Roger moaned, and wiggled beneath Harmon and the restraints of the ropes. "That was so fucking hot. But really quick, babe. Please tell me you can keep going."

Harmon looked down at his cock. It was still throbbing hard and showed no signs of going anywhere anytime soon. "Yeah, I think so."

"Good. Slide down my stomach, man."

Harmon slid down Roger's chest and stomach, and stopped about halfway down.

"Slide down some more," Roger said softly.

Harmon moved another couple of inches.

"More."

"But then I'll be sitting on your cock," Harmon laughed.

"Exactly," Roger said, and lifted his hips as much as he could. "Sit on it."

"I don't . . ."

"Sit on my cock, babe. I want to fuck you."

"Roger, really, I don't think . . ."

"Shut up and sit on my dick, Harmon. I want . . . I need . . . to fuck your ass."

Harmon looked down at Roger. He was still tied up and blindfolded, and unable to move more than just an inch or two in either direction. And yet he was forceful and dominant and in control. His hard cock throbbed powerfully against his smooth and flat stomach, insisting on attention. And as much as Harmon tried, he couldn't resist Roger or his demands.

"Okay, but just be careful, okay? I don't normally . . ."

"Yeah, whatever," Roger said flippantly, and thrust his hips up to meet Harmon's ass. "Just fuckin' sit on my cock, man."

Harmon was thankful that Roger couldn't see his smile or how hard his cock was bouncing up and down in front of him. He leaned back a little and spit on Roger's big dick, and then slid down so that his hole was just barely touching the hard, red head.

"That's it, baby," Roger moaned. "Just a little more."

Harmon pushed his back farther, and gasped as the head of Roger's cock slipped inside. He took a deep breath and waited a few moments until his ass stopped feeling as if it were being stabbed with a thousand needles. When the needles turned to a warm, tingling sensation, he slid another couple of inches of Roger's thick cock inside him, and shivered with pleasure as he was invaded.

"Damn, dude," Roger gasped as he slid farther inside. "You're so fucking hot and tight. You feel incredible, man."

Harmon thrust his ass down the last couple of inches, until he was sitting completely on the big dick. He felt his ass dancing around Roger's cock, even though he wasn't intentionally doing it himself, and he smiled as he saw Roger's face turn pink and watched him struggle to slide even deeper inside him.

"Is that what you want?" he asked.

"Oh, God, yes," Roger moaned. "Fuck my cock, baby."

Harmon slid his ass off the cock until only the head remained inside. When Roger squirmed beneath him to try to keep his dick inside, Harmon slid back down it quickly, and then up and down again. His ass felt as if it were on fire, but as oddly as it sounded, it felt better than anything he'd ever felt before. He rammed his ass up and down the big dick like a piston charging at turbo speed, and then slowed down to where he was barely moving at all.

His cock was red to the point of almost purple, and bounced up and down in front of him frantically. It leaked a large amount of precum that dripped onto Roger's chest and stomach. A part of him wanted Roger to see his cock and how powerful it looked right then. But a bigger part of him was glad that the only knowledge of him that Roger had was the way his ass felt wrapped around the big dick and how good it made him feel.

"Oh shit, man," Harmon whimpered as he picked up the pace again and pounded Roger's cock. "I'm so close. I'm gonna cum."

Even before he finished the sentence he started shooting. The jizz flew everywhere, landing on the blindfold and Roger's face, his chest and stomach, and the blankets on either side of them. Harmon's entire body quivered for a few moments and then he collapsed on top of Roger's chest and torso.

"Fuck, baby," Roger gasped as he pounded faster and harder into Harmon's ass, "I'm gonna cum."

Harmon pushed himself off of Roger's cock, and slid down so that his face was only a couple of inches from the fat head. A second later several shots of warm cum splashed across his face, covering every inch of it.

Roger was still panting heavily as Harmon lifted himself up and leaned in to kiss him on the mouth. "Wow, man," he whispered. "I taste my cum all over your lips."

Harmon carefully removed the blindfold from Roger's eyes, and wiped away a strand of cum from under his nose, and then kissed him again.

"Fuuuuuck, baby," Roger said, "you're even more beautiful than I imagined."

Harmon smiled. "Thanks. And you are a hell of a lot sexier than I ever thought. How the hell did you get tied up so well?"

Roger laughed, and blushed a little. "A good friend of mine tied me up and blindfolded me right before you got here. He barely left before you walked in. You might even have run into him on the way in."

"No, I didn't see anyone. But I was concentrating on making sure I had the right place. I hope your friend didn't help you with this," Harmon said as he wrapped his fist around Roger's slowly shrinking cock. "I get jealous easily."

"Awww, you don't have anything to worry about, babe. He's straight, but I think he was kinda getting into it while he tied me up and blindfolded me. But this is all yours, if you want it," Roger said as he flexed his cock in Harmon's hand.

"Oh, I definitely want it."

"Good. Now can you untie me so I can kiss you properly?"

Harmon carefully untied Roger, and pulled him in close for a kiss. Then he lay down on the bed, and pulled him into a spooning position. He hugged Roger tightly from behind, and kissed him tenderly on the neck and ears.

"I'm starving," Roger said as he pressed his naked ass against Harmon's soft cock. "You ready to grab a bite to eat?"

"If we must. But I could easily just fall asleep with you here in my arms."

"That's sweet, but I have got to eat something. How about we go grab a burger and shake, and then we can come back here and go at round two."

"Oh, all right," Harmon sighed dramatically. "But this time I wanna be tied up and fuck you."

"Oh yeah," Roger said as he jumped out of bed. "That's what I'm talkin' about!"

III.

"You're an idiot," Heather said as she sprinkled more cinnamon on her white chocolate mocha and sat down next to Roger. "You do realize that, don't you? A pure, unadulterated idiot."

"Way to be supportive," Roger said, and stirred his hot chai.

"Hey, I am not here to support your psychosis," she said as she kicked off her flip-flops and set her feet in his lap.

"What kind of fag hag are you?" Roger asked, and massaged her toes. "That's exactly your job description."

"Well, it's a good thing I do this work on a volunteer basis, because I'm exercising my right to change the job description."

"You're no fun," he said, and pushed her feet back onto the floor. "Just my luck to get the one radical hag who goes all mutiny on my ass. You're supposed to worship the ground I walk on, and do everything, absolutely everything, that I tell you."

"Well, I will never worship the ground you walk on, let alone do everything you tell me to do. You drew the short fag hag straw on that one. But I do love you, Roger, and I care about you. I want you to be happy, and it pisses me off to see you hijack your own happiness."

"I am not hijacking my own happiness, Heather. You're so

melodramatic. I invited him over, didn't I? I met him in person and we . . . made love."

"No, you didn't. You had Zach tie you up and blindfold you, and then you had meaningless, emotionless sex with the hunky prison guard."

"Yeah, but after that, we made meaningful, emotion-filled love. And that was only the first time. We've gotten together four times now."

"Mmm-hmm," Heather said, and blew on her mocha before taking a big sip. "Which you felt completely uncomfortable with, and hurried him out the door afterward. You were much more at ease with the blind anonymous bondage fuck. I can tell just by the tone in your voice, and the look in your eyes. You're a hot mess."

"I am not. I'm just cautious. You know how many guys I let in, and then they just used me. All they ever want is my money. And not even my money, but my family's."

"But Harmon is not them. He's different."

"They all seemed different, Heather," Roger sighed. "None of them walked into my life with a sign on his forehead saying, 'I'm only here to fuck you so that I can weasel my way into your family and take all their money.' They all seemed nice and sweet and really into me. Do I need to remind you of Travis?"

"No," Heather said, and turned her attention to the traffic outside the coffee shop window. Her best friend had been beaten nearly unrecognizable when he'd stood up for himself and denied his boyfriend what was being demanded of him, and insisted on being respected. He'd spent four days in the hospital after the encounter. "But not everyone is a Travis."

"What about Daniel, who stole my credit cards and charged almost five thousand dollars' worth of electronics?"

Heather sighed.

"Or Rudy, who stole and then wrecked my 'Vette?"

"Okay, you have a point," she said, and reached over to hold his hand. "But honey, you can't shut yourself off to the world because of a few bad apples. From what you've told me, Harmon seems really different. He's been into you for a couple of months, even before he met you. He had no idea that your family owns half of California or that you're gonna be the first openly gay president of the United States. He only knew that you were cute and adorably funny and smart as hell. And he liked it."

"And I really like him, too," Roger said slowly, and barely audibly.

"I know you do. Or at least I know you could, if you'd let yourself go and just do it."

"I just don't want to be hurt again."

"I know you don't, Boo. But you're never going to love if you don't open yourself up to being hurt. That's just the way it works."

"Well, it sucks."

"Life sucks, babe. But remember, no one can hurt you unless you give them permission to do so."

"You're such the philosopher."

"Bite me. You know it's true. And you're hurting yourself more than anyone else is."

"What do you mean?"

Heather fidgeted with her almost empty coffee cup.

"Oh, God. Don't start with that again."

"Well, it's true. You're still carrying that torch for Corey, and until you blow that one out, no one else will ever be enough. You'll keep attracting the undesirable bums who are only interested in your money, and you'll keep putting up a wall to block out the good guys who really do wanna know you and love you for who you are. It's just the little game you've devised to keep holding out for the one guy you can't have, and shouldn't have. Not for a lover, anyway."

"I hate you," Roger sulked.

"Of course you do. That's your job description." Heather laughed, and looked up at the TV in the corner of the room. "Oh my God, Roger."

Roger looked up at the TV.

"We apologize for interrupting your regular broadcast," the news reporter stated, "but we have some breaking news tha: we feel is important for public safety."

Roger's eyes were glued to the view of San Quentin in the background behind the male reporter. His heart pounded hard, and he found it difficult to swallow.

"A little over an hour ago, a large riot broke out in San Quentin prison. For well over a year now, the gymnasium has been converted into a large cell not dissimilar to a stockyard overfilled with cattle. Racial tensions have been riding high from the very beginning, and experts have stated vehemently that the system was at risk of a catastrophe if the oldest prison in California did not remedy the situation. Well, they didn't, and now the predicted worst case scenario has happened. Over five hundred men in the gymnasium cell are in the middle of a massive violent riot as we speak. We have confirmed at least two prisoners dead, but are quite sure that that number will be much higher when all is said and done. Three guards are being held hostage, and their fate is unknown. And we have just learned that two death row inmates have escaped. Rumors are rampant that the riot was started as a distraction for the escape. The two escapees are considered extremely dangerous, and the public should be very cautious until they have been captured."

"Oh, God," Roger squeaked. "Three guards."

"Is Harmon working today?" Heather asked.

"Yes. Oh, God." He jumped up and ran out the door, and Heather ran after him.

*　*　*

For the past fifteen minutes, the violence had tapered off and the gymnasium was relatively quiet. But Harmon knew that was just temporary. He'd never been in a riot situation this large before, but he'd attended enough trainings and had learned enough about their dynamics to know that each side was just taking a breather and working up a strategy. They were in the eye of the storm.

The rectangular gym was fairly evenly split into three sections, and barricaded by overturned bunks. The Latino population took up a narrow strip that ran the length of one full wall. The White and Black inmates split the remainder of the room in two, and all three areas were clearly defined by a wide empty corridor separated by the metal beds now lying on their sides.

"You don't want to do this, man," Harmon said to Larry Williams, the inmate who'd handcuffed his hands and shackled his feet, and who thrust a homemade knife to his throat every few minutes to show that he was in charge, at least of the White section of the gym, and that he meant business.

"Shut the fuck up, bitch," Williams said, and spit into Harmon's face. "They told me you were pretty fuckin' smart, but you're sure not acting like it right now. You're actin' stupid, and if you know what is good for you, you'll shut that pig mouth of yours. *Capiche?*"

"I just don't want you to get into any more trouble than you . . ."

Williams swung around and pressed the filed-down toothbrush against Harmon's jugular vein. "Go on, man," he said through gritted teeth. "Give me a reason to shove this through that fat neck of yours. Not like I need one right now, but go ahead and give me one if you want."

Harmon closed his eyes and turned his neck a little, but didn't say anything.

"Good boy," Williams said, and walked away to continue talking with his small group of conspirators, who were pointing at a larger group of Latino inmates on the other side of the room.

Harmon looked across the room and saw Adam Pollard. His face was frozen and expressionless, a talent that didn't take long at all for new prisoners to master. Harmon thought he would make an excellent poker player, but he also knew that for Adam this expressionless demeanor was not a game. For him it was a matter of survival.

Adam caught Harmon's eyes, and slowly shook his head no, and then looked away. He moved out of Harmon's line of sight.

Any other day, and under normal circumstances, neither of them would be in the gymnasium at that time. Adam was not housed in the overcrowded gym, but in one of the cells on the main floor. In fact, the entire nine months he'd been at the famous prison, he'd never once been inside the gym. He'd heard enough about it, and had never really had a desire to see it for himself.

And Harmon wasn't one of the guards assigned to the gym. He had enough seniority to be given the easier task of watching over the relatively quiet Badger Unit. Though home to some of the prison's more violent inmates, most of them had been incarcerated long enough to settle into a sense of calm and compliance. He was big enough and built up enough rapport with his prisoners that he very seldom ever had a problem with anyone. Others had complained about some "troublemakers," but Harmon often wondered if it wasn't just the guards bitching, because he'd never really dealt with any of it, not even in his earliest days on the Q.

But the day had started out good, and only gotten better. Adam had been informed that he received several extra points for good behavior and helping out some of the counselors with several computer problems they'd been experiencing for several months. As a reward, he'd been granted two hours of extra recreation time of his choice, and he naturally chose to spend the time in the computer lab. Rather than walk around the maze of hallways that they usually took on their midnight jaunts, Harmon had chosen to cut through the gymnasium, and cut their travel time in half.

Halfway across the crowded floor, however, a loud exploding sound reverberated through the gymnasium, and a second later the hall was filled with screaming voices, and beds and personal items started flying. The two regularly assigned guards were grabbed immediately, and seven or eight big men jumped Harmon just as he was reaching for his gun. They disarmed him and had him cuffed and shackled in less than a minute.

The inmates immediately segregated into their separate race blocks in just a couple of minutes. It was obvious that this little uprising was not happening spontaneously, but had been carefully planned out. Harmon and the other White guard were forced to the floor in the middle of the White section of the gym, and the Black guard received the same treatment in the Black section. The first half hour of the riot was pure violent hell. Fists and beds and anything else not tied down flew in every direction. Blood was everywhere, and Harmon saw a couple of guys being dragged lifelessly over to a corner.

That had been a couple of hours ago, and since then he'd seen several more people killed, a couple of fires started near the doors, and heard the sirens go off in other sections of the prison a couple of times. He knew the whole place was in lockdown, and wasn't surprised when he saw through the windows a battalion of SWAT officers snake their way around the gymnasium. It was surrounded now, and he knew there was no way anything good could come out of this. He figured they had possibly another half hour at the most before the SWAT team crashed through the doors and windows and overpowered the hostile prisoners.

Harmon wondered if he would make it out alive. There was no doubt that the ringleaders of each of the three gangs would be killed. They wouldn't allow themselves to get out of here only to be punished more, and they all prided themselves on their sense of martyrdom. The only question was how many others would perish with them.

He caught Adam's eyes again, and saw them sparkle, and then his favorite prisoner put his finger to his mouth and winked. When Adam walked over to the prisoner who'd just threatened him, and whispered into his ear, Harmon couldn't help but wonder if he'd misjudged the attempted assassin.

Adam Pollard walked over to Harmon and kicked him in the side and grabbed him by the arm.

"Get the fuck up and do what I tell you, fucking pig," Adam said roughly. He leaned in close to Harmon's ear. "Sorry about the kick," he whispered. "Just play along and say as little as possible. This will be over soon. The cavalry is here. But I need to get you away from them." He nodded at the three leaders of the gangs, who were now standing chin to chin in the middle of the room, pushing and yelling at one another again.

He dragged Harmon to the back of the room, and when he was sure no one else was looking, he shoved him behind three bunk beds that had been overturned and provided a decent barrier against the violence.

"Stay here and don't move," he said. "Don't make a sound, and if someone sees you, pretend you're dead."

"But Adam . . ."

"Shut up, asshole," he yelled loud enough for the others to hear. Then he whispered, "Just do what I say, and if you believe in God, then you might wanna pray, too."

Adam jumped up and ran into the crowd, where he was lost.

Harmon closed his eyes, and tried to breathe normally. Less than five minutes later, three loud explosions rocked the gymnasium. Screams bounced from the four walls, and several gunshots rang loud through the room. Ten minutes later it was all over. All the prisoners were lying face down on the ground, more than fifty SWAT officers had their guns aimed right at the heads of exactly the right key players in the riot, and prison officials were hurriedly handcuffing and carting away the prisoners five at a time.

"Are you all right, sir?" one of the SWAT cops asked as he flung the bunk beds aside and helped Harmon to his feet.

"Yeah, I'm fine," Harmon said as he shook his hands to get the circulation going again once the cuffs were released. "Where's Pollard?"

"Who?"

"Adam Pollard. He's a prisoner."

"I don't know, sir."

"Adam!" Harmon yelled, and pushed past the SWAT guy as he staggered through the gym, looking for his friend.

"Over here," Adam yelled back. He was being handcuffed and lifted roughly to his feet by another guard over by the door.

"You all right?" Harmon asked as he approached him.

"Bernacke, you can't talk to this prisoner," the guard said sternly. "He's going to solitary, and you've got to go see the warden for detox."

"Shut the fuck up, Holmes. I'll take him from here."

"You can't do that."

"Watch me." He removed the cuffs from Adam's wrists and handed them back to the guard. "Come on, Pollard."

They stepped over a few prisoners still on the ground and walked out of the gymnasium. They walked in silence as they turned right and then left, and wound their way through the maze of halls.

"Thank you," Harmon said with a crack in his voice as he opened the door and waved Adam into the computer lab.

"You're welcome," Adam said, and reached down and squeezed Harmon's hand, and then walked into the room.

IV.

Roger wrapped his leg around Harmon's and pressed his naked body as closely into the big guard's as possible. He couldn't stop smelling Harmon's neck or caressing his arms and back, or kissing his mouth. And it took every ounce of energy in his body to keep the tears behind his eyes there, and not falling down his cheeks.

"It's okay," Harmon said. He kissed Roger's nose, and hugged him tightly. "*I'm* okay. I promise."

"I just can't believe how lost I felt when I was watching the news and knew that you were stuck inside there," Roger said, and wiped his nose with the back of his hand. "I couldn't stop thinking about what I'd do if you died, or just how much I'd lose."

"But I didn't die, and you didn't lose anything."

"I know," Roger said as he hugged Harmon tighter.

"But I have to say I'm a little surprised by your reaction."

"Why?"

"Well, I didn't think you were really that into me. Honestly, whenever we have sex, it doesn't seem like your heart and soul is into it. I mean, don't get me wrong, the physical part of it is always amazing. But I never really felt like you were emotionally into it.

So this," he said as he wiped a tear from Roger's eye, "is a little shocking."

"Oh, God, I'm so sorry," Roger said, and kissed Harmon several times on the lips. "I wasn't being fair with you. I always had this wall up around me because I was afraid."

"Afraid of what?"

"Of you. Of me. I don't know, really."

"You're afraid of being loved, aren't you?"

Roger tried to hold his reaction in, but the audible gasp couldn't be denied, and neither could the tightening of his entire body against Harmon's.

"It's okay, you know," Harmon said. "There's nothing to be afraid of. I knew the very first time I met you that I loved you. I know that sounds a little ridiculous, but it's true."

"Harmon, what am I supposed to do with that?"

"You don't have to do anything with it," Harmon said. "It's not yours to do something with. It's mine. You only have to be yourself, and allow me to be me. If you ever decide that you love me in return, that will be wonderful. But if you don't, that's okay, too. My love is mine to give, it's not yours, nor is it your responsibility. Your only decision is what to do with it. And I have confidence in you that you'll do the right thing."

Roger smiled, and kissed Harmon on the nose and then on the lips. "Make love to me, baby."

Harmon turned Roger over so that he was lying on his right side, and hugged him tightly as he kissed his neck and back. His cock was already hard and it slipped between Roger's ass cheeks with a comfortable familiarity. He slowly slid his fat cock up and down the length of the crack, relishing the way the friction warmed his shaft.

Roger turned his head back so that he could kiss Harmon on the lips, and at the same time he raised his left leg, exposing his hole.

Harmon broke the kiss, and turned Roger around so that he lay on his stomach. He moved down his lover's back, kissing every inch as he moved closer and closer to the smooth mounds below him. As he slid between Roger's long legs he spread the creamy white globes, and kissed his way between them.

He licked around the puckered hole, flicking his tongue so that it barely made contact with the pink skin. He knew it drove Roger crazy, and smiled to himself as he heard him moan lustfully and wiggle his ass around frantically. Harmon grabbed both cheeks in his hands and spread them even farther, and then slid just the very tip of his tongue inside.

"Oh, fuck me," Roger squealed, and raised his ass higher off the bed, trying to get more of Harmon's tongue inside him.

Harmon pulled back, denying Roger the full impact of his tongue, and reached beneath his lover to squeeze and pull on his cock. It was fully hard and throbbed hot in his hands, and he thought he'd never felt anything so hot and exciting.

When Roger whimpered pathetically, Harmon slid the full length of his tongue deep inside his hot hole. He knew there were few things that Roger enjoyed more than being eaten out, and he'd been told on more than one occasion that few guys could eat an ass better than him. He slid his tongue deep inside the tight hole several times, and then pulled it out completely and licked and flicked around the sphincter for a few seconds.

"Oh my God, babe," Roger said breathlessly. "I need you inside me so bad. Please fuck me."

Harmon got onto his knees and spread Roger's legs farther apart. In this position, Roger's hole was completely exposed, and Harmon thought it was possibly the most beautiful sight he'd ever seen. It was pink and smooth and puckered, and it twitched with a fevered anticipation. Harmon's fat cock bounced in front of him and dripped a large gob of precum just from looking at it.

He spread the precum around the hole with his cock head, and then slipped just the head inside.

"Don't tease me, baby," Roger moaned, and wriggled his ass around Harmon's cock head. "Give it all to me. Now."

258 / *Sean Wolfe*

Harmon leaned forward and slid his entire cock deep inside Roger's ass.

"Oh, fuck, man," Harmon grunted. "You feel so amazing, Roger. I'm not gonna be able to hold out very long at all like this."

"No, please, babe. Make it last. I want you to fuck me forever."

"I'll try."

Harmon stopped sliding in and out of Roger's ass, and counted slowly to ten. He thought of George Burns and Bea Arthur and Carrot Top . . . anything that would help him slow down the inevitable. But Roger wasn't making it easy. His ass gripped Harmon's thick cock and squeezed and milked it with a pressure that he didn't think possible. It wrapped around his shaft and pulled it deeper and deeper inside, where it was hot and moist and tight.

He pulled all the way out. It was the only way he could keep from shooting his load all over or all inside Roger.

"No, please," Roger moaned, and thrust under him on the bed.

Harmon slid between Roger's legs again, and dove back in with his mouth. He slid his tongue in and out of the hole slowly at first, and then with quickening strokes. He didn't dare touch his own cock, and tried hard to keep it from rubbing against the blankets as he tongue-fucked Roger's hungry hole. After a couple of minutes, he thought he could slide his cock back inside without risk of immediate ejaculation.

"You ready for my cock again, baby?" he asked.

"Oh, God, yes!"

He moved over to the head of the bed and hugged Roger lovingly. He pulled him close, so that he was spooning him, and kissed him tenderly on the neck and shoulders. "I love you," he mouthed behind Roger's head, so that he couldn't see it.

Roger lifted his left leg again, exposing his hole, and this time Harmon slipped his cock deep inside in one move. He kept his cock there, without moving, for a couple of minutes, and then began slowly sliding in and out. Roger's ass started doing that thing it did again, and Harmon wrapped his arms around his lover's chest and held him tighter as he picked up the speed and fucked him more intensely.

Roger wiggled around a bit until he was lying on his back and Harmon was sliding in and out from on top of him. He reached up with both hands and caressed Harmon's face, and then pulled him down for a kiss on the lips.

The feel of Roger's ass sucking his cock deep inside him, and the taste of Roger's tongue slipping in and out of his mouth and then sucking on his tongue was all Harmon could take. His heart raced painfully in his chest and he struggled to breathe normally. He could feel the orgasm building deep inside his balls, and knew that it was all going to be over in just a few seconds. He looked down into Roger's eyes, and saw that they were staring back into his own. And they were filled with tears threatening to spill over.

"I love you," Roger said softly, and pulled him down for another deep kiss.

"Ungh," Harmon grunted loudly.

He tried to end the kiss and pull out of Roger's ass, but Roger wasn't having either. He held on to the back of Harmon's head, forcing him to continue the passionate and frenzied kiss. And he wrapped his legs tighter around Harmon's waist, keeping him lodged deep inside him.

Harmon whimpered as his entire body shuddered and he emptied himself inside Roger's clutching ass. There were several strong shots that felt like he was shooting a cannon off inside his lover. With each contraction and release, his body shook more violently, and it felt as if his soul was being drained with each spurt.

Roger moaned as he shot off his own load. The first couple of sprays landed across Harmon's stomach, and the rest fell on Roger's own torso. He hadn't touched his own cock—he was still holding Harmon's face in his hands. But that didn't stop him from shooting off an extremely large load.

He finally broke the kiss, and Harmon rolled off and out of him, and onto the bed next to him.

"Oh my God," Harmon said as he caught his breath. "That was amazing."

"It sure as hell was," Roger said.

Harmon lay on the bed with his eyes closed for a few moments, waiting for his breathing to return to normal. He didn't say anything, and kept his eyes closed.

"You're wondering if I realize what I said, aren't you? Or if I meant it or just blurted it out in the throes of passion."

"Well . . ."

"I do realize, and I definitely mean it. I love you, Harmon. It's scary as hell, and I have no idea if I will do it right. But I do love you."

"You can't do it wrong, baby. And I love you, too."

INCH SEVEN

Big as Hell

I.

Brian Emerson looked around him and tried very hard not to look intimidated or starstruck. The moonlight shining through the skylight cast a soft white hue across the table, and the candlelight glow from his table and those around him added an aura of magic to the ambiance. Two tables to his left, Meryl Streep laughed comfortably with Steven Spielberg and patted the waiter's hand familiarly as he refilled her wineglass. Just to his right, Jack Nicholson entertained three giggling and blushing young women in miniskirts and stilettos.

He wasn't completely out of his element here. His family frequently stayed at the Beverly Wilshire hotel when they traveled to Los Angeles, and the staff welcomed them all by their first names. He'd eaten at Wolfgang Puck's famous steakhouse, Cut, a few times. But it had always been with his family, and as much as Brian prided himself on his independence and accomplishments, whenever he was with his parents he always felt like Barry Emerson's Oldest Son Brian.

But tonight was his night. His father was eight hours north in San Francisco, and had no idea that he was here. Sitting across the table from him was Warren Masterson, founder and CEO of

Masterson Builders, the third largest construction company in the country. Under other circumstances that might have been as intimidating as sitting across from his father. The CEO was tall and stout and strong, with a stalwart face that bore more than a passing resemblance to Winston Churchill. Most people were afraid of Warren Masterson, and that was not by accident or coincidence. But Brian had never been intimidated by the big man, and the two struck up a quick rapport.

Brian was at Cut on his own merits that night. Though Daddy's money had paid his way to Harvard Law School, it was Brian who'd put in the work and graduated Cumma Sum Laude, and it was he who'd gotten himself hired as the Assistant Lead Counsel for Masterson Builders right out of college. Now, a little less than two years later, he was having a private dinner with the CEO, and that could only mean that he was about to be promoted.

He wasn't really a steak kinda guy, and would have much preferred going out for sushi or even seafood. But he knew Masterson, and all of the other big wigs at the company, and 90 percent of the high-power people who ran 95 percent of big and successful companies came here to eat big, rich, and comically expensive hunks of bovine muscle. And so ordered the rib-eye steak cooked medium rare with creamy horseradish sauce, and polenta with caramelized sweet corn and sautéed chanterelle mushrooms for his sides. Masterson ordered a Maine Lobster "Louis" Cocktail with Spicy Tomato-Horseradish for an appetizer, the 32 oz. Porterhouse steak, which was meant to be shared among two people, and tempura onion rings and buttered Romano beans on the side.

"We all know I'm not one to beat around the bush or mince words, Emerson," Masterson said as he scooped the last of the lobster from his cocktail dish. "So, you probably know why I invited you here to dinner."

"Well, I'd like to think I do," Brian said as he gnawed on his rib eye slowly and tried to keep focused. "But I've been wrong about things like this before, and I really don't wanna be seen crying like a little girl who just lost her favorite Barbie doll in front of Winston Churchill and Meryl Streep."

Masterson laughed so hard a chunk of lobster flew from his mouth and landed on Brian's tie. "That's hilarious, Emerson. You're such a fag." He guffawed and swallowed the mouthful of lobster cocktail with a large and graceless gulp of Bordeaux Pauillac Merlot.

Brian giggled nervously, and diverted his eyes from Masterson's. That statement could easily cost the big man a serious portion of his wealth. But only if someone would ever actually have the balls to contest his arrogance and follow through with a lawsuit against him. Masterson knew, as did Brian and everyone else who worked for him, that no one would ever stand up and hold him accountable for the bigoted statement. It was one he used often, and without the slightest thought to the truth or possible truth of it. It was not intended as either a compliment or a cruel put-down, Brian knew, but simply the truth. Or at least Masterson's idea of truth.

"I'm hoping the words 'Sanchez Development Group' and 'Colombian government' are going to have something to do with the reason I'm sitting here enjoying my mortgage's worth of fine steak and wine tonight."

Masterson chuckled, and wiped his mouth as their steaks and sides were delivered to the table.

"They do, indeed. I don't have to tell you that this deal is very big. The biggest our firm has seen in at least ten years. It could be our biggest deal ever, in the hands of the right person."

"And you think that person is me?" Brain asked.

"I do."

"But what about Miller? He's Lead Counsel for the firm. I'm just his assistant."

"Miller is an idiot. He'd have the deal blown even before his plane lands in Bogotá."

"Then why is he your Lead Counsel?"

"Because he's my asshole son-in-law. I felt obligated. I just can't say no to my baby girl. Never have been able to."

"But . . ."

"Karen has been staying at home . . . my home . . . the past four nights. She and Paul have been having troubles lately. Serious troubles. She's filing for divorce next week."

"And you need a reason to fire him."

"I can't fire him for not making his marriage to my daughter work, Emerson. But I can promote you to Lead Counsel and demote him to Assistant. He won't stay a week under those conditions. You've got an outstanding record, Emerson, but I need you to really pull this deal off in Bogotá. You'll be a rockstar, you'll make the company half a billion dollars, and there will be no doubt that you should be Lead Counsel at Masterson Builders. Paul will leave in shame on his own volition."

"I'm honored, Mr. Masterson."

"Call me Warren. And you should be honored. This is a big responsibility for someone just out of college for two years. I'm putting a lot of faith and trust in you, Emerson."

"You won't be disappointed, sir."

"Good. I hate being disappointed. I'm not doing you a favor, son. I believe in you. I trust you with my company. Don't make me regret it."

"No, sir."

"Excellent! Are you going to eat that steak, or just push it around your plate like a pansy?"

Brian took a deep breath. "I don't really eat red meat, Warren. A little chicken or turkey every now and then, but mostly fish and vegetables. I used to eat meat, just not in a couple of years."

Warren Masterson burst into laughter, and pushed Brian's plate closer to him.

"You crack me up, son," he spat out between laughs and a couple of gulps of wine. "You're such a fucking fag."

II.

There were seven high-level executives on board Masterson Builders' private jet. Brian had only met two of them before today. The others had flown in from satellite branches across the country. Everyone sat alone, as far from the other team members as possible, and kept their earphones on and their laptops humming.

The Bombardier Global Express XRS jet cost more than $50 million, and was customized to Masterson's very precise specifications. Italian leather seats and upholstery; mahogany wood trim seats, bookcases and liquor bar; a galley more fully stocked than Brian's own kitchen, and a full bedroom in the back made it the epitome of luxury—a palace in the sky. Masterson often rented it out to superstar actors, musicians, and politicians.

Brian took a sip of his Scotch and leaned back in the leather recliner. He pulled up the shade on the window and looked out at the expansive space in front of him. The infiniteness of it always held him in awe, and he loved looking down at the white, puffy clouds. Though he knew it was ridiculous, they always looked as if they'd cushion a fall even from 35,000 feet and float him slowly down to the safety of the ground below.

The past three days had been mostly a blur. There was so much that he had to be briefed and prepped on, and both he and Masterson knew there was no way he could be up to speed in just three days. And that didn't even take into account his need to polish up on his Spanish skills. There was so much for him to think about and memorize and strategize.

As much as he had to think about, though, he couldn't get the "faggot" comments Masterson had made out of his mind. He wasn't a faggot, of that he was sure. But he had a lot of gay friends, and always felt uncomfortable around people when they made bigoted jokes or remarks about gay people. He always made a point of telling them it wasn't funny, and in fact rude and ignorant. But Masterson wasn't just anybody, and hadn't said anything that night, and it pissed him off.

Brian's little brother Roger was gay, and was one of the best people he knew in the world. And though he was certain of his own heterosexuality, he had experimented with a couple of other guys back in college, and he knew that gay people were not the hideous monsters or perverted sissies that his straight friends laughed and joked about.

His first experience with another man was during his junior year in college. He'd been walking back to his apartment after a basketball game, and had had way too much beer. His head spun, and though he wasn't exactly stumbling down the street, he wouldn't have been able to walk a straight line if asked to do so by the cops. He had to pee something fierce, and ducked into a dark alley to relieve his bladder. Halfway through, he was joined by another guy. He couldn't really see what the new guy looked like; it was way too dark. All he could make out was that he had dark hair and features, and was about Brian's height and weight. But he could see that his new friend had finished pissing and was stroking his cock as he watched Brian finish. When Brian finished shaking his cock and began to stuff it back into his jeans, the new guy reached over and squeezed it, and a second later was on his knees in front of him.

The dude was the best cocksucker Brian had ever felt, and in ust a couple of minutes, was swallowing his big load. When he was finished, the guy stood up, stuffed himself back into his pants, and took off running down the alley. Brain never knew who the man was, and never saw him again, at least that he knew of.

The only other time he'd ever messed around with a guy was even worse. He'd accompanied one of his best friends to a gay bar, and after an hour, his friend picked up a trick for the night, and left with him, leaving Brian alone at the bar. He'd just ordered a drink, and decided to stay and finish it. The guy sitting a couple seats away from him at the bar had been watching him all night. He was a few years older than Brian, maybe early thirties, with rugged good looks—a five o'clock shadow, a few tufts of chest hair peeking through the top of his shirt, and a backward baseball cap that made him seem younger than he probably was, and full of energy.

Though Brian never really thought about being attracted to another guy, he found himself sneaking glances over at the man, and smiling back when he smiled at Brian. The guy scooted over to the seat next to him, and laid his hand on Brian's knee.

"What's up, man?" the guy asked as he smiled and looked directly into Brian's eyes.

"Not too much," Brian said nervously. "You?"

"I was just about to leave. Wanna join me?"

"Where to?"

"My place. I live three blocks from here."

Brain smiled as he looked the man right in the eyes, and had every intention of saying thanks but no thanks.

"Absolutely," he said, and immediately felt his eyes bulge as his heart pounded in his chest.

"Sweet," the guy said, and took Brian's hand and led him out the door.

Back at the man's apartment, he was all business, with a definite focus. Without saying a word, he led Brian to the bedroom, quickly undressed him, and pushed him onto the bed. He ripped his own clothes off and slid between Brian's legs, and sucked his already hard cock with a desperation that Brian had never seen.

Brian's legs began to quiver as he felt his orgasm building immediately below his belly button. He was just starting to see fireworks when the man pulled his mouth from Brian's cock, and everything began to go bad.

"I want you to fuck me," the guy said.

"What?" Brian stuttered, still trying to catch his breath.

"Fuck me, man. Shove that big dick deep inside my ass," the man said as he crawled up the bed and began to position his naked ass right above Brian's cock.

"No, man," Brian said. "I'm not gay. Just suck me off, dude. I'm already close."

"Fuck that shit," the guy said, and slid his ass across Brian's hard cock head. "You need to fuck me and fuck me hard." He slid down another inch, so that just the head of Brian's cock slipped inside his ass.

"I said no," Brian yelled, and pushed the guy off of him and onto the floor.

"What the hell, man?"

"I told you that I am not gay," Brian said, and stood up to gather his clothes.

"You're a fucking cock tease," the man said as he pulled himself off the floor.

"Like hell I am," Brian said. "You came on to *me,* dude. I didn't say a word or do anything to make you think I was a fag."

The man laughed. "Except 'absolutely' when I asked you to come home with me."

"That doesn't mean I'm a faggot or that I am going to fuck you."

"You closeted queens are the absolute worst. You want cock and ass so bad you can almost taste it, but when you have it right in front of you, you can't deal with it."

"Fuck you," Brian said, and stormed out the door.

* * *

The jet landed smoothly and silently at El Dorado International Airport in Bogotá, and Brian couldn't get off the plane soon enough. It wasn't that the ride was uncomfortable. There was plenty of head and leg room, and he could walk around all he wanted, and even sleep in a real bed if he wanted to. As far as plane rides went, it was as comfortable as he could ever hope for. And it wasn't that he was claustrophobic or afraid of crashing to the ground. The truth was, he simply didn't like to fly.

The twenty-minute drive from the airport to his hotel seemed to take an hour. He'd traveled a little while in college, and he'd even visited a few "underdeveloped" countries, so he shouldn't have been taken aback by the overcrowded, poverty-stricken streets. But he'd always traveled with the highest level of luxury, and only went to the most posh and comfortable areas of those countries that catered to filthy rich Americans and Europeans. And so he was overwhelmed with the sight of rusted old busses filled to overcapacity with people hanging out the doors and spewing black smoke into the air as they sped through crowded streets; the low-hanging gray clouds that looked more like fog but released torrents of cool rain, and all of the insects that swarmed the entire city, but seemed to have a particular affinity for him.

"Aqui estamos," the chauffeur said.

Brian sighed loudly. "English, please."

"Here we are."

Brian saw the driver roll his eyes, but ignored him. He knew the man understood English pretty well, and spoke it enough to get by, and he'd asked him to speak English while working for Brian and his group. He hated the arrogance of the driver to refuse to speak English when specifically directed to do so. He supposed it was possible that the driver didn't understand his instructions, but he doubted it. The car company had assured him that the driver spoke perfect English, and so he had to have a decent education. He was just being stubborn, and it pissed Brian off.

"You can open my door now," he said tensely, and waited for the chauffeur to walk around and do just that.

Even though designated as such, 101 Park House Suites was not the five-star accommodations he was expecting. He'd been assured by Masterson that it was one of the best and most comfortable hotels in Colombia, and so he had a fairly specific image in his mind. That image included a high-rise building with enormous balconies, maybe overlooking a romantic river. It included lavish marble floors and oversized crystal chandeliers and sunken hot tubs in his suite and staff who attended to his every need.

Instead, 101 was a low-rise stucco building that resembled some of the low-income housing projects back home in San Francisco. Some of the units had a balcony, but they were barely large enough to hold a couple of plastic patio chairs, and nothing else. He didn't feel completely safe in the neighborhood at dark, and rushed to get inside as quickly as possible.

The interior of the hotel was clean, and he could tell that they'd at least made a respectable attempt at opulence. The floors weren't marble, but the imitation was not bad. The chandeliers weren't oversized or crystal, but at least they weren't bare bulbs hanging from loose wires from the ceiling.

Masterson had set him up in the Imperial Suite, for which he was thankful. It was a two-story, two-bed and bath suite with a full kitchen, and was impeccably furnished. A fireplace separated the master bedroom and a decent-sized den in the upstairs area, and the balcony covered both the bedroom and the lounge area. The master bath did have a sunken tub with hydrojets, to his surprise, and he knew he'd be utilizing that quite a bit.

After unpacking, Brian checked in with the other team members, making sure they were satisfied with their rooms, and made an appointment for the entire team to meet at seven in the morning to put together a plan. Just because they were thousands of miles from home did not mean that they could slack off on a Friday, and as much as he was sure they would bitch and moan about it, he also planned on having the team work their way around the big city, assessing it and getting a feel for the long and hard work ahead of them over the next couple of months. Their work of planning and developing the massive project was paramount in its success and he wanted the groundwork to be impeccable for the construction crew when they arrived to start building their team from local workers.

Back in his room, he poured himself a glass of wine, stripped his clothes off, lit a few candles, and climbed into the hot tub. The soft music wafting in from the bedroom, the warm bubbly water, and the sweet wine were exactly what his tired body needed after an extremely long flight, and before too long he was relaxed and felt himself give in to the fatigue. He knew he'd sleep well that night.

He hadn't noticed the phone on the wall only inches from his head, and when it rang, he jumped, and dropped his glass of wine into the tub.

"Fuck!" he yelled, and fished the glass out of the water and then picked up the phone. "Hello?" he yelled angrily into the receiver.

"Mr. Emerson?"

He thought it had to have been Masterson, and that's the only reason he'd even picked up the phone to begin with. No one else knew where he was yet. So when he heard the deep voice with the thick accent, he was more than a little perturbed.

"What the hell are you doing calling me right now?" he said. "I've barely been checked in for an hour. What did I do, forget to dot an 'i' or cross a 't' on the credit card authorization? I was assured you provided the highest level of customer service, but I have to say that I'm not impressed so far."

"Mr. Emerson, this is Manuel Sanchez. We have a meeting at ten o'clock Monday morning at my office. I called to make sure you arrived safely and had gotten settled in okay. But it sounds as if you're not completely satisfied with your accommodations."

"No, it's fine," Brian said, and sat up in the tub. "I'm sorry, Mr. Sanchez. I'm just tired and a little irritable. It was a long flight."

"I'm sorry to hear that," Manuel said. "I'm even more sorry to have to ask if you can possibly meet me in an hour."

"What? An hour?"

"Yes. I know it's unconventional and unplanned. But I'm afraid I must insist. I have a family emergency and must leave for Barranquilla on Saturday morning. I won't be back to Bogotá until Wednesday morning."

"But our meeting on Monday . . ."

"Yes, I know. My executive team will still meet with you and your men on Monday morning. But I will not be there. My mother has passed away, and I must accompany my younger sister to Barranquilla. There is no getting out of it. But I feel it is very important to meet with you myself. I believe you and I must be unequivocally on the same page from the very first stages of this project."

"Yes, I agree," Brian said. "But can we not meet tomorrow morning or afternoon? I've just settled in for the evening."

"No, that's not possible."

Brian waited for Manuel to elaborate. When he didn't, Brian became flustered, and stammered out, "Your English is excellent." He winced, and closed his eyes.

"Yes, some of us here in Colombia are quite well educated. And we take customer service very seriously."

Brian realized how stupid and arrogant he must have sounded earlier, when he thought the caller was from the hotel reception. "I'm sorry about that statement earlier. I'm just very tired. Are you sure we can't meet tomorrow, before you leave?"

"Quite."

He closed his eyes, and rubbed them with his thumb and forefinger. "All right, yes. Of course I can meet you."

"Excellent. I'll meet you downstairs at your hotel bar at ten-thirty."

"I look forward to it," Brian said, and hung up the phone.

III.

The bar reminded Brian of the rest of the hotel—modest and trying desperately not to look modest. The dark wood looked like authentic cherry, but was much too thin and smelled undeniably like several layers of Old English wood polish. The "leather" seats also looked cheaply constructed, and when Brian eventually sat in his booth and took in a deep breath, expecting to get an unmistakable whiff of aged animal skin, he was instead assaulted with the odor of plastic and chemicals. The dim lighting helped mask the charade, and the strong drinks helped even more. Brian supposed some guests might be fooled, and those that weren't probably wouldn't care after their second drink.

He spotted Manuel immediately. There were only four people in the bar, other than the bartender. In the middle of the bar was a middle-aged balding man in a tacky suit. He was sitting at a table with a much younger woman sitting on either side of him. The man looked greasy and when he laughed much too loudly his crooked and rotting teeth threatened to fall out of his gums and onto the table. The women were attractive enough, but wore way too much makeup, and their miniskirts exposed more upper thigh and nether region than would be socially acceptable in 127 out of

130 developed or semi-developed countries in the world. He'd never engaged the services of a prostitute before, but he knew one when he saw one. Brian knew undoubtedly that this was not Manuel Sanchez.

The only other person in the bar was sitting alone in a booth in the far corner from the door. The bar was dimly lit so that the glow from the dozens of candles could help set whatever mood each patron sought for his own purposes. From all the way across the room Brian couldn't make out what the man looked like, but as he made his way across the floor and his view of Manuel got clearer and more in focus with every step, he felt his feet get heavy and his legs begin to shake.

"You're late," Manuel said as Brian approached the booth.

Brain stared down at Manuel, and prayed that the rapidly growing hardon in his slacks was not visible. The man was more stunning than anyone he had ever seen. His skin was the color of the coffee Brian drank with four individual cuplets of half-n-half, and looked as smooth and soft as his silk sheets. His hair was black and shiny and stylishly cut with a little wave in it.

"I'm sorry," Brian said as he gazed in the sparkling and beautiful light green eyes that took his breath away and brought his quickly hardening cock to full mast. He looked at his watch. "But I'm showing that it's been exactly an hour since you called me and asked me to meet you here." He slid into the booth and waved the bartender over.

"Your watch must be slow," Manuel said as he took a sip of his martini. "My watch says it's been an hour and almost ten minutes."

Brian smiled uncomfortably, and remembered his earlier tirade about customer service. He also kept in mind that Manuel Sanchez, Jr. was the son of the wealthiest man in Colombia, and ran his father's conglomerate of over a dozen companies that provided the majority of the Colombian government's construction projects. It would behoove him to keep his mouth shut just this once, and so he bit his tongue.

"I'll have a double Chivas Regal on the rocks, please," he said to the bartender/waiter through his fake smile. "I apologize. And I promise that from now on my team and I will be early for our meetings. I know your time is valuable."

He noticed the very slight smile on Manuel's full, pink lips, and wanted desperately to lean across the table and kiss them.

"I will not pretend anything here, Mr. Emerson," Manuel said as he set his glass down and stared directly into Brian's eyes. "I am not very impressed with your work ethic up until now."

Brian hoped the plastic smile on his face was coming across as courteous, and not as pious. Other than his father, there had only been a handful of people throughout his life that had ever made him feel small or foolish. And he wanted to hate Manuel Sanchez for making him feel that way now. But that was hard to do when he couldn't stop thinking about how beautiful the man was, or stop wishing he could lick those full, pink lips, or stop his hardon from growing even harder and thicker and leaking precum all over the inside of his boxers and down the inside of his thighs.

"I highly resent the tone of voice you used when answering the phone this evening, when you assumed I was the hotel staff. It's very rude. And the pretentious remarks about the level of customer service were extremely disrespectful. We may not have all of the extravagant amenities that the finest hotels in the U.S. boast, but we work very hard to provide a comfortable stay and to make your time here as welcoming as possible, and we take much pride in our efforts."

"I'm sorry," Brian stammered. "I was just extremely tired after an exhausting flight, and I just wanted to relax. I don't know why this is bothering you so much. I wasn't attacking you personally. I was just expressing some frustration to the hotel staff. We'll be leaving a very generous tip, I can assure you."

Manuel snorted and took another drink, and waved the bartender over again. "You are only digging yourself into a deeper hole, Mr. Emerson. Actually, you were insulting me personally. My family owns the 101 Park House, along with eleven other luxury hotels in Colombia, Argentina, and Venezuela. And as I mentioned, we take much pride in our work and in our employees."

"Oh shit," Brian said as he felt his face warm with embarrassment, and he finished off his Scotch. "I'm very sorry. I did not mean to be disrespectful in any way whatsoever."

"Yes, I believe you. And that is what is most disturbing. To think that you could be that rude and inconsiderate of others without trying or intention is very disconcerting."

"Okay, look," Brian said tensely. He was never more aware of the Sanchez family's wealth and importance, or what this deal could mean to Masterson Builders or to him personally. And he also was never more turned on by another guy. His heart pounded hard in his chest, and he struggled to breathe normally. But he'd also had enough. "I've apologized, and more than once. There's nothing else I can say or do to express my contrition. You can either accept my apologies or not, it's up to you. But I'd venture a guess that there is very little that is more rude or disrespectful than to hold a grudge and not accept a man's apology. You don't strike me as someone who would or could make such a bad business decision. Either way, though, I won't sit here and be belittled or scolded. I've had a very long day and an even longer week, and I'm exhausted. Sometime we make mistakes when in that state. It's human. But my apologies are sincere and so is my desire to work with you. I hope you can be man enough to accept my apologies and to start over."

Across the table Manuel was staring directly into his eyes without blinking. Brian's heart felt as if Arnold Schwarzenegger had grabbed it with both hands and squeezed as hard as he could. The Terminator Arnold, not the governor Arnold. His throat constricted and forced him to breathe heavily through his nose. Visions of him standing in the unemployment line and begging for change on street corners flashed through his head, and he felt his face and neck begin to sweat heavily as the room closed in around him and began to spin.

Manuel grinned and raised his martini glass. "Very good," he said as he clinked his glass with Brian's.

"Excuse me?" Brian said, confused.

"I wanted to see that you had a sensitivity about you. Our culture is very different here, and an overarrogant personality will be met with resistance and inferior work from our crew members. It would not benefit either of us. I believe your apology was sincere, and I have faith that you will be more conscientious of your words and actions from here on out."

"I can assure you of that," Brian said, taking a deep breath and feeling the stranglehold on his heart loosen just a bit.

"You already have, and I appreciate that. But as important as it is to keep your arrogance under control, it's just as important not to let my men intimidate or walk all over you. They will try, I can guarantee that. It's just our nature here in Colombia, and in all of Latin America. Our men are 'macho' and feel they need to assert themselves and their superiority over you. That is why I tested you with my own arrogance and strong will. It will be a balancing act of gaining their respect and maintaining your leadership and supervision roles with remaining respectful and sensitive to our culture."

"I'm up for the challenge, Mr. Sanchez," Brian said, and then jumped so high that his knees hit the underside of the booth.

Manuel had kicked off his right shoe and planted his foot in the middle of Brian's crotch. Brian had been completely hard from the moment he approached the booth and set his eyes on Manuel, and now his hard cock was being caressed and stroked by the handsome Latino god's foot.

"I can see that," Manuel said, and increased the pressure on Brian's cock as he slid his foot up and down the length of it.

Brian felt his eyes bug out to what must have been comical proportions. He began hiccupping uncontrollably, and his entire body began to quiver.

"You look terrified," Manuel said as he leaned back in the

booth, but continued stroking Brian's cock with his foot. "Are you all right?"

"Mmm-hmm," Brian squeaked out.

"Do you want me to stop?"

"I don't think . . . I'm not sure this is . . . no."

Manuel stroked Brian's cock expertly with his foot as he signaled the bartender for another round for each of them. He alternated between sliding his foot up and down the length of the hard cock, and pressing it deeper into his crotch.

Brian felt his entire body begin to tingle as his breath became shorter, and his cock throbbed hard in his slacks. As the bartender approached their booth, Brian was horrified to realize that he was on the verge of an orgasm. He'd never cum without masturbating or having sex, nor had he cum while fully dressed, and certainly never in public. But he was, without question, about to blow his load, and he knew that even if Manuel stopped his foot massage he would not be able to stop it.

"Thank you, Carlos," Manuel said as the bartender set their drinks on the table. He pressed his foot deeper into Brian's crotch as Carlos turned and walked away.

"Oh, fuck," Brian whispered as his body shuddered and he felt his cock constrict and contract as several spurts of warm cum shot from his cock and dripped down the inside of his thighs. He closed his eyes and took a couple of deep breaths as he leaned back in the seat.

"Are you okay?" Manuel asked with a cocky smile.

"Yeah," he said softly. "But a little messy."

Manuel laughed, and pulled his foot away. The two men discussed their upcoming joint project and ironing out some of the early details. After about an hour, Manuel announced that he needed to get back home and pack for his trip.

"Don't you want to come up for a few minutes before you head out?" Brian asked with a little more desperation than he'd hoped for.

"I can't, really," Manuel said. He made sure Carlos was not watching, and then held Brian's hand and leaned over and kissed him on the lips. "If I come to your room now, I will not want to leave. And I have a very full day tomorrow and really do have to pack and get things ready for my trip on Saturday."

Brian's heart sank, and he squeezed Manuel's hand. "I understand."

But he didn't understand. He wanted Manuel to come to his room and he wanted to fuck him more than he could ever remember wanting anything in his entire life. It felt as if he'd die a long and horrible death if he didn't fuck Manuel's brains out in the next five minutes. This confused him a great deal, because he'd never had those kinds of feelings for another man before. He'd recognized his limited attraction to a few guys before, but never felt for a second that he was gay. He'd never once felt like he *needed* to fuck . . . to be intimate with . . . another man before. And now, to be denied that need was overwhelming.

"But I'll be back on Wednesday. We have a meeting together first thing in the morning, and we will of course need to be completely professional. But at the end of the day on Wednesday, instead of coming back here to your room, I wish for you to come back to my home. Are you in agreement?"

Brian smiled and felt his face blush. "Oh yes," he said. "One hundred percent in agreement."

IV.

The meeting with his own team and Manuel Sanchez' team was possibly the most difficult he'd ever been in. Manuel's words, ". . . we will of course need to be completely professional," were burned into his head and proved to be the toughest directive he'd ever been given. Manuel stood at the head of the table and led the meeting, introducing Brian and his team to the small group of the Sanchez Development Group elite management.

Brian couldn't take his eyes off of Manuel, nor could he slow down his heart rate to anything near normal. And try as he might, he couldn't make the erection in his slacks go down. When it was his turn to speak, he made sure to hold a binder on the table in front of his crotch to hide the indiscriminate evidence. Brian assumed he presented at least a modicum of professionalism throughout the meeting, because he didn't notice Manuel scowling at him at any point, and when he finished speaking, the group applauded.

But it was a struggle, and never any more so than immediately after the meeting, when Manuel excused himself and left for several other appointments. Brian didn't see him for the rest of the work day, and when he didn't hear from Manuel by seven in the evening, he resigned himself to a night alone. He was driving back to the hotel when his phone rang.

"Hello," he said as he pushed the button on his Bluetooth earpiece.

"Sorry, I had a really busy day today. A million meetings."

Just the sound of Manuel's voice sent Brian's heart racing, and caused him to gasp for breath. What the fuck was wrong with him? He didn't care.

"That's okay," he said as he focused on staying on the road. "I know you're very busy."

"Where are you?"

"About half a mile from the hotel."

"Turn around and go back toward the office. My house is about five minutes from there."

* * *

The house was on a sprawling estate, and behind a guarded security gate. Even with his own experience with wealth, the home took his breath away. The white stone structure was typical of Greek architecture, and was massive enough to be an all inclusive resort. It was illuminated with ground lights of various colors, and the quarter-mile driveway was lined on either side with large spewing water fountains.

Brian lifted and dropped the heavy iron knocker three times, and popped a breath strip into his mouth as he paced across the expansive porch.

Manuel opened the door with his hair still dripping and hanging into his face, and dressed in nothing but a pair of gray sweat shorts.

Brian gasped audibly as he took in the sight before him. Manuel's light green eyes and copper skin glimmered in the glow of the light on the porch. His chest was muscular and sculpted, smooth as the marble floors behind him. Small droplets of water clung to his tiny and perky nipples for several seconds, and then slipped down his torso and across the hairless abs that had ridges deep enough to bathe in. His legs were thick and strong, and his biceps were almost as big, with thick ropey veins running across them and disappearing into his shoulders.

"My God, you're beau . . ."

Manuel pulled Brian in to him and kissed him. His lips were strong and soft at the same time, and commanded every ounce of Brian's attention while they were attached to his own. He licked Brian's lips and then slid his warm tongue gently into his mouth.

Brian sucked on Manuel's tongue, and locked his knees to keep them from buckling beneath him.

"Vente conmigo," Manuel said as he broke the kiss and took Brian by the hand.

"Huh?"

"Come with me."

He led Brian up a long winding staircase and into the bedroom. He ripped Brian's clothes off quickly and threw them to the floor, and then tossed Brian onto the bed as he kicked off his own shorts.

"Holy fuck!" Brian said. "What the fuck is tha . . ."

Manuel lifted Brian's legs into the air and rested his knees on his chest so that his ass was exposed and in the air. He leaned down and kissed each ass cheek and then licked around the puckered hole.

"Oh my God," Brian moaned as Manuel's tongue skirted around his twitching hole and then slid slowly inside. "I've never felt anything like that before."

"Do you like?"

"Fuck yeah."

"Then shut up and enjoy it."

He returned to eating out Brian's ass, and as the moans got louder and more frantic, he slid first one finger, and then a second one inside the spit-slicked hole.

"Now it's my turn," Manuel said, as he stood up and moved toward Brian.

"I've never done that," Brian said tentatively as he squirmed beneath Manuel. "I don't think I could . . ."

"Suck my dick," Manuel said, and straddled his chest.

"Holy shit!" Brian gasped. "It's even bigger up close. I've never seen one that big. I don't think I can . . ."

"Bullshit," Manuel said, and slapped his long, thick cock across Brian's face playfully. "Stick out your tongue."

Though he wasn't a mathematician by any stretch of the imagination, he'd held his share of rulers, and he knew that the giant cock just a couple of inches in front of his face was longer than that. And as impressive as the length was, the girth was equally frightening. Brian couldn't wrap his fist around it, and was quite certain that his mouth wouldn't stretch wide enough to get even the head inside it.

But he thrived on a challenge, and so he took a deep breath and stuck his tongue out and licked the head of Manuel's fat cock. He'd seen a few uncut cocks before, in the locker rooms at school, but only from afar. He'd never seen one up close, and had certainly never felt or tasted one. He'd always thought that he'd be freaked out or disgusted by it, and so he was surprised about his reaction to it now that it was in front of him.

He slid the foreskin back and licked the head for a moment, and then sucked it deeper into his mouth. He loved the smooth, hard feeling of it, and the heat as it slid along his tongue. The taste of the warm precum that oozed out of the tip made him drunk, and he sucked on the head harder, not wanting to lose a single drop. By accident, as he was sliding the extra skin up and down the shaft while draining the precum, his tongue slid between the hard head and the thin sheath of skin. That was the very second that he realized he loved sucking cock, and especially thick uncut cocks, and devoured Manuel's monster.

He opened his mouth as wide as he could, until it stretched so far that the corners ached, and was able to take a couple of inches inside. As badly as he wanted to swallow the entire cock, he wasn't able to take more than two or three inches. But what he lacked in skill he made up in determination, and he attacked the hard cock with vigor.

His head spun with the excitement, and his cock dripped its own precum. From the second Manuel's tongue slipped inside his ass he knew he was experiencing a spiritual orgasm—every cell in his body tingled and caused the hairs on his arms and legs to stand on end. All of his senses were heightened, and he felt like he was on the verge of crying with every breath. It felt as if he would shoot his load at any second, just with the pleasure of sucking Manuel's cock.

And so he was completely unprepared when Manuel pulled his cock out of his mouth suddenly and dismounted his chest.

"What's wrong," he panted, and wiped at his sore mouth. "Was I doing it wro . . ."

Manuel grabbed Brian by the waist and flipped him over onto his stomach in one surprisingly graceful move. He slid between Brian's long legs and spread them apart with his knees, and leaned down and licked hungrily at Brian's smooth ass again. He spread the cheeks apart and ate at it vigorously, and then spit on the spasming hole.

"Take a deep breath," Manuel said.

"What?"

He planted one hand on each cheek and pressed his cock head between them and against the sphincter.

"No way," Brian said, startled. He squirmed and tried to sit up. "I can't take that. I've never been fucked before. It's way too big."

Manuel lay on top of Brian's back, pinning him to the bed.

"Just breathe deep and try to relax. It will hurt at first, but then it will feel good."

"No fucking way," Brian said. "I can't do it. You're frickin' big as hell. Let me fuck you instead."

"That's not going to happen," Manuel said, and slid his thick cock along Brian's crack.

"Come on, Manuel, I'm serious. I can't get fucked by that thing. It'll kill me."

"Kiss me," Manuel said, and leaned forward so that he could reach Brian's mouth.

As frightened as he was by the prospect of having his insides ripped open, Brian was still intoxicated with everything Manuel, and couldn't resist kissing him again. He licked at Manuel's lips and opened his mouth to accept his probing tongue.

At the same moment that Manuel slipped his tongue inside Brian's mouth, he also slid his cock head just inside Brian's ass. He wrapped his arms around Brian's chest and held him tightly as he slid an inch inside, and Brian cried out loudly and bucked beneath him.

"Stop moving and just relax," he said, breaking the kiss.

"Relax? You're fucking killing me. Get off of me. It hurts."

"No," Manuel said firmly. "I won't get off of you. But I won't hurt you, either. I promise. You'll be fine, and after a couple of minutes, you'll feel good."

"Fuck you," Brian said loudly. "You're too fucking big, and you're hurting me. Get off of me, Manuel. "

"No."

Manuel held him closer and kissed him on the ear as he slid another inch inside, and rested so that Brian could get used to the monster cock invading him even deeper. When Brian turned his head away to resist his kisses, Manuel moved with him and continued kissing and licking his ears while hugging him tightly.

"Please don't," Brian whimpered and tried hard not to cry. "Don't rape me. Please."

"I'm not raping you, baby," Manuel said, and slid the rest of his cock all the way inside Brian's ass and rested there. "I wouldn't be doing this if you didn't want it."

"Fuck you. I don't want you to do this. It hurts."

Manuel felt the ass wrapped around his cock relax, and recognized the cry of pain turning into the moan of ecstasy. "You want me to fuck your ass," he said as he slid halfway out and then all the way back inside again.

"Fuck you," Brian repeated, but this time with a tone of excitement in his voice as his ass involuntarily squeezed the cock inside him.

Manuel kissed him passionately on the lips again and slid slowly in and out of the tight ass. He pulled his cock all the way out of Brian's ass, smiling when he heard Brian whine, and then slid it back in until he was buried to the pubic hair.

"What did you say?" he asked as he nibbled on Brian's ear.

"Fuck you," Brian moaned, and kissed him back frantically.

Manuel fucked him faster and deeper for several moments, and then pulled all the way out again just as Brian began bucking his ass up to meet his thrusts.

"Tell me what you want," Manuel teased.

"Fuck me," Brian whimpered. "Please. Put your cock back inside me and fuck me."

"That's my baby," Manuel said.

He lay on his side and pulled Brian into a spooning position in front of him. When Brian leaned back into him and kissed him, Manuel lifted his legs into the air and slid his cock back inside him in one slow, long move.

"Oh, fuck, yeah," Brian moaned. "You're fucking big as hell. Deeper, man."

Manuel slid in and out of Brian's ass, slowly at first and then quicker and with more varied speeds and depth. He loved the way the tight ass squeezed his cock lovingly and slid up and down his long rod. He normally didn't have a problem holding out and outlasting any partner. But he found himself getting closer a couple of times with Brian, and had to slow down or stop completely and rest a moment, and smiled to himself and kissed Brian on the lips when he moaned and begged to be pounded again.

"Do you want me to stop, baby?" he said teasingly.

"God, no," Brian said huskily. "Fuck me, babe, please. Fuck me hard."

Manuel moved Brian onto his back and raised his legs in the air again as he slid between them. He slid his cock inside the now twitching hole slowly, resisting the temptation to slam into him relentlessly. He leaned forward and kissed Brian tenderly on the lips again as he moved in and out of the tight ass. When Brian kissed him back, he sucked hungrily on the warm tongue and licked his lips lovingly.

"Oh, God, baby," he moaned. "I'm close."

"Me, too," Brian said breathlessly.

Manuel pulled his cock out of Brian's ass quickly. He leaned down and took Brian's dick in his mouth and sucked on it as he beat his cock with a frenzied determination.

"Oh fuck!" Brian almost yelled. "I'm cumming."

A second later he felt his cock spew several jets of cum into Manuel's mouth. Manuel swallowed his cock deeper into his throat, which only caused him to quiver even more uncontrollably and shoot several more shots of cum deep into his throat. A moment later Manuel moaned loudly, and Brian felt seven or eight huge spurts of warm jizz splash across his still exposed and clutching ass, and across his balls.

Manuel collapsed between Brian's legs and then rolled off to the side of the bed as he collected his breath. It was several minutes before either of them said anything.

"Rape, huh?" Manuel said finally, as he pulled Brian closer to him and hugged him tightly.

Brian laughed. "Well, I didn't wanna seem too desperate."

"Do you still hate me?"

"Hell, no."

"Are you still mad at me?"

"Only if you don't fuck me again."

"Of course I will. Anytime you want me to."

"Tomorrow?"

"Yes."

"And Friday?"

"Of course."

"What about Saturday?" Brian asked as he turned his head to kiss Manuel.

"All day, and Sunday, too. And every day next week if you want."

"Oh, I want. I want very much."

V.

It had been six months since Brian had last flown on the Bombardier Global Express XRS jet, and time had flown by as quickly as the jet traveled itself. He'd extended his stay in Bogotá an extra eight weeks longer than had originally been planned. Had anyone told him before he'd left for Colombia that he'd have done that, and even more that he'd dread going home, he would have laughed at them. But Masterson was ecstatic with the progress of the project, and eagerly approved Brian's request for another eight weeks to finalize it and make sure the foundation was solid and ready to go for phase two.

He'd gone home a little over halfway through his stay for a one-week stretch to spend Christmas with his family in San Francisco. His little brother, Roger, was there as well, and he took him aside one afternoon while the folks served dinner at a homeless shelter.

"What's gotten into you?" Roger asked. "You've been like a little kid waiting to open his presents on Christmas morning ever since you got here."

"Can you keep a secret?" Brian asked excitedly.

"No," Roger laughed. "Because I'm a six-year-old girl in pigtails."

"I think I'm gay," Brian blurted out.

Roger stared at his brother, expressionless, and blinked his eyes several times. "Excuse me?"

"I think I'm gay."

"Brian, you can think you're late for an appointment, or you can think you like asparagus but aren't sure and might need another try at it. You can't 'think' you're gay. You either are or you are not."

"Okay, then I'm definitely gay."

"What the fuck are you talking about?" Roger said, and leaned forward so that he was closer to Brian. "Are you high?"

"No, I'm not high." Brian laughed. "You know I've been in Colombia for the past few months, right?"

"Yeah."

"Well, I met a guy down there. His name is Manuel, and he's amazing."

"Oh my God, you're Bubba's bitch?"

Brian punched Roger playfully in the arm. "More like Manuel's mamacita."

Roger gasped and stared at his brother. "Are you telling me you're a bottom?"

Brian raised a single eyebrow and smiled.

"Oh, hell, no," Roger said, and pulled one leg underneath him and sat on it. "The biggest jock in high school and college is now taking it up the ass?"

"I can't get enough of it," Brian said, and laughed nervously. "It's fucking huge, Roger, at least a foot long and as thick as my forearm. The first time he fucked me, I thought I was going to die. But now it's like heroin. I have to have it every day or I go through withdrawals."

"And you only *think* you might be gay?"

"Okay, so I know I'm gay. But I think I might be in love."

"What?" Roger shrieked. "I can't believe I'm saying this, Brian, but you can't be in love with a cock."

"I know. But Manuel is hot as fuck, and he's nice and sweet and smart and rich and . . ."

"Rich?"

"Yeah. His dad is the wealthiest man in Colombia."

"Well, Mommy and Daddy will be tickled!"

"Shut up!" Brian said, and sat next to Roger on the bed. "I'm serious, I think I'm in love with him. He's an incredible guy, and the fact that he's built like a Mayan god and has a cock that would make a porn star blush is just an added bonus."

"I assume you haven't told Carl and Jo."

"Of course not, and I'm not sure I'm going to."

"Well, they aren't exactly slow. I think they're going to figure it out when the grandbabies speak Spanish."

"Not hilarious," Brian said.

"What's the big deal. They're liberal. They don't have a problem with me being gay."

"I know, but that's you. You popped out of the womb singing 'Over the Rainbow.' But I'm different."

"Yeah, well this story isn't supporting that theory very well."

"You know what I mean. The folks love you and they accept you. They've had a long time to get used to you being gay because you have never been anything else. But with me it's different. I know you were joking about the grandkids, but it's not a joke. I know they want them, and they're expecting them from me. And since this is a new venture for me, you know as well as I do that they're going to think it's a phase or something I'm experimenting with."

"And are you sure it's not?"

"Yes. Manuel isn't my first. I did experiment with a couple of guys when I was in college. But it was just testing the waters with them, and they didn't stir my soul. They didn't mean anything."

"They didn't stir your soul? Oh my God, you're becoming Carrie Bradshaw. I'm gonna tell Danielle you're trying to take over her reign as cheesy romance authority of the world."

"Fuck you," Brian said, and pulled his brother into a headlock.

*   *   *

That had been two months ago, and he still hadn't told his parents that he was gay, or about Manuel. That was going to change in the next few days, though, out of necessity. But first, he had to have the very uncomfortable conversation with Masterson.

The plane landed smoothly and almost noiselessly, and the company limo was waiting for him. The ride to the office was way too short, and didn't give him near enough time to talk himself out of the nerves. So when he walked into Masterson's spacious office on the sixty-fifth story of the U.S. Bank Tower in downtown Los Angeles, his knees were shaking almost as badly as his voice.

"Have a seat, Emerson," Masterson said as he covered the phone with one hand. He threw a cigar at Brian. "You deserve this."

Brian had never smoked anything, and he particularly hated the smell of cigar smoke. He thought seriously about pushing the cigar off to one side of the desk, but the way Masterson was puffing on and looking at his own, Brian knew that his boss would notice the gesture, and would probably be offended. So, he stuck the cigar in his mouth, lit it with the lighter on Masterson's desk, and took a couple of small puffs.

And then he felt the blood rush up his neck and across his face, and he ejaculated a mouthful of spittle and smoke a couple of feet into the air as the first wisp of smoke tickled the delicate inside of his lungs.

"Oh my God," Masterson said as he hung up the phone. "Are you all right?"

"Yeah," Brian said weakly through a fit of coughs.

"You are such a fag, Emerson." Masterson laughed. "First you don't eat cow and now you are going to honestly stand there and tell me you've never smoked a cigar?"

"I've never smoked *anything*," Brian said as he steadied his hand on the arms of the chair.

"Nothing? Not even pot?"

Brian shook his head.

"How the hell did you ever get through college without smoking anything?"

"I studied. And I ate well."

"You're such a fag."

Brian took a couple of deep breaths, and decided he'd never find a better time than now. He smoothed his jacket and looked at Masterson in the eyes.

"Yes, I am."

"Yes, you are what?"

"A fag. I'm gay, Warren."

Masterson looked at Brian for a moment, and then burst into laughter. "That's hilarious, man. You didn't even break a smile. You're sweating a bit, but that's from the coughing fit. A smile would have been a dead giveaway."

"It's not a joke, Warren. I'm gay, and I'm in love with Manuel Sanchez."

"What the fuck are you talking about?" Masterson asked as he leaned back in his chair.

"I'm moving to Bogotá. For good." He looked at his watch, and prayed that it wasn't running fast. He couldn't bear sitting there with the bulldog staring at him any longer than he had to.

"This isn't funny," Masterson said as he leaned forward on his desk. "Not even a lit . . ."

The phone rang, and Brian saw Masterson's face begin to turn red.

"I told you not to interrupt me!" he barked into the intercom.

"It's Mister Sanchez calling from Bogotá," his assistant said nervously. "He says it's urgent and insisted that I put him through."

Masterson glared at Brian for a moment, and then hit the speaker button on the phone.

"Manuel, my friend," Masterson said warmly, never taking his eyes off of Brian. "How are you?"

"I'm fine, Mr. Masterson," Manuel said. "How are you?"

Brian's heart jumped in his chest at the sound of his lover's voice.

"Good," Masterson said energetically. "But why so formal? Please, call me Warren."

"I'm speaking with you formally because I have a business proposition for you, Mr. Masterson."

"A business proposition?" He sat forward in his chair and glared at Brian.

"Yes. I assume my timing is appropriate and that Brian has disclosed something of a personal nature with you."

Masterson closed his eyes and shook his head, and leaned back in his chair.

"Mr. Masterson, are you there? Warren?"

"Yes, I'm here. And yes, Brian did just reveal something very shocking about himself a few moments ago."

"Good. I was hoping I didn't ruin the moment."

"Oh no." Masterson laughed out loud. "The 'moment' was quite brilliant, actually. But I don't know what that has to do with your business proposition."

"I'm extremely pleased with the work Masterson Builders has done for us here in Bogotá, and especially under Brian's leadership."

"Well, he is our Wonder Boy."

"Yes, he is. I'll get right to the point, Mr. Masterson. My father and I are looking to expand our little project. We had it in mind from the beginning, but we wanted to see how it went here in Bogotá before committing to anything further."

"Expand?" Masterson asked excitedly.

"That's correct. We weren't sure that this type of project would work here in Latin America."

"Well, that was quite the risk you took without having a good sense that it would work."

"We believe in taking risks, Mr. Masterson. My father and I believe that nothing significant comes about without risk. High-end shopping plazas with spas and specialty boutiques with large and luxurious high-rise apartments atop it was quite the risk for us. Colombia is not known for its abundance of wealth or its high quality of living. We weren't sure that our people could afford to live here. But we had faith in the possibilities, and we wanted to see where the risk could take us."

"And from what I understand, it's paying off," Masterson said as he smiled at Brian and shook his head.

"Yes. Thanks to Brian's creativity and commitment to the well-being of our communities, we have found a way to make it work. All of the residential units have sold even before the foundation has been poured. And we have American and Colombian retail stores begging us to let them into the commercial contracts."

"Brian did all of that, huh?" Masterson asked.

"Well, our teams worked together on the details, but it was Brian's idea to offer the residential units to low- and middle-income families with a subsidy from my company and the Colombian government, in exchange for a scheduled number of community service to our churches, schools, and other civic organizations. We anticipate a very large economic revival in Bogotá with this project."

"Wow," Masterson said. "That's quite the accomplishment, Emerson."

"Is Brian there?"

"Hi, babe," Brian said cheerfully.

Manuel laughed. "Hi, cariño. I didn't know you were going to be there in the office."

"I almost chickened out and didn't tell him. I was a little late, so I didn't get out before you called."

"So, what is your plan for expansion, Manuel?" Masterson asked.

"We want to build another project on the other side of town, in one of our poorest slum areas. Same quality of apartments and all the amenities, just like here in downtown. Maybe some different stores, to give more retailers the opportunity to get in with us."

"A second project? Are you sure you can sustain that?"

"Quite certain. But that's only the beginning of our expansion plans. We have property and investments in Argentina and Venezuela as well. A few hotels and resort properties that we want to transform into Villas de la Gente, just like the ones in Bogotá."

"A few, huh," Masterson said. "How many is a few?"

"Eleven more, for a total of twelve. We anticipate each project to take about two years from start to finish, and we wish to complete one before beginning the next. That will put Masterson Builders in Latin America for at least the next twenty-four, twenty-five years."

Brian smiled as he saw Masterson begin to breathe heavily and wring his hands.

"And I'm estimating, taking into account our current contract and a reliable rate of inflation, that our deal could mean upwards of three billion U.S. dollars for Masterson Builders. If you're interested, that is."

"Oh, I'm interested," Masterson said excitedly.

"Good. I only have two stipulations," Manuel said.

"I'm listening."

"My father and I do not want the projects to be managed from executives thousands of miles away. If we are to do this, we will want Masterson Builders to open offices here in Bogotá."

"That makes sense, and will not be a problem."

"Excellent. The next is that we want Brian to oversee the projects. I can't imagine any of this without his leadership and innovation, and we will not be interested in moving forward without him."

"So, he'd have to be there for the next twenty-five years, huh?" Masterson said as he leaned back in his chair.

"Yes. He'll be available to travel, of course. We both plan on extensive visits to the U.S. But we need him here full-time. I want him here."

"I'm sure you do," he said with a chuckle. "And I can't imagine a better president for Masterson Builders Latin America. I think we can work something out, Manuel."

"That's what I wanted to hear, Warren. I'm looking forward to working with you. I'm planning a weeklong trip to California next week. Let's plan on sitting down and working out the details, yes?"

"Perfect."

"All right then, I'll let you go. I look forward to seeing you next week."

"Me too, Manuel," Masterson said, still grinning ear to ear.

"Bye baby," Manuel said. "I love you. I'll see you in a few days."

"I love you, too, babe."

The phone clicked and the line went dead.

Masterson shook his head, and leaned forward with his hands clenched in front of him. He glared at Brian for a full three minutes before saying anything, and Brian knew better than to be the one to break the silence.

"You blindsided me," Masterson said finally.

"I'm sorry," Brian said. "It wasn't intentional. I just need to be there with Manuel, permanently. It's not easy getting a permanent resident status there unless there's a good reason to be there. And the project really is phenomenal. Manuel and his father have more money than God, but they wouldn't throw it away like this if they didn't believe in it. We think it has the potential to transform the country, maybe even all of Latin America. It was Manuel's idea to expand, and it was a great way to keep me there. We just thought it was a win-win situation for everyone."

Masterson stood up and moved in front of the desk, and handed Brian another cigar. "Here, smoke this. Don't be such a pansy."

Brian lit the cigar and inhaled more carefully. He still hated the taste and smell of it, but he didn't choke this time.

"Walk with me," Masterson said as he wrapped his arm around Brian's shoulders. "This calls for a drink."

The two men walked down the hall, and laughed as every head in the office turned and watched them leave.

"Three *billion* dollars!" Masterson yelled as they walked outside. "You must be one hell of a fuck, Emerson."

"Well, I try," Brian laughed. "But the truth is, I love him, Warren. I have to be there with him."

"Jesus H. Christ, Emerson," Masterson said with a laugh. "You're such a fag!"

INCH EIGHT

No Looking Back

I.

"You did what?" Carlos yelled at Ricky.

"Carlos, you don't understand. You get hooked on the shit and you can't go without it or you get really sick. I tried to stop, really I did."

"Bullshit, Ricky. We've been sharing this room for six months now, and you've contributed a whole twenty dollars. You blow all your money on that shit. I'm tired of it. I can't keep carrying the weight for both of us, man. You said you were going to carry your own."

"Do you want me to get sick?" Ricky asked as he scratched his arms nervously.

"Damn it, Ricky, you're sick now. Can't you see that? You're sixteen years old and you can't even see a life ahead of you. All you see is where your next fix is coming from. That's sick, Ricky, and I'll be damned if I'm going to stand around and watch my best friend die like that. I want $100 from you every week for your portion of the rent."

"Carlos, I can't afford that."

"Like hell you can't. Cut the dope, Ricky. I can't afford to keep supporting you."

"Why not," Ricky asked, becoming sarcastic, "you make three or four times as much as I do. I know you have at least a couple thousand dollars saved up."

"How long do you think that will last? And even if it could last, why should I play your mother and support you?"

"Exactly! Why should you play my mother and tell me how to live my life?"

"Ricky, I'm your friend. I'm worried about you."

"You mean you're worried about your precious money."

"That's not fair, Ricky."

"Life isn't fair, Carlos."

Ricky began pulling some clothes from the bureau and threw some toiletries into a backpack.

"What are you doing?" Carlos asked.

"I'm leaving. I don't want you to *support* me."

"Put your things down, Ricky," Carlos said, and began taking them away from Ricky.

"Leave me alone!" Ricky yelled, and pulled the clothes from Carlos.

Carlos grabbed them back and Ricky jumped on his back and began hitting him on the head and neck.

"Ricky, stop it," Carlos said as he tried to throw Ricky off of him.

Ricky landed a punch in Carlos' face, and Carlos snapped. He punched Ricky in the ribs with his elbow and when Ricky dropped onto his back, Carlos hit him in the face with his fist. Ricky landed on the floor with a heavy thud and put a hand to his eye.

"Oh my God," he cried, "you hit me in the eye."

"Jeez, Ricky, I'm sorry. I didn't mean to hit you, man."

"Yeah, just like your dad didn't mean to beat you, right?"

"Shut up."

"Just like your mom didn't mean to screw around behind your dad's back, right?"

"Shut the fuck up or I'll beat the hell out of you, Ricky."

"Why not? You're halfway there already."

"I'm going out now. I don't want you here when I get back."

Carlos turned and walked out the door, slamming it behind him. He walked out into the cool night and headed for Geary Boulevard. He needed time to cool down and think.

He knew he was wrong to have hit Ricky like that. He just blew a fuse and couldn't help it. And that scared the hell out of him, because it reminded him way too much of his father. But he also knew he was not wrong to have tried to straighten out his friend's life. Ricky himself had told Carlos he wanted to go straight, and was excited about his offer to help. That was all he was trying to do, and Ricky had no right to go off like that. Carlos knew they both needed time alone to cool down, and everything would be all right later tonight when Ricky joined Carlos in front of Supremo's Pizza.

A black sedan pulled up and interrupted Carlos' thoughts just as he reached his home base. Carlos got in the car and smiled at the handsome man, thinking how good it would be to make up with Ricky after this trick was over.

* * *

"What's your name, son?" the middle-aged man asked.

"Does it matter?"

"Well, I like to know the boys I allow into my home."

"And knowing my name means you know me?"

"Well . . ."

"My name is Dick."

"Very appropriate," the man said, staring at Carlos' huge hardon. "Dick what?"

"Dick Tracy," Carlos said. He was losing his patience. "You already said you weren't a cop, so what's with the third degree?"

"I just want to know if I can trust you. You won't tell me your name, so I'm not sure that I can."

"Well, I'm not a murderer or a thief, you can trust me about that. I'm just here to do a job. I'm going to fuck you long and hard, just like I do my girlfriend. Maybe even longer and harder, just to show you how much you can trust me."

"That sounds good to me."

"Of course it does. But I'm not asking for your approval. Shut up and lie down. My dick is starting to ache for your ass."

The man lay down on his back and Carlos walked over to the bed and rested his hard cock on the man's face.

"Beg for it!" Carlos commanded.

"Please let me suck your big dick. I need it."

"Then suck it. Swallow it all the way down your throat and suck the cum out of it."

Carlos shoved his cock into the man's mouth and tried to push it all the way in, but the man choked. He obviously was not used to swallowing cocks as big as Carlos'. Carlos settled for pumping the fat rod in and out of the man's mouth, letting him wet it.

"Turn over," Carlos ordered, "I want to fuck your ass."

"No. Just let me suck it. I don't think I can take one this big."

"I already told you, I'm not asking you. I'm telling you to roll over and let me fuck you."

"Look, kid, I'm not paying you to get smart. Just let me . . ."

Carlos slapped the man hard across the face and turned him over onto his stomach. The man tried to protest and turn back onto his back, but Carlos was too strong for him. He pulled the man's arms behind his back and laid his own body on top of the man's back. His cock was still hard, and pressed between the flabby cheeks of the man's ass.

"You can either shut up and go along with me, or I can take you by force. It's up to you. Either way, I'm going to fuck your ass. Now which will it be?"

"Okay, okay," the old man winced through gritted teeth. "But please, just take it easy."

Carlos lifted the man's hips and positioned the fat head of his cock at the entrance to the man's ass. Then, in one hard push, he rammed his big dick deep into the loose tunnel.

"Oh, Jesus Christ, that hurts!" the man screamed.

"Stop kidding yourself, old man. Your ass is as loose as the Grand Canyon. What have you been shoving up there, a baseball bat?"

"Please," the guy cried. "It really hurts. You're too big."

"Shut up. It only hurts for a minute. If my girlfriend can take it, so can you."

Carlos began to pump his cock in and out of the ass with a savage brutality. It took a lot of hard work and fantasizing, because he had told the truth; the flabby ass was really loose. Without much pressure against his cock, it took a long time for him to come. He finally did though, but it was about as exciting as blowing his nose, and felt like barely more than a dribble.

The man lay perfectly still while Carlos stood up and wiped himself clean with the towel the man had set at the foot of the bed before they'd started.

"You can pay me now, and I'll be gone."

"Pay you? You're lucky I don't report you."

"And you're lucky I'm not a murderer or a thief. Now just shut up and gimme the five hundred."

The man paid Carlos grudgingly, and Carlos left. He heard the door slam behind him and the locks bolted shut. He started to walk down the street to catch the bus that would take him back to Geary Boulevard, but only made it half a block before he had to stop and throw up.

Half an hour later he was standing in front of Supremo's.

"Hey, Blanche," he yelled at one of the queens across the street. "You seen Ricky?"

"No, I haven't, baby," Blanche yelled back. "Haven't seen him all night, which is kinda strange, don't you think?"

Carlos remembered the fight they'd had earlier, and the inevitable black eye Ricky would surely have. Ricky didn't like going out whenever he'd been beaten up, and usually stayed in the room and got stoned and drunk for a couple of days. "Nah. Actually, I remember he didn't feel very well when I left earlier. He's probably still in the room. I'm gonna go check on him."

"All right, baby. You know I have a freebie waitin' for you anytime you wanna take me up on it."

Carlos laughed. "Thanks, Blanche. I'll keep that in mind."

He walked the few blocks to the motel, regretting the fight they'd had earlier and wondering just how much making up with Ricky would cost him. Ricky would undoubtedly work the fight for all it was worth, and Carlos was sure he'd be out a couple hundred dollars' worth of food, clothes, and even cash before it was all said and done and Ricky forgave him. But he didn't care. Ricky was his best friend, and Carlos deeply regretted the fight. He'd gladly give him the money in order to be best buddies again.

When he walked into the room it was dark. He turned on the light and saw Ricky lying on the bed. He thought it odd that Ricky was sleeping at this time of night, and walked over to the bed to see if his friend was okay. As he got closer to the bed, he saw a large rubber strap wrapped tightly around Ricky's skinny bicep. A long needle was still lodged in his arm, and a peanut butter jar lid and a book of matches were lying next to him. A small amount of blood had dried on his arm where the needle had pierced him.

"My God, Ricky," Carlos yelled, and ran over to the bed. "Ricky, wake up man!"

He lifted Ricky's head from the pillow and slapped his face hard two or three times. He started to remove the needle from Ricky's arm, and then realized the trouble that could cause, and left it alone. He put his ear close to Ricky's mouth, and when he realized his friend wasn't breathing, he tilted Ricky's head back and began breathing into his mouth. But Ricky's mouth, and in fact everywhere Carlos touched him, was already cold and turning a light blue. Tears filled Carlos' eyes and he sank to the floor beside the bed. He held his head in his hands and cried.

Ricky was dead.

Grief overcame Carlos and he climbed onto the bed and across to the other side of the bed, away from the needle and works still attached to Ricky's arm. He wrapped his arms around Ricky's cold, stiff body, and hugged his friend and cried on his chest.

"Don't be dead, man. Please don't be dead. You're my friend, Ricky. You can't die. You can't!" Carlos screamed.

His words came out in staccato bursts, and seemed to evaporate even as they left his lips. He hugged Ricky even tighter, and his arm knocked the needle from Ricky's lifeless arm. A small trickle of blood oozed out from where the needle had been, and dried before it hit the mattress.

"Don't leave me," Carlos whispered into Ricky's ear. "I need you, man. Please don't die, Ricky. I love you."

Carlos ran out of words for his friend and simply cried. He cried for Ricky, for his rotten life, for his missing love, for his shattered dreams. After about twenty minutes the tears dried and Carlos sat silent with grief for his best friend.

He knew he had to do something, but he was afraid. He was afraid to call the police, but afraid not to as well. He couldn't think straight, and decided to take a walk before doing anything irrational. He walked out of the room and toward Geary Street, not really sure why. He certainly didn't trust anyone there enough to talk to about Ricky. But there seemed nowhere else to go, and no one else to talk to.

And then he remembered that Corey was home from school for Christmas break. He hadn't spoken to him in a little over three months, but he'd spoken with Mr. and Mrs. Baker a few times, and he'd visited Martina a couple of times a month since he last saw Corey. He'd changed his cell number right after their last argument, and up to now had had no desire to speak with him. But now he couldn't think of anyone he wanted to talk with more, or anyone he wanted . . . needed . . . to see more.

He pulled up the Bakers' number in his cell directory and prayed that someone would be home. He knew these few days before Christmas were hectic for a lot of people, and he was certain that the Bakers would have at least a dozen engagements to attend.

"Hello?"

"Oh God, Martina," he cried into the phone. "Thank God."

"Carlos?"

"Yeah, it's me."

"Baby, what's wrong?"

"Please tell me Corey is home."

"Yeah, he's here. The whole family just got home from some charity function. I think they were delivering toys to a homeless shelter."

"I need him," Carlos cried, and slumped to sit on the ground against the wall of a convenience store.

"Carlos, you're scaring me, baby. What's wrong?"

"Please, Martina. I need him."

II.

Twenty minutes later Corey's black Ferrari rounded the corner, and the tires screeched to a halt. Corey jumped out of the car and ran over to Carlos.

"Babe, what happened? What's wrong?"

Carlos wrapped his arms around Corey's neck and cried loudly. His legs gave out and he crumpled in Corey's arms.

Corey carried him over to the car and slipped him inside the passenger seat.

"Carlos, are you stoned?" Corey asked as he held Carlos' cold face in his hands. "You look like you're in shock and you're as white as a ghost."

"Yeah, sure. Because I'm Mexican and I'm a hustler and do all of those horrible things that are so beneath you, then I must be stoned, right? I don't do drugs, Corey. Don't you know me well enough to at least know that? I just found . . . I just found . . ." He began to cry hysterically again, and could not finish his sentence.

"Hey, Carlos, don't cry. It's okay. I'm sorry, I didn't mean anything by that stupid question. Just tell me what's wrong."

"My friend. He's dead."

"Oh, God, I'm so sorry, Carlos. Can I do anything?"

"He's still in my room. I don't know what to do. The needle . . . the blood," Carlos blurted out almost incoherently. "I tried to wake him up, but he just laid there. He was so cold. A big needle . . . he was so sad."

Carlos began to shake and he stammered unintelligibly.

"Calm down, Carlos. Just go slow and tell me what happened."

"We got in a fight earlier tonight. He kept buying dope instead of helping me with the rent. We got in a fight and I told him to leave. I went back three hours later and when I walked in . . ."

"Slow down, Carlos. I know it hurts, but you have to tell me what happened. I want to help you."

"I walked in and saw him on the bed. At first I thought he was just sleeping, but when I got closer to him, I saw it. There was a needle in his arm and some drugs next to him. He was dead. I couldn't do anything to help him. God, I shouldn't have hit him. He was trying so hard, and I just kept bitching at him. I killed him. Jesus, I killed Ricky."

Carlos' head fell back onto the headrest and his eyes rolled back in his head. Corey slapped him across the face and shook him. Carlos remained awake and stared blankly at him.

"Carlos, that's nonsense. You did not kill Ricky. Now tell me where he is."

"Rainbow Ranch Motel."

"Where's that?"

Carlos looked out the window to get his bearings.

"Just around the corner."

"Okay, Carlos, we're going to go over there. I'm going inside and check on Ricky. You stay in the car, okay."

"Okay."

Corey drove to the motel and made sure Carlos was going to be okay, even though he was shivering and crying. He instructed Carlos to stay inside the car, took a deep breath, and then went inside the hotel room. He came back about two minutes later, almost as white as Carlos had been earlier. He sat behind the wheel and said nothing for several minutes.

"He's dead," Corey finally said.

"I know."

"We have to call the police," Corey said, and brushed his hands through his hair distractedly. "Carlos, you have been with me for the last five hours. We went to dinner and then to a movie. We came back here so you could get a jacket, and found Ricky dead."

"What movie?" Carlos asked numbly.

"Have you seen the new Spider-Man movie?"

"Yes."

"Can you tell the police what it's about?"

"Yes."

"Then that's what we saw. It's playing at the Corona, on the other side of town."

"Okay."

"Carlos, Ricky has a black eye and a cut on his lip. Did you do that?"

"I told you, we had a fight. It was a small fight, and I accidentally hit him in the face. He was jumping and yelling at me, and I was just trying to push him away. I swear I didn't mean to."

"I believe you, Carlos, but the cops won't. Did anyone see you hit Ricky, or does anyone know about the fight at all?"

"No."

"Then there was no fight, all right, Carlos. You tell the cops you and Ricky were joking the last time you saw him and I'll back you up. For all they know, someone came in later and they got into it after you left with me for the movie. Then Ricky OD'd. Got it?"

"Yes."

They called the cops and were on their way an hour later. The investigating police knew Ricky well, and knew he and Carlos were friends. After talking with the motel clerk and a couple of the other hustlers, they had no reason to believe Carlos was involved in any way, and let Corey and Carlos leave after only a few questions.

* * *

It was just after midnight when they pulled into the garage. Corey knew his parents would have gone to bed already. When he saw the kitchen light on, he knew Martina would be waiting for them. He and Carlos walked into the house through the back door, which entered onto the kitchen.

"Oh, thank the baby Jesus," Martina whispered when she saw the two boys. "What happened, baby?" she asked Carlos as she rushed to him and hugged him tightly to her bosom. "What's wrong?"

Carlos looked at Corey with wide eyes, but didn't say anything.

"His best friend just died," Corey told her. "Carlos walked in and found him. He's a bit shaken up."

"Oh no," Martina said, and held Carlos at arm's length. "I made hot chocolate," she said as if that would make everything all right. She let go of him and worked hurriedly to pour all three of them a cup.

"Thank you, Martina," Corey said as the two boys accepted their cups. "I know you're anxious to hear all about it. But I think Carlos is still a little in shock, and maybe it would be best for him to just go upstairs and sleep."

She looked hurt, and crossed her arms across her ample breasts. "Yes, of course," she said finally. "Take your cocoa with you. It'll help you both sleep better. I'll make a nice, hearty breakfast for tomorrow."

"Thanks, Martina. You're the best."

"I know."

Corey and Carlos went upstairs, and Corey undressed Carlos and helped him get into bed and under the covers. Carlos was asleep in less than five minutes. Corey sat in bed next to him, watching him sleep and brushing the hair from his eyes whenever he tossed and turned. About half an hour after falling asleep, Carlos began crying and thrashing around a bit, and Corey lay next to him and wrapped him in his arms until he quieted and was sleeping soundly again. He, too, began to get sleepy, and he undressed and crawled back into bed and hugged Carlos tightly to him as he drifted into sleep.

* * *

Corey floated toward consciousness slowly, trying to open his eyes, but not being able to do so for a couple of minutes. He wasn't sure if he was dreaming or really waking up. He felt an incredible warmth wrapped around his cock, followed by an increasing pressure that slid up and down the length of his dick.

He moaned and lifted his hips off the bed, driving his cock even deeper into the warm wetness, and forced his eyes open.

"Babe?" he said sleepily.

Carlos let the big cock slip from his mouth, and slid up the bed so that he was lying right beside Corey.

"I'm so sorry, Corey," he whispered, and held Corey's face in his hands as he kissed him.

Corey slipped his tongue inside Carlos' mouth, stunned that it tasted so sweet and was so warm and wet, even after all the crying Carlos had done.

"Sorry for what?" he asked when Carlos broke the kiss.

"For being such an idiot before. I love you, Corey. I've loved you since the first time I met you. And when you weren't here with me, I felt like I was lost. I don't ever want to feel that way again, baby."

"You won't have to," Corey said, and kissed Carlos lightly on the nose. "If you want me, I'm here for you. I'm yours."

"Please don't ever leave me again, baby," Carlos said, and snuggled up to Corey and kissed his neck.

"I'm not going anywhere."

"I want you to make love to me." Carlos whispered into Corey's ear.

"Oh God, babe," Corey said as he rolled over onto his side so that his back was pressed against Carlos' chest. He pressed his ass against the hard cock behind him. "I would love that."

"No," Carlos said, and turned Corey back around to face him. "I want *you* to fuck *me*." He reached down and squeezed Corey's dick as he rolled over and spooned Corey with his ass rubbing against his lover's big cock. "I want you inside me."

"What?" Corey asked, a little dazed. "Are you sure? I thought you never bottomed."

"I haven't. But I want to now. I want to feel you deep inside me more than I've ever wanted anything. Will you fuck me?"

"You better believe I will."

Corey rolled Carlos over onto his stomach. He lay on top of Carlos' back, rubbing his cock up and down the crack of the hard, smooth ass, and kissed him on the back of the neck. He licked behind Carlos' ear.

"I love you so much, babe."

"I love you, too," Carlos said, and wiggled his ass against Corey's cock.

Corey licked down Carlos' back, kissing every inch of his spine. When he reached the hard, marble smooth globes of his ass, Corey spread them gently with his hands, and licked around the hole for a moment, and then slid his tongue deep inside.

"Oh my God," Carlos moaned as Corey snaked his tongue inside his tight ass, and wiggled it around. "Fuck me. Please."

Corey spread Carlos' legs and moved onto his knees between them. His cock was throbbing visibly, and bright red and dripping with precum. Though not quite as huge as Carlos' fat cock, his was not small by any stretch of the definition. It was almost eight inches long, and six inches around. He'd been too big for a few guys who considered themselves accomplished bottoms, and so he was concerned that he might hurt Carlos.

Corey turned Carlos around onto his back, and kissed him passionately on the mouth. "Babe, I want to make love to you so badly I can taste it. But are you sure? You told me you've never been fucked."

"I haven't," Carlos said, and leaned back and kissed Corey.

"I'm pretty big."

"Yeah, I know. I want you inside me."

He looked at Corey's giant cock with mixed emotions. The size scared him. There was no way he'd ever be able to fit it all into his mouth. On the other hand, he wanted it so badly. It was a beautiful cock—long and thick, light skinned with short, blond pubic hairs. The balls were large and packaged in a silky-smooth sac.

Carlos closed his eyes and licked the head of the big dick tentatively. He tasted a drop of precum that had accumulated and swallowed it without thinking. He liked the sweet taste. He opened his mouth wide to suck in the entire head. It fit snugly inside his mouth and he was proud of himself as he rolled his tongue over the smooth head.

In almost a year that he'd been hustling on the street, Carlos had only sucked cock twice, and both times were awkward and lasted only a few minutes. The guys he tricked with weren't really interested in his cocksucking or bottoming talents, they wanted only one thing from him—his phenomenal cock. But with Corey's big cock in his mouth, he took a liking to cocksucking at once. The feel, the taste . . . it all fascinated him. His courage grew and he began to swallow more of the big dick into his mouth. When the head reached his tonsils, he choked and pulled off the dick.

"You have to relax your throat muscles if you want to deep-throat it," Corey said. "But you don't have to take it all, Carlos. It feels good just like you're doing it."

"No. I want to swallow it," Carlos said, with a lust he never knew could exist in him. "How do I do it?"

"Just yawn and swallow at the same time. Keep your throat muscles relaxed."

Carlos began sucking the big dick again, taking one inch at a time. When the head reached his tonsils this time, Carlos yawned and swallowed at the same time. His eyes grew wide as he felt the entire length of Corey's eight-inch dick slide slowly but effortlessly deep into his throat. He felt his esophagus expand to accommodate the thickness, and he was amazed when his nose was tickled by Corey's pubic hair.

Corey moaned loudly and began to move his hips so that he was fucking Carlos' throat.

Carlos accepted the dick gladly and was so caught up in the new sensation that he didn't realize that Corey was repositioning them both so that they were in a sixty-nine position. He loved having his cock sucked, and especially by Corey. When he was tricking, he didn't really care for foreplay, and wanted to get down to business and get it over with as quickly as possible. But he wasn't tricking now, and his cock throbbed at the thought of Corey swallowing it. He was surprised, therefore, when he felt Corey's tongue licking at his balls and the space between them and his ass instead of sucking on his shaft. Corey was still pushing his big dick in and out of his mouth as he tickled the sensitive area between his legs, and when Carlos moaned in delight, he wasn't sure whether it was from the feeling in his throat or the one between his legs.

Corey's tongue worked its way to Carlos' ass hole and licked around it until it relaxed enough to let his tongue slip just inside. He was getting close to cumming already, but he wanted to fuck Carlos more than anything he'd ever wanted before in his life. He filled Carlos' tunnel with saliva and moved him onto his back.

His dick was wet from the sucking Carlos had given him, and he was more excited than he'd ever know before.

Carlos knew what was about to happen, and he was nervous. But he was just as excited as Corey was, and he offered no resistance as Corey lifted his legs and let them rest on his shoulders.

"Please take it easy, Corey," was the only outward sign of Carlos' nervousness.

"I will, babe, I will."

Corey placed the head of his dick at the entrance of Carlos' ass and gently pushed forward. Carlos was nervous and tight, so the big head resisted entry. Corey leaned down and kissed Carlos' nipples, nibbling and kissing his way up to his neck and chin. When he finally reached his destination, and his tongue slipped into Carlos' mouth, Carlos relaxed completely, and Corey's long, thick dick slid all the way into Carlos' ass in one slow, smooth movement.

Carlos' eyes flew open, and his mouth tightened painfully around Corey's tongue. Corey remained perfectly still, allowing Carlos to become accustomed to the big dick in his ass, and continued kissing him softly.

Carlos moaned painfully, and tried halfheartedly to pull himself off of Corey's cock, but Corey held him still, and kept his dick embedded deep in the tight, warm ass. When Carlos finally relaxed a couple of minutes later, Corey took his cue. He slowly started to move in and out of Carlos' ass with long, slow strokes. The deep pain slowly faded into a dull, throbbing pressure, and Carlos began to move his hips in rhythm with Corey's.

Corey broke the kiss and began to pump himself harder and faster into his lover. The tight ass was better than any feeling Corey could ever remember feeling, and several times he got very close to cumming, and had to stop completely and catch his breath.

Carlos could sense when Corey was getting close, and would stop moving his ass, and tell Corey not to shoot yet. He beat off as Corey fucked him, and he loved the sensation of his ass tingling while Corey fucked him, and the feeling in his cock as he stroked himself.

Corey was surprised at how fast Carlos took to being fucked, and especially that he wanted it to last a long time. He'd figured Carlos would want to hurry and get it over with.

After about half an hour of the lovemaking, however, both boys were too close to stop, and it was not surprising to either of them that they came at exactly the same moment. They connected on so many levels that it just seemed natural.

Corey pulled his giant cock out of Carlos' clutching ass and began to slide his fist over it at the same rhythm of the fucking he'd been giving Carlos. He came hard and furious, spraying his cum all over Carlos' face and stomach. At the same time, Carlos' dick let go with an equally large load, covering Corey's sweaty body with hot, sticky cum.

Both boys were exhausted. Corey fell to the bed beside Carlos and they lay next to one another, trying to catch their breath. Carlos scooted over and rested his head on Corey's chest.

The two lovers fell asleep almost immediately, and didn't wake up until Martina knocked on the door a few hours later, announcing breakfast.

III.

Once he stepped inside the motel, Carlos was hit hard by the impact of the night before. The smile that he'd had all morning immediately left his face, and his eyes filled with tears as he walked into the room.

"Are you okay?" Corey came up behind Carlos and put both arms around his back and torso and kissed him on the back of the neck.

"No, not really."

"Let's get your things and get outta here. There's no reason for us to stay here."

"I was his only friend." Carlos sat on the bed. A tear rolled down his cheek.

Corey walked into the bathroom and began to gather Carlos' things.

"He had a very good friend," Corey said as he returned to the main room.

"I want him back, Corey. I miss him. It's not fair. He was too young to die."

"I won't argue with that at all, baby," Corey said as he took the clothes from the bureau. It wasn't difficult telling Carlos' clothes from Ricky's.

"He wasn't happy, you know. He hated his life. He wanted to quit hustling and go back to school. I was supposed to help him. I guess I didn't do such a good job, huh?"

"You did a great job. Is this yours?" Corey held up a stack of bills.

"Yeah."

Corey put the money in the bag with Carlos' clothes and walked to the door.

"Let's go, Carlos."

"Corey . . ."

"I said let's go. Now."

Carlos stood up and walked out the door and to the car. Corey returned the key to the clerk and joined Carlos in the Ferrari.

"Feel like an ice cream?" he asked Carlos.

"No."

"Then where to?"

"I want to talk to his mother."

"Carlos, I don't think that is such a good idea."

"Okay. I'll walk then. See you later."

"Like hell you will," Corey said, and started the engine. "Where did he live?"

Carlos directed him to Ricky's house, and when they got there, both boys sat silently in the car.

"I'll wait here. Don't be too long, okay, babe? It won't do any good to brood in grief. It just makes things worse."

"I just want to tell her I'm sorry."

"Okay. I'll be here when you get back."

Carlos got out of the car and walked to the house. Fido barked out a series of mean yelps and Ricky's mom opened the door even before he got to the porch.

He saw a very different woman from the one he'd met before. He immediately regretted calling her Mount St. Helens and laughing at her. Her eyes were red and swollen; her face ashen white and she smelled of vomit.

She recognized Carlos immediately, and grabbed him, pulling his head to her huge breasts and hugging him. She was crying uncontrollably, and Carlos was equally helpless against his own tears as they fell down his cheeks. She pulled him inside and closed the door behind them.

"Carlos, what happened to my baby?" she cried.

"I don't know, ma'am. We got into a little argument. I told him I wanted him to give up the drugs. He said he couldn't. I yelled at him and left. When I came back a couple of hours later, he was . . . he was . . ."

"Oh God, son." She looked to the ceiling, tears covering her face. "I'm so sorry I failed you, baby."

"Mrs. Bennett, you didn't fail Ricky," Carlos was still trying to stop crying himself. "You did your best."

"Does this look like I did my best?" she asked as she waved her hand around the mess in her house. "I raised my baby like a pig. I didn't care about anything but myself. I couldn't even be a mother to my only baby boy."

"Mrs. Ben . . ."

"He tried to talk to me last week, Carlos. He said, 'Mommy, I feel trapped. I want to become a better person. I want to be like Carlos.' Do you know what I did? I laughed. I laughed at him, Carlos, and I said, 'Not everyone can be Prince Charming.'"

Ricky's mom blew her nose loudly into a dirty paper towel.

"Then I borrowed some pot from him. God, Carlos, my son came to me crying for help, and I laughed at him. I killed my baby, Carlos. I killed my little baby Ricky."

Mrs. Bennett cried hysterically, and Carlos could find nothing to say to comfort her. She finally cried herself to sleep, leaving Carlos alone in the house.

He walked into Ricky's room and looked around. Nothing had changed. The same dirty clothes were strewn around the room; the same half-eaten bologna and cheese sandwich lay rotten on the desk, and presumably the same roaches scattered when the light came on.

Carlos sat on Ricky's bed and once again tried to imagine living Ricky's life. Were there any good times for him? Had he ever had a friend sleep over or had a birthday party, even as a kid? Had his father ever taken him fishing or had a man-to-man talk with him? Looking around him, Carlos was hit full force with the strikes against his friend. He got up and turned out the light.

Inside the front room, Ricky's mom was still sleeping. Carlos saw she was still crying, even in her sleep. He bent down and kissed her on the forehead, and left five $100 bills under her coffee cup on the table.

He walked back to the car and sat silently for a long while. He wanted to cry some more, but he was drained. It seemed like all the tears that could be shed for Ricky had passed. Corey sat silently with Carlos, staring straight ahead, down the block.

"How about that ice cream now?" Carlos asked.

"Sure. You all right?"

"I don't know."

"Well, ice cream works miracles. Let's go."

IV.

"I don't think I can go in there," Carlos said as he stood outside the giant Catholic church.

They weren't in the main sanctuary; there were only a handful of people present, and most of them were dressed in their street working clothes. The church was one of many in the city that doubled as a hot meal kitchen for the thousands of homeless people in San Francisco, and Ricky had frequented it almost daily. They had a small chapel located in the back of the building, abutting the alley, and no one ever used it, so they'd agreed to allow Ricky's friends and family use it for their memorial service.

"Of course you can," Corey said. He took Carlos' hand and walked with him to the back of the church. "You have no choice. And even if you did, you know as well as I do that you not only *can* go in there, but that you have to."

Carlos sighed. "You're right. But I don't want to."

"I'm sure of that. But I'm here with you, babe. You'll be okay."

They walked into the chapel, and Carlos gasped audibly. He knew there wouldn't be a hundred people attending the service. But he'd expected at least a couple dozen. The queens and hustlers on the streets always talked about how they were a family, and how they looked out for one another. Carlos was pissed that of the thirty or so that they frequently hung out with, only two had bothered to show up for Ricky's service.

In addition to them, there were only five other people in the chapel: two of the sweet ladies that helped serve warm food to the homeless through the church, Ricky's mom, and two men next to her. The one sitting right next to Ricky's mom looked to be about Corey's age, and was dressed in jeans and a long sleeved t-shirt and a baseball cap. The other looked to be in his early forties, and was dressed in a moderate suit.

Carlos and Corey tried to sit down in the last pew in the back of the chapel, but Ricky's mother looked back to see who'd walked in when she heard the heavy door shut, and noticed him.

"Carlos!" she cried out loudly, and struggled to heave herself up from the pew. Unsuccessful, she waved him over frantically. "Come here, Carlos. Sit with me."

She pushed the two men next to her down to the other side of the bench, and beckoned Carlos to join her.

He didn't want to. In fact, there was probably nothing he could want less. But Ricky's mother was insistent, and she started making a scene when he didn't immediately join her. She wailed loudly, clutched at her fat neck, and complained of chest pain. Carlos knew instinctively that it would only get worse if he didn't sit next to her.

"I'm sorry, baby," he said as he squeezed Corey's knee. "I think I better go sit next to her, or she's gonna really get dramatic."

"Go ahead, babe," Corey said, and kissed him gently on the lips. "I'll wait for you back here. She needs you right now a lot more than I do."

Carlos walked up the aisle and sat next to Ricky's mom, and cringed as she threw her arms around his neck and rocked him violently in her massive breasts.

"Oh, my baby!" she wailed as she cut off his breath with her death grip on his neck. "What am I gonna do without my baby Ricky?"

Carlos knew that Ricky and his mother had a very strained relationship at best. They weren't close at all, and he doubted seriously that her life would change dramatically with the loss of him, other than she might have to find a new pot supplier. But he hugged her tightly and brushed her sweat and tear-stained hair from her face and kissed her on the cheek.

"You're not gonna be without Ricky, Mrs. Bennett," he said. "You know he's up in heaven looking after you. He's your angel now."

That drew another glass-shattering wail from her as she slung her hefty body against the back of the pew and stretched her legs out in front of her. "My baby's an angel," she yowled loudly, and fanned her face with her hands. "He's looking out for me."

"I'm Justin," the younger man sitting next to him said. "She'll be okay in a few minutes. She just needs to make sure she's being noticed, and then she'll settle down."

"I'm Carlos," he said, and shook the boy's hand. "How did you know Ricky?"

"I'm his older brother. That's my mom," he said, and nodded toward Ricky's mother, who was now making a production of taking deep breaths and collecting herself.

"What?" Carlos said. "Ricky never mentioned that he had a brother."

"Yeah, I'm sure he didn't. We're not really proud of our family, you know. We don't talk about one another very much. I've been living with my dad in Philadelphia for the past ten years. We haven't really kept in touch very well with Ricky and Momma."

"Wow. I would never have guessed you were brothers."

"I know. We were about as different as night and day. But I did love him. I missed him a lot after we moved. I was hoping that once I moved to LA and started UCLA that I'd be able to come up and visit every once in a while. But I guess that won't happen now."

Carlos looked over at the man sitting next to Justin, and felt his heart stop in his chest.

"Oh, I'm sorry," Justin said, "this is my . . . Professor Norman."

"Call me Rich . . ."

Carlos and Richard stared at one another, confused at first, and then suspiciously, and then confused again. To Carlos it looked as if he were looking into a magical aging mirror. Richard Norman had the same full head of thick black hair, the same turquoise blue eyes that sparkled mischievously, the same twin dimples on either side of his full pink lips—and the exact same dark brown mole on his left chin. Richard had a few wrinkles that Carlos didn't, and he had a thick black stubble across his chin and lips that were absent from Carlos' face for another couple of years yet. But otherwise they looked like mirror images of one another.

"Hey, you guys look alike!" Justin said.

"Oh my God," Richard said as he looked at Carlos. "How old are you?"

"Seventeen," Carlos said, barely audible, and without taking his eyes off of Richard Norman.

"You're Lydia's son, aren't you?"

Carlos' eyes filled with tears and his chin quivered as he nodded his head. All of his life he'd felt like an outcast and that he was missing an important part of his life. Though he loved his mom and Rosie very much, and he knew they loved him as well, he'd never looked into his father's eyes and seen anything similar to love coming from them. He'd known why for several years, and he knew all about Richard Norman. His mother had never lied to him, and felt it was important for Carlos to know the reason behind Juan Cortez' rage. But that didn't make any of it easier for Carlos as he grew up.

"Sweet Jesus," Richard whispered.

Carlos dropped his head and began to cry harder than he could remember ever having cried.

"It's okay, baby," Mrs. Bennett said as she hugged him. "Ricky is looking out for you, too."

"Please tell me you don't hate me," Richard said.

"Do you guys know each other?" Justin asked, confused.

"I don't hate you," Carlos said, and he wiped his nose with his sleeve. "I just have so much that I want to ask you and talk with you about. I feel like I've missed out on so much."

"So do I, son. So do I."

"Son?" Justin said. "Is this your son?"

"Yes."

Carlos cried harder, and leaned over Justin to hug his father. "Please don't leave again."

"I'll be right here," Richard said, and wiped away his own tears.

"I'm gonna go back and sit with my boyfriend for now, but I want to talk with you after the service."

"I'd like that," Richard said.

Carlos hugged Mrs. Bennett again, and then walked back to Corey.

"Are you okay, babe?" Corey asked as he scooted over to make room for Carlos on the aisle.

"I think so. I'm not sure. That's my dad up there with Ricky's mom."

"Your dad? I just saw you hug him. From what you've told me, you'd never do that with your dad."

"Not my mother's husband. My dad. My real dad."

"I don't get it."

"It's a long story. I'll tell you later. But I was definitely not expecting this, and I'm not sure what to do with it."

"Can I help?"

"I don't think so. But I'm gonna wanna spend a little time with him after the service. Do you mind?"

"Of course not. Do what you need to do, and then gimme a call when you're ready for me to pick you up and take you home."

"Home?"

"Yeah. If that's okay with you."

Carlos smiled, and hugged him tightly. "I love you," he whispered into Corey's ear.

"I love you, too."

V.

"You look like you've just discovered the meaning of life," Corey said as he stroked Carlos' face.

It had been a long and exhausting day for both of them, and they were finally lying in bed, with only the light from several candles to see one another. Carlos had spent more than two hours visiting with Richard, and couldn't wait to share the story with Corey. And Corey couldn't help but cry as Carlos related it to him just an hour ago.

"Not exactly," Carlos said, "but it has been an amazing day. As sad as I was to have to say good-bye to Ricky, I met my dad for the first time in my life, and I finally feel like a part of me that has been missing my entire life has finally been found and become a part of me."

"Well, that makes sense," Corey said, and kissed Carlos' neck as he stroked his hard cock. "That's exactly what happened."

"I know," Carlos moaned as his cock was stroked and his neck tingled with Corey's kisses. "But I was afraid that I wouldn't be able to feel that way. That I'd gotten too hardened."

"I don't think that's possible, babe. You have an amazing heart, and an incredible capacity to love, and to be loved."

"You think?"

"I know."

"Good," Carlos said as he turned around and kissed Corey on the lips. "Because I want you to fuck me again."

"Serious?"

"Yeah. You felt so good inside me. And I felt so loved when you fucked me. I want to feel it again."

"You are loved. I love you. And I'd love to fuck you again, babe."

"Then do it."

Corey rolled Carlos onto his stomach, and spread his legs as far apart as they'd go.

"Okay, then. Just relax, and breathe deeply," he said as he kissed Carlos' ass.

Corey let a large ball of saliva fall from his mouth and onto the hole between the two brown globes. He placed his cock head right at the puckered sphincter, and pushed slowly.

"Ungh," Carlos grunted and tightened every muscle in his body as Corey's cock head slipped inside his ass.

"Want me to stop?"

"Don't you dare. Just go slow. I want every inch of you inside me, but I just need to go a little slow."

"Okay, babe."

Corey slid another inch inside Carlos' ass, and then rested for a moment or two before sliding another in. It took him a few moments to get all the way inside, and another few for Carlos to get used to the length and thickness. But once he did, he was like an addict jonesing for his next fix.

"Oh God, baby," Carlos moaned as he thrust his ass back deeper onto Corey's cock. "Fuck me."

Corey grabbed Carlos by either side of the waist and pulled him into him as he thrust his cock deep and hard inside him. He'd had dozens of sex partners, and most of them he'd considered pretty damned good. Of all of those experiences, he'd only bottomed for a handful, and so the vast majority of his action had been as a top. He considered himself pretty damned good in bed, and a good judge of great sex. And with all of that, he could say undoubtedly that this was in the top two best fucks he'd ever had. The other was when Carlos fucked him when they first met.

He slid his cock deep inside Carlos' ass, and kept it buried there for a long moment. Not because it was part of his style or technique, but because if he slid in and pulled out too close together, he'd blow his load immediately. The wet warmth of Carlos' ass muscles milking his cock was way too much for him to deal with coolly. With each thrust, either in or out, he had to grit his teeth and think about every ugly, gory monster in his favorite horror films to keep from shooting.

But Carlos had no such worries, and began to buck back onto Corey's cock with unbridled fervor. He lifted himself up on his hands and lifted his ass off the bed, impaling it deeper onto the fat cock. When Corey tried to pull out, Carlos thrust his ass even harder onto it, and refused to let go.

"Oh my God, baby," Carlos said breathlessly. "Fuck me. Shove it deeper into me and make love to me."

Just hearing Carlos say those words, along with his unrelenting ass wrapped around his cock, pushed Corey over the edge.

"I love you so much, babe," he whispered into Carlos' ear as he pumped into and out of his ass frantically. "I'm gonna cum."

"Give it to me, Corey," Carlos moaned. "I wanna feel your load all over my back."

"Oh Christ," Corey grunted as he pulled his cock out quickly.

He pushed Carlos down onto his stomach and held one hand on the small of his back. With the other hand he stroked his cock a couple of times, and then let go of it completely. He moaned as the first couple of spurts shot over Carlos' head and landed on the headboard in front of him. The next several shots landed on the back of Carlos' head, his shoulders and his back. The jizz just kept coming, in long-range missile-type projectiles, and thick dripping globs that slid down his long shaft, onto his balls and ultimately onto Carlos' still-gyrating ass.

"Fuck, babe," Corey said as he lay on top of Carlos' cum-covered back. "I'm so sorry. I wanted it to last longer, but I couldn't hold back any longer."

"That's okay," Carlos whispered as he turned around and kissed Corey on the lips. "I've never felt anything that felt that good before."

"It was all right?"

"It was amazing."

Carlos kissed Corey softly on the lips, and then began to cry.

"Whoa, whoa," Corey said as he held Carlos' face in his hands. "What's wrong? Did I hurt you?"

"No, not at all," Carlos said as he wiped the tears from his eyes. "My dad wants me to move to LA so we can get to know each other."

"What? No. No, please don't do that."

"I haven't ever known him, and I feel like I need to."

"I love you, Carlos," Corey said as he pulled Carlos to him and wrapped him in his arms. A single tear rolled down his cheek.

"I love you, too, baby. Don't cry, please."

"I had to go for three months without you in my life. It was the worst time in my life. I don't want to ever be without you again," Corey said.

"You don't?"

"No, I don't. If I ask you to come back to New Haven with me, please tell me you won't break my heart and say no. I know your dad wants to get to know you, and I don't blame him. We can go visit him all you want, I promise. In fact, if you come and live with me for the next six months, then we can move to LA after I graduate. I've always wanted to live there anyway. Just please don't say no to me. I can't imagine not having you by my side for the rest of my life."

"What? You want me to move to Connecticut with you?"

"Yes. I want you to live with me. I want you to be my lover, and I want you to share the rest of my life with you. I need you in my life, Carlos. Please say yes."

Carlos curled deeper into Corey's torso and hugged him tightly.

"Are you crying?" Corey asked when he felt Carlos shaking.

Carlos nodded his head and turned around so that he was being spooned lovingly by Corey.

"Please say yes," Corey repeated as he kissed Carlos' neck and ear.

"Of course I'll be your lover and move in with you. I can't imagine my life without you. Promise we can move to LA after you graduate?"

"Absolutely. Whatever it takes to make you happy. I want you to be happy."

"I am happy, baby," Carlos said. "You make me happier than I've ever been. But you can make me even happier."

"How?" Corey asked, and kissed him back. "Just tell me, I'll do anything I can for you."

Carlos rolled Corey over onto his back and lifted his legs. "I gotta fuck you now. My cock is begging to get inside your ass. Can I?"

"Hell, yeah," Corey said, and spread his legs apart. "I was afraid you were turning into a total bottom on me."

"Not a chance," Carlos said. "I love fucking you, baby. But I also love you fucking me, so we're gonna share, okay?"

"Whatever you say," Corey moaned. "Just shut up and fuck me now."

Carlos spit on the head of his cock and slid it deep inside Corey's ass in one quick and graceless thrust. "I'm so sorry," he said breathlessly as he began thrusting in and out slowly. "I just need to fuck you."

"Do it, babe," Corey moaned and lifted his ass up to meet Carlos' impaling cock. "Fuck me harder."

Carlos slammed his cock all the way inside Corey's ass, and smiled when Corey moaned and shook his head from side to side. He pulled his cock all the way out and then thrust it back in before Corey could catch his breath.

"I love you so much," Carlos said as he leaned down and kissed Corey on the lips. He slid in and out of the tight ass slowly at first, and then more fervently. "Please don't ever leave me. I need you more than anything."

"I won't," Corey moaned, and wriggled his ass around Carlos' fat cock. "I never want to leave you. But, God, Carlos, fuck me harder."

Carlos lifted Corey's legs higher into the air, and then fucked his ass relentlessly. It didn't take long before he felt the orgasm building deep in his balls.

"I'm gonna cum, baby," he whispered.

Corey impaled his ass all the way onto the thick cock, and grabbed Carlos' ass, holding him deep inside his ass as he squeezed it with his ass muscles.

"I'm serious," Carlos grunted. "I'm cumming."

"Cum inside me," Corey moaned.

"Are you su . . ."

He held himself perfectly still as his cock thickened inside Corey's ass with each contraction. His entire body quivered as he unloaded himself deep into his lover's guts. After he felt the last spasm rack through his loins, he pulled out and collapsed on the bed next to Corey.

"I'm exhausted," Corey said with a yawn.

"Me too," Carlos said. "Just hold me and let me fall asleep in your arms. And one more thing, baby?"

"Anything."

"Make sure I never look back. I used to always tell Ricky to never look back, and to always look forward. Please don't let me look back. There's nothing back there for me."

"No looking back, babe. Only look forward. I'll be right there with you."